Binding ARBITRATION

Binding ARBITRATION

ELIZABETH MARX

Binding Arbitration

Book design by Maureen Cutajar
www.gopublished.com

Cover Design: Alexandra Fomicheva
alfoart.com/about.html

Thanks to Jennifer Ames for use of photo to create cover.

ISBN-13: 978-1477470732
ISBN-10: 1477470735

For Tim, if I am a diamond in the rough, then you're the precious metal that holds it in place.

1

THE HIT THAT PULLED ME FROM THE GAME

Aidan 11 a.m.

Thirty years of experience in locker room antics hadn't prepared me to manage the filming of a thirty-second television spot with six six-year-old fairies.

They say life imitates baseball—if that was the case, then mine should be silver plated peanuts and gold encrusted Cracker Jacks, but I hadn't had a prize fall out of my cardboard box in weeks and Sailor Jack and Bingo had jumped ship.

The ump laughed, before singing to the tune of Take Me Out to the Ball Game:

Take him out of the bullpen,
Pay him for an endorsement.
Give him some pixies and faerie dust,
He won't care until all his seams bust.

Most guys with a clear conscience hear their own voice in their heads, but I'm a professional baseball player and a turn-of-the-century ump commands mine. Ever since I took a tumble on the side of a mountain last year, the ump's been running a continuous color commentary.

When my agent, Fletch, arranged what he considered an 'easy' gig, the ump enjoyed my discomfort more than a beer guy enjoyed extra innings at a scorching doubleheader in July.

The ump sang his ditty, until the glitter that shook free from the rafters felt like it was sluicing through my cranium. I imagined shoving his old-fashioned, Boston-style cap down his throat and silencing him for a few bars. Oh yeah, and at the weirdest times I'd see him, too. Nobody else, just me. Right now he was standing on the bench in the set's Styrofoam dugout.

My co-stars had shred the baseball field backdrop. The fairies were tramping around the bench like trolls searching under a bridge for three Billy goats. If they didn't find something to entertain them soon, they'd move onto the gruff, over-paid baseball player *du jour*.

How had I found myself in such an irritating predicament?

There was a time when the sight of an experienced catcher squatting over home plate and a freshly packed mound was enough to make my fingertips itch for the seams of a ball and a broken-in mitt. Before the game became endorsements and contracts, it had been about the applause of the crowd and locker room pranks. Back then; throwing ninety-five miles-per-hour fastballs had been enough to raise gooseflesh. Once upon a time, that amounted to more than all the material wealth and fame.

"Six beautiful girls can create a lot of chaos." The make-up guy startled me as he re-powdered my t-zone. "Don't sweat those chiseled cheeks off, honey." He patted my rear with his bare hand. He had to know we ballplayers did that only with mitts on.

I closed my eyes to avoid the glare shooting from the camera lights. Sweat trailed down my back and into my too-tight uniform pants; the costume department had neglected to provide a cup. I chafed, even as sweat flowed into my uncomfortable pink-and-black shoes--much too much Pepto Bismol pink to be called cleats. Though if there'd been a bottle of the liquid stomachache relief I'd take a hit straight from the bottle.

That doesn't aid your kind of heartache, kid.

I ran my hand through my hair, and when I drew it away, my palm sparkled with pink glitter. The director had stormed off the set in search of aspirin, returning now with a cold pack against his temple. The producer corralled my co-stars below the lights again, where they splattered equipment with fairy dust, which a weary cameraman dusted away before he zeroed in on me again.

They had already poked, pummeled, pulled, pinched, (in the butt I might add), and smacked (not on the lips, thank God) me into speechlessness. When my eyes beseeched the make-up guy for assistance, he blew me an air kiss and winked. I ump pantomimed the makeup guy; blowing air kisses through his mask.

Things were crumbling faster than fairy mounds under an ogre's club, so I accessed my father's deep, serious voice. The one I'd successfully used to contain even the rowdiest females. "You fairies need to behave."

They glared at me, before they danced around me hand in hand, chanting back and forth, Mr. Bandage and Mr. Bondage.

"My name is Band-Aid," I said, all salt and vinegar.

"And we're pixies not fairies," the petite brunette of the group retorted, before she narrowed her fire-breathing-dragon eyes on me. I saw my own reflection in her irises.

Reflections are so easily changed by action, but magnified by neglect.

I shook my head, clearing it. There was no way I was going to let the ump call this game against me.

A boisterous, screeching pixie was hanging from each of my arms when the phone at my backside began ringing. One of the pixies pried the phone out of my pocket. I wrestled it from her grasp and shrugged them off. They dropped the pretext of civility, curling their cotton-candied colored lips back to reveal their hunter's teeth, snarling for fresh meat.

I glanced at the caller ID window of my man-phone. Every guy I knew was preprogrammed into it, but it was an unknown number.

I replaced the phone, unanswered, and worked up a megawatt smile before turning back to the pixies, hoping to coax them into collaboration. If charm didn't do the trick, I was going to have to resort to bribery to ensure their cooperation or this commercial might never fill time slots between Tinker Bell's Parade and My Little Pony.

The phone danced against my back end again.

Star light, star bright. How many bimbos can dial a number right?

Exasperated with the voice in my head, I pulled the phone out and growled, "What?"

"Aidan?" The woman's voice was a haunting melody, whispered tones that sang to me in my dreams. Her voice coursed through me and threatened to bring distinct appendages to attention.

"Yeah?" My mind refused to place the voice, but the caller, whoever she was, should've known I was off the market. Wasn't that the advantage of a celebrity engagement?

"Aidan, its Libby." Her throat cleared. "Elizabeth Tucker."

Another sharp liner—hit right back up the middle off a fastball I left in the center of the plate—came at me hard. The room spun with its impact. I swallowed several gasps of oxygen before I was able to clear my tongue from my windpipe. "Be still my beating heart."

"You have a heart?"

As evidence to its existence, I could hardly hear past its thumping. "I don't have time for a stroll down memory lane."

"I'm honored you remember a lane." She sighed with a deep, seductive tenor before her voice tightened as sharp as a drill. "I know you're in town, and I need to speak with you, even though you must be extremely busy." Her sarcasm scratched about as subtly as glass shards against a cornea. "I wouldn't dream of taking up more than ten minutes of your time."

"I'm in the middle of shooting a commercial." As if on cue, the pixies giggled.

"I know the importance of beer commercials. Or is it razor blades?" She gave a scoffing snort. "Either way, I'm sure you can spare ten minutes off your multimillion-dollar stop watch."

I almost dropped the phone. Libby's heated language crackled through my eardrum; she rubbed words together like sandpaper against flint—scorching my hand. "I'm a busy man."

A redheaded pixie goosed me to get my attention. I grunted in reply, which set off another round of hysterical giggling. Maintaining my temperature with Libby and my composure with the glittery little girls of the harem proved more challenging than satisfying the suits in the front office.

"You and your playmates can roll around the set all morning, for all I care. But I need to see you, two-thirty at Gutheries on Addison." Her voice mocked me with its sugary tone.

"You better watch it, cutter, I might think you actually have emotional nerve endings."

She groaned and the silence stood still.

"Listen jock-boy, if you don't show up, you'll need more than a band-aid to close the gaping lesion I'll split open."

"Forget it. Have you stopped reading People Magazine, babe? I'm a celebrity. And I don't show up at anyone's beck and call."

"I know exactly who you are, that's why you're going to show. You wouldn't want the sordid details of your personal life splashed all over the cover of the Spectator." I could hear her teeth grind together. "I need to see you face to face."

"Why don't you schedule a meeting with my agent, he handles the scorned women. If he thinks you have something to say, maybe we'll have a sit-down."

"You can sit your ass down at Gutheries."

"Let me give you his number."

"I have his number."

If she already had Fletch's number, I could only assume he'd given her mine. He was a dead man. No, death would be to kind. I'd hang-glide off the Sears Tower, because that would add considerable gray hairs to his crimson coiffure.

"Look, I have any number of ladies to have a drink with." I winked at my pink entourage encouraging their laughter.

"I'm thrilled for you." I imagined her narrowing those fiery emerald eyes. "But if you don't want your thirty-three-point-seven-million-dollar deal to run afoul, I suggest you show up this afternoon. Feel free to bring Mr. Fletcher along. Bring your mommy, daddy, manager, masseuse or anyone else who'll give you moral support. But get your ass there!"

"Why you smart-mouthed, little..." I looked around at my audience. Several of their faces lit with smiles while they pushed me. My plastic cleats slipped through a mound of glitter, further lubricating my accelerated descent. Unable to catch my balance, I tripped over a heavy electrical cord and toppled over. As I turned to get my bearings, a traitorous light stand landed on my face. I shook my head, trying to clear the pyrotechnic sugar plum fairies from dancing in my head.

And sometimes a woman hurls a fateball that leaves you on the disabled list, the ump chortled through his brown leather mask, his gravelly voice packed as hard as the infield.

Libby's words reverberated through me as I tried to eject the ump from my head. 'The gaping lesion I'll split open.' A shot of raw pain blinded me, ricocheting from temple to temple. The last gash she'd left me with had barely scabbed over; I'd rather be traded down to the minors than see her.

My phone was still cradled in my death grip, when a petite pixie kneeled down and examined my face. "You're going to need a huge band-aid for this." She patted my cheek; her green eyes flickered like the stardust that sprinkled her concerned brow.

I felt the throbbing swell of my face. "I'm not bleeding."

She stilled me by placing her hands around my wrist, her concerned expression focusing on me intently. "You don't bleed on the outside, Mister. All your hurts are on the inside."

Another ragged flash of emotion fizzled through me and bottomed out in my stomach. The little girl's eyes were focused on my wrist, which started to tingle. My other hand connected the phone with my ear again. I wasn't sure what words I intended to use but it didn't matter. I was listening to the dial tone drone.

My wrist seared. The burning snaked around my wrist like a lit charge. I held it up toward the lights, which captured and then reflected a thin chain of shimmering points. I rubbed it, but it was melded into my skin. I was torn between the shock of its radiant appearance and the facts that Libby had the audacity to not only threaten me, but to hang up on me.

Me! The number one celebrity athlete in all of Chicagoland.

The old arbitrator in my head groused in his sarcastic upstate New York accent, **Glittery mirrors reflecting the soul, linked together by memories so old.**

2

COURTROOM ANTICS

It is the trade of lawyers to question everything, yield nothing, and talk by the hour. Thomas Jefferson

Elizabeth

"Libby, Mr. Caster is on line one," Vicki's voice chirped through the intercom. "Your mother is on line two."

"Tell Jeanne to swallow another Xanax for her antics, no more Bozo costumes on my credit card, and her buffoon-sized, red-and-pink glittered saddle shoes better not come within a hundred mile radius of Chicago."

"Your mother is your cross to bear." Vicki grunted. "And you need to get to the courthouse."

I wondered how my best friend, who never wore a watch, kept time better than Raymond Weil. And deciding between the lesser of two evils—"I'll take line one."

There were no preliminary salutations before my boss started his diatribe. "I'm turning over a new client to you. If you can get Mr. Pervesis off," he chuckled at his own joke, as Mr. Pervesis was a high profile pedophilia case. "It could earn you a partnership."

I have more work than any other associate and I can't bear another pervert. "I just turned down a *pro bono* case. With everything that's going on, another case would bury me."

"This gentleman's already had three attorneys."

"You are aware of the additional outside obligations I have right now." *Life or death kind of responsibilities.*

"I hope you're keeping Accardo happy." He lowered his voice. "But not too happy."

I looked at my watch; if I didn't get a move on my client might have me fitted for the Saks Spring concrete shoe collection. "Send me the file. I'll work Pervesis in next week."

My boss' panting reminded me of a man taking hits from an oxygen mask. "I'll deliver the case file personally."

I preferred the silent innuendo of his beady eyes, to the vulgar, oxygen-starved, catfish-out-of-water style breathing. If he came to my office I'd witness whiskers twitching in anticipation of his frisky fingers pawing me.

"Miss Tucker?"

"Court in fifteen minutes." And I hung up before he could say my name again. Sometimes I swore he garbled Fuckher, instead of Tucker, through the phone.

I go by Elizabeth, and I'm as precise about the letter of the law as I am my name. I don't respond to Beth or Betty or, heaven forbid, Liz or Lizzie. And only those near and dear call me Libby.

In what would appear diametrically opposed to that statement, I'm a criminal defense attorney in one of the largest law firms in the city. Whitney, Brown and Rodgers' reputation was built on substantial connections to cops, crimes, and conspiracies that filtered through generations of Chicago families. Our cases run the gambit from Skid Row *pro bono* work to the North Shore elite, where quite often we polish brass off their gilded-edges.

I caught the elevator and pushed through the heavy glass lobby doors on my way to the street. A damp breeze off the lake kept everyone huddled against raised coat collars and made cabs a commodity so hot they could have been exchanged at the Board of Trade. So I hoofed it to the Daley Center in my silver, three-inch, faux lizard-skin boots.

Crossing the plaza, planters filled with ripe plum, vibrant red, and burnished gold mums heralded the season. Pumpkins decorated haystacks. Scarecrows displayed the hometown team's jerseys—Sox, Bulls, Blackhawks, and Bears. Wouldn't you know the Cubs jersey had to be number thirteen? Band-Aid was everywhere. It was a miracle that his sphere and mine hadn't already collided.

In the lobby of the Dirksen Federal building I forced my frozen fingers to deposit my briefcase on the x-ray machine and reset my mind on my job, the only thing keeping me sane.

I was representing Tony Accardo III, the grandson of Tony the Big Fish Accardo, who had been the greatest mob boss the Chicago outfit has had since Al Capone. My Mr. Accardo had recently inherited a horse racing park through his grandfather's estate, and I was representing him on tax evasion counts involving said entertainment venue in Villa Park. I reviewed the books myself, and they looked on the up and up. Whether they were the sole set of books, I couldn't say.

Mr. Accardo developed real estate all over the city and had recently opened a supper club, making him appear as legit as possible. His personal life was squeaky clean, no abused girlfriends or illegitimate kids, the guy didn't even have a parking ticket. But who was I kidding, he wasn't the kind of guy who parked his own car.

He unwound his six-foot frame as I approached, placed his phone in his hand-tailored suit pocket, and took my briefcase. He kissed me on both cheeks, offering his elbow to escort me into the courtroom. When he put his hand over mine, a guttural hum escaped him. "You could use some warming up."

I pulled my hand from his grasp. "Let's speak in private." I glanced about, trying to ascertain if we had an audience.

He leaned in closer, placing his lips a hair's breadth away from my ear. "I would love to be alone with you, but I have a tail." He nodded in the direction of the water fountain. "Blond guy, who's pretending to read the paper." He sighed. "Mmm, you smell too good to be a lawyer, too."

Only by willful determination did I remain unaffected, but I elbowed him a safe distance away anyway. No matter how attractive the packaging—and Mr. Accardo was no slacker in that department—

-I was determined to keep things professional. He was born with just the right kind of Italian DNA: tall frame, olive skin, piercing blue eyes, and a chiseled jaw line. The stubbly surface of his chin made his face appear shadowy. There were secrets in those darkened recesses, the kind that led women into dim corners and dangerous situations.

I glared a warning at him, before clenching my teeth. "You would appear more professional, and therefore more confident, if you'd maintain a reasonable distance from your attorney."

His brow tangled, causing a scar over his right eyebrow to move toward his hairline. The single flaw in his perfectly proportioned face didn't make him deficient; it made him look determined. He took a step back. "It was a cheap shot to get next to you, but the copper irritates me. I thought I'd give them something new to mull over down in the satellite truck." He spoke as he held the door open and we found empty seats in the back of the gallery as the case before ours was still underway.

"Try to behave, Mr. Accardo."

"Accept my deepest apologies, and please call me Tony." The corners of his lips folded into a sly smile.

I dug through my briefcase for his file. "Stop. For good."

"I have no intention of giving up so easily." He winked.

His eyes beckoned from my periphery. A woman could get lost in eyes like that, the surrounding framework of black lashes making them appear even bluer. The bluest I'd ever seen. Almost.

I scanned the courtroom. The DA assigned to the case wasn't in the gallery, but his superior was. Although everything seemed in order in the mahogany chamber, I couldn't set aside my suspicions. "Mr. Accardo," I whispered. "Remember to remain impassive during the proceedings, no matter what happens."

He drew an eyebrow up, and raked his gaze around the perimeter of the room. The door behind us opened and the Assistant District Attorney assigned to our case sauntered in.

Jackson Xavier Wagner had been a former classmate of mine at Northwestern, and he was an exceptional attorney. We had managed to remain friends, despite the fact that we were on opposing sides of the bench. He strolled to a seat behind the prosecution's table. His boss, Eve Moore, pushed off the wall and took a seat alongside Jax and whispered in his ear. Moore was known for her hard-nosed prosecutions and soaring conviction rates. I watched Jax's classic profile, but his facial expressions gave nothing away. Moore turned and pinpointed our exact location with a piercing gaze.

Tony gave her a dazzling smirk. She acknowledged him with a slight nod of her head. As soon as Moore turned away, I elbowed Tony and gave him a narrow-eyed examination of my own, before watching Jax's brow furrow and Moore grimace.

"They're up to no good," I whispered.

"Yeah?"

I shrugged a shoulder. "The bozo in the corridor isn't watching you around the clock for fashion tips. This is more than a fishing expedition." I let a single eyebrow clear the frame of my glasses so he'd catch the magnitude of the situation. "The Feds cast a wide net, one large enough to ensnare a Blue Barracuda."

He instinctively blanched at the reference before a slow smile took his face. "Your brains traverse your beauty."

"And your old-world charm, animal magnetism, and dazzling eyes aren't about to sidetrack me."

The judge's gavel brought me to attention. "Case number one-zero-zero-nine-nine-nine, the State of Illinois vs. Anthony Accardo." The court reporter scoffed and Judge Foreman gave her a look before he asked Jax and I to approach the bench.

He placed his hand over the microphone and nodded at the bailiff. "Jax, what the hell is going on in your office? This trial was supposed to start today. Then, I get a note that you need a continuance. For what, I'd like to know? Either you have the evidence, or you don't."

"The state doesn't believe in wasting the court's time. The District Attorney's office begs your apology in this matter, but the State wishes to bring additional charges against Accardo."

I felt Jax's eyes fall on me. My lawyerdar hit the cautious zone, but I steadied my expression.

The judge glared through his thick glasses, and when his hand went to his chin, he expelled a heavy breath fogging them up. "What the hell is going on, Jax?"

"The state would like Mr. Accardo remanded into custody."

"Like bloody Hell." The judge grabbed a bottle of Mylanta and took a sputtering gulp straight from the bottle. "What in Sam Hill are they teaching you youngsters at Northwestern Law School?" He backhanded his mouth.

Judge Foreman was known for strange outbursts and tangents. Before he got too far off on one, I thought I might jump in. "Your honor, if the state wishes to bring additional charges against Mr. Accardo, that's their prerogative." I smiled at Jax, even as I gave him the evil eye. "I assume the surveillance detail pertains to these additional charges?"

Jax dropped his head, shaking it like a drenched golden retriever shedding rainwater. "He has surveillance because he's a flight risk, Libby."

"Don't you dare 'Libby' me, Jackson Wagner."

"Don't you care to know what the charges are?" The judge took the forms and reviewed them through his oversized gold-rimmed glasses, coming to a quick conclusion. "They're doozies."

"The DA's office has it out for my client, who is nothing more than a law-abiding citizen. Since we're all assembled, the charges can be read in open court." My overconfidence had always irked Jax. "Your honor, I would like the record to reflect my opposition to the manner in which this was arranged."

"Always look toward appeal, Ms. Tucker."

Jax was smiling like a puppy with a new bone. I maintained my composure by smoothing the lapel of my blazer on my way back to the defendant. I was barely planted before the judge cleared his throat in the microphone and said, "The State of Illinois is bringing the additional charges of racketeering and aggravated assault against Anthony Accardo." The courtroom erupted as Judge Foreman dropped his gavel.

Jax stood and cleared his throat. "Your honor, the state would like Mr. Accardo remanded into custody until his defense is ready to respond to the charges. We wouldn't want him flying the coop on his private jet or sailing his yacht away."

I got to my feet. "Your honor, Mr. Accardo's defense appeared today in response to a continuance. If the state wanted the pleasure of taking my client to jail, then they should have gotten an arrest warrant. They cannot march into the courtroom and levy additional charges and try to revoke his bail all in one stroke. The charges, while grievous, have not been proven and no one is in imminent danger."

"That's not what our key witness would say. He's in critical condition at Cook County Hospital," Jax retorted.

I turned on Jax like I was animal control and he a rabid coyote. "How long has the security detail been on my client?"

"Approximately ten days."

"I assume a warrant was issued for this surveillance."

He nodded his head and handed it across the aisle.

"When did your material witness become hospitalized?"

"Three days ago."

I snatched the warrant and scanned it. "Ah, you've been following my client for ten days, and three days ago your surveillance detail allowed him to assault a state witness?" I tried to play naïve, but an eyebrow rose in accusation.

"Of course not. The state alleges that Mr. Accardo arranged for the assault. He wouldn't do it himself."

"I see from the warrant his phone has been tapped. How did he arrange for having a man beaten? Smoke signals?" I let him chew on that kibble for a bit.

"I object, your honor!" Jax leaned over his table.

"It wouldn't be a circus if you didn't." Judge Foreman dropped his gavel to steady the courtroom that was all abuzz.

I leaned on my knuckles in the same manner and stared Jax down. "Are you going to charge him with being rich, Mr. Wagner? What's next, too attractive? Is that a crime now, too?"

Judge Foreman dropped his gavel over the laughter from the

gallery. "Order, I want order in this courtroom!" He pointed his gavel at me, "You've made your point, Ms. Tucker. Don't go so far as to make a mockery out of my courtroom."

Wagner grumbled out, "Your honor . . . "

Judge Foreman stopped him with a glare. "I am going to let the bail stand. But I am going to require Mr. Accardo to relinquish his passport before he leaves the courthouse. Happy?"

I smiled, knowing I'd won this round. Tony touched the sleeve of my suit jacket. I looked down at his passport. The man was prepared for any eventuality.

"Approach," the judge said as he cleared his throat, "Ms. Tucker, I expect you and Mr. Wagner in my courtroom next Wednesday to start this trial."

"But, your honor, that gives me only a week to prepare."

He smiled when he said, "Next Wednesday, same time. I'm sure your client is looking for a speedy trial." Before I had a chance to continue my rebuttal, he was moving forward. "Did the two of you go through school together?"

"Yes sir, we did," Jax said.

"Did she kick you in the ass there, as often as she does in my courtroom, Mr. Wagner?"

"Yes, but she kicked everyone's ass there, sir. She didn't single me out."

Judge Foreman gave Jax a knowing look. "Too bad for you." The judge winked at me. "Libby, keep up the good work."

"Your honor, I didn't do anything," I protested for effect.

"This is the first time all day that this room has been quiet. Every man in this courtroom is watching your backside right now. The quiet does my old ticker good." He tapped on his heart with his free hand.

"You do realize that borders on sexual discrimination, your honor," Jax said, insulted for me.

"You hear me say anything sexual? Discriminatory?" He harrumphed. "Miss Tucker can take a compliment when kindly meant." He glared at Jax before addressing me again. "Now, sashay back to your counselor's table so I can be done with this farce for today."

Jax didn't know the judge as well as I did. I'd been his clerk while in law school, and he was the least discriminatory judge on the bench in Cook County. Foreman was giving me a subtle reminder about the only case I'd ever lost. An Illinois Supreme court case I'd left being his clerk to third chair. A case so insidious, that it almost took down all the chairs on either side of the case and the largest law firm in Chicago.

After Judge Foreman dismissed us, I took my time assembling my briefcase. I let Mr. Accardo precede me through the swinging gate. I stopped to put on my trench coat, and when I looked up, I saw Eve Moore and Tony evaluating each other as if they were sizing each other up for a future battle.

When I reached for my briefcase, Mr. Accardo refused to relinquish it. "Can you tell me what just went down?"

"Maybe you can tell me." I cast a look at Eve Moore, but she was speaking with Jax and a frantic police officer.

We stepped into an empty client lounge, as I examined the new charges. I knew the conversation between Accardo and I would be akin to the Pope taking Satan's confession. "The assault charges are for one Vito Serrelli." I eyed his response over the rim of my glasses. "Someone you know?"

"He grew up on the Northwest Side. His family owned a grocery store and meat market. His older brothers ran numbers out of the butcher shop in the back, and his elderly uncle Charlie sold drugs from under the cash register."

"What would you know about a mob family, growing up on the North Shore with silver spumoni—" I smiled. "—in your mouth?"

"All of the families are related, by blood, or by marriage. I liked to slum when I was a teen, and it drove my father crazy. Whatever happened to Vito wasn't my doing. He's an informant with a serious drug habit. Either can land you in the hospital."

I watched his calm confidence, either he was the best liar I'd ever seen or he was declaring the truth. Not that it made a difference in my capacity to defend him.

The firm set of his jaw softened. "I hope when this is resolved you'll consider going out with me." His tone was as deep and rich as a glass of burgundy, and seduction was his usual ploy of distraction.

His aqua eyes pierced me. I had to force my eyes away by blinking. "There is a strict code of conduct between lawyers and their clients."

"I can get another attorney, but it's not every day I meet a beautiful, well-educated, Catholic girl. My mother would beat me with a stick if I let you get away."

I extended my hand. "Vicki will contact you to set up an appointment to go over the game plan for the new charges."

He brought my hand to his lips. "I'm not giving up."

"You're going to have to." I started through the door and then turned back. "Mr. Accardo, you would do well to remember the best way I can help you is if I have all the necessary information to assist you in fighting these charges."

"I have no intention of letting these charges stick." He tilted his head and a wry smile lit his expressive face.

"I hope you don't think batting your eyes at Eve Moore will help your case. She'll eat you for lunch."

"That's the same observation many people make about you."

"Don't underestimate me, Mr. Accardo. I can make Moore look like a Sunday school teacher. If I had to, I could roast you alive for lunch and use your charred skin to weave a bread basket for dinner."

His shocked reaction dissipated as he followed me to the elevators.

Two uniformed officers stepped off the elevator, removing their hats in salutation. "We're looking for Tony Accardo." I pivoted and gauged Tony's response, when he caught sight of the police he looked grim, but he didn't seem surprised. He put his phone in his trench coat pocket when the officers took a step in his direction. "Mr. Accardo, we have a warrant for your arrest.

I blocked the officer's path, examining the warrant. "Mr. Accardo, if I don't leave now I'll be late for my next meeting. It's urgent. Otherwise, I'd go with you to the station. I'll call the judge."

I watched them cuff him. "Hopefully, you won't spend the night."

I jumped into the elevator before the doors closed. It was 1:45pm, and my next dance with the devil was at 2:30pm.

If the demon I was meeting was still as slippery as Jax Wagner and Tony Accardo were, I was in for another battle. I might just have to lay waste to several males in my path to get what I needed for the only one of them that counted. I hailed a cab with a shrill whistle and made my way out of the Loop.

Out of a pan of purgatory and into a kettle of confession.

3

PITCHER VS. CUTTER

Cardinal rule for all hitters with two strikes on them: never trust the umpire. Robert Smith

Aidan 2:15 p.m.

Survival instinct is the reason I initially refused this meeting. Exposure being the next justification, because a potential scandal was the last thing I needed right now. I paced the sidewalk in front of the plate glass window, refusing to glance at my own reflection. I was avoiding the consequences of the only game, in thirty odd years, I hadn't seen to completion.

Curiosity is what lured me here, like a die-hard Cubs fan to the seventh inning stretch. I wanted to face her and ease my conscience by laying all the blame on her locker room floor. I glanced at my watch and pitched myself across the threshold.

"Palowski." The bartender sneered from behind a beer stein she was polishing, as if she were expecting me.

Gutheries was a local hangout two blocks from the ballpark in Wrigleyville. While I'd been here before, it wasn't a regular haunt. I enjoyed the earthiness of its roughly carved bar and rugged, wide-plank flooring, but I lived in Lincoln Park, and neighborhood bars are a dime a dozen in Chicago.

The soft Irish ballads playing in the background gave me the impression I'd stumbled into an Irish wake, which wasn't reassuring.

Whiskey fumes and fish-n-chips filled the air, threatening to bring the bile up from my stomach. I shook off my nausea and concentrated on the sepia photographs that hung on the plastered, whitewashed walls. The turn of the century photographs ran the gambit from immigrant families in tattered clothes to beefy stock yard workers slaughtering cattle right off boxcars. The vast majority of the images appeared to have last been cleaned during that same era.

I was waiting at the ascribed place, at the assigned time, like a cosseted schoolboy. I retreated to a table farthest from the surly barmaid, keeping a direct bead on the door.

Strike one, the ump grumbled.

The bartender focused on the trash bags in her hands. "What'll it be, glitter-boy?" The feeling she'd like noting more than to incinerate me along with the trash at the rear of the establishment snaked up my spine.

"Pale Ale."

When she returned, she banged the beer on the table, a spray of foam danced across its top sloshing onto the sleeve of my coat. No napkin, no nuts, no apology. She returned to her post in the watering hole and snapped the pages of the *Tribune* up in front of her, effectively obstructing me from her line of sight, but I heard her whispering into her cell phone.

A few gulps of beer later the small silver bell at the top of the frosted glass door chimed on a blustery wind. A tall woman, whose expensive boots looked like they'd never step foot in a place like this, swept through the entry and forced the door shut. She shook off her trench coat exposing a navy suit. Her lengthy chestnut hair was pulled back into a chic French twist with a silver barrette exposing a classic profile.

Her briefcase strained her delicate features, but at the same time anchored her, if only for the hesitant moment between each determined stride. I couldn't pull my eyes away, as I stared at her from behind my shades. My pulse accelerated.

The woman took in the interior with a wide sweep of her head as the lenses of her glasses lightened. It wasn't until she started toward me with her boots clicking the hardwood that I realized this ravishing woman was the one I never thought to see again.

That would be a curve ball.

All these years later, I couldn't allow myself the luxury of a full recollection of time spent with her. That might've required admitting I'd never scratched my itch for her out. All the numerous women, every shade from platinum to strawberry-blonde, couldn't dish out half the heartache a wild-haired brunette cutter had put me through with her flaming green eyes and a mouth so lush it made my tongue ache to taste it.

I swallowed a long swig of beer, the steely grain helping me bottle my reaction. I attempted to reconcile what I was seeing with what I had expected. She still had it—if not more of it—that special something some women have that first draws men's attention then buzzes their brains into crushed barley.

She hesitated in front of the table. I refused to stand and I didn't remove my Oakleys. Let her stare at her own likeness, while I took my time studying the perfectly sculpted lines of her face, which lead to a defiant chin.

Libby tossed her briefcase between us on the tabletop, as if that paltry item could provide a barrier between us. I grinned at the thought of it until my dimple ached.

She perched on the edge of her chair.

I spun my beer bottle on the graffiti-riddled wood.

I watched her green eyes blink in agitation, her opal skin blanched to ivory and her overly generous lips flattened out. She threaded her hands together like an angry teacher about to reprimand an unruly schoolboy. We stared each other down.

"You've grown even more beautiful with time." I saluted her charms with my bottle, arching a brow in challenge.

Her eyes enlarged for a second; the rest of her demeanor was a veiled mask of harnessed hostility. "Smarter too."

She's cute, cute, cute for a cutter,
She ain't easy to fluster.

I ignored the ump's baritone. Libby's calm demeanor gave the distinct impression that she was an Elizabeth now. "You always were too smart for your own good."

I thought I saw an instantaneous spark of pain, but then her eyes bored into me. "Obviously not, or we wouldn't be having this exchange."

"Does that say something about me, or you?" I grinned.

"Whatever, I don't care to rehash the past. And thank you, but no, I don't care for a drink."

"I don't see what else we would have to talk about." I shuffled in my seat, making to leave like a rude jerk.

She put her hand on the sleeve of my leather jacket, holding me in place with those serious eyes, which I had been able to read once upon a time. "Don't you?" A red flush crept up her neck, as she jerked her hand away, shaking it.

"Why don't you dispense with the mystery, and tell me what you want? Just be prepared to get in line like everyone else."

Libby swallowed. Whatever it was, she wasn't any happier about asking than I was about waiting. She fished around in her briefcase and pulled out a computer printed form. "All I need is a blood sample." She pushed it toward me with a perfectly manicured hand.

My eyes scanned the title on the form and my hands clinched the beer bottle. She held out all this time, never asking for anything. I was about to get my biggest one-year paycheck, and somehow she not only knew the exact figure, she wanted a share. She thought I owed her something. I pushed the lab form back at her. "Why on earth would I want to do that?"

Her long dark lashes met her cheeks and her voice wobbled over words that had much of the emotion sucked from their core. "Because my child is dying from Leukemia, and you might be the only chance he has to live through the rest of this year."

Strike two.

It was the second sucker punch I'd received today. My chest felt like someone had dropped a two hundred-pound barbell across it when I didn't have a spotter. When I caught my breath, I took in her serious bearing. Whatever I had anticipated this meeting would be about, it wasn't some concocted story to see me again or even to blackmail me. She might've tried to check the volatility of her words, but the fear that washed her face was right below the surface, ready to erupt from her quivering lips.

She blinked in rapid succession before looking at me. She was angry and hurting and there were other emotions I couldn't read in her fathomless eyes. But none of that could appease the beast raging in me. "You kept the kid?" I seethed.

"No one knows about your relationship to my 'kid' and I'd prefer it to remain that way. All I need is a blood sample to eliminate you as a viable marrow donor, so I can move onto other international sources." She stilled her shaking hands on the table. "If you're a match, and you want to do something for someone other than yourself, the whole process is anonymous."

"You kept the kid all these years, and you never told me. You are one cold-hearted—"

"You listen, Mr. Band-Aid, and you listen carefully. I'll speak painstakingly slow, and I won't use any prodigious words."

Her glare captivated me, she reminded me of a tigress circling its unsuspecting prey.

"I did you an enormous favor by walking away. I knew you didn't want any distractions. The most important thing in your world was a shot at the majors, and I gave it to you. Nothing to care about except ... " She bit into her lips. "I knew what you wanted. I never once asked you for a damn thing."

"Until now," I grumbled.

"Listen, I never sang you a sob story while I walked the floors with a sleepless baby. I never contacted you when I busted my butt and still came up short. I never sold the story to the tabloids when I didn't have rent money or my son needed new shoes. I never did a single thing, except once, for a very short time, I was dim-witted enough to care about you more than I did my own future." She looked around, recalling herself. "For that, and all the other things I didn't do, you're going to give me that blood sample. I knew you once ... " She shook her head. "I thought I did, anyway. I know you have some decency in you, somewhere. You wouldn't let an innocent child, even if he is mine, suffer."

I had a son, a son who needed me. The heartache was so acute I wanted to reach across the table and choke her so she wouldn't be able to speak another word of the truth I had refused to acknowledge, the one true regret of my thirty years. She was the only thing that hadn't gone off exactly like clockwork. I had planned seduction and conquest and all I'd gotten for my troubles was yearning and consternation.

It was unconscionable, what I'd done, but what haunted me was how easily I'd set it all aside. If the media got a hold of this story, no amount of charity work would redeem last year's *People* magazine's Most Influential Sportsman.

I had never shirked a responsibility in my life. But seeing her reminded me I wasn't the man I'd been raised to be, or even half the man I wanted to be.

"Be honest with yourself," her voice wavered. "You didn't want him. I understand you had another plan for your life, but whether you wanted him or not is irrelevant now, because he's here. He's a major part of my world, and I'm going to lose him if I can't find some way to save him." I watched her gulp down the lump in her throat and perhaps a piece of her pride, in which she seemed wrapped like armor. "I can't stand to ask you, of all people, but I love him enough to suffer any indignity to give him one more minute of life." As she slid the form back toward me, the first tears skimmed down her cheeks. "That's why you should give me the blood sample."

In that solitary moment, the moisture of her tears washed away all the built up barriers that made her the woman she was today. And what sat before me now was the vulnerable, beautiful girl that I almost once…

Some of my anger washed away on the tide of her tears. I couldn't deny a thing she'd said. I hadn't had the guts to show up for court, so I'd signed the termination of parental rights forms. I'd thought she was giving the kid away and I couldn't stand witness to it. But she'd always had an inner strength, and I should have known she would have found a way to keep her child, if she had a mind to. "What's his name?"

She pulled out a five-by-seven snapshot and laid it over the lab request. "Cass Christian Tucker."

I looked at the photo; a small smiling face stared back at me. He was missing some teeth, but he had a single dimple. It was a face as familiar to me as my own, except he had his mother's eyes. I traced his smile before I looked at Libby. "Tucker?"

"Yes, Tucker. You were too busy signing autographs, I suppose, to show up for a hearing." She glanced away and sighed. "I didn't think he should suffer the disappointment of looking you up someday. If by some miracle you're a match, we can say it was random. Cass' doctors don't know who you are. They've assured me the person's identity would remain that way. If you do this for him, for me, you'll never hear from us again. You know I can keep that promise."

She'd eliminated me and kept the kid, she knew him from the moment he was born, he probably loved her and hated me. Now, aren't those the most selfish things to think? But I thought them, and I reveled in the fact she had wronged me again.

I let time tick off as I gathered my thoughts. "But I would know he exists."

She nodded. "You knew you had a child somewhere."

"Yes, but I didn't think he was with you," I ground out.

She drew in a sharp breath. "I see." She bit down on her lips again. I could sense her weighing what she wanted to say. "You feel the need to punish me because I had the guts to stick it out and keep and care for what was mine."

"You should have told me you kept him instead of leading me to believe you were giving him up for adoption."

"Those documents severed your parental rights. There was no indication of adoption. You received bad legal advice."

I acquired an interest in the label on my beer bottle. "My lawyer never saw the papers. If the club found out that I had an illegitimate kid they might have rescinded my contract. Baseball is America's game, and we're supposed to be squeaky clean."

The center of my forehead became her sole focus until her blazing eyes met mine. "You believed what you wanted to."

"Yeah, and I believe I should be cautious around you. Who knows what kind of a scam you're running. Maybe you want the blood to prove paternity." I pushed the computer form back.

"If you can look at that photo and doubt he's your kid then you might need more than your head examined."

"Maybe all you're after is some money."

"I always knew about your filthy money. Pay attention, jock-boy. Do I look like I need it?"

I'd examined her thoroughly. She didn't exude destitute-little-girl-barely-getting-by. Her designer watch fit too precisely to come from a street vendor on Randolph and State. The pearl David Yurman necklace that hung between the folds of her silk blouse skimmed across her breasts at just the right length. I had paid for enough jewelry to know quality.

"Maybe you invented this crap so you can mess around with my head again."

"If your head is screwed up, it has absolutely nothing to do with me. I spent only one night with you, and we weren't playing mind games from what I remember. Don't flatter yourself into believing I'm here out of anything more than life-or-death desperation." Her words drew my attention back to her face, her perfectly highlighted hair, her flawless complexion and makeup.

No, the evidence suggested she didn't need cash, but it didn't seem plausible in my mind that she had money of her own. There was no wedding ring; it was one of the first things I'd noticed. "Did your boyfriend set you up?"

She closed her eyes, mumbling words under her breath before looking heavenward. "I worked and paid for everything I have. For Christ's sake, I graduated from the same Big Ten University as you. Did you think I was living in a trailer park with Billy Bob?"

I couldn't get a word out.

She laughed at my shocked expression. "You did, didn't you? You are such an egomaniac. Did you think I didn't have it in me to pick myself up, dust off the worn knees of my jeans and go on when you didn't speak to me at graduation?" Her voice quivered. "You're still a conceited, spoiled, spineless bastard."

I'd been too shocked to speak to her that day. She'd said she was taking classes here and there, but ... "You went out of your way to make me believe you were a cutter, and not a whole lot more. How was I supposed to act when I saw you walk across the stage with a growing belly?" I rubbed my jaw in agitation.

"How about manning up? They teach that at spring training?"

"My mother and father were there. If I had spoken to you that day—sooner or later they would have figured it out."

"Over the years, I sometimes wondered if I made the right decision about involving you in Cass' life, but you've solved all those doubts today." Her mouth narrowed and her eyes crinkled. "All you ever talked about was your grand plans, as if being a professional baseball player was the equivalent of finding the cure for AIDS, or winning the Nobel Peace Prize."

I sat up straighter in my chair and moved toward her, trying to get in an angry retort of my own.

"You only wanted me to be a cutter. You used me and threw me away like the trash you thought I was. I know you saw me waiting under that oak tree for you after graduation. I had every intention of telling you I was keeping my baby. When you got there you put your overly educated girlfriend holding out for her MRS. Degree in your sports car, and you didn't have the guts to look me in the eye. Even if I wasn't the woman you wanted—what kind of a man would completely ignore the woman carrying his child?"

I ran my hand along my jaw-line; the calluses on my fingertips matched my callousness back then. I'd ignored her, acting out of a sense of hurt and betrayal. I'd wanted to give her a taste of her own medicine. "You were supposed to go to that clinic in Indianapolis in March. You promised you would do what I wanted. You disappeared, not leaving me a single word. I had no idea how to find you."

She shook her head in disbelief. "That's what it all boils down to. I was the first person to refuse you and mean it?" She reached across the table and swiped my glasses off my face. The Oakleys sailed across the table and over the edge, shattering.

"You told me no before that." In spite of the black eye, I smiled my cockiest grin. "Eventually, you said yes."

She regarded my eye. "It appears that someone has recently emphasized what a crass pig you are. And for the record, I was drunk. You didn't ask, you just took what you felt entitled to for time invested in the cutter girl who wouldn't put out."

I reached across the table and locked her forearm against the tacky tabletop. "You might have been a little tipsy, but you climaxed every time I did. I took that as a definite sign of agreement." I released her arm in increments, letting her know there was truth in what I'd said.

She moved to her feet abruptly, digging her nails into the table to maintain her balance. She looked down her aristocratic nose at me. I felt her quiet determination not to spill another tear in front of me. "I can't imagine we have anything else to say to each other. The doctor's name and information is on the form. If you care to help Cass, do so." She leaned over the table, placing that superior pout across her lips. "If not, go fuck yourself, Palowski."

She picked up her belongings and walked to the bar where she threw some money down for the bartender. They spoke a few hushed words before a deafening silence thundered through me.

She never looked back. I willed her to, but she'd never bent to my will before. Why would she start now? But I was going to teach little Libby Tucker that no one walked out on Banford Aidan Palowski unless I was of a like mind. And thus far, there was a colossal abyss separating her way of thinking from mine.

The ump flipped off his mask and danced a little jig on the bar top. **For its one, two, three strikes you're out—**

"Shut up," I bellowed.

The two suits at the bar having a late lunch turned and examined my lunacy and me. The bartender just laughed.

—At the same old game, he sang, straightening his bow tie.

4

EVIDENTIARY HARPOON

Evidence given and then retracted with the sole purpose of prejudicing the defendant in the eyes of the jury.

Elizabeth 4 p.m.

It felt so much worse than I expected, seeing him again. The only consolation was that he looked shoddier than I expected.

Don't get me wrong. He was still one of the most beautiful men I'd ever seen, but he looked tired. Maybe it was just the shiner, but there was some vulnerability in his eyes that I'd never seen before. Something was weighing on him, and had been for a while, from the look of him. It could've been his career, or even the bimbo he was marrying, but I certainly had no reason to spill tears over it, so why was I crying?

My phone buzzed. I pulled my head off my tear-soaked briefcase as my Indian cabdriver extended a tissue. I focused my bleary eyes on my caller ID, although I already knew who it was.

I was on the edge of losing everything, and Matt Caster had the threads of my survival dangling from his fingertips. He was going to see how he could make his puppet dance. "Elizabeth, why was Tony Accardo booked this afternoon without his attorney at his side?"

"Because, Mr. Caster, I cannot be in two places at once."

"Well, wherever you were, you weren't at Cook County."

I bit my tongue. "Judge Foreman is gone for the day anyway; there is no way to avoid a night in county. He's not the first Harvard Grad to spend the night on the city's dime."

"He better be the last client of yours to do so, or you're going to have to find a very persuasive way to maintain your position in this firm." Heavy oxygen mask breathing again.

I wanted to gag, but instead I made a crackling sound and said, "Sorry ... going under post office ... talk later ..." And I hung up on Rat Bastard.

The phone started ringing again and I involuntarily clicked it on, even though I had no desire to talk. "Hello, Jeanne."

"Elizabeth Ann, I've been calling you all day. Why haven't you called me back?"

"Jeanne, I have a job and a lot on my mind right now." How many years could one get for smothering a sniveling mother?

"That's the reason I'm calling. I dragged all your cousins down to the lab in the last few days. You have that Dr. Seuss call down here, and get these results. How's Cass feeling? Why don't I come up and stay with you all, and help you?"

I put my leather briefcase strap into my mouth and chomped down. The only reason I didn't buckle it around my throat and cinch it tight was the thought of Cass spending the rest of his life taking care of Jeanne. The image was about as appetizing as dining on road kill in Death Valley with Satan.

"Elizabeth Ann, have you heard a word I've said?"

"Yes, Jeanne, I'm here." I sighed. "Cass is feeling okay. I will call Dr. Seuss to get the test results from your lab. Maybe we'll get lucky and get a match."

"Elizabeth, have you contacted Cass' daddy?"

"No comment." If Jeanne found out about Aidan, she'd think she'd won the jackpot at Wednesday night bingo. She would be all over him for God could only imagine what. And that would be a bitter embarrassment.

"Give me his name. I'll look him up on the Internet. I could help from here, if you don't want me up there."

"He's had opportunities to claim Cass, and he didn't. We live in the same city, and he's never looked for us."

"That explains why you moved all the way to Chicago."

"Jeanne, I did not come here to be close to Cass' father. I came here to go to law school, and this was where I got a job. There are two lawyers in French Lick; it isn't likely I'd get a job to support you there."

"But this is where your roots are."

If French Lick has roots, I'm cutting down every tree in the county. Scratch that, I'm starting a forest fire. "I'm never coming back to French Lick."

"You're gone up there, and your brother is living the high life in Florida. I thought by now you'd get tired of city life, come back home, and get married."

"Jeanne, who is there in French Lick to marry who has a speck of sense?"

"There was a Junior Cox or David Bazin, Penny just left him, and he was always sweet on you. If you had been nicer to him, you could have gotten him to marry you instead of her."

"You want me to give up my career to come back home so I can be the wife of an adulterous hardware store owner? Are you sure you don't have fewer expectations, or have your meds finally thrown you for a loop?"

"Elizabeth Ann, my medications are just fine. Some day Cass will be grown, you know, and you'll be alone because you were too scared to give anyone a chance. Good afternoon to you."

She hung up on me, which was our normal way of ending discussions, but usually I was the one doing the hanging.

I reclined against the headrest of the cab, thinking about what Jeanne said about being alone. Few people got all the love they felt they deserved in the world. I had decided at a very young age that it was better to fold my heart into a neat little envelope, never letting anyone in, rather than deal with the pain.

Had I decided that all at once, or had I folded it up piece by piece? A father that didn't want me, a mother incapable of parenting me, abandoned with total strangers.

I did unfold that envelope for a short time, but it only left me hurting worse. No one chooses her parents, but I had chosen Aidan Palowski, I had chosen the man who had stamped my envelope "postage paid," along with the other letters he'd received. I had never been marked "special delivery" for anyone other than Cass.

I realized this afternoon, sitting across from Band-Aid Palowski, that Cass was the only stamp of approval I have ever needed.

5

MEETING IN MY BULLPEN

Catching a fly ball is a pleasure, but knowing what to do with it is a business. Tommy Henrich

Aidan 5 p.m.

I should have benched myself—impossible-to-remove-glitter-and-all—but instead, I beat the red boxing bag until I had blisters on my knuckles. I thought of Libby, and I slugged it harder, as if I could release all my frustrations in an upper cut. My trainer, an easygoing guy, stumbled backwards. "Hit the showers, Band-Aid, or I'll blacken your other eye."

Water cascaded over my aching head, steam surrounded me, but I couldn't hammer the images from my head. *Cass Christian Tucker*. C.C. Tucker would be a great baseball name.

Noise blared from my phone, vibrating off the metal lockers, pulling me out of the solitude of the shower. Vanessa had chosen an incessant rap song ringtone to ID her calls. I couldn't muster the resolve to deal with my fiancée now. I was willing to admit to myself that in the great scheme that was becoming my life, her assets weren't out-weighing her liabilities.

6 p.m.

I slid my new sunglasses back into place as the doors of the hospital elevator opened. An older, debonair gentleman stood against the paneled wall. I pushed the button for the 14th floor.

He looked up from the handheld device he was frantically shaking. "Technology," he said continuing to stare. Appraisers always spelled trouble. The hair on the back of my neck rose, coming to sharp points beneath my shirt collar.

"Mr. Palowski, I'm Winslow O'Leary from the Tribune." He extended his hand in my direction.

Crap. I shook it. "Nice to meet you." O'Leary put the go in gossip. He was an entertainment reporter, and he wasn't averse to investigating anything illegal, unethical, or immoral.

"I hope you're feeling well." He looked me up and down.

"I'm one-hundred-percent. Just here for a visit."

"The fourteenth floor has oncology offices."

"I might need to go back to the information desk, then." I examined his selection on the same keypad. "They validate your parking?" I asked for effect.

He raised his eyebrow. "Anything you'd care to share?"

"What kind of story did you say you were covering?"

"I didn't, but I'm tracking prescription drug card fraud." He folded his arms across his middle. "As a matter of fact, a corporation called CUX keeps coming up. It's funny, me running into you, seeing how your fiancée is on the board of CUX."

"I have no comment on any of Ms. Vanderhoff's holdings. We keep our personal and professional endeavors to ourselves."

"You keep your personal endeavors to yourself, and she keeps her business practices to herself." He raised a wiry eyebrow.

"If you so much as print you saw me in the elevator, I'll call your editor. I'm sure he's familiar with all the ins-and-outs of the new HIPPA guidelines." The elevator chimed, and I held the door open. "I think this your stop. It was nice meeting you."

He moved to the door, and then chuckled. "I've never heard anything other than exemplary things about you, so I'll give you a piece of friendly advice: someone of an intimate acquaintance might be involved in illegal activities."

That girl isn't worth all the bullion in Vanderhoff Hall. All that

glitters isn't gold.

That encounter gave me pause, as I stepped off the elevator. But Mr. O'Leary would have to run up four flights to determine my destination and he was much too distinguished to sprint for a story.

Dr. Rothstein's office was at the end of an elegantly appointed hall. I stepped to the receptionist's counter where an elderly, gray bearded fellow was reading the sports page.

As I approached, he stood and left the paper forgotten. "You must be Mr. Palowski. I'm Dr. Rothstein, but everyone calls me Dr. Seuss." He pumped my hand while he examined me.

He had the straight back silver hair and beard, prominent nose, and oversized glasses of his namesake. His lab coat was bright yellow, covered with characters from Dr. Seuss books—Thing 1 and Thing 2, Cat in the Hat, Horton the Elephant. He couldn't have been more than 5'-6", but he walked with the confidence of a starter as led me to his office.

I was pleasantly surprised to find his office decorated in a sports-theme. Brass plated, plastic trophies lined the shelves, pennants hung like valances above windows. Baseballs sealed in Plexiglas boxes, and framed newspaper articles from sports pages, gave the office more prestige than if it had been festooned with his framed diplomas. When I took in the first article, it was about a kid playing little league; he'd hit a grand slam in the bottom of the 9th to take his team to sectionals. "This is quite a collection, doc."

"None of them made it to the Majors, or the NFL, but many of them played in college. A few even made it to the Olympics.

"It's a terrible thing to tell parents that their child has cancer," he took his seat behind his desk and waved at all the memorabilia, "so when I give that diagnosis, there has to be some optimism that their children can also survive."

"This is a powerful way to say it."

"Cancer's a powerful enemy. Leukemia had a twenty percent survival rate around the year you were born. Now we're up to an eighty percent survival rate. Many of our new treatment options didn't exist five years ago." He tapped on his desktop. "Cancer isn't a death sentence anymore. I fight it with anything I can—and hope is a powerful healer." He motioned me to a chair. "So what can I do for you, Mr. Palowski?"

"I've come to talk to you about Cass Tucker."

"Aha, you're the anonymous donor." He had his fingertips steepled in front of his face with his elbows resting on the desktop. "I see the resemblance." He eyed my facial contusion curiously.

"What are Cass' chances for survival?"

"His cancer has a ninety percent cure factor, if we find a bone marrow donor."

"I'd like some of the specifics." I stared him down.

"I'll give you some pamphlets. Cass has Acute Lymphocytic Leukemia, the form of cancer most common among children. Acute Leukemia is associated with the rapid growth of immature blood cells, which makes the bone marrow unable to produce healthy cells. If you're a viable donor, I will sit down with your physician to discuss the danger of the procedure. The side effects are minimal for donors, but you would want to make sure that you had your personal business in order. Your next of kin should be notified, and you will need weeks of recuperation."

"And what about Cass' case specifically?"

"I'm sorry Mr. Palowski; I will keep your confidence, just as I'm keeping Cass' now.

"I left blood samples in the Lab. I ran into a reporter in the elevator so I'd appreciate your discretion."

"I heard Mr. O'Leary was in the building, that old coot can be quite tenacious." He leaned over a file cabinet, pulling out brochures. "But if your involvement here works out, you could raise donor awareness, sponsor and star in a public service announcement. The National Leukemia Foundation would love to have someone of your stature as a spokesperson."

"Yeah. The guy who abandoned his kid," I muttered.

"To quote my namesake: 'Sometimes the questions are complicated and the answers are simple'." He shook his head. "Did you and Elizabeth know each other at Indiana?"

From the first moment I laid eyes on her, she was trouble to my concentration, my libido, and my mental health. After six weeks of pursuit, I'd trapped her between my upraised arms against a bookcase, somewhere betwixt Shakespeare and Voltaire. "I want the witchcraft in your lips," I'd whispered.

Instead of arguing, she'd grabbed me by the ears. She's been all soft lips, liberal tongue, and nipping teeth. I'd contributed a willing body and a vulgar groan. She'd drawn away, licked her lips, and ducked under my arms. When she was about three yards from me, she'd tilted her head up like a siren on the bow of a ship and pursed a devil-may-care smile at me before she curtsied.

She'd challenged me to pursue her, and I'd intended to, but when I pushed off the bookcase it fell backwards. I tumbled in a heap of literary tombs. I could still hear her laughing when the library's elevator doors chimed closed.

"Yeah," I said, answering the doc's question, "Before she set me up."

"She got herself pregnant all by herself?" Dr. Seuss asked, his wrinkled brow drawing my gaze again. "I'm not quite as old as I let on. I remember well enough all the places you can go."

"I participated in the act, but not the outcome."

"She must have known at the beginning of her pregnancy that she was accepted at Northwestern. She wouldn't blow that to set a trap, even for a pro-athlete."

"Northwestern University?"

"Yes, Northwestern Law School."

Holy mother of God. "She went to Northwestern Law School?"

"She's a criminal defense attorney."

I stood abruptly. The moment he gave me the literature I shook his hand and left. I started dialing numbers. I was getting a thorough background check on Elizabeth Ann Tucker.

I like that Dr. Seuss fella. 'You have brains in your head. You have feet in your shoes. You can steer yourself in any direction you choose'. Choose the right path, kid.

I imagined strangling the ump with his plaid bow tie.

7:30 p.m.

The rap song blared through my cell, every fifteen minutes, like clockwork. I was sick of pushing the reject button. "Yeah?"

"Banford, darling, you've been a naughty boy."

My real name is Banford Aidan Palowski, and I was known around Chi-Town by many names; Palowski to critics, Band-Aid to adoring fans, Aidan to my friends and family. No one called me Banford to my face, even my mother. Vanessa said it made me sound very east-coast-old-money.

"I've been calling you all day." There was blaring noise in the background and glasses clinking together.

Crap. "Sorry Vanessa, I've had an eventful day."

"Me, too. The photographer was late. Then my dumb-twitted assistant, Melinda, spilled coffee all over the Valentino I was supposed to wear for the shoot. She had to shop for a new dress, and the shoes she selected were cheap Franco Sartos. Who would wear shoes without leather soles? Did you know they don't have a Ferragamo shop in San Fran? That's why I've been calling you. I thought you would be a dear and pick them up for me."

"You could have had them overnight them to you." I picked up the mail off my foyer floor.

"I'm over my limit."

"What?" I almost dropped the mail.

"My card was declined. It's the end of the month, Banford."

"It's the eighteenth. How have you spent your budget?"

"Come on, Banford, don't be such a stickley. We can afford whatever I want. Please, let's not fight about money."

"It's stickler, not stickley." Deep breathe. "We set the budget so we wouldn't fight about money. You've blown through twenty grand in eighteen days. Do you realize most families in Chicago live on a quarter of that a month? I meant what I said. I won't marry you if you can't be financially responsible."

"It's the off-season." She huffed. "Why can't you just relax, pick up my shoes, and send them to me instead of being such a trollop about money? Or is it a toll?"

Does Goldilocks know most people consider her a trollop?

"It's being droll, not a trollop, and a toll is a fee you pay on the highway." I closed my eyes. She was a sweet girl, but sometimes, God, she was challenged. "I have better things to do than to shop for you," I finally said.

"Oh really? What's so important?" She let the silence linger. "Working out three times a day?"

I hesitated. I wasn't going to mention Cass. "The clown for my Halloween fundraiser didn't pass his background checks."

"That's real save the world stuff, you know?"

"I have decisions to make." *Life or death decisions*. "Forgive me if I don't return your calls, or give a flying fig about your Ferragamos." When she started to whimper, I ended the call. No matter how many labels Ferragamo, Valentino, or Franco Sartos stitched in soles, I didn't have time for her or silly shoe shopping.

The realization hit me like a stiletto to the head: she was never going to grow up. I couldn't face a forever of this kind of nonsense . . . not with the seriousness of my current situation. I couldn't coddle her like those canine cockroaches.

In the kitchen I dug around in the Sub-Zero, constructed a sandwich, and grabbed a beer. Before I was able to get a bite out of my sandwich, the doorbell rang. Fletch was a crumbled mess on my doorstep. I'd never seen him without a suit coat on and his tie knotted in a perfect Windsor, but the former was draped over his shoulder and the latter's knot dangled in the center of his chest. "You look like hell," I said.

"Yeah well, your eye looks like shit." He followed me into my study. "I could use one of those." Fletch pointed toward the beer as he threw his sports coat, and then himself, into a chair.

"Dick Doyle wants you to testify to the Senate subcommittee about steroid use in professional sports."

Who is named Dick anymore? "Am I being subpoenaed?"

"Of course not. He read the *People* magazine article. He wants someone to testify about clean living in baseball. The hearings aren't until the new January session, so I booked it."

"I'm not interested."

By then, kid, the whole world will know you cut deeper than any Band-Aid could cover.

"You need all the positive PR you can get," Fletch said.

"You didn't come here for that. What's the bad news?"

"I tried to get Mrs. Landscale to settle. She's moving forward with the lawsuit."

"Crap."

"Crap is right. I pushed up your contract signing on Friday with the front office to noon. We should have it signed, sealed, and delivered before it hits the news."

"I want to settle. How much does she want?"

He looked resigned. "Five million."

"What? Is she crazy?" I had met Mrs. Landscale at her husband's wake. She was distraught but sane.

"She says you intentionally risked their lives."

"She has no idea what was said between us, and I was the only one left alive."

"That's what she's most displeased about, that you're still alive. She insists her husband would have returned to base camp, when the weather turned."

A chill ran through me.

Fletch regarded me. "It's true? One more of your adventures that took you to death's door? I've never seen a guy with more to live for, who's willing to throw it all away."

"I would not throw my life away."

"No, you just take it to the edge as often as you can. Someone else got hurt because you went too far. Two kids don't have a father now." He threw me a dirty look. "This is going to be the worst public relations nightmare."

"Pay her." I pulled a long drag from my beer.

"Are you crazy? That guy wouldn't have even made two million in his entire life. There's no way I'm paying five."

"Pay her. Certified funds. Tomorrow."

"I am not paying her more than a quarter-million."

"Pay her Fletch." I rested my head against the headrest, resigned. "I have bigger fish to fry."

"There's more to this change of heart." He spoke through the doorway as I retrieved his beer. "This morning, you were convinced you'd never give her more than the quarter million. I know you feel bad, but regardless of your adrenaline-junky highs, it was a white-out, and even you can't order those."

I gave him a look of blank resolve as I handed him a beer. He was worth every penny I'd ever paid. "Sometimes I wish we could talk as friends, without you trying to position things," I said, reclining in my office chair.

He smiled wryly. "What happened between you and Tucker?"

I shook my head no, and stared resolutely at my computer.

"If you don't tell me, I'll pay her office a call."

"You gave her my number and me no heads up she's a big time criminal defense attorney."

"I only know two types of broads: those I've fucked, and female lawyers I should've done before I got married. She falls into the latter category. She's one hot number, but I asked around, and no one I know ever got to first base with her."

I reached across my desk and grabbed him by the loosened tie and pulled his face up until our eyeballs locked. "She's not just another notch in a belt."

"What's she to you?" He laughed in my face. "The one who got away?"

With my other hand, I slid the knot of his tie back toward his wide pipe. "I've asked you nicely."

"Okay, okay." He was struggling and choking. "All right she was more than a piece of a—"

I glared and he stopped himself.

"It's obviously a sore subject. What does she want?"

His blood, guts, and tears on a silver platter.

"It's a private matter."

"You gave up your right to privacy when you became a professional athlete and a client of mine."

"Yes, but Libby didn't."

"Libby, is it?" He arched a brow in accusation. "You're going to have to tell me what's going on sooner or later, so you'd better cough it up. I can't take any more shitty surprises."

I crossed my arms over my chest and sat back farther in my chair. "Her son is dying of Leukemia. She needs my help."

"Don't you have to be related to be a donor?"

It was the kind of silence that came before an avalanche.

Fletch's face became so red I thought he might ignite. "You have a kid, and you never told me? You asshole! You haven't been paying child support." His Irish Catholic rage-o-meter blazed up his neck through the tips of his ears. I thought it might spew a river of red rage out his eye sockets. "She's going to clean your clock! Why didn't you tell me?"

"I knew she was pregnant, but it was right before I'd been called up to triple A. When I told her I wanted her to have an abortion, she disappeared, and about a year later I received termination of parental rights papers. I signed them and sent them back. I assumed that meant she was giving the kid up."

"You aren't supposed to assume a damn thing! You pay me to make sure your conjectures are correct. Why the fuck didn't you show me the papers?"

"I didn't want anyone to know." I met his eye. "I didn't want to be pressured into doing the right thing."

"Doing the right thing?" He ground out in agitation.

"Coerce me to into being a father. I wasn't ready."

"If you didn't want to be a father you should've keep your bat and balls in your pants." Fletch was silent for a minute solid. "And for the record, what the fuck would the right thing have been?"

"I don't know. Marry her and give the kid a name."

"From one friend to another," he looked up from his hands, "if you thought she was giving the kid up for adoption, then why the fuck would you think I would tell you to marry her?"

"I didn't want to get married. I wanted to concentrate on my baseball career. So I signed the papers, thinking she wanted to give the baby away, and I would forget all about it. I wanted it to go away, and it did."

"You thought you'd force her hand. If you weren't going to help her, she'd have no other choice than to give it up."

"Believe what you want, but that's bullshit, Fletch."

"You didn't count on her being as tough as nails." His eyes narrowed. "She worked her ass off to get through law school. She probably had debt up to her eyeballs, and she was carrying your dead weight. You are one lucky fuck. She could have ruined you."

I never asked myself why, because then I'd have to admit she was the better person. She let me walk clean and clear and never held it over my head.

"I'm curious. What did it take to forget?" He got to his feet and paced up and down in front of my desk. "Did hang-gliding in the Amazon make you forget? Did parachuting in the Grand Canyon? Did trying to climb an impossible mountain in the middle of a blizzard make you forget?"

I shook my head. "It's been eating away at me forever."

"And rightly so." Fletch whittled words together in silence before the sharpened barbs would fly, you'd be impaled before you realized the splinters had pierced you skin. I wasn't used to being on the receiving end of his rancor.

"You're an idiot! You had the chance to have a woman like Elizabeth Tucker, and instead you found a shallow immature bimbo to marry. Do you know what happens to your gene pool when you marry someone that ignorant?"

"For the record, I couldn't have her. Libby, that is."

"Obviously you did at least once." He shook his head. "Have you thought about what you're going to do now?"

"I had the blood test run, and I saw the kid's doc." I took in a deep breath. "I'm going to do whatever I can to help him."

Silence stretched out between us, filling the chasm the storm left. "I'm speaking as your friend, here. You clear your calendar, and make yourself available twenty-four/seven."

"Done." It was the least I owed Libby and my son.

"I knew you were too much of a choir boy—no booze, no drugs—of course not, that would have hindered your perfection on the field. Sheez, I should have realized why women weren't your vice—because you couldn't have the one you wanted!"

"Shut up, Fletch."

"This gives me a whole new perspective on your out-of-control cravings for the adrenaline rush. If you fill your senses with the rush, you can avoid feeling anything real."

"Don't start that psychobabble stuff with me. The next thing I know you'll be watching Oprah with your wife."

"I happen to like Oprah. And leave *my* wife out of this."

"And I enjoy extreme sports."

"This isn't about your hobbies. I'm talking about financial responsibility. Pay her all the child support she's due. Twenty percent of every dime you've ever made. You might have signed termination of parental rights papers, but this is one gig you're going to live up to."

"I have no problem with that."

"Now, speaking as your attorney, this will give us the bargaining chip we need in the wrongful death case." He ran his hand across the stubble on his jaw and walked the length of the room a few more times. "No jury is going to award Mrs. Landscale five million dollars when your kid is dying of Leukemia."

"What?"

The third ball right against the breastplate, folks.

"When this story gets out, you're not going to pay Mrs. Landscale much of anything. It was a tragic accident, after all, and you understand all about tragedies yourself. You've missed the first ... how old is the kid?"

"Six."

"You've missed the first six years of your kid's life, and now he's dying." He smirked.

"What kind of crazy spin are you going to put on this?"

"Just enough spin to keep your money in your bank account."

"So much for high moral standards."

"Don't you dare talk to me about morals, when your shit got us into this, and it's going to get us out." He narrowed his gaze. "You're going to help Elizabeth and the kid any way you can. You're going to pay all his medical bills. You're going to negotiate a reasonable settlement in the Landscale wrongful death suit, which, once her lawyers learn your son is dying of cancer, they'll gladly accept. And then you're going to graciously take your child support money back, when Elizabeth Tucker throws it in your face. The home run of the whole thing is that you're going to look like a fucking hero, when all is said and done. Whether the kid lives or dies, you come out looking better than you have in years."

"This is a kid we're talking about! Whether he lives or dies is important to Libby."

"You abandoned your kid to play in the majors, when you already had more money than God." Fletch turned on his heel. "All I'm doing is picking up the pieces as best I can."

This is the kind of thing agents have done for the game. Heartless bastards.

I took the ump's cue. "You're heartless."

"Heart is when you put others first in the line, and that's where my family is. My heart came from nothing, now it beats on greenbacks. I wasn't born with the luxury of a golden glove up my ass." He picked up his suit jacket before parlaying his final jab. "You're ashamed of me for getting us out of this any way I can? Well I'm ashamed you're here in the first place. You've always been cocky, but I never once pegged you a coward."

Fletch stormed out of the house.

I picked up the first thing I could lay my hands on and rocketed it across the room. A spilt second later it met with my flat screen television and both shattered into thirty-three-point-seven-million little pieces.

That little tantrum cost you a good inning of work and you missed the strike zone by a mile.

"Yeah, well, some things are worth paying for."

6

(NOT) LOVE AT FIRST SIGHT

Fire is never a gentle master.

Elizabeth

Cass hooted as the pinball machine's score tabulated, flashing red and white as it dinged. You would never imagine by looking at him that his body was failing him. In spite of being poked and prodded by two specialists, he was having a good day and he'd earned the evening at Dave & Buster's.

I used to be able to bribe him through doctor visits with candy, but today he'd said, "I'm six now, and I'm looking for bigger payoffs." I'd swung around looking for Aidan—it was the kind of thing he'd say—and I'd tried to smile when he said it. It's funny how biology trumped environment sometimes.

Madi ran up to our booth, eyeing her father, before turning her puppy-dog-pout on me. "Aunt Libby, Cass won't listen to me. He never does what I say."

Before I could respond, Cass came alongside Madi looking about as innocent as a choirboy caught with his hands in the collection basket. "You're a girl. You can't boss me around." He was serious, and his smile was so broad that the dimple in his right cheek might cut his sharp little tongue out.

Dr. Steve Dubrowski smiled at his daughter. "You've got to stop being so bossy, Madi. Nobody likes a know it all."

"But you said I was the smartest girl in the world."

I pulled on one of Madi's long brown braids and noticed pink glitter dotting her cheekbone. I whispered conspiratorially, "The trick is to make him want what you want."

"I'll use my Pixie Powers, like I did on butthead."

"We don't call people butthead." Steve smiled at his daughter. "Here are some more tokens, go play until dinner."

Cass took the coins, and Madi, in the direction of the claw.

"Pixie power?" I asked Steve.

"Her grandmother put Madi in a commercial this morning." He gave me a grim smile. "She's trying to turn Madi into her mother, minus the character flaws, of course."

I put my hand over my mouth in mock disgust. "And you found nothing appealing about Danielle in the least?"

He cocked his head to one side. "That's enough about my ex-wife who dumped us for a cabana boy. What happened with super jock?"

"I think the parlay between our children succinctly sums up my conversation with Band-Aid Palowski."

"The guy's dense. I'd give you anything you wanted."

"That's because you're a giver, and he's a taker."

"No, I'm interested in taking." He winked.

I was saved from rehashing a conversation with the man I would love only as a friend, when Vicki bounced up to the table performing a nervous twitter with her hands. New age hocus pocus, maybe. "What did you get yourself into now?" she asked.

"The devil wants a slice of my soul." I shied away from Steve's gaze. "But I maneuvered a bail hearing for Accardo."

Vicki was my closest friend and glowing at seven months pregnant. She could no longer see her feet, or the color of her hair, I assumed. It was as black as midnight on a moonless night, with a single shaft of electric blue running down the larger side of her part. Yesterday, that stripe had been tangerine on blonde. "What?" She ran her hand along the darkest part of her hair. "It's a fabulous color, and it matches your mood."

I was used to her eccentric behavior—I blamed it on her weed-riddled parents.

We'd both hailed from cutter-ville. Cutter originally referred to someone who worked in the local stone cutting industry, but it became a derogatory term used by Indiana students, akin to townie.

While I was on Nose-to-the-grindstone-gravel-road, Vicki was traveling along Live-a-little-lane. Both of us expected to end up somewhere better than a dirt path in Southern Indiana. Each of us had our own ideas about how to arrive at our new destination. I had a route mapped out, and Vicki ... she didn't care to read a map. In her estimation, it was always more fun to fly on the edge of your broomstick with a bare backside.

"What happened?" She probed again.

My mind drifted back to the confrontation. "A serious miscalculation on my part, and he was pissed."

Aidan's confidently sprawled form among the sea of empty chairs at Gutheries had made me shake on the insides. He still had that animal magnetism that drew me in and those piercing blue eyes that could cut the flesh from my bones. Any semblance of the guy I once knew was buried beneath the cocky, confident arrogance he exuded. Aidan had eyed my approach, sinking further into his chair. His long, denim clad legs splayed out in front of him in the casual manner of a man who knew exactly where he was, where he had been, and what he wanted once he got to where he was going. I felt the first twinges of defeat. "Having my tonsils removed by a Volvo mechanic would have been more fun."

"He's pissed you want help?" Vicki prompted me to go on.

"I had entertained doubts that he'd show up, but the threat to his contract got his attention." Baseball was his God and his life centered on its worship. "He thought I gave Cass up."

"Uh-oh." Vicki paled. "Jenny said he was in a snit and talking to himself before he left."

"He called me and told me where and when he wants to talk to me about what he wants in exchange for his DNA. And I'm not talking Dashing, Noble, Arrogance."

"He asked you out? I don't see the problem with that. He's still hot."

If I had a Vicki doll, I'd toothpick her irises. "I'd like to tie him to a totem pole and set fire to it."

Vicki tapped her fingertips against watermelon-shaped stomach through her gauzy embroidered tunic, and waited for me to back down. "He's always compelled you to combustion."

Better not comment on the Mu-Mu; she was getting a little prickly about the maternity clothes issue. "What you call compelling, I call manipulative." I waved my arms around as if willing God's intervention. "All I want is some DNA."

"Are you sure?" She asked perkily.

Steve groaned.

"I guarantee you want to see him more than I do. Dealing with him has always been a nightmare, and I have enough on my plate right now." I gave her a look that, roughly translated, meant: keep your matchmaking fairytale dreams to yourself.

She smiled at my frown and stared off in the direction of the kids. "There's one way to find out if dreams do come true."

Vicki believed in dreams. Hell, she conjured them. She'd fallen in love with the Fed Ex guy. "I could also believe peacocks can fly to Timbuktu, but they prefer to prance and preen. Oh wait, that describes Palowski and his cunning agent perfectly."

In the interest of her happy *chi* and keeping a harmonious relationship with Steve, I said, "He's engaged to what's-her-face … . the one with the practiced-pose-on-the-cover-of-some-trashy tabloid. Which proves he's as superficial as ever."

Vicki stopped my rant with a kohl-rimmed eye roll. Voodoo priestess translation: I know what's best for you.

"Yeah," I retorted. "If I want to know what life on Mars is like, you know best. Otherwise, I'm still the well adjusted of our pair. Ask the doc his professional opinion." And I indicated Steve with a nod, knowing that he'd take my side.

Instead of doing so, he got to his feet. "I better check on the kids before we have to pay for a Claw machine."

I tried to smile Steve's frown away. It made me sad that he

wanted more, but we'd only be friends. What was wrong with me? He was the holy trinity of dating: straight and sexy, gainfully employed, and matrimonially inclined. Vicki wasn't trying to dismiss Steve as a possibility for me because she didn't like him; it was just that she had an affinity for a *Gone With the Wind* kind of saga.

I should be irritated with her, but if it weren't for Vicki busting her tattooed ass, I wouldn't be a lawyer. Vicki stayed with Cass while I'd gone to law school. At night, she worked jobs ranging from a topless cocktail waitress to 911 operator. She'd even done phone sex, while she was a 911 operator, which was a mess to dig her out of.

When I passed the bar exam, she went to secretarial school and took her first professional job. It was a thorny transition for a woman more akin to being an Egyptian Priestess than a legal assistant. I brought her on board at my firm and, because of her help, I was on the fast track to make partner.

"I should have saved myself the hassle and subpoenaed him into giving me the blood sample."

"Neither of you admitted it, but that doesn't mean there wasn't something between you." Vicki huffed off in the direction of the ladies room, probably to whip up some sort of love potion or bend a voodoo doll to her will.

I sighed, as Steve tried to coax the kids into another game. Here I was, seven years later, aching all over again because he still refused to give me any part of himself. What had been a bloody tournament of wills between us then could still run cold with spiteful emotions now. Only this time I would lose the only part of him I had kept for myself—Cass. I gave up two long-harbored dreams the day we created our son—Harvard Law and love.

In my reflection of the world, love lived only on pages of a southern depression-era novel. And let's face it: Aidan Palowski was no Rhett Butler.

Elizabeth, 8 years ago

Vicki pulled me, and I tripped over the stairs into the alcove's pool table at McCleary's. He was bent over the green felt and mahogany surface. His eyes focused on me, and for the first time in my life I felt like I was a strange, exotic, thing. Unusual enough to encourage another human being's pursuit of me to the end of the world. My body jerked strangely in reaction to his examination, and then a slow smile spread to the corners of his generous mouth.

Time came to an otherworldly halt, as we were caught in the vortex of the other's reflections, my eyes bound to his crisp crystal blue depths. I didn't believe in love at first sight. In fact, I didn't give much credence to love at all, but his whole personality seemed resolutely focused on my being, as if he could see under my skin, through my veins, right to my heart.

The increased beating of that very organ awakened me out of my stupor when he came toward me, extended his hand, and we exchanged names. His warm fingers brushed mine. In an instinctual reaction, I stepped away, but he held fast. "Elizabeth is a beautiful name."

The moment we touched, I came alive, humming with a thin layer of perspiration beading my skin. Streams of subconscious desire leapt through my body. I looked down at my feet.

"Everyone calls me Band-Aid." He hadn't released my hand, but gave it a gentle squeeze, forcing me to look up. He had a single dimple in his right cheek. I willed my hand to stop tingling and for the baby hairs on my arms to relax.

As we played pool, I stole glances at him under my lashes. My throat had grown tight and scratchy, despite my liquid refreshment. Afraid that I would say something stupid, I kept my thoughts to myself, but I wondered if our friends noticed the sparks dancing between us.

"So?" His rolled-up shirtsleeves brushed against my bare arm. "I've seen you somewhere before. Are you a sorority girl?"

"Do I look like one?" I took off my glasses and breathed onto the lenses before cleaning them with the tail of my shirt.

"Well, you have that 'uppity' look about you, and you haven't put two words together."

"Maybe you're confusing uppity with plain old shy."

"I've been looking for half an hour, and there's nothing plain about you." His intense aquatic eyes seemed to be puzzling out my behavior. "Where do I know you from?"

"I work at the Waffle House on Kirkwood."

"If I'd seen you there I'd be a regular by now." He smiled. "If I win, you'll go out with me?"

"Are you trying to distract me so that you can catch up on points?" I smiled as I bent over to take my shot.

"I was working up the nerve."

I wiggled my backside, which he was watching, while I took my follow-up shot. Without looking up from the table I said. "I somehow doubt nerve has ever been a problem for you." I sank another striped ball into the side pocket. "You're not going to win." I set up the final shot.

"How can you be sure of that?"

"I'm about to make this simple shot and win." I couldn't stop myself from pouting when escape was within my reach.

He moved closer as I leaned on my stick, studying the table. He put his hand on the lower part of my back, and leaned into me. His spicy, masculine scent filled my senses. "I, for one, hope you can't make that shot, so I can take a shot with you."

As I leaned over the table, I smirked over my shoulder, sinking the ball into the outside corner pocket. "Too bad, so sad." I gave him my stick. "You won't mind putting that away for me, will you?" I recovered my drink, Vicki, and our purses, and we made our way into the throng of the bar. His gaze followed and burned through my backside once again.

Vicki caught my eye. "Those were some serious fireworks."

"He's just a jock playboy. It didn't mean anything."

"Did you check out his bod? He's built like a long, tall tree I'd be willing to climb."

"There's a lengthy line of lady lumberjacks with scraped knees crying in the shadows of his mighty limbs."

"Come on, there were actual sparks flying." Vicki bumped my

hip with hers. "I considered sunglasses to help with the glare."

"Sparks lead to fire, fire to flame, flame to burning, and then I'm toast. I know an incendiary device when I see it, and no matter how enticing the packaging, I'm not playing it with him."

"He has the hots for you." Vicky reiterated.

"I'm not interested."

"What are you not interested in?" His silky Midwestern twang filled my ears.

I hadn't seen his approach, but I smelled him. The golden God, who towered over everyone in the room, swirled around me.

"You," I said.

"Really? I could try harder."

"You're not my ilk."

"Really? What kind of ilk am I?"

"Jock, pretty boy, all the girls chase you, thinking they'll be the one to snag you." I resumed playing with the lime in my Absolut and cranberry. "You're prince charming; they're all damsels in distress. Yada, yada, yada."

"Afraid you can't measure up?"

"I'm not interested in stumbling among the masses."

He took a long swig of beer before he swiveled my stool toward him so he could examine me. "I hardly think you stumble all the time, and you already stood out from the crowd. That's the first time I've lost a game to a girl and didn't throw it."

"You lost because you were too busy checking out my ass."

"Checking you out was worth losing my competitive nature." He tipped his beer bottle into my highball glass. *Clink*

"What do you want from me?"

"How about a date?"

"Nope."

"Sex?"

"You have a girlfriend."

"Why would you think that?"

I put my hand over his right hand and strummed my fingertips over his bare ring finger. "Your class ring is probably hanging among some lovely coed's perky breasts right now."

"Did you say perky breasts?"

"You keep up better than most jocks." I saluted him.

He had enough decency to blush, as he looked at his hands absentmindedly rubbing the white line across his finger. "We have a very open relationship."

"I'm sure you have an open relationship, and I'm sure she doesn't know about your extracurricular activities. Thanks for the offer, but I don't play second string." He was the finest thing that had ever given me the time of day, but I wasn't going to be a plaything for some batboy who didn't know that everyone has feelings. Even us small town girls.

He kept staring, willing me to look at him. When I gave up, and our gazes met, he smiled. "You know, any other girl wearing those glasses would not appeal to me at all, but there's something different about you, Elizabeth Tucker."

"These librarian glasses enhance my ability to call a spade a spade."

"Wow. Who burned you so bad?"

"No one." I sighed. "Everyone."

"You were more fun when I had you corralled in a small room, unable to speak."

"Guys always lose interest, once I start talking."

"I like to listen to your voice, even if I don't know what you mean half the time. I'll catch on sooner or later." He picked up my hand from the bar, his thumb tracing the lines in my palm. "You have the prettiest hands. You talk with them."

It was all I could do to keep my seat. I'd just been plugged in. All my senses were set ablaze. As ridiculous as it sounded, I knew exactly what it would feel like to touch him again. I would ignite. It would burn so badly and so deep that I wouldn't be able to breathe or think or feel anything else.

And that's exactly what had happened. I had been toasted to a crisp heap of broken heart. Superstar jocks don't take cutters to the Rose Well House at the center of campus at midnight, to pledge their undying devotion beneath its sparkling dome. That privilege was reserved for girls of status.

And now seven years later, he'd insisted that I see him again. What does a girl have to do to get a little anonymous DNA?

7

AWAY GAMES

Bench me or trade me. Chico Ruiz

Aidan 5 a.m.

"Disposition, Band-Aid?" David asked as he took my bag.

I slid into the coal colored interior of the limo, where I found a *Tribune* and a Dunkin Donuts black coffee. "We'll talk. Just let me jump-start my brain." I saluted him with the Styrofoam cup.

"Nice shiner." He snickered. "Up late?"

David and I had played baseball at IU together. He'd been a great first baseman, but not such a hot student. When his GPA bottomed-out, he was cut from the team; it wasn't long until he flunked out, and then he bummed around Bloomington until everyone else graduated. When he came to Chicago, I invested in his limo business, not because I thought it would be profitable, but because he was lost and needed some direction. But he made a go of it and finished school, and now he's busy signing contracts with every major sports organization in Chicago.

"Not for the right reasons. I couldn't sleep. I need to have a difficult conversation with my parents."

"The truth will set you free." He laughed.

"Six years overdue."

"I thought you might be flying out to see Vanessa."

"She's first up, and she won't be happy when we're done."

"You finally releasing her from that hare-brained life-time contract she suckered you into?"

"I thought I could marry her, but I can't." I ran my hand through my hair. If I can't confide in my best friend, who can I count on? "Someone reminded me how it feels to really want someone."

I gazed out my window. We had just merged onto the Kennedy Expressway; traffic was sparse heading for the airport. "You never gave me your scouting report on Vanessa."

"Hard to tell which one of you has been more spoiled, but I've known you a long time. When you dig deep there are some everyday good guy values." He hesitated and he cleared his throat. "Vanessa, on the other hand … if you dig deep with her, all you'd find is decaying peroxide bottles."

"Don't hold back now."

"Palowski, she's the dumbest thing you've ever done. She has a greedy heart that only a bookie could love."

I threw my head back against the headrest. "You could have told me sooner and saved me the trouble of buying a fancy ring."

"Sooner or later you'd start to think with the right head."

I'd say my vision had been clouded where Vanessa was concerned, but it might have been delusional blindness.

"I saw Libby."

"I know it's a sore subject, and you're not going to want to hear this, but Libby's the only girl that ever changed you." He nodded in the rearview mirror. "At the time I resented the hell out of it.

"I thought she distracted you from the team—and from winning." David paused, smoothly changing lanes. "You always were perfect at everything, but something about her made you shine."

"She kept the kid. He's sick." I tried to rub the ache out of my neck. "She's a criminal defense attorney."

"I know." David scratched at his collar. "I shuttled attorneys from her firm to a Christmas party. She ignored me."

"Well, you used to call her Little Libby Nobody."

"I didn't say I didn't deserve it. I was an ass. I knew as much about women then as I did about making the dean's list."

"Why didn't you tell me you'd seen her?"

"I tried to hint around about it, but once you were engaged I didn't want to interfere."

"Aren't best friends supposed to?"

"My Granny taught me, if you don't have anything nice to say, shut your pie hole."

9 a.m.

I slipped into the BMW 645 rental, put the top down and made my way onto the freeway. One of the things I loved about California was the cars: Ferraris, Lamborghinis, Porsches, and Bentleys stretched across the landscape.

I didn't know for sure, but I assumed Vanessa would be at the Ritz. I preferred the St. Regis Hotel for the character and history, but my fiancée thought the most expensive equaled the best. Plus, her family owned it.

Vanessa's celebrity wasn't birthed through education, hard work and ambition. It flowed through boarding schools, Swiss bank accounts and largesse. Vanessa vaulted to the media's attention through calculated planning, publicity and public outbursts. It didn't hurt that her father was one of the richest men in the world, owning hotels that spanned the globe from Bangkok to Bolivia.

But she was going to be Daddy's problem again. I had been working through this decision before I knew about Cass, but with the reality of him everything else seemed to crystallize on fast forward. There was no way I would be able to devote myself to establishing a relationship with him, if I had to babysit a spoiled grown up.

I pulled up on Stockton Street under the columned pediment, which would have been better displayed on the mall in D.C. than wasted on a hotel. The valet opened my door, "Hey, you're Palowski, on the Cubs, right?"

"That's me." I handed him a fifty-dollar bill. "Do me a favor, don't garage my car. I won't be long. An hour tops."

The front desk rang Vanessa's room. I heard Melinda on the line, and Vanessa screaming in the background: "Who's calling so early in the morning?"

As if this was the predawn hour, I thought as the elevator jolted to a halt on the seventh floor. Her assistant met me at the door. She was dressed and ready for the day.

"Why don't you take the beasts down to The Terrace, and have breakfast on me?" I waved some bills toward her.

"Maybe she'll feel better when you're done with her."

"Don't count on it. It's not that kind of *tête-à-tête*."

She didn't seem panicked. "Are you breaking your engagement?" She asked curiously, before she smiled. "I quit. Give me one minute to grab my bags. Nothing could get me to come back knowing that. I'll leave the canines at the front desk."

"That bad, huh?"

"You have no earthly idea." She dumped what was left of her toiletries into a carry on.

"Call David to pick you up when you get back to Chicago."

"If you think … the only things she takes lying down are those that please her." She bit her lips and I wondered what other revelations she was keeping to herself.

But I didn't have time to ask, I was mentally preparing for a woman-made earthquake. This wasn't going to go down smoothly, but I hoped I wasn't going to have to refurbish the room.

The darkened suite was eerily quiet when I knocked on the bedroom door. I turned the knob surprised it wasn't locked. I made my way to the windows and pulled one side of the blackout panels back to illuminate the luxurious cavern.

"I don't care if the King of Prussia is here!" She shrieked from behind her silk eye mask. "Revoke him from my room."

This is what I reap for giving her a vocabulary builder. I sat on the edge of the bed.

Palowski, Goldilocks isn't as well rounded as the practice balls in the dugout.

"That's one of your problems." I ran my hand through my hair.

"You never care what anyone else wants."

Her lips contorted into a naughty smile. "Banford, you didn't have to bring the Ferragamos purposefully. You could have shipped them, but I'm peachy–cleaned you didn't." She threw her covers back invitingly. When she shifted, her gown wound up around the top of her tanned thighs. There wasn't a lot left to the imagination, undergarments had been an optional apparel item since she'd received her first bra.

"I didn't bring shoes, and I didn't come for that—either." I tugged the covers over her bare assets.

"Oh my God, you got cut from the team." She flapped her hands. "We can have more time to play together."

"What? No, I told you I'm signing a new contract tomorrow."

"You did?"

"That's just it, Vanessa. You're so wrapped up in your own life that you never listen to what's going on in mine."

"What are you trying to say?" If she noticed the condition of my eye she didn't comment. But panic and fear began to rise in hers. "You love me, Banford. I know you do."

"No, Vanessa, I don't love you, not the way I should. We enjoyed each other's bodies. I thought I felt something more, but it wouldn't be right for us to marry. You're not ready to settle down and have a family. I'm sorry, but we don't want the same things. You hate Chicago, you don't want to be a player's wife; you want to be a princess and jet setter."

She pulled herself up onto her knees as she started to cry. I hadn't seen the fake tears for what they were in the past but I gauged them correctly this time. "This is about the money. I'm sorry, Banford. I'll be good from now on. I'll live on the budget, I swear. I love you, Banford. Please, think of what you're doing. Daddy already booked the Plaza for our wedding."

"I don't want to be tied to a little girl who's living in a woman's body. You can keep the ring, sell it and buy as many Ferragamos as you want." I watched the crocodile tears dry up and her jaws snarl on a death chomp.

"Do you know who I am? I'm going to be one of the richest women in the world when daddy dies. Do you think you can use me and be done with me whenever you want?"

"We used each other in equal measure. I've tried my best, but it's not enough."

Before I caught the first tremor of movement, she lashed out with her nails drawn. I felt blood run down my cheek in the wake of the burning claw marks. I stood and pushed her off me, she bellowed, her lungs heaving, hurling accusations. "Does this have something to do with someone named Libby?"

I froze, my knees going weak on the patterned carpet. "What?"

"You said 'oh Libby', when you climaxed once."

I did? I forced myself to move toward the door without looking back.

"You've been cheating on me, and when I find out who the little bitch is, I swear I'm going to make her life miserable."

What she lacks in brains, the leech makes up for in venom.

On the Pacific Coast Highway I passed the opulent painted ladies with giant picture windows overlooking the Golden Gate Bridge and San Francisco Bay. I had been so stupid, not only about Vanessa, but about Libby too. If I was calling out Libby's name in my sleep, perhaps something bigger than my guilty conscience was at work.

Were the tangled workings of my principles reining me back to her all along? Did Cass get cancer, so I'd have to see her again? So I'd have to deal with what I'd done wrong? Maybe I deserved more than a black eye and a bloodied face. Until I'd met her, I had never had a reason to look in the rearview mirror of my life. Now it seemed I needed a major backwards glance.

I avoided oncoming traffic along the winding road and narrowed paths populated with drivers who'd attended a few too many wine tastings. My parents bought a small vineyard in Napa Valley when I went to college. I always considered Chicago home, but my younger brother, Avery, was a surfer, basking in Pacific waves every chance he could. He was a junior at Stanford this year, and I hoped he wouldn't make the mistake I'd made in college.

The Italian-inspired villa sat in a clearing, shaded under two-hundred-year-old Spanish oaks. The deep-set stone veranda wrapped its arms around the entire perimeter of the house like my mother's arms circling our family. The stucco exterior was painted butternut gold and the roof boasted red clay tile. Two turrets housed front and back staircases and stained glass windows. Huge, timbered oak double doors marked the entrance. The front façade was covered with purple bougainvillea, reaching up to the third story balcony—my parent's favorite respite.

I arrived under the shelter of the giant oaks at the sprawling gate, where Big Al, the handy man, met me. "It's been too long. Your dad's out on the back patio, I think." He took off his Cubs hat and scratched his head. "Do what you can with that face before she sees it."

"I already did something with it."

His laughter went deep into his chest where it rumbled around. "What's the other guy look like?"

"That's the problem. It wasn't a guy."

Big Al rubbed his chin, before nodding me through.

When I reached the front door I rang the bell and, after several moments, my father swung the door open. He stood at the threshold in starched boxers and a crisp ruffled apron. His chest hair stood out around the edges, making him look like some butler in a BBC comedy show. He searched the veranda. "I was expecting your mother."

"If you thought it was Mother, why didn't you answer the door?" I stepped into the front hall.

"Umm . . . I'm the butler."

"I don't think protocol allows for answering the door in boxers, Jeeves."

"What's with the bruising and scratching?" He examined both sides of my face, before we continued to the kitchen.

As I was about to respond, my mother flew in through the back door. She had on a transparent top that revealed a white lacy bra Victoria's Secret couldn't have made any sexier. A short black skirt stood out around her waist with about twenty rows of ruffles under it, and fishnet stockings stopped just above her knees with red ribbon laced through the tops and tied in a bow. She was teetering in six inch, red stilettos. I couldn't pull my eyes away fast enough.

A flush leapt across her cheeks but she recovered quickly, smiling in my direction, then glaring at my father in turn.

"Son, this is Frenchie. I just promoted her to downstairs maid." He elbowed me in the ribs like one of the guys in the locker room, eyebrows working up and down in conquest.

"Aidan, your visit is so unexpected." Her flush pooled in her cheeks before creeping down her neck.

"I guess you could say so." I looked back at my father. "So this is what you took early retirement for."

"Among other things." He winked at my mother. "Then, of course, there's golf."

"Michael Banford Palowski." She nervously played with the ruffles on her matching apron. "You couldn't have called me, and warned me he was coming?"

"I didn't know he was coming until he came, Frenchie."

"You stop the double entendres." She stepped toward me.

"This is serious, look at his face! What happened?"

"If you think I'm having this conversation with Frenchie and Jeeves, you're both crazy." I backed away, biting the inside of my cheek to keep from laughing. "I'm going out onto the patio and I want you both appropriately dressed."

Heading for the French doors, I heard my father say, "Yes, let's go slip into something more comfortable, Frenchie."

My mother yelped. "Michael, when you and I are alone, I'm going to make you pay for this."

"You listen to me, Frenchie, when we're alone next, you'll be smiling from crown to stilettos."

I heard their bedroom door slam shut. I barely made it to a

chair. I threw my head back taking in the clear blue sky. Thank goodness I didn't show up ten minutes later, or I might have found Frenchie riding the Eiffel Tower.

My dad reappeared wearing chinos, a white linen shirt, and sandals. He had an opened bottle of wine and handed me a glass.

I took a swig of wine. "Great timing runs in the family."

My mother appeared, wearing a sundress with an embroidered cardigan sweater tied around her shoulders. My father and I both looked at her and burst out laughing.

"What?" she asked.

My father grabbed the little red crown that she had neglected to remove from her hair, placed it on the table and slid the third glass of wine toward her.

Dad spoke up, "Why don't you start by telling us what happened to your face?"

I squared my shoulders. "I broke off my engagement today."

"Thank heavens." My mother drew in an audible swig of wine. "I told you he'd figure it out on his own. Aren't you glad we didn't butt in? Aidan wouldn't make that kind of a mistake."

"Why don't we let him talk before we decide?"

I rubbed my hand across my temples, gathering my thoughts. "Dad's right. I did come to tell you about Vanessa. But that's not even close to all of it and not nearly as important as what else I have to say."

"It can't be all that bad." Frenchie gulped wine.

"Dammit, Kat, let the boy speak."

I swallowed down the lump in my throat. "I have a son."

Their eyes were huge. "Where? When?"

"It happened in college." I swirled the wine in my glass, wishing it was alphabet soup with letters that would help me form the right words. "I met a local girl in Bloomington. She was so beautiful. She still is. We formed an odd friendship, which was all she wanted, and of course I had a girlfriend. Things changed, and I wanted more, but when that didn't happen I was determined to forget her, even though it felt like I lost my best friend. I wanted to be with her. That was the summer I went back early to IU to condition for football. I wasn't all that interested in football, but it got me closer to her."

"Who is she?" My mother asked.

"Elizabeth. Libby."

"I don't remember a Libby," Mom interrupted.

"That's because I didn't talk about her, but I thought about her." *Constantly.*

"I was able to stay away from her for two days before I broke down and went to go see her. Our friendship resumed most of the fall, but occasionally I would slip up and hit on her. She resisted me, making it all the more challenging."

Neither of my parents spoke, but my mother's hand was permanently pressed to her chest.

"I came home for Christmas break. I lasted a couple of days before I drove back to school."

"I remember that," Mom whispered.

"I found her that night in a bar with her friends. We had both been drinking, one thing led to another. It was the first time in months I slept in peace. And it wasn't because of the alcohol, I was ecstatic that I'd finally claimed her."

"Why didn't you introduce us?" My father asked.

"Honestly, I was afraid that I couldn't hide what I felt for her from Mom. It didn't matter anyway. She told me that the whole thing was a big mistake, and she couldn't see me again. I begged her to give me another chance but she refused to listen.

"One day, I found her behind the Waffle House, where she worked, retching. I tried to help her, but she told me I'd done enough. I didn't understand what she meant, but then she told me she was pregnant. It was February, and I knew I was going to be called to triple A as soon as I graduated. I wasn't thinking straight, I told her to get rid of the baby."

"Oh, Aidan why would you do that?" My mother paled.

"I thought about the majors, about your disappointment in me. But mostly I thought I couldn't concentrate on baseball if I had a screaming infant and a wife at home. Libby was enough of a distraction. I didn't think I could take more.

"I thought I'd convinced her. I made an appointment, but she never showed. When I went looking for her, everyone said she moved back home and they refused to tell me where that was.

"I didn't see her again until graduation day. I thought she was a smart cutter with aspirations to get out of southern Indiana, but she graduated *summa cum laude*. I watched her walk down the aisle alongside me, five months pregnant, with her head held high."

"Son, why didn't you go after her then?" My father asked.

"I was so torn up inside I didn't know what to do, I was ticked she'd hidden from me right under my nose. I was mad that she didn't need me. I was angry that she was still more beautiful than any woman I'd ever seen. But I ignored her, the only person who I'd ever cared about more than myself."

I looked up at my mother, who was crying. "I saw her. There was something about her. She was standing across the street under an oak tree in a yellow, old-fashioned dress. I remember thinking she looked lost. I couldn't imagine why a pregnant girl was all alone on her graduation day. Oh my God, after all these years, when I think of your graduation, I remember how beautifully sweet she was." She put her hand over her mouth.

"A few weeks after I started in the majors, I received papers asking me to forfeit my parental rights."

"Aidan," my father said, his lips thinned to a line.

"Baseball was my passion, but that day, it lost some of its luster. It was the first time I considered what its achievement might cost.

"I figured Libby wanted to give the kid away. I signed the papers and sent them back. I never confided in anyone about it, except for David." I burned my copies of the papers, but I can still taste the ash in my mouth. "I tried to forget. Sometimes, I think I have, but over the years it hasn't hurt less.

"Yesterday, Libby asked me to meet her." I put the snapshot on the table. "She kept the baby, a boy. His name is Cass. He needs a bone marrow transplant."

"Have you seen him?" Dad asked as he eyed the photo on the table, but refused to reach for it.

"Not yet, but I intend to. I don't know how long it will take before the media catches the story, but I wanted you to hear the truth from me." There was a solemn silence for a full three minutes before my mother spoke.

"What's wrong with him?" My mother asked looking away from my father's ashen expression.

"Leukemia."

"We could be tested, too," my mother said.

"The donor pool comes from parents or siblings."

"Son, I don't mean to sound crude, but are you sure he's your son?" My father asked.

"He looks just like Aidan when he was boy." My mother picked up the photo and passed it to my father who hesitated before taking it. "He looks like Andy, too. He's beautiful. But why didn't she come ask you for help all these years?"

"She didn't want my help. Didn't need it either. She's a big-time attorney in Chicago."

My mother and father exchanged glances.

"I should've found them, made sure Libby was okay and that the baby was in a good home, but I was just a little boy with a bat and a ball and a game to play."

"You're entitled to more than just a game," Mom said.

I looked both my parents in the eye. "I didn't behave the way you expected me to. The longer I let it go, the heavier it hung over me. It's the only thing I've been ashamed of."

My father clapped my shoulder. "Every decision has costs, every action consequences, but inaction often leads to remorse."

"I am going to set this right with her. I want to know him. It's not right for a boy not to have a father. But until I can get this sorted out, I need you to learn two simple words. 'No comment.'"

My father hesitated, searching my mother's face.

She nodded to him silently.

"I'm not going to tell you what to do because you're a grown man, and you know right from wrong. I've made mistakes in my life, too. Things that hurt your mother, things that were hard to forgive, but that forgiveness started when I told her I loved her. Maybe you should start there, too."

I looked up from my hands. "It's not about love, Dad."

"It's always about love: love of the game, love of self, love of a woman." He shook his head. "Start with I'm sorry. It's the best advice I can offer. If you're lucky, maybe she'll forgive you someday."

I willed my mother to tell me what mistakes my father referred to, but she looked me squarely in the eyes before saying, "No comment."

I looked at the ump in my mind's eye. He straightened his bow tie, further ignoring me by practicing the hand signals that secured his induction into the Hall of Fame. I prodded him with an elbow; he looked up and smiled through his mask. **No comment, kid, no comment.**

8

DISCOVERY

Discovery: the methods used by parties to a civil or criminal action to obtain information held by the other party that is relevant to the action

Elizabeth

The cars and pedestrian traffic raced past me with clamoring horns, hurried conversations, and hectic footsteps traversing the Magnificent Mile. I dragged myself over the Chicago River, admiring the Parisian inspired bridge houses and reminded myself it wasn't as if I was headed for the guillotine.

The twinkle-lights adorning the leafless trees danced on the evening breeze. Every store along the way displayed the latest fall fashions. People walked quickly here in the city, eager to reach their Friday evening destinations. Occasionally, you'd see people with Chicago guidebooks looking completely lost; they would stare up the length of a skyscraper, as if the answer to their logistics problems were at the pinnacle. I'd climbed to the top of these buildings through education and hard work, but was that going to be enough to save my son from the precipice on which he was teetering?

The fresh air helped clear my head and strengthen my resolve not to lose my temper. The opposition wouldn't have called for a meeting, if they weren't willing to offer some kind of concession. But I couldn't help feeling like a chicken with her neck stretched across the chopping block, the edge of the shiny blade perched at my jugular.

Aidan had acquiesced to supplying a blood sample. I prayed with equal measure that he'd be a match and that I'd find another anonymous one. I was running out of options as quickly as Cass was running out of time.

I reached the Omni and was relieved; my red patent leather heels weren't broken in for walking that far, and my feet were throbbing. I glanced at my watch, as the bellman opened the door and ushered me in on the tip of his hat.

The 737 Restaurant was in the corner of the building, with floor to ceiling windows overlooking Michigan Avenue. The modern interior was layered with mahogany accents and a neutral décor. The marble bar top was a sharp counterpoint to the lighted glass liquor shelves stacked a story high behind it. I ordered a glass of Shiraz and enjoyed the view, perched at a high-top table.

I felt the presence of someone and looked up to see a tall man pulling out the stool next to me. He was in his mid-thirties, in a tailored to perfection Brook's Brothers suit.

"Do you mind if I join you?"

"I'm expecting someone."

"I'll keep you company. I'm Rob Forrester." He looked down the bar haughtily, as one of his comrades saluted.

"I'm Elizabeth Tucker."

He smiled over the rim of his scotch. "I've seen you at the courthouse." He had medium blond hair that was gelled straight back and his eyes were the exact shade of Milk Duds, making me long for Friday movie-night at the Rodgers house. "You're an attorney, but you don't look like one this evening."

"Criminal defense."

"I'm strictly family law." He took the stool confidently. "I wasn't criticizing your clothes; you look like the sexiest librarian I've ever seen."

I didn't say anything. I stared at him over the top of my retro glasses, helping to cement the image he had of me.

"Unfortunately for you, fella, she's my sexy-librarian."

I jumped. Aidan swarmed around the intimate setting like a thunderous cloud. He was dressed in black Italian loafers, black jeans, and a black dress shirt, un-tucked and unbuttoned at the bottom, and a black Armani sports coat. A dark scowl dominated his perfect features making his crystal blue eyes vibrate.

Robert shifted to his feet with the finesse of an athlete, extending his hand toward Aidan.

Aidan looked at his hand but refused to take it.

The unspoken territorial antipathy between them had nothing to do with me. I was just the insignificant property that started their land dispute. *Which one would draw his weapon first? Better yet, whose was larger?*

A sardonic smile filled Robert's face as he examined three distinct gouges in Aidan's cheek. "You might need stitches for those, or maybe butterfly Band-Aids."

"I'm the Band-Aid, and she's the balm." Aidan pointed to me, as if I were an inanimate tube of jock cream waiting to be rescued from the shelf in his medicine cabinet.

Robert crossed his arms in a cocky stance.

I have to admit that I was flattered, but the time had come to put an end to their conversation. "Both of you need to back off." I put out my hand in Robert's direction, he took it but instead of shaking it, he kissed it. A thrilling jolt hit my stomach, but Aidan's glare bottomed out the delight. Uh-oh.

Robert's eyes met mine. "I'll be in touch, Elizabeth."

Aidan put his arm around the back of my barstool, claiming possession of me. "Don't waste your energy. We're tied in a nice tidy knot." He placed a delicate kiss on my temple, exactly the way he had done at school. "I've missed you," his whispered words brushed my neck as his sapphire eyes explored my neckline.

I caught my breath and concentrated on watching Robert stride away, drink in hand.

The testosterone level dropped several degrees. Aidan put his hand on my forearm, capturing my attention. "I do not like walking into a bar and finding you entertaining some Bozo."

I laughed, despite the steely determination set in his jaw. "Let's get a couple of things straight. I wasn't entertaining him because he's a colleague. And last time you and I spoke in person, you didn't seem to care if I continued to draw air."

"I wasn't myself the other day. I apologize." He met my eye when he said that. "When someone from your past materializes out of thin air, you need time to think it through."

"Robert was harmless."

"He's as harmless as my Aunt Fannie. When a guy says 'sexy' in any part of a conversation, he means that he wants you for sex."

I drew my hand over my mouth in mock horror. "I would have never picked up on that myself, but I can handle my private life without any assistance." I prayed that my cheeks weren't pink.

"You could, but your private life has become intertwined with my private life. Rule number one: no other guys."

"Right." I rolled my eyes.

"I mean it, Libby. No other guys." He squeezed my forearm.

"Listen, all I need is a little blood sample. If you're a donor, you can donate anonymously. No one knows the connection between us, and I'd prefer for it to remain that way."

"That's tough." He drew his brows together like he was going to throw a curve ball. "You gave up your likes the moment you dialed my number. Everyone is going to find out you let the big-time-jock knock you up, so you might want to think about how you're going to respond, because we're sticking this out together."

Was he a maniac?

He hit me with the good old-fashioned stare-down he used on me so many times in college.

"You meant dumb jock right?" I slammed my wine glass down. "I'm surprised you're ready to admit you're the father, me being so far beneath you and all."

He slid the glass out of my grasp ignoring the jab. "We know you find me irresistible when tipsy." He smiled several heartbeats of that coy smile that induced countless Chicago women to toss their supple bodies at his feet. "I can't have you losing that pretty head of yours tonight." His eyes became softer.

It riled me.

He placed his hand over my mouth, and I swallowed my angry words. He looked at me with such intensity I wanted to back away from him. "If you ever tell me to go fuck myself again, I will put you over my knee. After the pleasure of that, I'll wash your filthy mouth out with peroxide." He took his hand away, rubbing Vivacious Vixen lipstick down his jeans.

"I'm sure your threats work on all the girls with an IQ under sixty, but women with brains can think of more elegant rejoinders." I tilted my head and smiled back at him before saying, "Screw you!" I picked up my belongings, ready to stalk off, but he had a handful of my tweed skirt balled up in his fist.

"You walk away, cutter, and I assure you it will be minus this skirt." He pulled on my clothing, testing his grip. "Do you still wear those lacy thigh highs?"

I regained my seat with as much dignity as I could muster, embarrassed that he was playing me. The same old tricks, but now the dog was bigger, bolder, and had a longer leash.

"Mr. Palowski, I pride myself on my excellent negotiation skills." My face burned in agitation. "Tell me what you want." I tried to untangle his fist from my skirt.

But he held me in my seat. "Here's the way it's going to be. One, no other guys. Two, no cursing; for heaven's sake, you're a mother now. Three, I want to meet Cass. Four, when the time is right, I want to tell him who I am. Five, until I tell you otherwise, you let me run the show. We'll start with dinner to discuss three through five. The first two are self-explanatory."

"Negotiations over." I moved to stand.

The man tugged on my skirt again. "You look nice in this suit but even nicer in your underwear." He raised a brow. "I would know."

With every intention of wiping his pretty boy smile off his perfect stubbly jaw, I said, "I don't wear underwear."

He had the courtesy to blush, shaking his head in mock defeat.

"No one fights better than you, Libby."

"I need to get home to Cass. Sorry, no dinner tonight."

"Really? That's interesting. I phoned over to the Rodgers' house and Suzy said I could keep you out as late as I wanted. If you want to check on Cass, though..." He removed the phone from his breast pocket and handed it to me with a congenial smile. "She said Cass was having fun at movie night."

"How do you know the Rodgers' number?" I chewed on my lip.

"The same way you knew my cell. I have connections, babe." He pursed his lips, which made him seem both determined and sexy.

I glanced over at the slick iPhone and wondered just how many playboy bunnies' numbers the thing could hold.

"If you want to fight, let's have dinner first. I need the energy." He waved toward the hostess. "You want to make a call or not?"

"Not," I said, as I slipped him the phone. I had forgotten how big he was, until he put his hand over mine, his fingertips purposely rubbing the inside of my wrist. I flinched away.

The perky hostess took us to a table in the corner of the room where the two walls of windows intersected. Aidan's hand rested on my lower back. Maybe he thought I'd make a run for it if he didn't hold me in place.

The table afforded a view of the beautiful glazed terra cotta sculptured historical building across the street. The tables on either side of us sat empty, creating a sense of uncomfortable intimacy. His fingertips brushed my shoulder as he helped me adjust my chair, before taking his own.

Perky gave us our menus, and laying it on thick for baseball's hottest hunk. She winked as she sauntered away. Aidan opened his menu and with acute nonchalance removed a small note. He ripped it in half, then quarters, before discarding the pieces in the center of the table. His eyes went back to his menu.

I pushed his menu down. "You might need that later."

"I have a strict rule." He flicked his menu. "I only work on one girl's number at a time. I'm still laboring on yours."

"You just said you had all my numbers already."

"I'm talking about your number, meaning I've figured you out." He placed his menu at his elbow. "I tried all these years. You're a little harder to decipher than most."

"I'm sure you didn't lose any sleep over it."

He eyed me but didn't respond as the waiter approached with a friendly smile halting that vein of conversation, thankfully. Aidan requested a bottle of wine before he proceeded to order a three-course meal for the two of us. "I'll let you pick the dessert." He looked at me tenderly as the waiter stood patiently at the table. "I assume you still love desserts."

If we were lovebirds on a date, the sparrow-haired seducer was out to have the insignificant finch for dinner. What the cannibal didn't know, however, was I wasn't irrelevant anymore. "That's fine, you high-handed rat—"

He pinched the inside of my knee.

"Bastard." I glared at him. The waiter chuckled as he melded away. "Get your claws out of my skirt."

"I'll be in more than your skirt, if you continue."

"In your dreams, Band-Aid."

"We have serious things to discuss, and we won't be able to discuss them if you're constantly thinking of a comeback."

"God knows you never thought of coming back."

"Save the sarcasm for someone in the minors." He raised a wing-swept eyebrow. "Truce?" He patted my knee and removed his hand. "Tell me how you managed law school with a baby."

I blinked the shock away and glanced from my hands, playing with my napkin in my lap, to meet his well informed eyes.

"I'm sorry you had to do that on your own. It's amazing what you've been able to accomplish with a baby."

"He's not a baby anymore, and it beats living in a trailer park in southern Indiana." I swallowed a long drink of wine. "Plus, I can concentrate on more than one thing at a time."

"That one I deserved."

"What do you want from me?" I quipped.

Before Aidan responded, another man towered over him. His

left arm rested on Aidan's chair while his right hand pumped Aidan's hand. A petite woman stood alongside them. What she lacked in height she made up for in sultry presence. Her curves started at the golden highlights in her coppery spiked hair and continued to her purple pointy-toed boots. She had all the right equipment, in all the right places, and unlike Aidan's fiancée, this woman appeared all natural.

When Aidan stood, I pushed my own chair back and rose to face none other than Cyrus Fletcher. I cringed inwardly.

Cyrus Fletcher was the slickest sports agent in the Midwest. He was notoriously known as a contrary peacock counselor whose ego and influence was as expansive and as vivid as the preening bird. 'Fletch' flounced through courtrooms with the same self-importance feathering most of his clients.

He was uniformed for the evening in an Italian three-piece suit, precision-cut for his angular frame. His hand-tailored pink shirt was starched so stiffly it doubled as body armor. His necktie was 100 percent silk, as smooth and as eye-catching as the most vibrant of peacock feathers. Not a hair on his crimson colored head was out of place, except for the spikes he wore across his forehead.

Other attorneys swore the man didn't sweat, and I concurred. But if you ever listened to a peacock cry, you'd understand why God made it so beautiful, because the cacophony was less than pleasing.

Aidan had greeted the woman with a friendly hug, and then eyed Fletch before turning back to me. "You two are already acquainted?" His cheek twitched, along the crest of the bone.

Fletch looked at me, and then back at Aidan. "When we met, she called me a narrow-browed, dim-witted, cave-dwelling ass-hole."

I cleared my throat. "I said ass-wipe, not ass-hole."

Fletch ignored my halfhearted attempt at smoothing things over. "Elizabeth, this is my wife, Tricia Stone-Fletcher."

We shook hands, and she beamed a smile before taking me in more seriously, tapping her lip with a polished fingernail.

"What are you newlyweds up to?" Aidan asked.

"Celebrating," Tricia whooped, as she produced a white plastic pregnancy test. Aidan leaned away, suppressing his knee jerk reaction.

I, too, blanched before whispering my congratulations.

Aidan slapped Fletch on the back. "Fast work, old man."

The waiter arrived with our first course. "I'll let you enjoy your dinner." Fletch guided Aidan back into his seat by applying pressure his shoulder. As I resumed mine, I overheard him say, "I received a very distressing call from your fiancée's lawyer."

Judging from Aidan's volume, he wasn't interested in keeping their conversation private. "I tried to reach you by phone, text, and e-mail today."

"I was busy commemorating."

"The white stick says mission accomplished," Aidan laughed.

Fletch's wife tugged at his sleeve, and he turned on her.

"Tricia, you're going to wrinkle my best suit."

She looked at me apologetically—"Men"—before turning back to her husband. "Remember. No business tonight, no crack-berry, no baseball players, just baby talk." Her manicured hands were resting on her hips.

Fletch scoffed in response, before he turned on me. "One last thing, she's more skillful in her use of obscenities than I am." Fletch had the audacity to wink at me as he walked away.

Aidan grumbled into his salad. "How'd you two meet?"

One of the perks of being a lawyer is the perfected direct stare. If you don't have it down by the end of the first year of law school, you're destined to be a tax attorney. I directed mine on Aidan. "I was representing Johnny Buck, who hooked up with that NBA rookie, Albertson, for some 'Bloomingdale Bidness'."

Aidan raised a brow in question.

"They were selling 'exclusive' merchandise out of the trunk of Albertson's Mercedes for drug money. He's as hard-headed and as pimply as the basketball he dribbled into the courtroom."

"John Buck, the real estate investor's son?"

"Generations of Bucks have skillfully bent and stretched the length of the law in Chi Town."

"And you're the Buck's attorney."

"Fletcher was Albertson's lawyer," I answered. "After a confrontation in the ladies lounge, where Fletch cursed me out, I lambasted him with a few choice words of my own."

Aidan chuckled under his breath. "That's it?"

"No, he said, 'any woman with a mouth like mine he wanted in his bed.' And I told him where to shove it."

"Are you involved with anyone on a personal level, or do you consort solely with your clients?"

"That's none of your business."

"Everything you've done is my business. You have my son, and I want to know about your lives."

"My private life has nothing to do with this transaction."

"This is much more than a business transaction." He took a fork full of lettuce. "How old was Cass when he walked?"

"Ten months. Why?"

"Tell me all about him." Aidan smiled. "I meant what I said earlier. I'm sorry, and I intend to set this straight."

"Aidan, this is a lot more complicated than saying a few I'm sorrys. I have to think about Cass' feelings and his future. He has no idea who you are."

Although, it wouldn't hurt for Aidan to see Cass once, his curiosity would be quenched. I reconsidered, saying, "I'll let you meet him, but you need to keep in mind the seriousness of his condition. I don't want to do anything that would upset him."

"I've thought of little else since I saw you. Every boy needs a father, and I want to be a real father to him."

"But someone who's playing at fatherhood out of a sense of guilt can do more damage than good." What little food I'd been able to get down, rolled in my gut, threatening to come up. I brought a shaking glass of water to my mouth. "You haven't had a lot of time to think this through. The hardest part of being a parent is doing what's right for your child, even if it's not easy on you.

Maybe you'll discover that letting him go will be the best for him. It might even be the best for you."

"This is going to turn my life into a circus. Granted, it's one of my own making, but I'm willing to pay the price of admission into the fun house. You don't like the idea of having to deal with me. This time you can't disappear. I know where you live, where you work, and I will track you down, if I need to."

"I can deal with you. It's all the other stuff. Be realistic. You're a public figure. You're contract negotiations are a feature story on TMZ. You're personal life is fodder for Twitter and Facebook. I don't want Cass put on display. And I won't permit anyone making him part of your byline. He's a little boy who's been sick for several months, and he wouldn't understand the sudden media glare."

"People are going to find out as soon as they see us together. For crying out loud, he looks exactly like me. My mother said that, first thing."

"Your mother?" I gulped.

"I showed them the photo you gave me. They offered to be tested. They want to get to know their only grandchild, too."

"Why did you have to tell your parents? You didn't even know if I would let you see him!"

"I knew you'd be sensible enough to give me what I want, since I am more than willing to give you anything you want."

"Cass thinks you're dead," I blurted out, keeping my eyes focused on the table.

"What?" The angry furrow in his forehead pinched.

I had seen him do that on the evening news, and once in the middle of a game, when he got a questionable call from a crusty umpire. Maybe the ump deserved it; I didn't.

"As far as I was concerned, you were dead and buried. I would've never seen you again, and you would've never known anything about us, if Cass hadn't gotten sick. I'm already sorry I brought you into this."

His voice strained, deeper as he spoke in clipped tones. "Whether you like it or not, I'm going to know my son. You need to find a way to resurrect me immediately."

"You would garner more cooperation if you learned to ask me rather than demand." I moved before he had a chance to put his talons on my skirt. "Don't call me, I'll call you." I pulled out a few bills and dropped them on the table before making my way through the dining room.

But apparently, Aidan still had the ability to silently stalk his prey. I didn't know the vulture was hunting, until the elevator chimed open and he circled in right on top of me. He held the doors open for two older ladies already on board. He beamed them with a charming smile, before saying, "Ladies, would you mind letting us ride downstairs alone? I need to flesh a few words out with this gorgeous gal, and they might not be something you could stand hearing."

"Aren't you that baseball fellow from the Cubs?" The lady with the blue-grey hair cackled.

"Yes, I am."

Both of the ladies eyed me. I prayed they wouldn't leave me alone with the bird of prey. They shuffled off. "You aren't going to hit her are you? Cause you look madder than Hell."

The other cawed, "It takes two flints to strike a fire."

"I won't hit her. You have my word."

"I saw you in *People* magazine with that tramp Vanessa Vanderhose." The other old lady spoke. "My first husband liked hussies like her. Couldn't tell a good woman when he saw one."

He flinched. "I'll take that under advisement."

The blue-grey haired lady leaned on her cane heavily. "You scratch the other cheek if he gets fresh."

She continued to mutter other oaths at him as the elevator doors slid shut. He stood next to me in the elevator like a concrete image of an owl with his arms crossed across his taut torso. I could feel his angry reflection radiating off the polished door as it shut. I would have jumped out behind the little old ladies if I thought he would let me get away. I counted seven seconds before he pushed the emergency stop button, and we came to a jerky halt.

9

LEAVE THE GENTLEMENS AGREEMENTS ON THE FIELD

All I want is my case to be heard before an impractical decision-maker. Pete Rose

Aidan 8:07 p.m.

"Elizabeth Tucker, rule number six." I closed the gap between us in the jolting elevator. "You do not walk away from me, when I'm not done with you."

"Aidan Palowski, I will walk away any time I damn well please. You taught me how."

"Fine," I grimaced. "If you're doing whatever you want, then I'll do as I please." I caged her in the corner, searching her eyes, and when she didn't surrender, my lips, of their own volition, descended. In reflex, I claimed her; my lips branding us together like tobacco to the inside of a bottom lip.

The kiss was gentle only for a second, before I parted her lips, and took her tongue. A soft cry whimpered in her throat. My arms wrapped around her, pulling her against me with force. When I sensed her surrender, I drew her bottom lip between my teeth and nibbled, much tastier than nicotine, but just as addictive. I struggled to pull away. "You curse at me, walk away from me, or do anything to irritate me, and I'll do this again," I whispered. "You'd better believe I'm going to take it a little further every time."

My angry tirade had turned into a seduction. I couldn't think straight, my lips tingled, and Libby was shaking.

"Now, I'm going to let you go. If you don't want to end up flat on your back on this elevator floor, you'll behave." She didn't respond and I squeezed her hip. *How had my hands gotten there?* "I'm going to be a gentleman, and take you home."

I stared, hypnotized by her blazing green eyes. I took my time untangling her body from mine. I set the elevator on its way and straightened my jacket, as the car descended. I handed her a handkerchief from my pants pocket. "Your lipstick's everywhere."

"Seriously, a handkerchief." She took the square of monogrammed linen reluctantly, and dabbed at her swollen lips. "I don't like you, Palowski."

I smiled, like a boy who got caught with tobacco stained fingers in a no smoking zone. "I know, babe, I know."

After all this time, after all of the other women, I was stalking the one girl I forbid myself to think about. I tried in earnest to recall one other beautiful face, but all I could see was Libby's soft features and swollen lips. The scent of her, in the confined space, throttled my sanity.

I held the elevator door open. "Let me call for my car."

"I'm going outside for some fresh air."

"Trying to ditch me?"

"The thought had crossed my mind."

"You can run, but you can't hide. Not anymore."

"Oh right." She crossed her arms, fending off the chill. "You're the one who runs away. How silly of me to forget."

"I wasn't ready to grow up then, but that doesn't mean I'm not a grown man now." I took off my sports coat and draped it over her trench, holding onto the lapels as it brushed the top of her knees. "I know you've never screwed up, but you have to realize: the longer I let it go, the harder it was to face you."

The wind lashed around the corner, ripping strands of her hair out of their knot and swiping them across her angry face in violent torrents.

I continued: "Do you think it's easy to face you, when you've made such a success of yourself? With a kid on your own, and all I have to show for myself is wins and losses in a record book somewhere?" The smell of fall swept off the lake, hinting at the frosty weather that would soon lock us up until spring training. But when I examined her from head to toe, I closed my eyes, warming unexpectedly.

David pulled up in front of the hotel and exited the car. He pulled his cap down, as he opened the door. I ushered Libby toward it. She halted, resting her hand on the door frame, and met David's downward gaze. "I know you." She paused for a moment more. "You're one of the bad baseball boys."

David cringed. "Where you always this hot?"

"Yes, but my I.Q. excluded me from your dating pool."

"Little Libby can still dish it out," David chimed in before she could finish.

"I hope you drive—" She glared giving the limo a once over, "—better than you grovel." Libby slipped into the backseat.

As I started to sit down, David muttered. "Hot damn, Palowski, maybe you do know how to judge raw talent."

Taking advice from the guy who was benched for academic under achievement? The ump saluted me in the rearview mirror.

Libby removed her glasses and cleaned them on the hem of her pencil skirt. When she stared over the top of the black horn-rimmed spectacles, her vibrant eyes challenged me to learn what was going on inside that pretty head of hers, even more than her evasive answers.

"Drop me at the L," she ordered.

"I would rather take you to my car and then take you home."

"Whatever." She positioned her briefcase between us before she started twirling a strand of her hair around her finger.

David slid the glass up, leaving us in a silent cocoon. I rested my hand alongside hers on her briefcase, brushing it. "Why didn't you tell me you were going to graduate? We spent a lot of time together."

"You saw me at the library with a book bag." A ragged breath slipped past her lips. "You should have figured it out. Ours was a secret dalliance, which didn't require truths or obligations. The imaginary universe existed only in our minds."

My thumb brushed the back of her hand, hoping to get her to look at me, see me. "You think I pursued you a year and a half just to get you into bed?"

"I think you were Romeo chasing after Juliet until you'd invested too much time to give up empty-handed. But I wasn't some pitching record you could capture, and then sit on in glory. I was a person with thoughts and dreams that weren't an extension of yours. That was the error between us—you were focused on a goal, and I had my heart set on dreams."

"You could've told me." I rubbed her chilled hand, letting the electricity course through me. "What was your dream then?"

"Harvard Law," she sighed. "I lost it the day Cass was conceived. It seemed so important, but it hardly matters now."

That wasn't the dream I'd anticipated her having, but somehow it was more important. "You were going to Harvard?"

"I planned on it, but I was wait-listed. By the time I got in, I knew I couldn't go to the east coast with a newborn."

"You gave it up so you could keep the baby?"

"Yeah, I didn't have enough of your single-minded determination. You were going to the majors. Nothing was getting in your way. I've never seen anyone more determined on a path that he pays no heed to anything else."

Just when I started to feel complimented she cleared her throat and continued.

"At first, I respected you for it." She replaced her glasses but wouldn't look at me. "Then I hated you for it."

"I never disregarded you." I sighed. "After I found out I was going to the majors, I begged you to come with me."

"In exchange for aborting my child." She turned and glared at me. "Is that what you're still angry about? That I didn't choose to follow you around and forfeit my child's life?"

"Up until I received those papers, I assumed you would've hunted me down and insisted on my financial help. It's what most girls would have done"

"I'm not most girls. I'm the product of forced affection between parents who could barely stand each other."

"I didn't know where you came from or how that would have any bearing on your decisions. But that's not all my fault. I always listened to you, Libby."

"I did what I had to do. You did what you wanted. Nothing can change that." She brushed her fingertips across her brow.

"I could have afforded to take care of you."

"The price wasn't in dollars, Aidan. It was in time, sleepless nights, and sweat and tears." She grunted. "We'll see how long you can last. About how much you can give, when it doesn't involve cold, hard cash."

"You better get used to the idea of me knowing my son."

"You should grow accustomed to the reality that everything that's worth having isn't traded on NASDAQ. It's not sold at Nordstrom, and your utterly overflowing bank account gives you absolutely no credit with me. The sooner you define your own limitations, the better for everyone, especially Cass."

"What do you want from me? Blood? I'll give you that. DNA? I'll give you that, too. Tell me what you want, and I'll bust my butt trying to give you whatever you need. I can't make it up in a day, or a week, or even a month, but I can make it up, if you let me. I handled things poorly back then. I didn't think of everything at stake, and I was wrong, but aren't you doing the same thing now? Are you doing what's best for me and for Cass? Or are you doing what's easiest for Libby, and to hell with everyone else?"

"Don't confuse your past behavior, with mine now. They don't equate because I have something real to protect." The quiet sound of tires on the road stretched out between us.

Once we reached my block, I spoke to David. "Once around to make sure the coast is clear." The massive maples overhanging the parkway shielded the streetlights; its giant arms cast eerie shadows as leaves rolled over the deserted sidewalk.

There weren't any news trucks camped on the parkway, so I was hoping the breakup wasn't that big of a story after all.

Yeah right, the headline reads: 'Baseballs Golden Glove Dumps Heiress'. Google hits on your name just skyrocketed.

It was exactly the kind of thing I didn't need right now. Libby wrangled her gaze out the window, searching for some unseen threat. "Anything you want to fill me in on?"

"I broke my engagement with Vanessa yesterday."

Her head skipped away from scouting out the shadows.

"My best guess is that she's planning some retribution."

"Great, just great, these are exactly the kind of media circuses I tell my clients to stay out of at all costs. Now you're dragging Cass and I into the center ring with you."

David saved me a retort by bringing the car to a stop in front of my house. There didn't appear to be anyone on the street, as we exited the car. "Thanks, I'll be in touch."

He whispered, "Good luck, Band-Aid. You'll need it."

Libby started toward the sidewalk. I caught up with her, fishing keys out of my jacket, which was wrapped around her slender frame. She came to a dead halt, and I walked right into her from behind, steadying her at the hips. Over her head, I caught a glimpse of a featureless woman standing in the shadows on the sidewalk. I moved in front of Libby, as the woman started toward us. I caught the first flash of light before the cameraman stepped into view from his evergreen nest. As the woman moved closer, I realized it was Vanessa's recently unemployed assistant, Melinda.

"Melinda, what in heaven's name is going on?"

"I wanted an exclusive on your breakup, but I have the feeling it's become a lot more interesting. I'm a journalist for Harmsworth Publications." She examined Libby.

Harmsworth Publications owned the *Spectator*, the magazine that had hotter dish than TMZ. "Crap."

"You've been together all night." It was an accusation.

"Listen, Melinda, you haven't acted professionally here. You posed as Vanessa's assistant for three months."

"I'm an investigative journalist covering the story from the inside. Do you think it was fun for a Vassar graduate to work for a high school dropout who doesn't know there's no difference between tuna and chicken of the sea? Whatever I get out of that, I've earned. Trust me. Now, why don't you give me an exclusive with your new friend?"

Libby swung on me, poking me in the chest with her finger. "You have exactly two minutes to get rid of her and that cameraman—minus the photos—before I go absolutely ape shit."

I pulled Libby into my arms speaking over her head. "I'm not giving you anything." I turned Libby about, placing the keys in her hands and pushed her up the front stairs of my building.

I grabbed the photographer by the lapels of his coat. "You want to print pictures of me? That's fine; I'm a public figure. She's not. If you show one hair on her head, I'm going to have so many lawyers up your derriere you'll be able to recite the constitution out your nose." I let him go and straightened his lapel. "Do we understand each other?"

The balding man looked at Melinda before nodding in the affirmative and took a step away.

"Come on, Aidan, I know you're a good guy. Let me help you out here. You're going to need it."

Libby had reached the glass door and was arguing with the keys as I evaluated Melinda. "What is that supposed to mean?"

"She's coming after you. Haven't you talked to your lawyer? I have information that can offset all the negative publicity she's going to throw at you. Names, dates, locations."

I nodded my head in Libby's direction. "You eighty-six her, and I'll give you a sit-down."

"I'll do what I can, but my sources report you had a tail on you at the restaurant. Someone else might've picked up on the story already. If they did, then I have to go with what I have."

I looked up and down the street gauging how much I wanted to say. "Be fair when you write the story."

"I'm not after you."

Libby was mumbling under her breath as she tried to force the bolt to turn over. I reached around her for the keys, which were shaking in her hands. "It sticks sometimes, babe." I drugged myself with a long deep breath into her hair. She smelled like homemade apple pie.

Libby stepped into the foyer, before the Victorian, mirrored coat rack that took up the entire wall opposite the front door. Her beautiful likeness in my mirror caught me off guard. I struggled to think past our joined reflections.

She slipped off my coat and held it out to me, as if she couldn't wait to be rid of it.

"Let me show you around. I need to check my email. Then I'll take you home." I flicked a light switch; the illumination shimmered over walls and sparkled in Libby's hair.

When she moved into the vaulted living room, she focused on the painting hanging over the mantel.

"Renoir?" She stepped closer. "It's breathtaking." Her eyes never looked back at me. "It must have cost a fortune."

"Unfortunately, the original is in a museum." I looked away. "And they wouldn't part with it."

"It's odd that a jock would buy a portrait of a woman."

"You're a little old for stereotyping. Or do you call it profiling?" I laughed. "You said it yourself. She's beautiful."

She turned on me, the serenity of the spell broken, looking around as if unsure about her environment.

"My office is in the back." We walked through the connecting dining room and into the custom designed kitchen where she paused, her eyes surveying the room.

Antique white glazed cabinets set off the granite countertops. Stainless steel appliances matched the pressed tin ceiling and molding. The red cast iron stove seemed to draw her to the stained glass Victorian window over the sink.

"Do you need a kitchen like this for soup and sandwiches?"

"Someday, I hope, my wife will want a big family."

"I can't imagine Vanessa Vanderhoff slaving over that stove in a pair of Pradas."

She's right. You need someone who smells like an easy bake oven.

"That's one of the reasons why she isn't going to be Mrs. Palowski." I gestured for her to precede me into the study; while I gave the ump the 'I'm going to slit your throat sign'.

Libby stood just inside the casement, examining the wires protruding from the wall; they looked like alien antenna reaching beyond the surface ready to snag her signal. She sat on the other side of the desk, in one of the oversized armchairs, which seemed to swallow her up. As I listened to, deleted, and saved messages, I tried to keep my eyes off her, but it was as if the beating of her heart was a beacon I couldn't ignore. She drew her stocking feet up alongside her, her eyes fighting to stay open as she relaxed. Most of her hair had worked its way loose and she seemed as peaceful as Renoir's woman on canvas.

That's why you bought the piece of art, kid.

I studied her now. On a subconscious level, that painting reminded me of her subtle tranquility. She had managed to grow lovelier with age. Faint lines around her eyes only made her observations seem keener. Her freckles had faded like script on a piece of paper left in the heat of the sun, until they were just faint traces.

I thought she was asleep, so I let her rest, while I opened the mail. I tried to find it interesting, but my eyes kept wandering back to her. She mumbled in her slumber. The phone broke the silence and rocketed her awake.

"Hello."

The person spoke on the other end.

"No comment," I said before hanging up.

She was wide-awake now. "Between whatever happened to this wall behind me, the reporter greeting us on the stoop, and that call, I have a feeling all hell is going to break loose. Tell me what's really going on."

A lawyer, when properly informed, knows when to pass on a case. Better ease her into the disaster that's your life.

"I broke up with Vanessa, and it's going to get ugly."

She didn't seem convinced. "Why'd you do that, when you knew it would draw attention?"

"Because I couldn't deal with what Cass needs if I had to babysit her." I drew my eyes away from the mail to look at Libby directly. I took a deep breath, blowing it out through my nose. "The relationship wasn't going anywhere, so it's better if we go our separate ways."

"Does she think it's because of Cass?"

"She doesn't know about Cass. I just told her it's over, the end, Amen."

"Did she think she could dig her way back into your heart with her nails?"

I smiled. "Only after she begged."

Libby snorted and it made me yearn to touch her. "What was there?" She pointed toward the blank, but dented wall.

"Flat screen TV."

"Did it fall all by itself?" She asked mockingly.

"No, projectile intervention."

"What sort of projectile?"

"An iPhone."

"The infamous estrogen-free phone I presume?"

"Last year's model."

"Trading in all last year's models?" She smirked. "I can't wait until I make you really mad."

"We already discussed that, remember, in the elevator."

"We need to come to an understanding that doesn't involve physical violence perpetrated on my person."

"I never threatened physical violence." I didn't look up for her response. "It was sexual retribution, I believe."

I glanced at her, and her face was finally flush, but she managed to utter. "There's no way I'm doing things your way."

I smiled at the thought of getting to her.

Keep it up, kid, and I'll have to eject you.

"That's certainly your choice but a deal's a deal."

"I don't want an arrangement with someone whose price of cooperation always outweighs his benefits." She bolted to her feet, clutching her briefcase, before she yelped, and fell back into the chair grabbing her stocking-clad foot. I moved around the desk and went to my knees to pry open her bloodied hand.

"You stepped on glass. Let me get it out for you."

"I'll get it out myself." She slapped my hand away. "Where's the bathroom?"

I picked her up before she could refuse, carried her to the bathroom and deposited her on the edge of the tub.

She pointed toward the door. "Out."

I leaned into the doorway.

She turned on the faucet and stuck her foot under the cold cascade. Then she pulled it out and tried to locate the glass.

"You're going to have to take your hose off."

She glared at me, before her expression turned blank and her eyes rolled back in her head. I caught her before she fell into the tub. I sat her on the toilet. "I'll get it out." I gave her a cold washcloth. "You try not to pass out." My hand ran up her leg to remove her hose.

She flinched and her skin ran to gooseflesh.

When my fingertips brushed the top of her thigh-highs they froze. Our gazes collided. I cleared my throat. My hand trembled, as I peeled the sheer silk away from her translucent skin. I dug in a drawer for tweezers, thanking God my hands had something to do because the room came alive with the current running between us. As I dug for glass, she balled up a fistful of skirt and bit perfect crescents into her bottom lip.

"We're going to work this out between us, like friends." I caught her eye. "The best thing for Cass is for us to get along, so we can make good decisions for him."

"You can make yourself believe anything you want, Palowski, but don't con yourself into believing we're friends." She clenched her teeth, balking when I went a little too deep with the tweezers. "You have no rights, where Cass is concerned. And I will make decisions without any interference from you."

I pinched the pad of her foot to further open the wound.

"You made a game change when you called for my help. Now I want a say, especially where Cass is concerned. I have more practice dealing with the media. Once they get hold of this story, they'll rip you to shreds, if you don't let me handle it."

Libby screamed. "You don't think I have any experience dealing with the media?" Her other leg shot out and kicked me in the shin. "I'm a lawyer." She was panting. "For God's sake."

She tried to pull her foot away, but I pulled it back, almost dumping her on the floor. Her skirt slid to her hips and I could see the edge of dark lace.

"Let me handle it." I dug deeper in the wound.

She roared in pain like a fire-breathing dragon doused in glacier ice. "This isn't a game," she said between colorful curses about my balls on a bloody platter. "It's real life."

"Life's a game." I extracted the sliver of glass and held it up to the light, admiring the fact she'd remained upright.

The ump chuckled. **Quite a chunk of reflective material, isn't it?**

I glared over my shoulder at his imaginary presence in the hall before I turned back.

"You need to decide, if you want to be played, or be the player in control." I ran my finger over her arch urging her to relent. "Let me run this game my way. I can promise you a win."

She jerked away in response to my touch. I caught her ankle, but her head hit the porcelain toilet lid.

He's knocked another one out. And we aren't talking about a ball here, folks.

10

RESCUE DOCTRINE

Repentance must be something more than mere remorse for sins; it comprehends a change of nature befitting heaven.
Lew Wallace

Elizabeth

I refused to admit that I fainted, I just closed my eyes for a few moments and now my head had a gong going off in it. My skirt slid over the leather seat of Aidan's BMW like a base stealer sliding across home plate. I righted myself, gripping the armrest, hoping to squelch my throbbing head.

I wanted anonymous DNA. Instead, I got self-righteous apologies from a man who thinks empty words give him room to maneuver my world. In my wildest dreams, I never fathomed he would want anything to do with Cass. I should have listened to Suzy.

Neither of us spoke as we made our way down Lake Shore Drive, following the curves and natural delineations of the edge of the land as the roadway made its way around Lake Michigan.

The Frank Lloyd Wright homes along our route reminded those passing that Chicago had made its mark on architectural history by developing a truly American style. Loyola University flanked either side of the street, and we maneuvered around the medical school building, deeper into Rodgers Park. One of Chicago's cities within the city, it's bordered at the north end by an aging cemetery, where buried souls rested in prime real estate. Too bad I couldn't buy a plot in which to bury the past.

The last of the towering grave markers heralded our arrival in Evanston, the home of my alma mater, Northwestern University. We passed the limestone pillars, and the scrolling black metal gates that mark the entrance to campus. On the opposite corner sits Saint Mary's church with its arched stained glass façade. Depending on the time of day, the sun glistens off its colored facets in brilliant adoration of the cross. At this hour, it lay dark and dreary, tired of its struggle against a relentless enemy, who was as coy and charming as my own.

Aidan's fingertips brushed over the back of my hand.

I flinched from my meanderings.

"I know the address, but I need a little direction. Don't you people believe in street lights?"

"We people like our privacy," I grumbled. "Unfortunately some people don't pick up on that."

"Do you always wake up in a sour mood or is it the clunk on the head?" His smile glimmered off the dashboard. *Mr. Positive, with cloying regularity.*

"Unlike you, I have to be up at 4:30 a.m. to go to work."

"It's barely ten."

"The house is in the middle of the next block on the right. You'll see big planters. The gate should be open."

"You live on the lake side? With a gate?" He whistled when he took in the colonial mansion with a circular drive, and a detached coach house. "Your boyfriend must be rich."

"I don't have a boyfriend. I rent."

"Thanks for the score." He drove up the cobbled drive to the brick coach house, where Cass and I lived over the garage in a two-bedroom apartment. "I can make it from here. Thanks."

He looked from the main house to the coach house, and then to me. "I'll see you all the way in."

My head thudded, my foot pulsated, and I was too tired to continue my protests. "I have to get Cass from the Rodgers." I pointed toward the mansion with the pristine brick exterior and manicured lawn, which he was admiring.

"I'll assist."

"Couldn't we do this some other month?"

He opened his door and exited with a confident swagger. "No time like the present."

"You know, this will be like walking into a firing squad. They know what you did. Hell, they helped me through it."

"I'll be sure to graciously thank them." He straightened his collar and stood straighter.

Gingerly, I walked over the cobbles. The ball of my foot still hurt from jock boy's glass extraction. With my shadow on my heels, I rang the bell. "Let me do the talking."

"As long as I like what you're saying."

The bell gonged and I wished I could make Lurch appear. Instead, several long moments passed before Ollie opened the massive door. She was dressed in purple plaid PJ bottoms rolled down low across her hips, and a short-fitted lime green T-shirt that read 'mean people suck'. This was Ollie's mantra.

"Hey, Aunt Libby, Dad is in the library and Mom is at your place with Cass. He fell asleep, but he's fine." She stepped aside, before looking Aidan up and down. "Who's the old hottie?"

"Aidan Palowski, meet Olivia. Ollie, meet Aidan."

"Nice to meet you, Olivia, and I'm not old."

"There's a big difference between a twenty-year-old hottie, and thirty-year-old hottie. Trust me," Olivia said.

"Oh yeah, what's that?"

"One will get you a slap on the wrist, and the other gets you fitted for an orange jump suit. Do not pass go, do not collect two hundred dollars."

"Are you going to be a lawyer?"

"That's kind of a grown up question for a playboy baseball player." She tilted her head inspecting him closer.

I appreciated Ollie giving it to him, but I had other things to do.

"While you entertain the old guy, I'll say good night to your dad." I started, but a large hand stopped me.

Aidan winked at Ollie. "I've got to make an appearance with your aunt, but I'm going to be keeping my eye on you."

Ollie's color flashed. "Don't forget your bifocals." He moved right behind me, laughing. "I like that girl."

The library door swung open, and Max filled the jamb with his imposing figure. There was only one way to describe the Dean of Northwestern University law school—-big, loveable, teddy bear with the manners of a marauding Viking raider. "I've been worried about you, sweetheart." He drew me into a loose embrace before stepping into his heavily paneled study.

"I was forced to undergo less-than-amiable negotiations." I kissed his cheek. "Aidan, this is Dr. Maxwell Rodgers."

Aidan extended his hand. "It's very nice to meet you, sir."

Max ignored his gesture moving around the side of his desk taking command. "I wish I could say the same. I do appreciate your bringing Libby home, but she's in safe hands now." I had never heard a dismissive speech from Max before, but he didn't want Aidan in my life any more than I did.

"Contrary to what you want to believe about me," Aidan countered, "I was raised with excellent manners."

"Someone with breeding doesn't abandon the woman carrying his child." He lowered his voice to an almost caustic level. "An honorable man lives up to his responsibilities." He cleared his throat. "No matter what that cost him."

"I understand you want to protect Cass and Libby. I even understand your hostility, most of which I deserve. I made a monumental mistake, but I'm man enough to admit it. I'm even man enough to take whatever admonishments you feel appropriate." He didn't pause for air.

"From what I've pieced together, you took up the portion of their care that was mine and I'd like to thank you for that." He stared Dr. Rodgers down, like he was some rookie who just came up from triple A. "I hope I can seek your advice from time to time, since you know them better than I do." He glanced at me. "Especially, since Libby can be a handful.

"I hope I can earn your trust and demonstrate that I'm thoroughly capable of taking care of them." Aidan's gaze was direct. "Maybe you'll even see I'm well-mannered and honorable."

I held on fast to the arms of my chair to keep myself from shaking. *Had he rehearsed that speech? Because it sparkled.*

Max glanced at me, before relaxing into his leather-tufted desk chair, but he continued his appraisal of the younger man.

Aidan was rigidly planted in his stance, as if he'd stand there all night, if need be, to come to an understanding.

Max spoke grudgingly. "Take a seat, Mr. Palowski."

Aidan sat, never taking his eyes off the older man's gaze.

"I'm a tough man, but a fair one. Libby's more than a tenant, she's like a daughter to me, and the only thing that's kept me from running your rookie-of-the-year baseball ass through the ringer is her protest. Your success was at her expense, and for the life of me I can't imagine why. But those reasons are only hers. If you start this game, you damn well better finish it, because if she or Cass is injured, you'll be looking over your shoulder for the rest of your life."

"Max," I said in hopes of slowing down his lather.

He gave me the evil eye. "She says the word, and I'll take any avenues to ensure retribution, legal or otherwise." His glaring eyebrow dropped a fraction of a degree. "If you someday choose to care for Cass, then you will comprehend my feelings in this regard."

Aidan gave a slow, curt nod.

"Don't disappointment me, Palowski." Max extended his hand. "It's the bottom of the ninth, and you have the bases loaded with two outs. One mistake will cost you the game." Max shook Aidan's hand—a compromise, not a concession.

"Lucky for me, I'm the best closing pitcher in the league." It wasn't a cocky exaggeration, but a statement of fact.

"You're going to need more than luck." Max turned to me. "Libby, send my wife back to me." He glanced at Aidan. "I don't sleep well without her."

I leaned over the desk and gave Max a kiss. "Good night."

My heels popped over the corridor's parquet floor. The comforting scent of microwave popcorn wafted through my senses before the crisp moonlit air assaulted me.

Aidan didn't speak a word, but he followed in my wake.

"That conversation pretty much negates rule number five," I chuckled under my breath, "Do what I want the way I want it."

"Don't think so. None of his threats come into play, as long as I do what I promised. And I have every intention of living up to my end of the bargain."

We clanged up the corrugated green metal staircase of the coach house. I was fishing my key out when the door swung open.

Suzy was wide-eyed right inside the door. "Dr. Seuss called."

My heart rate kicked up. "Is Cass okay?"

"Yes, but Dr. Seuss has tried back several times. He said he tried your cell phone, too."

I patted my trench coat, then my suit jacket. "I must have forgotten it at the office. Did he say what he wanted?"

"No. He asked how Cass was, and then said he had some important news. He said you should call, no matter how late."

"I'll call right now." I hesitated. "This is Aidan." I hugged her so she wouldn't be able to read the concern on my face. "Thank you for sitting. I won't stay out this late again."

"Don't worry. Cass is always a peach."

Suzy grabbed her coat, which Aidan helped her into. She slipped out the door.

"I need to return this call," I muttered.

Aidan stepped further into the room.

"You don't need to wait," I said, dismissing him.

"I'll wait." He looked around. "There's plenty to read." He examined the floor to ceiling wall of books behind the sofa.

I went into my bedroom. With shaking fingers, I dialed the numbers that were illuminated by the filtered light coming though my open shutters. The phone rang three times before Dr. Seuss picked up. "Elizabeth, I have excellent news."

I held my breath.

"We found a match."

"Oh my God. How? Where?"

"Mr. Palowski gave us a sample on Wednesday night. The lab rushed it through with the others. I haven't looked at all the data, but we have a match. I wanted to give you the good news as soon as possible. My office will call Monday to set up the chemo schedule. Once we harvest the marrow, we'll be ready to move along. We've been lucky with this."

All I was able to get out was, "Thank you for calling," before I dropped the phone. Forgotten, it never made it back into the cradle.

The sobs I had carried hidden in my heart for almost two months broke free. I cried out in relief, joy, and sorrow all together. The grip cinching my heart loosened, as my muffled cries sang out rejoicing. My child would see the end of this year. He would live to see the snow fall and the spring melt it all away. With this hope, I too, could start to live again. Life would not take from me the thing I had cherished above all others. I tried in vain to staunch the flow of tears; my body shook with relief, taking me to my knees on the floor.

Gentle hands wiped the hair, soaked in salty tears, from my eyes. Strong arms wrapped around me, consoling my jerking sobs. Finally, I slowed enough to make out words.

"Libby, what's wrong? What's happened?" I heard Aidan's deep tenor; it was thick with emotion.

Words would not come; only sob after sob racked my body.

He moved away for a moment, the door to my bedroom latched shut. He gathered me up, carrying me to the other side of the bed, making it a buffer against the noise of my cries. When he settled me on my knees, he wrapped me in his strong embrace. He rubbed my back in long, steadying strokes, willing me to calm.

He spoke soft words too tender to hear, and I started to relax. As my body convulsed in the aftershocks of renewed hope and recaptured dreams, the pain in my chest eased. My arms were around his neck, and his face was buried in the side of my throat.

His mouth was tangled in my wet hair and once again at my ear. "Please, Libby. Please tell me what's wrong."

I pulled away and stared at him for a moment. I tried to speak, but only hiccupped. "They found a match. I can save him."

His smile sparkled in the bright moonlight. With a calm reverence, he stroked the tears away from the crests of my cheeks with the pads of his thumbs.

"Of course you can, babe." He placed me on the bed. He gently removed my shoes, my suit jacket, and my glasses. I pulled a pillow down into the center of my body wrapping myself around it before he pulled a blanket up over me. "Of course you will," he said before he brushed my tear soaked hair away.

In that fragile moment, I witnessed the miracle of the man Aidan Palowski had become. All the smug conceit vanished, the athletic ego evaporated. He could express tender emotions and gentle ministrations, where nothing predatory lurked in any part of his touch. I closed my eyes with relief for Cass—but terror for my own withered heart.

11

SQUEEZE PLAY

'You seem you spend a good piece of your life gripping a baseball, and in the end it turns out that it was the other way around all the time.' Jim Bouton

Aidan 7 a.m. (ish)

I came awake with a start. Something was stabbing me along my rib cage. "Mister, you gotta wake up," said a small voice that was more than a dream, and familiar.

My eyes blinked open to find a miniature version of myself standing at my head with a remote control in his hands. He was taller than I'd expected and he had Libby's eyes, radiant green with mischief.

"Where'd you get that shiner?"

"Uh..." Athletes are known for their finesse both on and off their respective fields, but I stumbled through my mind, trying to find words. Surely, I could have a conversation with my son.

"You're in my spot, mister." His brow furrowed, marking his displeasure. A mysterious cartoon character was emblazoned on his flannel PJ's and the creature was as much of a puzzle as my own son was. "Where'd you get the love handcuffs?"

"Uh..." I rubbed at the thin line of glitter on my wrist that appeared when a little girl held my hand and told me all my hurts were on the inside. I struggled to sit up. "Sorry about your spot, little man."

Cass had already made himself comfortable, where my head had been resting on a stack of pillows. "Once that kind of mark seeps in, it never fades away," he said, eyeing my glittered wrist.

A quiver ran through me.

Cass shrugged his shoulders breaking the hypnotic pull of our eyes. "My mom needs to rest. If she wakes up, she'll make me go back to sleep." Cass put his finger to his lips, flipping through the channels, immediately engrossed in Sponge Bob.

When Cass spoke again, I jumped; something about the way he looked at me had me on edge. "What's your name, mister?"

"Aidan Palowski."

"You must be Polish. My friend Madison Dubrowski is Polish. She's a ski too."

"I see."

He's not a catcher. You can use words with more than one syllable with him.

"Was my mom on a date with you?" He scrunched up his face, but his eyes were still engrossed with the TV.

"Sort of. Is that okay with you?"

Cass looked me in the eye. I'd never seen a kid with such a direct stare. "Are you her boyfriend?"

I thought about that for several moments. "I think that would be nice."

"If you're her boyfriend, will she kiss you?"

You'd have to do some major league convincing for that.

"Why?" I asked smiling.

"She's always kissing me. If you could get her to kiss you some of the time, that would keep her lips off me, it gets kind of yucky, and the other kids notice."

"I would love to help you out." It was a toss-up. What would be more fun? Convincing her or kissing her?

"Mister Pole-ow-ski, you know what else?"

"What?"

"My mom needs someone to make her laugh. She's sad a lot."

"That's probably because you've been sick."

He shook his head, but his eyes went back to the cartoon.

"I'll do what I can to make her laugh again."

"Mister Pole-ow-ski, if you could love her, I think that would be nice, just in case if I'm not here no more."

"Cass, you're going to be here." I couldn't help myself I reached out and brushed his hair away from his concerned face.

"But sometimes when mommy cries, I can't get her to stop. I bet you could make her stop. 'Cause you're big."

"It's not right to intimidate anyone with your size."

"What's in... tim... i... date?"

"When you force someone to do something because you're bigger or louder. It's when you push someone around."

"There are some big people I'd like to intima, intimi. What's that word again?"

"Intimidate."

"Or you could intimidate them for me, so my mom won't cry. What else would she need a boyfriend for?"

"Your mom has had other boyfriends before, right?"

"Nope," he said.

I looked at his solemn face, burdened with the weight of his mother's unhappiness. That's why kids needed two parents, so the kids would feel each parent looked after the other's happiness, freeing the child to find his own. I knew, because for a short, tumultuous time, I had lived with only one parent.

I watched Cass for a while before speaking again. "Do you have any baby pictures?"

"I have scrapbooks." He jumped off his perch, all smiles, as if this might be more entertaining than Sponge Bob. He went to an armoire, pulling open drawers, rifling through them before he lugged three binders back, putting them in my lap. He snapped the TV off, settling himself alongside me before he opened the book.

"That's my mom the day I was born. She went bowling with Aunt Vicki to get me to come out." He started to turn the page.

I stopped him. "Do you mind if I look at it for a sec?"

Cass frowned for a brief moment. "I'm on the next page, and I'm really cute."

"I'm sure you are, but so is your mom."

"Girls aren't pretty, when they have a baby in their pocket."

I wasn't sure if I should correct him. If he believed he was in her pocket, then that was as good an explanation as any I supposed. Better to save that particular talk for another time.

Libby had smiled hesitantly for the camera with her beautiful long fingers resting on her protruding stomach. She looked anxious, as if finding the real function of her body was a terrible combination of agony and joy. She looked young and fragile, but at the same time, confidence simmered in her eyes. A longing to step into that picture overcame me. I wished I could wrap my arms around her, kiss her temple, and tell her that it would be okay. My stomach twisted, knowing that the opportunity had passed, and I'd missed it.

Cass flipped onto the next page. A baby's hospital photo can only be compared to a mug shot, except babies are allowed to wear hats in theirs. His face was scrunched up and fiery red, he looked about as happy as some guy who was brought in for disorderly conduct. At the bottom of the page were two footprints about the length of my thumbs; I traced their size trying to imagine something so small and perfect.

On the opposite page Libby was in a gray hospital gown, holding a bundle in her arms. Her face was colorless, her lips pale and drawn. She clenched a handful of tissues. My arrogance had done that to her. What should have been a happy day with a healthy child in her arms had turned into a painful reality, while I had been off pursuing baseball dreams.

We went through the photos one by one, and he would tell me things about them and about his mother. In most of the photos, she looked exhausted, but her smile shone with happiness. There was a summertime shot of Cass lounging between her long, outstretched legs in tall grass. Cass was sitting up and Libby looked more like her sassier self. Her figure had returned to its former state. It was enhanced, and not in a bad way.

"Hey Cass, when is your birthday?"

"October ninth."

Exactly nine months later, at the tail end of the season.

Isn't there a saying about knowing your ass from a hole in the ground?

I shut out the ump's voice. "I just missed your birthday."

"I had a cool party with all my friends, but I had to invite Madi Dubrowski. You know what, Mister Pole-ow-ski? Girls can be a real pain in the butt."

"Really? Why's that?"

"Cause Madi wanted to kiss me for my birthday. Those females are kissing maniacs," he said, clearly disgusted.

I couldn't contain myself I chuckled. I picked up the second scrapbook, which Cass helped me leaf through, telling me about his first meal, his favorite toys, and his first steps. Then we came to his first birthday party. There were several pages for the happy occasion, held in the Rodger's house. I glimpsed a familiar-looking, older gentleman holding Cass in several shots. "Who's this man?"

Cass looked over my shoulder. "Oh, that's Grandpa Rodgers. He lives in the old folks' home a couple blocks away. We go visit him every Sunday after Mass. He don't remember so good any-more. Sometimes he thinks my mom is back at school again, and he asks her how come she keeps coming to work without her uni-form. Mom doesn't laugh at him though, she just tells him not to worry everything is okay at the Waffle House.

Old Mr. Rodgers owned the Waffle House. I'll be damned!

"I love the Waffle House." Cass sighed. "We go there whenever we go to Indiana. But my grandma ain't married to Grandpa Rodgers on account, he's only my grandpa 'cause he wants to be, not cause I have his blood. Do you like waffles, Mister Pole-ow-ski?"

Max Rodgers is old Mr. Rodgers' son. The elder Mr. Rodgers must have helped Libby, so she could finish up school at Indiana. I gave my attention back to Cass. "I like the pancakes better at the

Waffle House, the ones with apples, cinnamon, and whipped cream."

"Have you been to the Waffle House at Indiana Hoosiers?"

"I went to Indiana University, too."

He thought about that a few minutes. "Are you a lawyer?"

"I'm a professional baseball player for the Chicago Cubs."

"Me and Madi like the White Sox." Cass frowned. "Her dad took us to a game once. But we didn't watch too much 'cause me and Madi ate candy, peanuts, popcorn, hot dogs, soda, cotton candy, pretzels, ice cream, and Italian ice." He counted these items out on his fingers. "Then, we both had to puke. I barfed more than her, but she thinks she did 'cause she puked in the car on the way home, too. Who do you think the winner was?"

"I can't say. Haven't you watched the Cubs on TV before?"

"I don't watch sports. My mom says jocks are dumb."

She makes several relevant points about you, kid.

"You better not tell her you play baseball, 'cause she'll dump you. Once, I wanted to play T-Ball with Madi. She yelled at Mr. Dubrowski, and he was the coach."

"Would you let me teach you how to play baseball?"

"If my mom says it's okay, then I could try it. But I don't think I'll be very good."

"You'll be good at baseball. It's in your blood."

"I wasn't born with baseball in my blood, Mister Pole-ow-ski. I was born with cancer in my blood."

My heart sank. "It isn't your fault you've been sick. You're going to get better." I gave him a reassuring smile.

"I might get better for a while." He patted my shoulder, as if he wanted to console me.

"Maybe we can replace the cancer in your blood with baseball." I swallowed down. "We could buy you some equipment today, and play in the park. How would you like that?"

"Can we see if Madi can come, too?"

"How about just me and you and your mom today, and another day we'll invite Madi, if her mom and dad agree."

"You can ask her dad, but she don't see her mom because she runned off with some man. She comes around once in awhile. Besides, Madi has her dad and my mommy. Everyone loves Madi."

"Hmm." The question was does her daddy love your mommy, or vice versa? This was a deeper conversation than I'd intended, and I wasn't sure if I was ready to hear Cass' feelings on child abandonment.

Cass' stomach grumbled. "Hungry?"

"Kinda."

"Let's see what you have." The kitchen was straight out of the 1930's with white painted cabinets and Formica counter tops with a stainless steel edge. Cass climbed on a step stool, reached into an upper cabinet, and pulled out Raisin Bran and two bowls. I grabbed the milk. The fridge looked original to the structure in a sage green color with a stainless handle, when you closed it gave a suctioned clunk. The only new items in the room were a moveable center island and a Viking stove. I poured cereal, cut bananas, and poured milk while Cass arranged silverware and juice. I sat next to Cass into the booth that served as the kitchen table.

I noticed the laptop on the table as I started to eat. "Is this your mom's laptop?"

"No, this is mine."

"Can I use it for a few minutes?"

"I guess." He slurped his cereal. "What for?"

"I want to buy a car. Mine's only a two-seater, and I won't be able to take you and your mom places in it." Underneath the computer was a manila file folder marked 'Nanny'. I eyed it.

There were several dealerships along the Eden's expressway. I pulled up the websites and searched through their inventories, while Cass pointed to colors and options that he liked. We went back and forth until we found what we could agree on. I arranged for us to pick the car up, while Cass dressed. I wrote Libby a note that we'd be right back.

The Hummer was fully loaded; the tubular utility side step and fender flares were highly polished chrome. Cass wanted 'army man green' and I thought that sounded cooler than platinum or ebony. I signed all the X's and collected the keys.

"It's a big, mean, green, fighting machine." Cass chanted as he decided that the seventeen-inch aluminum wheels needed the attention of his wool hat.

I opened the rear door, motioning him into the vehicle with a nod.

I heard the stereo blast to life, as he worked his way into the driver's seat, adjusting it and the side mirror so he could see me. I signed a few autographs and told the salesperson that I'd pick up my BMW later. As I approached the door, he switched the car lock, shutting me out of my brand-new purchase. But I had a great follow up pitch: I hit the automatic starter and the engine roared to life.

Cass jumped back in his seat, as I got in, and we argued over the fact that, yes he had to sit in the back seat, and yes he still had to use his booster seat, and yes he had to wear a seat belt. Once he realized I wasn't budging on safety, he said, "Oh, all right Mr. Pole-ow-ski."

Every time I hit a pothole Cass gave an enthusiastic belly laugh that made me smile. I liked the kid from the first poke. He made fun what should have been a chore.

My phone started to ring as I made my way down Dempster Avenue. I answered using my Blue Tooth. "Hello."

"Where in hell are you and where is Cass?"

"Libby, you're on speaker." She groaned. "Cass is with me. We went out to pick up a car. We're on our way back now."

"You stayed at my place without my permission, and you introduced yourself to Cass without me."

"Cass figured out I'm your boyfriend. Although, as your boyfriend, he would like me to take up all kissing duties."

"What?" she screamed.

I smiled into the rearview mirror, knowing that Cass was listening to every word. "Babe, everything is fine, Cass is cool with the whole thing."

"Aidan, when you get here we are going to have words."

"Okay, babe, see you in a few," I clicked off. No sense getting her any more riled up while Cass was listening.

"Uh-oh, mom's mad." Cass' concerned face replied in the rearview mirror.

"I'll smooth it over with her." When we pulled the truck into the driveway, the ten kids on the front lawn playing flag football froze and stared. Cass bounded out of the car without a backward glance.

Olivia had a red ski vest on, a black baseball cap with REF embroidered in matching crimson and a whistle between her teeth. She blew it and pointed at me as she assessed me. "Did you stay over with Aunt Libby? 'Cause my dad would not like that."

"Will Cass be fine with you guys for a little while?" I smiled. "I need to talk to Libby for a few."

"I'm keeping my eye on you. I won't be afraid to blow my whistle, if I catch you making an error." She put the whistle in her mouth and started away, walking backwards.

"I promise." I made a cross over my heart. "No errors, Ref."

"If you think I'm gullible enough to fall for one of your shaky promises, think again. Aunt Libby told me all about you; about how far a guy will go to get what he wants, and how fast he'll disappear when he gets it." She didn't bother waiting for my response, but she blew the whistle, and watched the pile of kids come apart before her.

I found Libby fresh out of the shower with a towel tucked around her body, she leaned over the kitchen sink, watching the action below. When she threw her arms up into the air for a touchdown, she almost lost her towel. I cleared my throat and willed my tongue to stay in my mouth.

"Shit." Libby jumped, but she managed to keep her towel around her torso. "Don't you knock?" One hand was grasping her towel the other was on her hip. "Why'd you take off with Cass?"

"You've sworn twice. When you get to five, I get the towel." I took a step toward her.

"Like hell you do." She took a step back.

"Three." I stared at her, from turban wrapped head to pink painted toes. "We had errands. Cass said you needed the sleep."

She blushed and pulled the towel tighter.

I gazed down her body again. "You have a woman's body now."

"I'm bigger, I know. I had a kid, for Christ's sake."

"That was a compliment." I took another step in her direction. "Your curves should be illegal."

She veered toward her room. "I'm getting dressed."

"I'll hold your towel."

"Go fu—,"

I grabbed her arm as she tried to clear me. "The F bomb counts for two from now on. If you use it now, I get the towel."

She shrugged me off and slammed her bedroom door.

I peered out the kitchen window, locating Cass immediately. He was running the ball into the end zone. *Atta boy*. When he got there, he did a silly jig, but instead of rejoicing, his teammates were all pointing in the opposite direction.

He slapped the heel of his hand against his forehead before collapsing into a pile of leaves. Everyone laughed.

When Libby didn't reappear, I made my way back to the living room. Instead of browsing the titles of leather-bound books, I picked up one of Cass' scrapbooks and settled in the sofa.

She wandered in fifteen minutes later. My eyes strayed from the photos and involuntarily followed her until she took a chair alongside the sofa. She was dressed casually in jeans, a sweater, and boots. A pair of rimless glasses perched on her face.

She tossed her damp hair over her shoulder. "I don't appreciate you spending the night here. What did you tell Cass?"

"He assumed I was your boyfriend, and I thought it might be a good explanation for why I'd be around."

"You're not going to be around."

"I'm going to get to know him, and you're going to help me do it. You owe it to me."

"I owe you squat. You knew I was having a baby. Did you think

I would throw him away the way you threw me away?" Her hand rushed to her mouth, perhaps trying to catch the words.

"You think I threw you away? Did you ever think about how I was supposed to feel? You treated me like a one-night stand."

"I do not have one night stands, you arrogant ass." She threw an embroidered pillow at me, hitting me in the head before stalking off to the kitchen window to check on Cass.

I followed right behind her and watched the kids, who'd raked up huge piles of leaves again and were taking turns jumping from a giant oak into the cushion of its leaves.

Libby was white knuckling the edge of the sink. "How the hell did you expect me to feel, when I woke up in the boinking room? Like the love of your life?"

That room, and all references to it, had caused me more heartache than pleasure. Back then, Libby told my roommates that a room set aside for sex was disgusting and that grown men should not be maneuvering their sex based on the occupancy of a bedroom that was available on a first-come, first-served basis. They all looked at her, shocked and intrigued when she asked why they hadn't had the foresight to put in a drive-through window.

"I went looking for you as soon as I got in town that night." I ran my hand through my hair. "I didn't think you'd come home with me when you'd turned me down so often before."

Libby dropped her head down over the sink, her tears spilling into the drain. "I'd turned everyone down before that."

"What?"

She swiped her tears away. "Figure it out, genius."

"Libby, I didn't know. Why didn't you tell me?" Her face was awash with physical exhaustion and emotional drain. I gathered her to me, surprised with the yearning sweeping through me. I hadn't expected it. I anticipated lust because that was an emotion she could easily pull from me. But this tenderness made me want to shoulder her suffering. If she wouldn't let me I'd have to take a hard look at myself, and that pain would be agony. I'd made her bleed like this once before.

I have woken up cold and sweaty with the memory of the monumental mistake of the night we spent together. Not that I took her home, even when I knew I'd gotten her pregnant, I didn't really regret it. What I lamented was not speaking the words she needed, not telling her that night that I didn't think I could ever get enough of her. The truths, oaths and promises only amounted to wishful thinking now.

I pulled her deeper into my embrace. She came grudgingly.

Cass barreled into the kitchen, leaves trailing in his wake. "Mister Pole-ow-ski said he'd take us to brunch," he was smiling until he saw his mother's face. "I told you, she cries a lot. You got to make her feel better Mister Pole-ow-ski."

I rested my cheek in her hair, breathing in her fresh, hypnotic scent before wrapping my arms around her. She shivered.

Cass came over and wrapped his arms around us before saying, "I think you need to kiss her, Mister Pole-ow-ski."

I had no problem obliging Cass, but when I saw the terror in her eyes, I softly rubbed my roughened jaw along her tender one. My touch begged forgiveness.

With one hand on Cass' head and my other arm enfolding the three of us, I knew that somehow fate had transported me to the exact spot where I was supposed to be.

"Ahem!" A paper horn blew the serenity out of my head.

12

CROSS EXAMINATION

The question of a wise man is half the answer.
Solomon Ibn Gabirol

Elizabeth

When I thought things couldn't possibly get any worse in the three ring circus my life was becoming, and with Aidan's jaw perfectly aligned with mine, and Cass wrapping us into his embrace, I glanced up to find my mother marching through the kitchen doorway with a full face of clown makeup and a blistering red clown nose. One hand was full of balloons; the other brought a paper bazooka to her lips that she blew at us.

I jumped away from Aidan.

Jeanne's silly spiral pink wig was slightly askew; her Bo Peep cast-off dress enhanced her perfect figure, and she was brandishing purple floppy clodhoppers. She wore purple harlequin stockings, green glitter on her face, and a chartreuse jester's hat. I now knew she wasn't bluffing when my checking account had been debited two thousand bucks for BoBo's Clown College.

Aidan's eyes widened when he saw her. "Did I mention good clowns are hard to come by?"

Cass threw his arms open wide and ran to his grandmother. "Grandma, Grandma! I didn't know you were coming to visit. We're going to brunch. You want to come?"

"I don't know your grandma, but I'm Hildy, the Hillbilly Clown." She smiled exposing her darkened front teeth and enfolded Cass into her arms. What had I done to deserve this? It was one thing to be embarrassed by one's parent, but it was a whole other side-show to be mortified in front of your nemesis.

I glanced at Aidan, who smiled from ear to ear, as he extended his hand. "I'm pleased to make your acquaintance, Hildy. I'm Aidan Palowski."

Hildy kept Cass in place with one hand as the balloons floated to the ceiling. With the other she shook Aidan's hand.

She took in Aidan with a discerning eye. "Nice to finally meet you." She patted Cass' head. "How are you feeling today?"

"I ain't felt sick in three whole days. Mom made Dr. Seuss fix my medicine, so it don't make me sick no more."

"He's good that way. It makes me one happy clown." She smiled bending toward him. "Where are all your friends today?"

"Miss Suzy called them in for hot chocolate."

"Why don't we go down and see them? I think I might have some magic tricks up my sleeves." She pushed Cass toward the door and waggled her drawn-on eyebrows at me. "Why don't you meet us down there in about fifteen minutes? Then I'll get my spiral perm out of your hair." I wondered if she had a vanishing act, and if she could use Aidan as an assistant.

"We were going to brunch."

"I'm here to visit a friend in the city. I just popped by to see how Cass was doing. I had no plans to stay, since I hadn't been invited."

As if that had ever stopped her before. "Jeanne, you don't need a party invitation." And who pays a visit to someone dressed as a clown? And who was her friend in the city?

"Well, it's always nice to get them, anyway." She pulled on a lime green parka with a hot pink fur-lined collar. She might be fanatical, but she was fastidious about color coordination.

"They found a donor for Cass."

She shot Aidan a look. "I knew they would." Her clown shoes flopped against the metal stairs in a descending thump, thump.

Aidan's amused grin boasted his signature dimple. "That explains the eccentrics. How old is your mom? She's pretty hot."

"Jeanne is quirky, eccentric is too refined a word to describe her." I crossed my arms over my middle. "She's crazy, for God's sake."

"She wanted to make Cass feel better. Besides, if you look that good when you're her age, insanity won't matter."

"Jeanne isn't figuratively crazy, but certifiable." I glared through him. "She's been in and out of mental hospitals since she was thirteen." I grabbed bowls and cups off the table, taking them to the sink, with Aidan traipsing behind.

"She seems stable."

I glared at him with squinting eyes.

"All right, except for the clown getup."

"Drugs will stabilize the looniest among us."

"Is it genetic?"

I fumbled with a bowl. "It doesn't manifest itself until late adolescence."

"You're not concerned about it?"

"No, I never even thought of it until you just asked."

"So, this is why you were so secretive in college about your home life?" He asked, pilfering through drawers for a dishrag.

"Does it really matter?"

"Being an attorney, do you find it difficult answering other people's questions? I'm trying to get to know you, so I can help you both." He pulled the washed bowl from my hand and dried it. "Let's go to lunch. I'm starving."

"Fine!" I'd been out-maneuvered by a jock. If I didn't cooperate, there'd be a scene, and I didn't want to upset Cass.

We found Cass on the Rodgers' back patio sipping hot cocoa with a rowdy bunch. Max and Suzy stepped out through the sliding door, carrying a tray laden with sandwiches, and Max had two bags of chips in his broad arms. I had the distinct impression he was going to crush them when he took in Aidan. Max snarled a smile that made the Grinch look friendly. "Did you make it home at all? Your car was here when I made coffee this morning, but when I came out for the paper it was gone."

"Cass and I had a pick-up." Aidan tilted his head in the direction of the Hummer, as he helped Suzy with the tray.

Jeanne's car was gone, but it would have looked trivial against the hulking mass of green metal. Strange behavior even for my mother, she was usually clingy.

"Where are you headed for lunch?" Suzy asked.

I looked up for Aidan's suggestion, but he and Max had started toward the new vehicle.

"Did Jeanne run off with Huckleberry the Hillbilly clown?"

"She did some tricks for the kids, flirted with Max before the normal disappearing act, once she caught sight of me."

"As long as Max isn't one of her tricks, we're all safe."

"She thinks flirting with Max evens the score between us." Suzy laughed. "It doesn't bother me."

"It isn't your fault that you're a better mother to me than she ever was."

"And it isn't her fault, either. She's mentally ill. You're her daughter, and she wants to be the one you turn to."

"That's about as likely as Hildy the Hillbilly clown becoming the CEO of Ringling Brothers."

Suzy laughed and nodded in Aidan's direction. "I see where Cass gets his charisma."

"I'm not charismatic?" I folded my arms under my breasts.

"He could charm a flock of nuns out of their habits."

"Good reminder." Cass ran toward Max and Aidan, I thought he would plow right into Max's legs the way he normally did, but Aidan anticipated him and bent low and picked him up into his arms before brushing his hair out of his eyes.

I gasped in a strangled breath. They were beautiful together. Cass even draped his arm around Aidan's shoulder while Max and Aidan continued to talk. Aidan's head turned, as if he knew my exact position. He silently bid me to come to him.

"There was more between you two than what you told me."

My immediate response was to be angry with someone I considered an ally. "You're a flocked nun, I see."

She chuckled. "Birds of a feather, you and me together."

I resisted the urge to flap my arms; instead I waved them over my head goodbye. I put my arms up for Cass to fall into them, but my child refused the invitation, instead allowing Aidan to launch him into the beast of a car. The thing looked like some kind of military vehicle, especially since Cass kept calling it Tank. And I thought it a strategic move on Aidan's part.

Aidan shook Max's hand and steered me around to the passenger's side. I arched a brow in question, before he opened the door. He cleared his throat. "Max says no more sleepovers." He tossed me into the truck a little rougher than necessary. "Let me get your belt for you, babe." When he leaned over, his face was in my chest. I tried to plaster myself to the back of the seat while he fiddled with the seatbelt.

"Aidan?"

The belt clicked. "We'll sleep at my place from now on."

While he meandered around the car, I gazed back at Cass quizzically. The kid never put his lap belt on without an argument or a complaint. "Mister Pole-ow-ski has strict rules about seat belts, Mom."

I looked toward Mister Pole-ow-ski.

"He tried to talk me out of it earlier, and we came to an agreement," Aidan said.

"I usually bribe him with candy." I offered.

"He can drive any of my cars when he's sixteen, as long as I never see him without a seatbelt on between now and then."

"That's kind of a long term commitment for you."

Aidan grinned. "He wants the Beemer."

"No sixteen-year-old should be allowed to drive a BMW."

"He should, if he wants all the prettiest girls."

Cass giggled. I smiled, as his happiness warmed me.

My eyes returned to Aidan, when he whispered, "That's the pickup car, and this here is the make out car."

I tried not to giggle, but it was contagious. Aidan put his hand on my thigh and squeezed. "Where to, babe?"

"Clarke's. Go to Chicago Avenue and make a right."

He smiled into the rear view mirror toward Cass. "Did your mom tell you about the time I waited for her outside her work at 4:30 in the morning to give her a birthday present?"

"She told me my dad stood out in the cold one day to give her a present," Cass replied as his eyes moved between us.

"You told him we knew each other at IU?" I hissed.

"I'm not going to lie to him."

"You do an awfully good job at lying to yourself. Feel free to spread it around," I barked, resolutely focusing on not speaking again. I was trying to find a way to extricate myself from the situation without upsetting Cass. But before I had come up with anything, we were walking through Clarke's doors.

Cass waved at several of the regulars, who were lingering over the counter, some with newspapers, some with menus, and some with coffee stained smiles. Clarke's reminded me of the Waffle House, and it was Cass' favorite place lately.

The college-aged waitress approached, her thick black eyeliner, sharp short bangs, and pair of stubby spiked ponytails with hot pink highlights striping her head, tagged her slightly right of Goth. She was wearing a short black skirt with red tights. You might think the tights out of place but they were the exact shade of her lipstick. She barely glanced at us before she smiled at Cass. "Hey, kid, how's it going?"

Cass' single dimple bloomed deep in his right cheek. "Lori, what are you doing here?"

Aidan looked first at Cass and then at the girl again. I had never seen her before. I would remember the dog collar necklace.

"I just started here to make extra money. What'll it be?"

Cass' head rested on the palm of his hand on the table, a bemused smile stretched from ear to ear. "I'll have a plain cheeseburger and a chocolate shake."

"Can do, little man," she didn't look up from her pad.

"I'll have a turkey club and an ice tea," I said.

After a few moments of silence she looked up from her pad at Cass-a-nova. "Do you have any idea what your dad wants?"

Cass didn't respond to her outrageous misnomer. "Mister Pole-ow-ski, Lori needs to know what you want."

Aidan cleared his throat. "Same as Mrs. Palowski."

I kicked him under the table.

Cass stared after her as she clunked off in her Doc Marten lace-up battlefield boots toward the kitchen. "Who is that?" Aidan asked.

Cass gaped after her until she disappeared. "She's a teacher's aide at school, but she works in Madi's class."

I nodded in dawning realization. "That's why he pitched a fit when he wasn't in Madi's class."

"I just had a flashback of what I must have looked like the night I met you at McCreary's."

"I do not resemble that girl in any way."

"You're more sophisticated now, but once upon a time you had that same haughty attitude." He looked me up and down. "It must be some weird genetic attraction thing," he laughed as he said it. "Your son is quite the flirt."

"How could you have rubbed off on him already?" I looked at my watch. "It's only been, like what, six hours?"

Cass spoke in the direction of his love's exodus. "It ain't Mister Pole-ow-ski's fault. I've been in love with Lori since the first day of school. Isn't she the most beautiful girl in the world, Mister Pole-ow-ski?"

"As much as I can appreciate falling in love on the first day of school, she doesn't come to school dressed like that I hope."

"No Sister Mary Francis makes her wear normal stuff, jeans and a T-shirt, when she works." He looked at Aidan for a moment. "Can I take her for a ride in the Beemer?"

"Not a moment before your sixteenth birthday." Aidan turned on me, smiling. "Calls to mind your first crush, doesn't it?"

"Yes, but I wasn't six years old."

"How old were you?" He wiggled his eyebrows up and down.

"Twenty something," I said looking away.

"I'm growing a rapid appreciation for firsts."

Cass burst out laughing, "My mom has only loved one boy, and it was my dad. She told me so, Mister Pole-ow-ski."

Lori reappeared with our drinks. As soon as she set them down I grabbed mine, and gurgled some down, while she grabbed one of Cass' cheeks and gave him a sweet pinch before she shuffled away.

Aidan pointed toward Cass. "You need to go wash your hands before you eat."

"Oh man," he responded.

"I'm sorry was that 'Old Man'? Or 'Oh Man', I better get a move on it'?" A stern look that made veteran baseball players wince washed Aidan's face. Who knew he could be so adult-like?

Cass placed his napkin on the table. "Yes sir."

What would've been a three-minute argument or a bag of M&M's for me was one stern look from Aidan and a 'yes sir'. I was dragged closer to my nemesis. "I think you should explain exactly what you told Cass about his dad."

I drew in a shuddering breath. "The only thing that Cass knows about his father is that he is dead."

"And that you loved him."

"He did ask if I loved his father, and I told him I did, but what was I supposed to say?"

"So, you weren't in love with his father?"

"No, I was drunk."

"Let me get this straight." Stillness took hold of him. "You were an inexperienced twenty-two year old, and you spent the night with me because you wanted a one night stand?"

I dropped my head.

He pulled my chin up to look me in the eye. "Did you at least enjoy it, when I filled your body with mine?"

All of the heat of my body pooled low in my gut. "No, I did not enjoy it at all."

"You're lying, Libby. And to be blunt, for an attorney you're not very good at it." Cass returned and our lunch arrived, saving me from further questions. I ate, choking down the turkey club.

The boys continued with a lively banter about Halloween, school, Madi Dubrowski, and baseball. Aidan refused to try to draw me back into the conversation, and Cass seemed content to have his man talk.

I heard Cass say, "Earth to Mom, earth to Mom."

Aidan had the check in his hand. I snatched it away. The man had had the upper hand for too long, and I was going to level the playing field. "I'll take care of this."

"Have it your way, Libby. You always have, especially when it comes down to anything important." I couldn't reconcile the expression on his face. He steered Cass toward the door and made his way to Tank while I paid the bill.

Aidan was waiting with the passenger side door open for me. He didn't speak while he helped me in. When I couldn't get the belt out far enough to meet the latch, he shooed my hands away and took control of it for me. "The one thing I've learned about growing up is lying to yourself doesn't hurt anyone but you."

I started to speak, but he cut me off with a knowing look. "We'll talk about it later when were alone. Maybe you can spend the night at my house tonight."

"Maybe the Cubs will take the pennant."

He ducked his head past mine, looking at Cass. "Hey, Cass, how about a sleepover at my house tonight? I have a game room." Once again, he played his trump card.

"Yee haw!" was Cass' response.

"I'll let you decide what side of the bed you want." He didn't wait, before soundlessly closing the door on my response.

Cass was engrossed with the DVD player. *I am not sleeping with you*, I chanted it in my head over and over again.

Aidan was smiling from ear to ear. He got into the war machine, and the engine roared to life. The men had assumed command once again. "I never said we'd be sleeping."

I pulled my head out of my chant.

"I can still read your face, sometimes, Libby."

Yeah, great, I thought, as I concentrated on masking any response, that's frickin' outstanding.

13

DOUBLEHEADERS

In the great department store of life, baseball is in the toy department.

Aidan 1 p.m.

I was angry, but I knew it wasn't fair. Every person I had ever wanted I'd been secure in their devotion to me, before I'd ever put my emotions on the line. Except for Libby. I glanced at her defiant chin as we drove down Sheridan Road, knowing she wasn't going to engage me in conversation. "Where's your dad?"

"Your guess is as good as mine."

No wonder she had a spine of steel—and an aversion to men. The revelation was a new one. Even an arrogant jock should've figured that out in college.

I was silent for a few moments of contemplation. I'd played a significant role in the destruction of our relationship. I wasn't the victim I'd convinced myself I was, and she wasn't the villain. I slammed my hand into the steering wheel, drawing her curious gaze. "I forgot something I need to do for work." It was the only thing that I thought to offer up in explanation.

"If you need to work, we can go home." She smiled as if she had found an extra surprise in a Cracker Jack box.

"I promised Cass the sporting goods store and park."

I merged into traffic on Lake Shore Drive. I tried to gauge her response. I didn't want to force her into my world; I wanted to smooth her into it, but if push came to shove? I wanted to know the woman she'd become. I needed to know if there was anything between us worth salvaging. And Cass deserved a chance to have his parents cordial with one another.

I parked in an underground garage off Huron. Cass walked between us, holding our hands, unaware the occasional 'Palowski' acknowledgement. Libby came to a dead halt at a store front window and she smiled. I looked up at the sign and laughed.

Libby eyed me, while Cass tugged on my hand. "She has a thing about shoes. If she's goes in, it could be hours." Libby scowled at Cass, before smiling a shrug as we continued onward.

When we reached Nike Town, I said, "Go to the shoe store, we'll come and get you when were done here."

She hesitated for a minute. "Be good," she kissed Cass' cheek. I, in turn, kissed her temple before stepping into the doorway. It hit me, what I'd done, and I turned to see her blank expression frozen to the sidewalk. Then I shrugged and smiled.

Nike Town was full of sports enthusiasts hovering around the youth baseball aisle. Cass looked up at me. "Why is everyone whispering Band-Aid? Is somebody hurt?"

"My real name is Banford Aidan, Band-Aid is a nickname." I slipped his hand into a glove. "I clean up games that other pitchers might have messed up, so they use me like a Band-Aid."

Cass smiled a toothless grin, as he beat the palm of the glove. "Can you fix other kinds of hurts with your Band-Aids?"

I smiled at how his mind worked. "I usually put the hurt on the other team, not Band-Aids."

"You aren't going to put the hurt on my mommy are you?"

That's when realization dawned. This wasn't a game, or a challenge. This was serious business, and I had the opportunity to hurt or heal them. I had to tread carefully. "I would never hurt your mommy... or you."

We made our purchases, escaping without a single autograph. Cass carried his bat on his shoulder like he was an old pro. As soon as we entered the Ferragamo store, I located Libby; she slipped her coat on and nodded no to the sales clerk before heading toward us. "The last thing I should be doing at a time like this is shoe shopping."

I arched a brow and the sales girl swooped in. "Are you sure you don't want the vintage pair? They won't last the hour."

Before she could say no again I said, "We'll take them."

The sales girl didn't hesitate making her way to the cash register, and I ignored Libby's protests as they were rung up. Cass dropped his aluminum bat on the tile floor when he heard the total, clanging everyone's attention to us. Libby helped him, while I signed the slip and took the bag. When she stood up I thrust the package in her empty hands.

"Happy birthday," I said, as I directed us through the revolving door and onto the Magnificent Mile.

All she could get out was a sputter, and she fumbled into another woman on the sidewalk. The woman's face met mine as the good-looking guy with her helped steady Libby. "Hello, Amanda." She was as golden as I remembered her, back during our on-again, off-again college relationship.

Amanda cleared her throat. "How are you?" She recovered quickly. "This is Marc Carson, my husband. Marc this is Aidan."

Libby froze in place. The square parcel became a life preserver, and she was holding onto it for dear life.

I guided her by the elbow forward. "Amanda, Marc, this is my girlfriend, Elizabeth Tucker, and her son Cass." I said, meeting Amanda's eyes as she examined first Cass and then me.

A broad smile erupted over Amanda's face and cascaded over Libby. "It's very nice to meet you, Elizabeth."

Libby croaked out, "Likewise," before she took Marc's hand.

"Are you with Whitney, Brown and Rodgers?" he asked.

She stood a little straighter. "Yes, I am."

"I saw your appeals brief on the Sullivan case. I'm a judge, and I was hoping to hear your arguments in my courtroom, but the case was assigned to someone else's docket. Judge Foreman says you're one of the best and the brightest; he's a mentor of mine. I heard you have a perfect record and was hoping to see you in action." He smiled broadly. "He didn't exaggerate when he said you were the best looking defense attorney in the city, either."

Libby flinched at the compliment; she'd never taken them easily. "Thank you. It's a pleasure meeting you, too."

Cass tugged on my hand, drawing my attention back to his. "We have a busy day." I extended my hand to Marc. "It was nice seeing you again, Amanda. Congratulations."

As we strolled away toward the garage, Libby looked back over her shoulder as if to confirm what transpired. "He's one of the best judges in Cook County. He'll probably be the governor one day."

"You're on his radar now." I narrowed my eyes. "And not because of your briefs." I took the package from her. "Did he actually say you're the hottest defense attorney in the city?"

"He only meant it as a compliment."

"Just remember who your boyfriend is," I said as I slammed her door shut behind her.

"Yeah, right, I think it might be time to go home."

"Mom," Cass said. "I want to go to Mr. Pole-ow-ski's house and play his pinball machine."

"All right," she looked back at Cass who was working the DVD player. "We aren't going to run into any reporters, are we?" She whispered under her breath.

"Melanie was trying to get a comment on the breakup. She doesn't have a clue about . . . " I nodded my head toward Cass.

"What happens when everyone knows about Vanessa?"

"Reporters couldn't care less or they could camp out around the block. Depends on how much stink Vanessa puts up."

She rolled her eyes as I pulled Tank around the corner. I had converted a three story grey-stone into a single residence. The original nineteenth century facades on either side of the street seemed to wink at each other as we rolled down the avenue. I went down the potholed alley and parked the Hummer in the detached garage.

Cass peered through the backdoor window into the kitchen in awe. "This room is as big as our whole house."

Libby helped him out of his coat, as we stepped in. "That might be a slight exaggeration."

"At least half as big," Cass retorted.

"Let's go upstairs. I'll show you the game room." I tousled his hair. "You can come up, too," I said to Libby.

Cass' eyes glazed over at the sight of the Foosball and air hockey tables, but he went straight for the pinball machine. I gave him a handful of quarters and he smiled. He was barely able to see over the pinball machine, but he didn't look up from the game. I grabbed a folding chair and stood him on it.

"This is really cool, Mr. Pole-ow-ski."

"Yeah, but don't beat my high score." I turned to find Libby leaning in the doorway with her jacket pulled tight around her body. A beautiful smile lined her face. She looked relaxed and content, until she caught me staring at her. She dropped the smile, as she straightened out of the doorjamb.

"Opted for the game room, in lieu of a library?"

"We had fun in the library. Maybe I'll look into getting one." I pulled her down the hall. "Besides the game room, there are two bedrooms on this floor." I towed her to the staircase at the end of the hall. The third floor housed the master suite.

Her lashes swept her cheeks. "Are the big boy's toys up here?"

"Keep it up, and I'll start playing with you."

She stopped, and her rear was in my face, it was no hardship admiring her snug jeans preceding me up the narrow staircase. When I looked up, she gave me a glare. "What?" I asked as innocently as a little leaguer caught stealing second.

"If this whole floor is your bedroom, I'm not going in."

I impatiently pushed her hips with mine toward the landing. "This is the sitting room and dressing area." I looked through the arched opening. "My bed is way over there, so relax." I led her to a pair of plush chairs and coerced her into one, before I flicked on the TV and handed her the remote. "I've never had to compel anyone into it. Not even you."

Closets ran down both sides of the walls, and the mirrored

doors squeaked. My closet was full, but the closet across the span stood empty, on silent hinges. Libby was flipping through the channels as I stripped to my boxers when she turned back toward me, she took me in nonchalantly, glancing first at my face, then at my boxers then turning back, as if my body had no effect on her. But a red blush crept up her exposed neck, and stained her cheeks. She slipped out of her jacket.

I chuckled. "You need a fan?"

"Keep it up, and you might need a medic."

"You've already seen me naked," I said as I slid my boxers off. She never could resist a dare. It's how I'd gotten her to do most of the things I wanted her to do in college.

She turned in the chair and stared me down. Not down, but directly in the eye. She refused to look lower. I felt my face light up with a cocky grin.

"If you're trying to make me feel uncomfortable, don't bother. I see Cass naked all the time."

"This is hardly a six-year-old body." I chuckled and turned toward the bathroom.

"Nice butt, Band-Aid."

Libby was watching the news when I came out of the steam shower. I wandered over in my towel and took the chair alongside hers. She didn't look at me until I put my feet up on the ottoman and nudged her. A channel five news reporter was interviewing a tall, elderly priest with thick black-framed glasses on the stairs of a church. I bent forward, recognizing him as the pastor at St. Ignatius, where I'd attended Mass every Sunday during my childhood. "What's going on?"

She was so involved with the story that she barely glanced at me. "A Mexican immigrant and her son have begged the archdiocese for sanctuary, instead of turning herself over to INS. It's a standoff. She won't come out, and the police won't go into a church to arrest her. The priest is speaking in response to the women with the signs."

I took in the screen again where a few women were marching

back and forth with signs that read: MOTHERS FOR DEPORTATION. "What are the protestors' beefs?"

"They're a group of right wingers who think the woman shouldn't be given immunity just because her child is ill and can receive better medical care here than in Mexico. They're insisting she's a criminal."

"How much you want to bet that among those protestors someone employs an illegal alien?"

"You're probably right, but that won't help get her out of trouble. She needs legal representation."

"You're an attorney."

"I'm in criminal defense, not immigration."

"They say she's a criminal. If you do a little digging, you could make this whole business go away, I bet."

"When did you become such a humanitarian?"

"I don't like injustice. I know Father Schimkowski. Maybe we should pay him a visit and see what we can do."

"Why would you want to get involved?"

"I'd think you'd want to. She has a sick kid. You have a sick kid. Besides, you could put your law school education to good use." I looked at the TV for a few minutes. "Tell you what. I'll pay you to represent her."

"I have serious case overload, but this is the kind of *pro-bono* work I love." She looked at me. "I'll think it over."

My cell phone rang, and I got up to get it. "Yeah, Fletch."

"Did you buy a car this morning?"

"I'm fine. How are you?"

"Palowski, I don't give a shit how you are. Did you buy a hundred thousand dollar car on your Amex this morning?"

"It was spur of the moment," I answered. "I needed a bigger car, and Cass picked it out."

"Cass Tucker?" He bellowed. "As in your kid?"

"That's the one."

"What the hell's going on?"

"I'm taking care of it."

"Is Libby with you?"

"Of course she is."

"Don't tell me you spent the night with her."

"I'm afraid so."

"You were supposed to keep her close enough to take care of the kid and business. Not close enough to form an attachment. This is why Vanderhoff's attorney is on my ass."

"I'm sorry to hear that, but you're well paid, and I have a lot to do this afternoon. I'll talk to you later."

"Listen to me Palowski I have enough of your kicked-to- the-curb broads causing me heartache. Don't add Tucker to the mix. Get in, give her what she wants, and get out."

"Have a great day, Fletch. Tell Tricia I said hi." I hung up and went back to sit alongside Libby.

"I hope you're not involving Cass in any of your schemes."

"Speaking of Cass, he seems pretty at ease with me. Have you had him around a lot of men?"

She glanced at my towel. "No unclothed client consults."

"I'm glad to hear that."

"As a lawyer, I stand up to physical manipulation now. And a bare chest isn't all that jarring."

"I'm not trying to make you uncomfortable. I usually sit in that chair—" I pointed to where she was sitting, "—to cool down before I get dressed. It's a habit. I can sit with you, if you prefer."

Her eyes traveled over my shoulders, before she reached out, her fingertips tracing the length of the puckered scar there.

"What happened?" she asked.

I forced myself to concentrate on the words, rather than on her fingertips. "I had surgery."

"I never heard a word about it."

"Doc says I've got two, maybe three years, before its shot to kingdom come." I put my hand over her soft fragile ones feeling her warmth run through me.

"Are you upset?" She was still staring at small round scars where pins had been. "Does the club know?"

"It's not like I thought I could pitch forever. The media doesn't know, and I'd like it if it stayed that way." I gave her a soft smile. "But everything might come out anyway."

"If we stay away from each other, nothing will come out."

"That's not an option. I want to get to know Cass, and if that costs me other things, well, then, that's the way it is."

"I thought you didn't sign a longer deal because you wanted to be traded."

"Chicago is my home. I want to finish here. I've learned a few things over the years. Baseball is a business. And in business, if you're not honest, the competition usually eats you alive. I'll play one year at a time."

"You could have gotten millions more out of this deal?"

"What do I need millions more for? It's like you said, money doesn't buy everything." In that silent moment I held her gaze. "How many other guys have there been?"

She smiled like a canary feasting over crow stew. "How many other women have there been?"

I met her eye squarely. "Too many to count."

She flinched, but then composed herself. "Why are we having this conversation? I don't need to know your deepest secrets in order for you to get to know Cass."

"But you need to know them if I ever want you to trust me again. So I'll tell you things I'm not proud of, and you can let it help you decide what kind of man I've become."

"Your sex life has nothing to do with trust."

"I'm curious about yours." I raised my eyebrow. "It wouldn't be fair to find out, without trading information."

She put her hands over her ears. "I don't want to know, and I certainly don't want to trade."

"Then I'll give you insider's scoop." I looked at the TV before I went on. "After the night we spent together, I wasn't with anyone for a long time."

She pulled her head up, taking me in, but didn't speak.

"I couldn't bring myself to want anyone else."

Containing my own anxiety was like trying to get a baseball down my throat. "The first time I felt anything physical for anyone was graduation day, when I saw you and I wanted . . . " I swallowed trying to choose the right words. "You were five months pregnant, and the sight of you . . . well, my body reacted, and I couldn't stay in my seat."

"I don't want to hear this."

I crouched on my knees in front of her and forced her to look at me. "I was celibate all that time, thinking you would come back to me, and then I could say I'd been faithful to you."

A tear slid down her face and she smoothed it away with the back of her hand. "I thought it was all a game to you."

"It was a game until I realized that I was playing with feelings, my own included. I continued waiting, but when I got the termination of parental rights papers, I thought you were giving away the last thing that bound us together. After a year of celibacy, I went off the deep end. I binged for about two years before I was so dead inside that my pitching started to suffer. By then I had exhausted myself trying to find some sort of challenge in anything, and I moved on to extreme sports."

"You could've stayed with Amanda after graduation."

"I stayed with her for a while." I looked away abruptly. "But we weren't having a physical relationship, and she couldn't understand why. The only girl I wanted wasn't interested in me. Amanda knew something was going on, but I couldn't share you with her. Then, she found some evidence, and she left me."

"Evidence?"

"Some letters. Amanda asked what had happened between us, and at that point I owed her the truth."

"I never wrote you any letters."

I arched a brow. "I can write you know."

Her hand was over her mouth. "That must have killed her."

"She was outraged that I'd abandoned you pregnant. She was more furious about that than my neglecting her."

"A girl in law school bragged she'd spent the night with you." Libby's expression became grim. "Cass was only nine months old, and I hadn't thought of being with anyone. It reminded me that I was alive, but you were the one who was living."

"Does that mean you were watching?"

"I heard things, and I was at a party you attended two years ago. You seemed content."

"Why didn't you say anything?"

"For the same reasons you never came looking for me."

"Whatever else you think, I believed you gave the baby up. And while I was initially relieved, by the second day I was furious that you could give a piece of me away like that."

"Compared to the way you gave us away?"

"I didn't say it was right. It was just how I felt. So when are you going to answer the question, counselor?"

"Which question is that?"

"We're both adults. You had a right to find someone else."

"Who says I didn't?"

I jerked, as if she had slapped me. "If you don't want to tell me, that's fine but don't yank my chain." I got up and had started toward the closet, when she grabbed my wrist to stop me.

She looked from her fingers to my face. "Only a few," the words were so faint, I almost didn't hear them.

I continued a step before asking. "Is there someone now?"

Neither of our eyes sought the others. "No. My life is much too complicated for that now."

"Then we agree," I said.

"I'm glad we're clear on all of that."

"Yes we're clear." I pushed open the door, and Cass' voice roared up the stairs, asking when we were going to leave.

"I've grown up, but I haven't changed that much."

"I'm counting on that." She smiled smugly.

"I've always done whatever it takes to have my way."

The ump, who hadn't said a word all day grumbled, **All's fair in love and war, kid.**

I made a disparaging hand sign into the mirror. Let him learn to call that play.

14

PLAIN VIEW

A location or field of perception in which something is plainly apparent.

Elizabeth

"This was the hood, when I was growing up," Aidan said, pointing toward the tree-lined parkway. "My *bushia* used to tell my mother to stay out of this 'Beatnik Neighborhood'."

"If it was a bad neighborhood, why did you come?"

"My mother volunteered at the Chicago Historical Society. She helped the neighborhood ladies, giving away clothes, food and occasionally money."

It was the first thing he'd ever told me about his mother, but I had already seen her photo at his house. She reminded me of Jackie Kennedy, petite, dark, and perfect, with a kind smile.

I heard a snort and turned around to find Cass with his head slumped back against the headrest, asleep with his mouth agape. "He was up at the crack of dawn." Aidan chuckled.

"He's an early bird. But then ten minutes before we arrive somewhere, he conks out on me."

"We'll wake him up when we get to the ball field."

Lincoln Park was to my right and on the left, some of the best real estate in Chicago. The architecture was as diverse as the city. Tall high-rises, soaring glass and metal remnants from the sixties, gleaming back water and sunlight. These were interspersed with shorter facades from a bygone era. Richardson arches rested on columns over entranceways. Red brick beauties showed off Italianate trims and moldings. They all stood along the Parkway, each one so different from the next, but united along the street front.

"You're awfully quiet," Aidan said.

"Did you know Lincoln Park was once the city cemetery?"

"It was an army post first, then the city cemetery and then a small pox hospital. Before that, it was a remote swampland of muddy forest. Around 1860, some of the city's leaders decided it should be Lake Park. They dug ten miles of ditches to drain the lowland into the lagoons that are sprinkled through the park now. It was based on Haussmann's Park in Paris."

"Are you planning a career as a tour guide?" *Or did he remember my love of history?*

"No, I'm considering a much more domestic position."

"Hiring out for stud services?"

He laughed as he continued on with historical tidbits for a few minutes. "When my great-great grandfather started his business here, land was only one-hundred-and-twenty dollars an acre. His slaughterhouse was at Archibald and Clybourn, and he had several breweries down at this end of the park. All the cheap labor he could afford to employ was living in the neighborhood in between."

"Beer and Brats? I thought your family was affluent."

"Beer and Kielbasa. Brats are German. Kielbasa is Polish. They were prosperous, but that doesn't mean they didn't work. The first Polish immigrants to Chicago were nobles who fled after the Polish-Russian War of 1830-1831."

I looked at him over my rimless glasses with an air of disbelief. "That explains the noble arrogance."

"I've missed you busting my chops. Your mom's a little wacky and your dad skipped out on you, but I'd bet my signing bonus you're related to the Queen of England."

I twisted in my seat and glared at him.

"What? You were always so proper." His face brightened. "You were an English major."

I expelled a breath toward the steamed up windshield. We had pulled into a parking spot, and I could see two baseball fields. One of which was occupied by a group of kids. "English was my major, took you only eight years to figure that one out." I looked at my watch gauging how much longer I'd have to spend in the Polish Prince's chariot.

Aidan pulled his right hand through his thick hair, resting his open hand on the back of his headrest, stretching. The corded muscles of his chest flexed beneath his tight long sleeve T-shirt. He watched me, as I watched him, before he moved his hand to graze my hair. "We could make out, if you're not into family history?"

"What little I know of my father's side, English Quakers that came to America in the early 1700's. My mother's side is German, my fifth great-grandfather came during the Revolution."

"That makes you about as American as apple pie."

"He was a Hessian soldier who fought on the British side. He was marched up and down the colonies before being captured near Philadelphia. When the war ended, he was to be shipped back to Germany, but he didn't have the money for transport, so he indentured himself to a South Carolina Quaker. After two years, he ran off with the man's twenty-six-year-old daughter and a cow. They were married and had thirteen kids."

"You have a fertile family. No wonder I got you pregnant the first time."

I glanced back at Cass to make sure he was still asleep before I gave Aidan my best lawyers glare. "Proud of that, are you?"

"Just goes to show I'm extremely good at everything I do."

I slapped his leg so hard the whack of it stung my hand. "I'm surprised you remember with all the lovely ladies that have fallen at your cleats since." I looked away.

"I remember the night we spent together more clearly than any of the women in the last eight years." His fingertips brushed aside the curtain of hair I was hiding behind. "Why haven't you gotten married and had more kids?"

"I was working on becoming a partner."

Cass' voice pulled me from the game and questions I had no answers for. "Mommy promised me a brother when she found the right Mister. I want a brother, Mr. Pole-ow-ski, you know why?"

Aidan didn't seem surprised by Cass' voice. "No, why?"

"Cause then I won't be the baby no more," he said with the harrumph of a six-year-old.

"Seems like a reasonable request to me." Aidan shrugged.

I turned away and opened the car door, letting the brisk breeze in. "Let's go do what you do best, Palowski. Play games."

He came around the car to help me, but I already landed on firm ground. "I think, with all our successes what we've done best is sitting in this car." He touched the end of my nose with his chilled fingers. "And that, cutter, is no game."

I walked toward the fields, watching the dust kick up as the runners wound their way around toward home. Aidan came up behind me, as I stood holding onto the chain link fence. He dropped the gear. "All I want is a chance to make Cass"—he stared off into the distance as if weighing each and every word he plucked from the swirling dust and leaves—"happy."

He wants a chance to make mince meat out of my heart again?

Cass wandered toward the other field where the kids were playing a highly contested game. I looked back and forth between father and son, again struck by the similarities between them.

He took his leather jacket off, shoving it into my arms. "Put it on. It's cold out here." He pulled a Hoosier sweatshirt out of his duffle bag and once his head popped through the hole he started winding up his arms as he approached Cass, who smiled. "We'll start with this glove. We need to break it in." Aidan pulled out a can of shaving cream and sprayed a mound of foam on the glove, and Cass's eyes expanded at the same rate.

"Tonight before you go to sleep, we'll do it again. Put the ball in the pocket and tie some string around it so you can sleep with it under your mattress. That will help loosen it up."

Cass giggled as Aidan bent the leather, making it more pliable.

"See how this feels on your hand." Aidan slipped the soft and shiny glove over Cass' hand.

Cass slapped at his palm with his fist. "It feels good."

"What position do you want to learn to play?"

"You're a pitcher, right?"

"That's the hardest position. Are you sure?"

Cass smiled a crooked smile. "Yep," he said definitely.

"Okay, I'm going over to home plate. I just want to see your natural throwing."

Aidan barely got there when Cass launched a cannonball that flew past his ducked head and ricocheted off the chain link backstop. Aidan picked up the ball and smiled broadly. "I thought you never played before." He arched a brow.

Cass snickered, before peering at me under hooded lids.

"You've got some gas, but it doesn't matter how fast you can throw it, if you can't get it in the strike zone."

"Control the ball," Cass parroted, "got it."

Aidan went back to the pitching mound with Cass. "You've got a lot of raw talent, but let's see what you can do if I teach you some form." Aidan tossed him the ball.

"Index finger and middle fingers across the seams," Cass repeated holding the ball as instructed.

"Now step with the opposite foot toward the target, which is your mom in this case."

"The opposite foot pointed toward the target, got it."

"You need to have your shoulders closed Cass."

"Huh?"

"Your shoulders should be pointed toward your target. Now extend your throwing arm back behind you parallel to the ground, that's called the long lever. The throwing motion begins by rotating your upper body and your hips, while your arm makes an L shape at your elbow. Release the ball snapping your wrist while your arm follows through toward the opposite hip." Aidan maneuvered Cass' limbs to complete the movement. "Okay, do the whole motion for me without the ball."

Cass was concentrating on controlling all his appendages.

Aidan said, 'again' every time he wanted Cass to go through the movement from the start. They must have done it at least twenty times before Aidan put the ball in Cass glove.

I stood through Cass's first lesson with my fingers wrapped around the metal chain links, and my mind wrapped around the fact that Cass' had a father, one who had things to teach him. One who probably had answers to questions I'd been asking myself my entire life—'Why'd you leave me?'

The kids playing at the adjacent field were edging closer to our field. They were varying shades of tan, from light caramel to rich chocolate. Each speaking in rapid fire Spanish, the gist of the conversation revolved around whether Aidan was a 'real' baseball player, and who was 'man or woman' enough, one of the two little girls pointed out, to find out.

Aidan and Cass lobbed the ball back and forth for a few rotations before Aidan looked at me. "You going to hold up the fence, babe, or are you going to catch for us?"

"Me?" I squeaked.

"You can catch, can't you?" He tossed a glove at me when I came around the fence. I tested the mitt. It was broken in already, and I hated that I wondered how many girls had worn it.

"Okay, killer, let's see if your bazooka can get the ball to Miss Priss over there."

I got down in the catchers squat as Cass wound up and threw the ball, it smacked the center of my glove effortlessly. Cass jumped up and down. "I got it, oh yeah!"

I tossed the ball up into the air a few times, catching it easily while the two males congratulated each other, one on his coaching and the other on his 'natural' talents. Then I wound up myself— "Aidan." —and threw the ball.

He barely got his hand up in time to catch it, before he took off his glove shaking the sting out of it. He started toward me. "You've got some 'splaining to do." He was about a yard shy of me when he stopped. "Well?"

I put my hand on my hip and gave him a dismissive once over. "Indiana State softball champions, two years at French Lick High." Then I made my thumb and index finger into a gun and blew on the tip, I waited a moment before holstering it.

"By the time I figure you out, I'll be dead."

I mocked his tone, "That or you'll wish you were."

He closed the distance between us, pulling me by the lapel, kissing my cold nose, then nuzzling my neck with his cold lips. Cass snickered on the breeze.

"Don't make me use my gun on you," I grumbled, trying not to giggle.

"Mines bigger," he laughed against my goose pimpled skin.

Another snickering voice made us jump apart. "Hey man, Lola here says that she's seen you on TV. Is she just messin' with us? She says that you play for the Cubs?"

"I'll deal with you later." He winked conspiratorially before addressing the kid. "Lola is correct. I'm on the Cubs."

"Can we play baseball with your kid, Mr. Band-Aid?"

"We can only play an inning before it's too dark and cold."

The kids jumped up and down excitedly as we divided up into two teams. Cass and the biggest boy were captains. Cass must have felt some sense of loyalty because I was his first round draft choice while the other team took Aidan. The rest of the kids were picked from the biggest to the smallest.

Cass was pitching, and I was the catcher. They had a runner on first, who had been picked off on a grounder. When Aidan came up to bat, he fouled off Cass' first two pitches. "How about a little wager?"

"What did you have in mind?" I repositioned myself, so I could see Cass stumping the mound in nervous agitation.

"If I get a home run you cook dinner for us."

"And if you don't?"

"I'll buy you dinner and take you home. I'll even convince Cass that it was his idea."

"You're on." I nodded toward Cass, letting him know that I was ready. He wound up and let go. The ball slid over the plate.

"Strike one," Lola sang out in a sweet high-pitched voice.

The second pitch was almost as fast, but when it reached the plate it slowed down and dropped, Aidan swung and missed.

"Strike two."

"That kid of ours has talent." Aidan chuckled as he stepped out of the batter's box, kicking at his spikes with the bat. When he stepped back into the box he said, "I forgot, after you make us dinner you'll spend the night with me."

Cass wound up and it was a perfect pitch until Aidan made contact and it sailed over everyone's heads, but couldn't quite clear the fence. Before he dropped the bat, he said, "In the park homer," and started off around the bases at a clipped pace.

Cass was watching as the outfielder recovered the ball and threw it back toward the mound. Cass barely caught the ball, but he smiled a breathtaking smile at Aidan just as he was rounding third base. Then he wound up so fast that I didn't even see the ball coming.

A solitary thought throttled my brain. My stomach did a little flip. I think Cass was falling in love. I looked back trying to find Cass only to see the ball coming straight at me.

I did stop it though—with the middle of my forehead.

15

EXPAND THE STRIKE ZONE

Games played with the ball, and others of that nature, are too violent for the body and stamp no character on the mind.
Thomas Jefferson

Aidan 1 a.m.

The stairs creaking overhead startled me awake. A bright stream of light fell across my body through the cracked door, into the room where Cass and I were sleeping. My bad shoulder had become Cass' pillow and his new baseball glove was wedged into my bare armpit. Kitchen cabinets were opening and closing and I wondered what Libby was searching for.

Cass' covers were tangled around his ankles and I pulled them up as I placed my hand on his forehead, wanting to feel his skin one more time. He turned into my hand without waking and mumbled in his sleep, "I love you." Hearing the sweetly spoken words meant for his mother made me long for something that I hadn't known existed. I smiled as I slipped downstairs on silent feet approaching the light, to find Libby standing over the sink and wrestling with the Tylenol bottle.

"Need some help?"

She jumped, and the contents flew in every direction. I picked up two capsules from the floor, reached for a clean glass and turned on the tap before she'd caught her breath.

"Are you trying to scare the shit out of me?"

"Seven swears. I'm looking forward to settling up."

She took the capsules and tossed them back in a single swig while I admired the long column of her neck where it plunged into her revealing tank top. Max looked none too happy when he dropped off a bag for Libby earlier, but Suzy must have packed it with mischief in mind.

A thread's width of shiny silver chain rubbed against her satiny skin, something on the end of it dangled between her breasts. She peeked at my bare chest before taking a step back.

"I didn't want to go through your medicine cabinet." She picked up the empty bottle, and the chain swung free.

I picked up the end of the sparkling chain, as she rose to her feet. A small green enameled ring barely fit on the tip of my finger. "What's this?"

"A ring." She tried to turn away. "Sorry I woke you." She moved to go around me, but I refused to relinquish the chain.

"This ring looks familiar to me." Because I had given her that ring, for Christmas, the same night I had given her Cass. Seeing her face light up when I put it on her finger was as thrilling to me as watching her climax in the soft moonlight.

"I'm going back to bed." She pried it out of my fingers. "If Cass wakes up he'll be scared."

"He's not the one afraid. Besides, Northwestern's marching band couldn't wake him up. I'll make you a cup of tea."

When I came upstairs, I placed the tea tray on her lap and squeezed in next to her against the upholstered headboard. She startled, when the hair on my arms brushed her satiny skin, she squirmed. Instead of calming, I had to choke back a reaction. "Done pouting over the bet?"

"I don't pout. I took a screwball to the head. I have a headache."

I chuckled. "I bet I could make you forget it."

"You need to keep your paws off me, or Cass is going to get the wrong idea."

I pushed her hair over her shoulder, so I could see the side of her face. "I called Father Schimkowski and told him we'd come by to meet Ms. Gutierrez after 10:30 Mass, then go to lunch. Or do you take Old Mr. Rodgers to lunch on Sundays?"

"Cass told you about Mr. Rodgers on Sundays?" She peered at me out of the corner of her eye. "That kid talks too much."

"He gets that from me."

"What makes you so sure I'm going to help Ms. Gutierrez anyway?" She set her teacup down on the tray.

"If you go to see an old man in a rest home every Sunday out of a sense of duty, I'm sure you'd want to help a single mother who's in trouble." I moved the tray to the nightstand. "Isn't that why you went to law school?"

"I went to make oodles of money so I'd never have to go back to French Lick and live near my relatives."

"What's going on with you and your mom?" Libby's mom smiled lovingly at her, but something rippled and quaked right below the calm surface between them. Perhaps her mother embarrassed Libby. I found her unusual, but no more so than any other parent, then again, Libby would feel it a reflection of her.

"Jeanne thinks that at twenty-nine I need to be parented. She didn't do such a hot job at nine, so I'm not interested in a repeat performance."

"But what was going on when she showed up today?"

"I have no idea why she showed up dressed like a clown."

"When I went home, I walked in on my parents playing maid and butler, your mom in a clown get-up is much tamer." I laughed, pulling her along with me as I descended into the covers, holding her against me until I felt her stop struggling.

She shivered. "Your hair is tickling me."

"You keep wiggling like that, and it'll be more than my hair tickling you."

She became stock-still. I spooned around her and my forearm rested between her breasts; her necklace fell into my hand. "Why'd you keep this all these years?"

"Stupid sentimentality, I guess."

"The chain it's on is so fragile; it's as fine as a strand of your hair."

"Cass saved his allowance, for I don't know how long, to buy it for me last mother's day. He said, 'I don't want to be the only thing that you carry from my father forever.'"

"He says these profound things." I waited until her breathing slowed before I whispered, "All day I've been trying to remember who Cass reminds me of. He makes sounds in his sleep like my brother Andy."

"I thought your brother's name was Avery."

"I had an older brother, Andy. He was nineteen when he died, right before my tenth birthday. He was going to Florida for spring training to play for the Marlins. It was cold and icy, but he insisted on driving the Corvette my grandparents had given him for his birthday."

When Andy hit a patch of black ice, and careened off a bridge into the Ohio River, a piece of each of us had died with him. In my childlike mind, I'd assumed he was my father's favorite, because he'd made it to Triple A right out of high school, and my father was a sports fanatic. My mother had wanted Andy to attend Yale, and then play ball, but my father had insisted Andy was old enough to make his own decisions. And he'd died because of them.

"I was jealous he was going to play ball all day, and I had to go back to school. He said I was coming to see him for spring break, and I was so mad I told him that I never wanted to see him again. When he died, I thought I was responsible."

Libby was quiet for a long time. "So you wanted to make it to the majors to take his place?"

"I know it's crazy, but I thought I was supposed to move up in the ranks and take Andy's spot. I had the notion baseball was the way to my father's heart. By the time I figured out that it didn't work that way, I was already in college, and I had to finish what I started."

Just like you're going to finish what you're starting now, kid, and this, you might even enjoy.

9 a.m.

Libby was already moving around in the kitchen. I dressed in slacks and a polo shirt and went down to the kitchen, where I found her standing over the stove.

She turned in anticipation of me, and my breath caught in my throat. She was dressed in a pale pink cashmere dress, ivory hose and boots. Pink, square-framed glasses, matching her lips perched on her face. Her necklace hung in the deep v of the dress, along with loose strands of her unbound hair.

"Suzy certainly knows your clothes," I said in greeting when the desperate housewife spun the spatula in her hand like a magic wand. "We made the front page of the entertainment section." She nodded to the paper in the middle of the plates, cutlery, and juice glasses and turned back to flip pancakes.

Chicago Cubs Player Plays the Field

By Winslow O'Leary, Entertainment Reporter

Word about the Windy City is that Cubs closer Aidan Palowski has been seen about town with a new lady on his arm. This is no **CELEBUTANTE**, but one of the city's finest criminal defense attorneys, Elizabeth Tucker of Whitney, Brown & Rodgers, the law firm that handles anything from crooked politicians to celebrity scandals. It's the law firm that's kept the Accardo family out of Cook County Jail since the early 1920s.

Speaking of celebutante scandals: sources close to the parties involved report that Band-Aid paid New York's Vanessa Vanderhoff a red-eye visit to San Francisco to close out the game with her. Sources say she **GETS** to keep the ring. He didn't take long to find a nice Midwestern girl and word on the street is that this new face is no second stringer. One has to wonder where and when the two were first acquainted. Both share Indiana University as their Alma Mater; they graduated the same year.

Perhaps an old love rekindled? The new couple has been seen in a local bar in Wrigleyville, the 737 Restaurant for a romantic candlelight dinner, where more than food passed between them, eyewitnesses report. And just yesterday, they were sighted together shopping on North Michigan Avenue, playing ball in Lincoln Park before she was **DUMPED** by a ball, which caused no serious injury but sent our lovebirds home for a quiet evening with Thai Palace take-out for comfort.

Things are never more exciting than when this Golden Glove is around town **AGAIN**, but this situation might be as sticky as cotton candy on an August afternoon since Ms. Vanderhoff, when asked to comment, said only, "We're on a temporary break." Which doesn't seem to jive with what Omni patrons observed watching Band-Aid close a new deal with a lady who's in a league of her own.

The ump laughed hysterically. **'Celebutante gets dumped again.' I love this O'Leary guy.**

I swallowed, willing myself to concentrate, but between the ump's laughter and Libby's backside, I was distracted. "The article's not all that bad and the good news is that it doesn't mention Cass." Her glare made me swallow the lust in my throat. "Obviously, a lot of people think highly of you."

She pointed with the spatula that turned from wand to deadly weapon. "I wouldn't be mentioned at all if it wasn't for you. I'm used to the main section, when I'm just listed as someone's lawyer. I don't like being fodder for entertainment reporters." She stacked pancakes on a platter. I watched as she poured more batter on the griddle and then she dropped diced apples on each one. The vision was enough to make me want to drop to my knees and propose.

I moved behind her. "Would you like to be fodder for a baseball player's fantasy?" I gave into the impulse to draw her into my arms. When she came grudgingly, our jaw lines connected and the sweet scent of apple pancakes and Libby engulfed me.

Too soon, she stepped away. "Stop puttering around, and wake Cass so we won't be late for church."

"Do you need to confess that you spent the night?"

"This accusation coming from a man who's slept with a troupe of Rockettes?" She raised a single brow.

"Maybe you just need to confess to libidinous thoughts." I pulled her back, pressing her arms around my neck. I didn't go to her lips, instead I placed kisses along her neck and down over the curve of her breasts. She threw her head back, closing her eyes, chanting under her breath. If my face wasn't buried in the deep V of her dress, I might've smelled the burning before the smoke detector squealed to life, careening us apart.

If that alarm hadn't gone off, my mind might have calculated how to get her out of her dress and onto her back so I could have my way with her while our child was asleep right over our heads. Where was the ump when I needed him?

On cue, I heard him laughing over the shrieking smoke detector. I scrambled for the broom in the butler's pantry, the handle of which I used to silence the squealing menace.

Libby was dumping the burnt pancakes in the trash when Cass barreled into the kitchen in his PJ's. "Mommy, what happened?"

I threw open a window. It only took a few minutes for the smoke to clear and the room to cool off with the fall breeze. My body was another matter.

"I burned something." She avoided me and smiled at Cass.

Did she ever! The ump chortled.

16

AGENDA, ALIENS, ASYLUM

Not ignorant of trials, I can now learn to help the miserable. Virgil

Elizabeth

Saint Ignatius was the largest church in Chicago. It was an older sanctuary where a balustrade divided the raised dais of the clergy from the parishioners. The high altar was gleaming mahogany set against the black and white tile floor. The dome over the apse was painted with scenes from the transfiguration; all its columns and supports were gold and gilded. It was an impressive restoration.

Soon, we were told to go in peace, as the procession of priests, deacons and altar servers moved down the wide aisle. Most of the congregation had filed out by the time Aidan made his way to the vestibule, where he was greeted in Polish, and Father Ski's outstretched arms.

Father Schimkowski was an elderly, balding man with gnarled hands, a sparse black comb-over and a protruding belly, which made me think of a comic book chef.

"This is Elizabeth Tucker and her son Cass."

"I'm very pleased to meet you. Aidan said you might be able to assist Ms. Gutierrez. The Archdiocese had sent over a lawyer to discuss the church's stance on taking refuge here, but there is a conflict with the Holy See on representation."

"I would like to assist her, but I am in another field of law altogether. I'm not sure how much I can do, but if I can't help, I might be able to find someone else who can."

"Whatever you can do would be appreciated. You may speak with her in the study in the rectory."

We strolled through what would have been a beautiful walled garden in the spring and summer, now the grass was turning brown and all the bushes were barren. It was a stark reminder of how helpless I felt only days ago, and how this woman must feel now. If I could help her, I would. We walked across the paved path into the darkened foyer of the rectory.

"Father, I'm afraid I might need a translator. My Spanish is rusty." At the stairs, sunlight poured through the stained glass window on the landing, sending a colorful spectrum from the coffered ceiling to the floorboards.

"Have no fear, her English is as perfect as yours."

Cass bolted up the staircase. When Aidan caught up with him, he bent low to talk to him, his hand resting on Cass' shoulder. They stood on the colorful shadows while Father Ski and I continued on.

"Elizabeth, Aidan has spoken with me many times about you."

"Father, what happened between us is better forgotten."

"But not forgiven?"

"He hasn't asked for forgiveness."

"God has not forgotten that the two of you created a family, even if that was not your intention. You came back into Aidan's life after all this time, and His reasons may be greater than your own. Aidan will make a good father."

"Father, I only contacted Aidan because Cass has leukemia."

Shock crossed his face before he looked skyward. He was silent for several minutes. "He works in mysterious ways."

Aidan and Cass appeared in the plastered corridor that smelled faintly of furniture polish. The small study's walls were encased with leather bound books, and in the center of the room sat a striking dark beauty at a library table. A little boy reclined at her feet playing Matchbox cars. She rose with old world poise and extended her hand. "I am Evita Gutierrez. I'm very pleased to meet you." She had a slight accent, but it was a cultured European one.

Evita wasn't just attractive, but exotically beautiful, with dark green, almond-shaped eyes, a straight nose, chiseled jaw, perfectly arched brows, and skin almost as flawless as the amber in the stained glass windows.

"I'm Libby Tucker, and this is my son, Cass. This is Aidan Palowski." When I looked at Aidan, he arched his brow at me. I expected him to be taken with Evita's exotic beauty, but he looked past her, to her son.

"What's your son's name?" Aidan squatted near the boy. Cass possessively wrapped his arm around Aidan's neck.

Evita spoke up. "Emanuel, but we call him Manny."

"I'll take Cass and Manny to the kitchen for a snack, so you can talk privately."

"Thank you that would be helpful." She instructed her son warmly in Spanish. "He has perfect English, Mr. Palowski, so don't let him try to convince you otherwise."

Aidan had each of the boys' hands in his as he approached me. I was admiring the old books and framed maps that hung off the bookcases when he kissed my temple. A sigh escaped my lips. Father Ski was holding the door open for the gentlemen's exit. I took a seat in the tapestry chair across from Evita.

"Life is complicated, no?" She seemed to be questioning herself as much as me.

I pulled a legal pad from my briefcase. "I have a feeling your story is less complicated than mine."

"No, we have all been fools once in our lives." She frowned.

"Why don't you tell me about yourself?"

"I'm curious, were you expecting an overweight, uneducated, illegal?"

"I try not to have preconceived ideas. It's good you're attractive. You'll look good in front of cameras, or a jury."

"I want to stay out of the public eye." She took a deep breath. "That's why I haven't greeted the reporters myself."

"Then why didn't you report to the INS as mandated?"

"The minute I touch Mexican soil, I'll be dead, and God only knows what would happen to my son."

"Why don't you start with your background?" I scrawled Uh-oh on my pad, as a sense of unease prickled over me.

"I was born in Mexico City to a prominent family. After private high school I attended the University of Mexico, where I majored in music. I am a jazz artist." She looked away briefly. "I haven't played a single note in over two years.

"The entire time I've been in the U.S., I've been apprehensive of doing anything that might give away my identity.

"I was getting by until Manny got sick; he was burning up with fever. I went to the emergency room in the middle of the night. With his diabetes, I couldn't wait for the free clinic the next day. They asked many questions I couldn't answer, so once Manny got a shot of antibiotics, we disappeared. When they searched my name, I showed up on Mexico's most wanted list."

"Wait a minute. Why are you on the most-wanted list?"

"Someone very powerful wants me back."

"Who?"

"El Patron."

A slither of warning raced up my spine.

"After university, I was on a concert tour. We partied all over Europe and the Americas. At the end of the tour, a group of us stayed in Colombia until the tour resumed in the fall. I was singing in the Ritz, in Bogotá, just for kicks. The most beautiful man I had ever seen came in, Enrique Espinoza. He watched me play and afterward he wanted to buy me a drink. But something about his demeanor made me refuse him.

"Men in that part of the world don't take rejection well, but instead of becoming belligerent, he left. But he would turn up wherever I was. He wouldn't speak to me but was somehow I felt him bending me to his will with his eyes alone.

"After several weeks, I met another man. I was leaving the club with him when Enrique's entourage stopped us. Enrique's bodyguard if I promised to never see the other man, they'd let him go. I made what I thought was a silly promise; I wasn't scared, only flattered Enrique had pursued me for so long. We spoke until the wee hours of the morning, and when he took me home, he didn't attempt to touch me. By then, of course, I wanted him to.

"I saw him every day for a month, and he never did more than kiss me. I saw the restrained desire in his eyes, but he refused to touch me. When we were alone one night he said, 'What you do with me is what you will become.' He asked if I understood, and I said I did.

But I had no idea.

"He was the most passionate man I had ever known, but at the end of the summer, I made plans to resume my career while he was away on a business trip. All my possessions were packed and ready to go, when he returned late that night. I thought we would spend one more glorious night together, but he told me I wouldn't be leaving the villa. I should have thought to be frightened, but I still wasn't, even when he took me to bed that night. I thought he loved me, and I couldn't imagine he would hurt me. In the early hours of the morning, I woke to find him gone. I was locked inside my room. All my possessions, anything he hadn't given me, were gone.

"When he came back a few days later, he said when he took something, he took it forever. Then he took me against my will." Her eyes welled up. "There was no more tenderness. I had no idea where to turn. I hadn't spoken with my family in three months, and I knew they must be worried.

"I was heavily guarded by men with automatic rifles.

"One of them was fond of me. He came to me in the middle of the night and delivered me to an abandoned airstrip, where I was smuggled by private plane back to Mexico.

"My family was scared to receive me—by then I was pregnant by the Colombian drug merchant. They were afraid of what he'd do."

"Manny's father is El Cartel de Espinoza, El Patron?" I remained calm, but that wasn't how I felt, my stomach flinched.

"I found a mission for unwed mothers, and I had Manny there. The nuns took pity on me and smuggled me across the border into the U.S., where I've been hiding since."

"And you've been running from him for six years?"

"I have spoken with my sister in Mexico. She said Enrique's been there several times looking for me, he's determined to have his only child, and I, back. Illegitimate or not, he wants his son to follow in his footsteps."

"Are you certain he's after you, not just his son?"

"Every time he tied me to his bed, he made it clear he would never let me go. He had to pull a lot of strings to get me on the most wanted list, he's desperate."

"Yes, he has friends in high governmental places."

"They have a saying: *plata o plomo*, silver or lead. Money or bullets, whatever method he uses, he wins. I need another identity, and the last thing I need is to be seen on TV."

"Let me ask you this." I gnawed on my pencil. "Do you know anything that could help U.S. intelligence find Espinoza?"

"I know the layout of the citadel, his ranch. I know the Colombians sell to dogs, drug dealers, the Dominicans in the south and the Mexicans in the north and a few names of associates."

"Okay, I want you to write down every detail, everything the man ever said. Every place you went, any dates of business trips, a time line of the period he kept you prisoner. Even what seems inconsequential could be important. The more you write, the more you'll remember.

"And Manny's diabetes, is it manageable?"

"Here, it is."

"What do you know about the protesters out front?"

"I worked for one of them, until her husband asked me to share his bed. When I told his wife, she threw me out and refused to pay me. I took her Rolex watch and pawned it. I made more than what she owed me, so I returned the difference . . . in cases of condoms to reiterate her husband's proclivities."

"Don't worry about them." I smiled at her ingenuity. "Don't let anyone serve you papers, and stay in this Church."

Evita nodded.

"I need to speak with some other attorneys about your case. I might need assistance, as this isn't my area of expertise. But I do know how the criminal mind works, so that might aid us with Espinoza. If we can give the Feds some information on him, we might have a chance to strike a deal. I'll get back with you in a day or two, but I'll try to get rid of the protestors in the mean time. I need her name and her husband's name, too."

As Evita wrote, I scratched notes about contacts. If I found her a position she was uniquely qualified for, that might help her illegal status. "I want you to start practicing the piano, you'll need a job, and that might be a place to start."

She looked at me skeptically before sliding the information across the table. "Ms. Tucker, thank you for speaking with me. When this is over, I'll find a way to repay you."

I looked at the list of names. "Try not to worry."

We found the boys playing together in a corridor off an expansive office. Father Schimkowski was sitting behind the desk with his black shirt sleeves rolled up, resting his elbows on the desk. He was listening to Aidan intently. His glasses were on the tip of his nose and too large to be fashionable, but he pushed them up and smiled when we entered the room. He got to his feet. "Done so soon, then?"

"Yes, Father. I'm going to take Manny back upstairs now, he has some school work to do," Evita said to him.

"Ah, *Mamì*, come on, it's Sunday."

"Thank you again, Ms. Tucker, I look forward to hearing from you." Evita scolded her son in Spanish on the way out.

"We should be going. I'll be in touch with Evita."

"I will walk you out." Father Ski came around the desk extending a parcel wrapped in ribbon to Aidan. "There's a back entrance to the parking lot."

"I need to go out the front of the church and have a few words with the protestors."

"There's a mob of reporters out there," Aidan said.

"Maybe I can get them to stop harassing her, if I speak with them. You and Cass go out the back with Father Ski."

"Babe, if you're going out the front I'm going with you. Father, can you take Cass around the back and we'll meet? That way his face won't end up on the front of the sports page."

Cass interrupted. "But I want to be on the sports page."

Father Ski turned Cass away from us. "We'll meet you out back in a few minutes."

Aidan arched an eyebrow. "You sure you want to do this?"

"I've confronted all sorts of people before."

"People, no problem. Cameras, problem."

We made our way through the massive doors and down the stone steps. I approached the group of women with a smile on my face. They all smiled in return, but they were looking at Aidan. "Good afternoon, ladies."

"Aren't you Band-Aid from the Cubs?" asked the curly-haired woman with the large nose and over-tweezed brows.

Aidan nodded yes in response to her.

The woman beamed back at him, and the others twittered.

I snapped my fingers to garner her attention. "You wouldn't happen to be Paula, would you?"

"Yes, I am," she looked at me for a brief second before honing in on Aidan. Her friends, Frick and Frack, were so enthralled they lowered their protest signs.

"Paula, I'm Ms. Tucker, the attorney representing the woman in the church. I want you to stop protesting out here."

That drew her back to reality. "Excuse me?"

"I'm asking you to stop harassing my client. If you won't do it voluntarily, I'll get a court order."

"We are not harassing her. This church is harboring an illegal alien, and we demand she be arrested and deported."

"Don't you think you've taken this far enough?"

Paula stuck her picket sign in my face. "We're exercising our constitutional right to protest. We have a permit."

I saw notebooks open and lens caps dropping. The media was picking up on the confrontation. "We all know you're trying to intimidate a woman who got the better of you."

"I know my rights, and I want that illegal bitch deported."

"I was going to play nice with you, until you called her a bitch. Now I'm going to exercise my constitutional rights as an attorney and speak to the media on my client's behalf. The big guy, who you can't keep your eyes off, and I are going over to those reporters. They're going to eagerly listen to whatever I have to say because I'm his girl, and what I'm going to tell them will shock them."

Paula snorted. "Shock them with what?"

"You three ladies have all had illegal-workers working for you. Not only did they work for you, but you paid them in cash." I paused for effect. "I can see by the looks on your faces that you failed to file any W-9's. But that's not the best part: your husband harassed my client while she was in your employ. Aidan, did I say sexually harass?"

"No, babe, but you just did now." He smiled and winked.

"After the sexual harassment took place and was reported to you, her employer, you fired her and withheld her wages. And now you're trying to further harass my client by bringing her status as an illegal to the attention of immigration officials, when before this incident occurred, none of you had any inclination to demonstrate for immigration reform. Furthermore, I understand your husband received a large shipment of condoms, which I can only assume he intended to use for nefarious purposes." I paused giving them time for the information to sink in through the Botox. "Or maybe it proves he hits on a lot of women. A short conversation with the reporters will get this all aired out."

The three women looked at each other. I tapped the frame of my sunglasses for emphasis and draped my free arm through Aidan's before starting away. The cameras were snapping photos of us. I was about to speak when I heard Paula scampering behind me.

"Ms. Tucker? Oh, Ms. Tucker."

Aidan leaned into me. "You're scary like this."

"It's time for me to settle my debt."

Before he could sputter, I had his lapels in my hands and was kissing him. Two seconds later, he took control of the kiss, and by then, the shutters were flashing away.

Paula cleared her throat. I pulled away momentarily to look at her. "We'll be on our way, Ms. Tucker. If you wouldn't mention this to the media, we won't be back."

"I'm happy you see things my way."

Aidan's arms slipped inside my coat and wrapped around me, and he was kissing me again. When he pulled away he said, "You used me, Ms. Tucker, for your own nefarious purposes."

"Don't try to tell me you mind."

"This picture is going to be everywhere, let's make it good." And before I could protest his lips melded into mine.

When I finally maneuvered a break in the suction he chuckled. "Everyone's going to know you're mine."

"A small price to pay to be rid of those idiots," I grumbled. "I need to get the media attention off Evita."

"So we'll deflect it onto us? I thought you weren't happy about the article this morning. What do you think is going to happen when these pictures come out?"

"You'll handle it like you said you would."

He pulled me against him tighter, smiling down at me, dimple and all. "What am I getting out of this deal?"

"What do you want?" I looked away hesitantly.

He straightened. "I need time to make a list."

I put my face against his hard chest; I breathed in his clean soapy scent and listened to the accelerated beating of his heart. Me, little Libby Nobody, made baseball's bad boy tremble.

I took in another clear deep breath before I looked up into his eyes. "Remember, I'm a seasoned negotiator."

He took my hand and pulled me along the sidewalk. "And I might drag the contract out for so long it goes into binding arbitration."

17

NANNY NEGIOATIONS

Next to religion, baseball has furnished a greater impact on American life than any other institution. Herbert Hoover

Aidan 1:30 p.m.

Pizza at Pizzeria Uno is cheese nirvana, and Cass worshiped at the cradle of the deep-dish pan, devouring three slices. When we returned to Tank, I had an eye on the road, an eye on Cass in the rearview mirror, and a finger on the automatic window in case he turned green. He made it all the way to Evanston without tossing his cookies, so I assumed that we had cleared the tower.

The Sunny Sky Retirement Home was on Chicago Avenue in Evanston, anchored on either side by a VA building and a dry cleaners. The walkway was littered with cigarette butts and men with stringy ponytails and decrepit fatigues. Each wore a guarded expression from suspicion to culpability, but when they eyed our approach several of them high-fived Cass.

Sunny Sky was modern; the walls along corridor were dotted with children's artwork. Cass raced ahead and pointed. "This is mine, and this one is Madi's." We sailed past the visitor's desk with a bright smile from the receptionist. It seemed everyone knew Cass and Libby, and everyone perked up in their presence. Orderlies, nurses and other visitors greeted them. Every patient we encountered had a few words to say to them. The brief conversations ranged from Cass' health to Libby's love life. I raised my eyebrow a few times.

One wheelchair bound lady with a red fedora and a purple terrycloth robe poked me in the chest with her cane. "Are you the bloke who knocked Libby up?" Why she had a cane when she was in a wheelchair puzzled me.

Libby placed a hand on the ladies shoulder. "Mrs. J., you recall we decided not to discuss each other's love lives. I promised not to ask about Mr. Zalinski or Mr. Tveter, and you promised not to continue to ask me who knocked me up."

"But that was after I already told you I was carrying on with both of them. And you didn't fess up to any liaisons."

Libby twisted a piece of hair around her finger, as the old lady rolled away.

I cough laughed. "What exactly does 'carrying on' mean?"

She tilted her head coyly. "Homerun."

As we continued down the hall, we passed a closed door, behind which there was huffing and puffing. I looked at Libby, wondering why she wasn't inclined to stop and see what was going on.

"The nurses call that the boinking room. The Monroe's are newlyweds."

"Very funny, Miss Priss." I turned her away from the scene.

Cass was in Mr. Rodgers room, before we stepped inside Libby stopped me. "He has Alzheimer's, so he might remember me and he might not. I go along with whatever he says, okay?"

Mr. Rodgers was working over a stringy wedge of pizza. He hadn't changed from his days at the Waffle House except he was a little more hunched and a lot more cantankerous. "You're late, Missy. Don't you hear that racket out there?" He smiled at Libby fondly, "Get your uniform on, we got customers to feed."

"Grandpa Rodgers, this isn't the Waffle House, and mommy is a lawyer, not a waitress no more."

Mr. Rodgers looked up and Cass grinned, "I know you're hungry, son. I'll get a waitress to serve you in just a moment."

Cass just smirked, shook his head, then he scrunched up his

nose and put one hand on his belly and the other over his mouth.

Folks, it's time to clear the stands. The ump grumbled.

Before I could react, Libby grabbed a garbage can and had it under him. When he finished the first wave, she helped him into the bathroom. "Do you remember when Aidan said two pieces was enough for a boy your size?"

"Yes, mommy..." Before he could say more, another wave hit him. Libby closed the bathroom door.

I looked around the spacious room; it wasn't as antiseptic as a hospital room, done up in warm hues of burgundy and hunter green. The man had one hell of a TV with a supersized remote.

I pulled the letters from my breast pocket; my fingertips caressed the envelopes that were etched with Libby's name in my scrawled script. I wondered, and not for the first time, where life would have taken me if I had delivered these letters and the promises they held. I couldn't bear to read them yet, so I replaced them and they reverberated, the collected pledges changing the rhythm of my heart.

"I remember you." Mr. Rodgers pointed his razor-sharp chin and knife at me. "You're that baseball player who ruined Libby."

The speech was hauntingly familiar. "Libby isn't ruined, and Max already put me through the wash and rinse cycle. I have no intention of hurting anyone. You have my word."

"What's your word worth? I won't be around—" He waved his hand over his head in a circle. "—too much longer, but you won't sleep another night through, if you hurt her. I'll make your life hell all the way from the grave, if I have to."

I'd hit an all time low. A death-bound man was planning retribution from the grave, if I didn't do the right thing.

"You'll do the right thing, all right, or you'll be sorry for it for the rest of your days." I jumped when he responded to my thoughts. I heard a sound and looked up, half expecting to see the Grim Reaper, scythe in hand.

Libby leaned over me with a concerned look on her face. "Are you okay? You look as white as a ghost. Are you sick, too?"

I got to my feet unsteadily; I glanced back at Mr. Rodgers, who was snoozing over his plate. Of course, I was sick. Sick with guilt for the way I treated them and with each reminder my shame crystallized until I could see through all its sharp points to my own pain. "No, I'm fine. How's Cass?"

"I think the worst of it's over, but would you mind taking us home? He could use a bath and a nap. He needs some down time; I can't be sure if he ate too much, if it's his meds, or just too much excitement. His clothes are a mess."

"Let me see what I can do." I stepped around her, "I'll strip him out of his clothes and I can wrap him in my sports coat until we get him home."

"Are you crazy? That's an Armani jacket. Use my trench coat; it's from Old Navy."

"I'll take care of it." And I skirted by her to collect Cass. "You say your goodbyes to Mr. Rodgers."

Neither of us spoke, as I helped Cass out of his clothes before washing his hands and face again. Then I wrapped my sports coat around his shoulders, which brushed the top of his Nikes. "Do you want me to carry you?"

"Are you mad at me, Mister Pole-ow-ski?"

"Why would you think that?"

"Cause I didn't listen, and now I made a big mess and we got to go home instead of going to the park."

"I'm not mad, but next time you'll listen to me when I say enough is enough."

"Yes, sir, enough is enough, got it."

"We can go to the park after school tomorrow, but you need to rest." I tousled his hair. "We don't want you to get sick."

"I don't know if we can play after school 'cause I got to interview a nanny tomorrow."

"Tomorrow?"

"Mommy wants to hire someone to pick me up from school instead in going to Afterschool Club, that way I can take naps when I need my Chemoteruppy, and Dr. Seuss says I need the

Chemoteruppy, so I can get all better with new bones."

"Don't worry," I assured him. "I promise I'll come and see you tomorrow, and the day after, and the day after that, too."

"You know what, Mr. Pole-ow-ski?" He looked up at me with eyes as pure as clover.

"What, Cass?" As I bundled him against my shoulder, he wrapped his arms around my neck and I struggled with my emotions. Instead of the noose tightening I felt I could breathe easier.

"We're going to be best buds."

"Best buds, got it," I parroted him as I picked up the plastic bag with Cass' clothes and found Libby securing the blankets around Mr. Rodgers, before kissing him on his forehead.

Cass fell asleep about five minutes into the ride, but I was able to wake him and give him a quick shower without a meltdown. It felt natural when I read a book and tucked him in; he was sound asleep before I closed the door.

I found Libby looking like she needed a tuck-in, herself. Her booted legs rested over the edge of the coffee table, her head dangled across the back of the cushions and papers were strewn around her.

She startled when I unzipped her boot and dropped it to the floor. I held her gaze, while I drew my finger down the inside of her leg to remove the second one. As soon as it was off, she jumped again to tuck her legs under herself protectively.

"You're a nervous thing this afternoon." I sat down.

"Don't you have somewhere else to be?"

I put my feet up on the table and sank further into the cushions resting my linked hands across my abdomen before I gave her a smile. "I have somewhere I'd like to be, but you'd need to let me take off your clothes first."

She flushed, before turning to look straight ahead. I knew she could only resist my heated glance for so long before she'd have to look to see what I was up to. My hand darted out to tug playfully on the cashmere belt of her dress.

She batted my hands away. "Don't you need to go home?"

"We need to talk about a couple of things."

She looked at me from the corner of her eye. "Like?"

"Cass told me that you are going to get a nanny for him."

"Chemo can be very draining. There's a lot of running around involved, and we need the extra help."

"I'll do it, and you won't have to waste your time going through all these resumes."

"You don't have any experience taking care of kids."

"Cass has been happy all weekend, and I want to spend time with him. This is the perfect solution. Plus, I work cheap." I waggled my eyebrows.

"Somehow, I don't think I can afford you."

"You can, but I'm live-in help."

"Absolutely not."

"Come on, I'll be a good boy." My dimple was aching.

She cocked her head to one side. "No deal, baseball boy."

"Come on, Libby, don't be so stubborn. You need the help, and I want to spend time with Cass. This is just what the doctor ordered. You can go to work, and not have to worry. You know you can trust me, and I work for free."

"If you want me to trust you, you'll have to promise me no hanky-panky."

I prefer hanky-spanky.

Shut up. Get out of my head. "If you don't want me to touch you, don't put me in serious lip locks in public, then pretend it never happened."

"I killed two birds with one stone; I distracted the reporters and settled my profanity debt." She thought that made all the sense in the world until another thought washed her face. "Are you trying to exchange DNA for a roll in the sack?"

"I'm not dignifying that." I closed my eyes for a moment, trying to find a whisper to grab onto, so I wouldn't wrap my hands around her neck. "You used my celebrity for your own purposes, so you don't get to count that toward your debt."

"You know, Palowski, I don't like the world where you get to make all the rules. I didn't make it through three years of law school to be steam-rolled by a jock. If you want to participate in Cass' care for awhile, then you're going to have to do it on my terms."

"No."

"Fine, I'll hire someone. Until then, Steve will help me. Thanks for your offer." She rose in her stocking clad feet and extended her hand. "It's been nice seeing you again. Good luck next season."

It was just the kind of dismissal that drove me crazy. She was the only person who could rub words together to start an eruption the fire department might not be able to contain. I grabbed her hand and pulled her into my lap, moving her defiant chin around until I was looking her in the eye. "Who's Steve?"

"Steve's daughter goes to school with Cass."

"Madi Dubrowski, whose father doesn't have a wife?"

"Did you pump my entire life story out of Cass?"

"No just anything he remembers about men in your life."

"You know what? I'm tired. It's Sunday night, and I have to be at work early, so why don't you go home and leave me to take care of my own problems just the way I always have—alone!"

"You're not alone anymore; and you're going to let me help. What time do you leave for work?"

She crossed her arms and gave me a decent stare down.

"You're acting like a prissy brat."

"Alpha males are so hard to reach sometimes that you have to knock them over their heads with a sledgehammer."

She could knock you over with a feather most of the time.

I gave her a pinch on the derriere.

She yelped.

"I'll kiss it for you, and make it all better." I leered toward her. "What time did you say you leave for work?"

"Usually around six." She rubbed her backside, twisting in such a way that her chest was on serious display.

I stood abruptly, almost dropping her before steadying her. "I'll be here. What time does Cass have to be at school?"

"8:15. Are you sure you want to do this?"

What he really wants to do is take you into extra innings.

"I'll be here at six."

She followed me to the door. When I stopped on the landing to say goodbye, she honed in on my pants. "I've heard ice works wonders for that." Before I could reply through my clenched teeth, I was staring at the closed door. I'd heard of guys going oh-for-five or oh-for-ten—but I was going oh-for-Libby.

You are so out of your league, and I'm not referencing the kid, here. The ump's gravelly voice spliced through my lust. **You got about as much chance of making her biddable as I have of watching you close out the final game of the World Series.**

I jogged down the stairs. "You really work my nerves."

Nerves won't get you anywhere in this game—this series is all about heart.

18

CELEBUTANTE

A sign of celebrity is often that their name is worth more than their services. Daniel J. Boorstin

Libby

I opened the Gutierrez case file, after researching some case histories last night, my best shot at aiding Evita was with supplying information to the FBI. I dialed the local office where I knew a field officer. I wanted to get her take on what the bureau would need on Espinoza in order to make all of Ms. Gutierrez's immigration problems go away.

"Libby, you always go for the gusto." Gwen Foley laughed and said, "Can I throw in immediate citizenship for the woman?"

"Is that a possibility?"

"If you can get me names, dates, and locations, I can see what I can do." Her voice dropped to a caustic level. "This is one dangerous guy. The Espinoza cartel usurped the Medallion cartel that was formed in the early seventies. As the Espinoza family rose alongside them, they posed as legitimate businessmen. They were into counterfeiting and kidnapping before they expanded into smuggling cocaine from Colombia to Bolivia."

"The acceleration of crimes is common in most organized crime families," I said.

"Yeah, but the Espinoza's weren't just any syndicate. The father was known as the 'Lord of the Skies', he was worth twenty-five-billion, when he overtook the Medallions."

"How'd he do that?"

"Bribery and assassination. He wiped out the entire Medallion family, the women and children, too."

I felt the urge to panic breathe, but Evita needed help and it was something I could be proud of buried amongst the heaps of garbage I usually dealt with.

"The son is worse than the father," Gwen continued. "If he gets his hands on your client, she'll go missing, and there won't be DNA evidence to prove she ever existed."

"Is there any good side of this for us?"

"We'd love to make him the next poster child for the war on drugs. You get us info that can help with that, and I can get your client a whole new identity."

"Thanks, Gwen. I'll be in touch."

My anxiety manifested itself as a migraine. I was about to call Vicki for some Imitrex, when I heard earsplitting bickering in the outer office. I teetered behind my cherry desk, trying to retrieve my stiletto from the shoe-sucking abyss. I bent under the desk to retrieve it as my office door slammed open.

I could hear Vicki's raised tone. The other woman's voice was pinched in a high, nasally sort of way, somewhat cultured in intonation but lacking something. I retrieved the runaway shoe, stumbling to my feet.

Vanessa Vanderhoff towered over my desk. She looked better in pictures than in person. But a predator's reflection lurked behind her glassy smile.

Vicki waited to pounce, protruding belly and all.

Vanessa took me in and squeezed her upper lip and her nose much the way a butcher would look at bad meat.

I stood to my entire five-feet-seven-inches, plus three-inch heels, yet she loomed over the room, like a bloodcurdling, blonde Amazon searching for boy scouts to dismember. Her ice-cold blue eyes made me want to pick up a weapon in defense.

"Would you like me to call security?" Vicki asked. "I swear to Buddha, I tried to put a kibosh on her."

Suddenly, the intruder's large Marc Jacobs bag, which was hanging off her skeletal shoulder, started to move and yelp. It continued its yip yip, yipping. A minuscule head pushed out so that two black beady eyes bored into me. The dog scrunched up his nose and mouth just as its master had.

"We exterminate rats in this building." The skinned rodent had a Don King hair pouf on the front of his head.

"Do you use poison, or traps?" The celebutante turned on Vicki, shooing her fingertips toward the door, but instead of being dismissed Vicki, moved closer to the desk.

"Should I bring coffee, Ms. Tucker?"

"Yes, cream and equal for me, and a large soy latté laced with arsenic for Vanessa." I took my seat gesturing for Vanessa to do the same across from me.

Vanessa poised her size two Heine on the edge if the chair. "As we have never been introduced, I would prefer Ms. Vanderhoff." Her voice registered, it had the practiced precision of someone who learned diction from a computer-generated voice.

When Vicki heard that, she turned back toward me with a raised finger. "Climb it, Tarzan."

I chuckled. Vicki knew a bit about monkey business.

"Snitty if you will, Ms. Tucker, because when I'm through with you, you won't have many laughs left."

Did she mean snicker? If Vanessa hadn't been born into one of the wealthiest families in the world, God knew, she'd be a small-town-lifer bumping any trucker with a Slim Jim.

Vanessa pulled out a European cigarette and a sterling silver embossed lighter. The cigarette teetered on her bottom lip finding its groove in her lip lines.

"You light that and the sprinklers will go off. Unless you like the Gucci wet-dog look, I'd save that." I took off my glasses to clean them, wondering if Vicki would be able to locate arsenic. Could you sprinkle it over the foam, like they did with cinnamon at Starbucks? Or would I have to cram it down Vanessa's skinny latté neck?

"Aidan must have been attracted to your brains in college. You don't seem to be his type."

"I'm not a type." I readjusted my gleaming glasses.

"You're flawed in so many categories it's hard to pinpoint where exactly you fit. But it all boils down to you being the smart girl who wears description glasses?"

I rolled my eyes at her. "Prescription?"

"Don't try to sideline me."

"Sidetrack?" I squinted at her.

"I can hardly find what else he would find attractive."

"It's the boobs. Unlike yours, 'plastic' did not make these possible."

"Does he enjoy the sarcasm?"

"He did all weekend." I paused. "What can I do for you?"

"I want you to stop seeing Aidan."

"I'm not." I extended my hand. "So you've wasted a trip."

"I came here to make you an offer you can't refuse." Vanessa reclined deeper into her chair and smiled a viper-like smile. "I understand why someone like you would be infatuated with a man like Aidan. But I assure you, he belongs to me."

She stood and made a short circuit of the room looking at the various photos of me and other noteworthy Chicagoans. She stopped directly in front of my framed diploma from law school. "You're ordinary. You went to college, you have a mundane job, and you'll never make the kind of money I make."

"That's because I make my living in front of a court room, not on my back in a hotel room."

"You come from different piers." Vanessa's eyes wandered over me as she approached my desk. "Give him up now, before I move toward measures that will hurt you. I want him back, and I want you to be the one to deliver my special message."

Vanessa rifled through her cavernous bag and pulled out a manila envelope accompanied by chorus of yips. She reclined into her chair. Her facial expressions were stiff, or maybe that was just Botox.

"I doubt he'll listen. I don't know why you think someone so ordinary could sway his *sphere* Ms. Vanderdumb."

Every ounce of facial color drained, and even Estee Lauder wouldn't be able to put the glow back in her chiseled cheeks. Her eyes became as murky as a river overflowing its banks and the blue contacts couldn't conceal the deepening brown of her eyes. "Well, Libby," she said it in a long drawn out LIBBEEEEE.

I cringed. "It's Elizabeth to you."

"See what you think of this." She extended the manila envelope in my direction but not quite far enough for me to reach it.

Instead of leaning over, I walked around my desk and grabbed my stainless steel letter opener, with which I could've gouged her swamp water eyes out.

"How's baseball's golden mitten going to look, when this hits the tabloids?"

I slid the photo from the envelope in slow motion—a nude man kneeled behind bare white buttocks that rose from a rumpled bed. The woman's face was hidden between long streaks of blond hair and dark linen. The man was anchored onto the woman's hips, and in the throes of passion, but he was easily identified as Band-Aid Palowski.

"With my money, pictures can be altered to show just about anything. What if we put a man in that photo, in my place? What would the world think then? You know how he feels about his career. I don't believe any baseball players have come out yet."

"He isn't gay." I stifled a laugh. He wasn't the pliable kind of man; he had the kind of will a steelworker would find difficult to bend with an industrial strength blowtorch and soldering iron.

"If it's photo-shopped, I could make you a believer."

"Anyone who knows Aidan knows he is the most testosterone-driven male around." Not that there's anything wrong with men who like other men, but no one will believe it. "He's slept with half the girls in Chicago, and they'll all crawl out from under his bench to get their fifteen seconds of fame."

Vicki hurried into the office with a huge vase of peach colored roses. I directed her to the coffee table by the sofa, but snatched the card, squeezing it into my palm.

"They just arrived, Ms. Tucker, sorry I haven't located the arsenic yet. You've had several urgent calls from Mr. Palowski. Should I patch him through the next time he calls?"

"Yes, Vicki. Ms. Vanderdeaf and I are done." I whispered conspiratorially, "The arsenic wouldn't work; you actually have to have a beating heart to succumb to poison."

As Vanessa collected her things I reclined in my chair and crossed my ankles on the edge of the desk, her head shot up.

"Those are vintage Ferragamos. My mother had a pair of them years ago. Where did you get them?"

"Michigan Avenue, trunk show." I started to sort through a stack of legal tablets.

"Those had to cost several thousand dollars."

"Yes, they did." They were the most comfortable shoes I'd ever worn, and the spicy brown patent leather gleamed around my foot. They were from the seventies, but they looked like they had just stepped off the pages of the October issue of Vogue—pointy toes, spiky heels, and all.

I looked up at Vanessa's narrow eyes. "He bought you a pair of vintage Ferragamos? He hates shopping."

She flung the envelope with the hateful photo at me and I got to my feet wielding the letter opener in self-defense.

One of her rat dogs parachuted onto the carpet from her bag and was yipping. He started running in circles around the legs of his masters' chair. He sniffed and then lifted his leg.

Vanessa bent, opening the beast's haven, and he hopped in. "Good boy, CoCo." She stood as straight as an arrow. "You can send me a bill for that, but I won't pay it."

Something deep inside me broke open in the light of her willful sense of entitlement. "Remember who got the flowers and the Ferragamos," I said to the slammed door.

The sweet scent of the roses overwhelmed the scent CoCo had left. I brought the flowers to my desk, settling them on the edge, blocking the last location of the beasts and their refuse.

There was something special about the little envelope I had clenched in my fist; perhaps it was the proportion of the card to the magnitude of the messages it brought. I thought of all the Happy Birthdays, Congratulations, and just-because-I-love-yous and a minute card never seemed large enough to carry the enormity of all those sentiments. Slipping the little card out of its nest I read it twice.

Libby, thank you for giving me something to look forward to for the rest of my life—Cass. Aidan.

Vicki came into the office sniffing. "I know there was a bitch in here. But why does it smell like dog piss?" She examined the carpet with the toe of her shoe. "What did the skank want?"

I handed her the envelope. "I need to clean this stench."

Vicki stood transfixed, her mischievous grin becoming slightly flushed. "I'll do that for you," she said absentmindedly. Her eyes never left the photo as she traipsed behind me in the direction of the bathroom cleaning supply closet.

I cleared my throat and held the door open for her. "I think not Vicki. You've had to clean up enough of my messes." When she looked at me over her shoulder, I finished my thought. "You're pregnant, and this is a hands-and-knees kind of job."

"He looks pretty choice on his knees, if you know what I mean." She came to a dead halt. "Are you insinuating I can't get in this position?" She pointed to the picture.

I swiped it out of her hand and went through the restroom door. "I'm sure you can. But I'm not convinced you could get back up again. Besides, it's dog pee, not baby pee."

"You win, getting up posed a slight problem this morning." She swatted her Mu-Mu to find the shape of her stomach before staring at me knowingly.

We rifled through the broom closet, I grabbed a roll of paper towels and Vicki handed me a rusted can of carpet cleaner. I was out the door when I realized that she wasn't behind me. I heard the stall door clang closed. I heard Vicki's voice echo off the tiles, "Sorry, Lib, if I even look at a toilet, I have to go."

I stuck my head back in the room. "Anything important that needs my attention?"

"Aidan did call for you twice and Rat Bastard called down from upstairs several times saying he wanted to see you."

"Great, just what I need right now. About a case?"

"Nope he just said, and I quote, 'tell her I want her.'"

"I'm going to disinfect my office. Patch him through, if he calls back down."

"Whatever grinds your gears."

I was on my hands and knees blotting, spraying and cursing the bitch, whether it was the bitch dog, or bitch master who irked me more, when a shiny pair of wingtips appeared in the circle of foamy carpet cleaner.

I looked up long legs, knowing immediately who it was: my boss, Mr. Matt Caster, a senior partner, fondly referred to as Rat Bastard. He neglected to offer me assistance to my feet.

"I like you on your knees, Elizabeth."

It was one of the least offensive things he'd said of late. I still held out hope he'd get compacted by a garbage truck, hit by a Metra train, or free fall from an elevated train station.

Rat Bastard was one of those obnoxious middle-aged men who were superior only in his own mind. He was a tall, stocky man, past his prime with thinning hair and a twitching mustache. His grey eyes were cold, cynical, and calculating—so focused on his pursuit that he refused to take in all the information. A bad trait for an attorney, but his ego permitted little else.

He hadn't specifically said *sleep with me and I'll take your career places*, but he rubbed up as close to it as he could.

"What can I do for you, Mr. Caster?" I knew one day I was going to slip up and call him Rat Bastard. If it weren't for my health coverage, I might have let it slip months ago.

He took in my desktop and the large floral arrangement. I rested my rear against the center of the desk, crossing my arms over my chest. He looked at the flowers again and raised an eyebrow in question. I refused to answer.

"Boyfriend?" He finally gave in and asked.

"Yes. Aren't they lovely?"

"I didn't know you were involved with anyone. Are you sure this is a good idea, with what's going on with your son?"

"I appreciate your concern, but my personal life is just that. Personal."

"When you needed time off for your son, you didn't feel the need to keep it so private."

"For clarifications sake, I have more personal and vacation days coming to me than any two lawyers combined. I also have someone to care for Cass, so you have no worries in regards to my ability to do my job. But thank you for your concern for the well being of my child."

"I came to speak with you about the Accardo case. These are very serious charges, and he's a very important client."

"I know. That's why I arranged for bond. The trial starts on Wednesday, and I am up to speed. The DA's charges won't stick. Mr. Accardo has a tail, probably the FEDS. Whatever is going on is bigger than these charges. Is there a problem?"

"No, he sung your praises for fifteen minutes. I can't figure out why."

"Because I'm a damn good lawyer."

"Is he the new boyfriend?"

"Sorry, that crosses attorney-client privilege."

"You're my associate before you're his lawyer."

"I have nothing else to say. If you have further questions, I think you should direct them to Mr. Accardo."

He took a step toward me, invading my personal space. His sour breath grazed my cheek. I refused to turn toward him, staring at my office door.

"Sooner or later you will give me what I want, and it will include, but not be limited to, you down on your knees."

He leered and leaned into me. I continued to stare at the office door, awaiting my rescue. If Rat Bastard was suddenly projected out of our solar system, my skin would still crawl with the memory of his proximity. I slid a few inches away, wishing it were light-years.

Rat Bastard picked up a wedge of my disheveled hair and brought it to his nose, then licked it. "The color of your hair is beautiful, Elizabeth. Does it match the other? I can't wait to run my fingers through it all. I do hope you have a full bush. I dislike the shaved snatch." As he relinquished the hair he rubbed it against where he assumed my nipple would be.

My eyes remained glued to the door. Any second now, Vicki would burst through it. She never left me in here alone too long with Rat Bastard.

As if I willed it, the door silently opened and the entire door-frame was filled with a pair of wide shoulders, and blue eyes villainously sly, focused on the hand that was on my breast.

19

DEFENDING THE MOUND

Every pitch, perfect or not, is a potential home run.
Preacher Roe

Aidan 10 a.m.

Vicki's kohl-rimmed eyes bugged out so far from her sockets at my prompt arrival that their golden centers appeared like a warning lights blinking off a rain slick bridge. I was irked when she told me to take a seat in the waiting area after she called me down here. I scratched at the glitter ring around my wrist in agitation. No matter how many times I washed, the glitter lingered.

"Where'd you get that?" Vicki asked.

"Some kid? Why?"

Vicki shook her head. "I had one, once."

I gave the voodoo-priestess a shrug that said whatever. The only thing about Vicki that had changed since college was the number of exotic hair colors she wore at one time. She still had the ability to look at me like she was examining my soul.

Vicki moved to Libby's office door and crooked her finger for me to follow. "I considered arsenic for the original problem, but you can handle this manifestation." She threw open the door shifting her width for my view. "Mr. Palowski, you need an appointment." I crammed the doorway as Vicki skittered away.

I stood stock still, studying the grotesque scene.

My feet started in their direction, ready before the rest of me, to do him bodily harm. I would have done the same for any woman, but no one would treat Libby like this while I drew air.

The man had enough sense to step away, but he was still several miles from where he should've been. He changed his body language, and his sneer melded into a submissive smile as I approached. The smirk vanished as my fist met his mouth.

My follow-through uppercut sent him flying across the desk, knocking off a vase of flowers. The rat landed in a sprawled pile on the other side of the desk with pieces of baby's breath festooned his thinning hair. His twitching nose squirted blood, which saturated his already wet shirtfront.

In the remoteness of my mind I heard Libby say, "Oh shit."

He was trying to gain his feet, but his hands slid through the water and he ended up in a crumbled mound, after his chin met the edge of the desk in a resounding whack. When his stunned mouth opened to speak, two of his teeth went flying.

Libby saved a stack of legal pads and a manila envelope from the water as I stalked around the desk. The louse had enough sense to back away on his elbows as I tracked him with my wrath.

"If you utter another despicable word, I'll bury you alive and dance on your grave."

"I think you misunderstood," he offered with a distinctive lisp as he swiped away blood. The two front teeth were a small price to pay in exchange for his life. And any price I'd have to pay was worth putting this middle-aged mongrel in his place.

"I comprehended every nuance." I thundered and shook my head in disgust at him. "If you touch her again, she's going to slap you with a sexual harassment suit so fast you won't have time for your head to spin. And, believe me, when I come riding into the courtroom in her defense, people will stand up and take notice. You'll be paying her until you have no teeth left." I loomed over him. I had a fleeting thought about what I had told Cass about intimidation, reevaluating my stance.

He nodded his acknowledgment as he struggled to his feet with a hand clasped to his mouth, trying to steady himself with the other along the edge of the desk. "We'll talk later," he mumbled through his fingers toward Libby, on his way to the door.

I stalked after him. "Her office door remains open. If it's something confidential, you meet in that lovely glass conference room down the hall so that anyone walking by can see you. I'll make sure Vicki understands that. I believe Mr. Rodgers and Mr. Whitney are golf buddies with Cyrus Fletcher, who happens to do whatever I ask."

He flinched at the mention of Fletch's name. "You won't need to involve anyone else."

I slammed the door in his wake and turned on Libby, who wore a combined look of stark relief and trepidation. I wanted her in my arms, but she backed away, along the desk behind her. "Are you trying to ruin my career? That was my boss you just slugged, for heaven's sake."

I grasped her wrist pulling her head onto my chest in that spot between my shoulder and clavicle. My body seemed designed with her in mind, she fit there perfectly; I felt a deep, drawn breath before I felt something wet. I drew my thumbs over her tears pushing them away as I looked into her face. "How long has this been going on?"

She had a far-off look in her eyes before she hiccupped an answer. "Too long, but it's escalated lately. He knows I'm going to be promoted and then his little perversion would be altered."

"It's over." I kissed her forehead. "Don't worry."

"It isn't over! If anything, he'll be even more vicious when he gets to me."

I pulled her chin up. "Trust me. He won't do anything. Fletch will take care of Rat Bastard."

She pulled away, a crazed look taking hold of her eyes. "Where'd you hear that name?"

"Cass." I looked around. "What's that awful smell?"

She knotted her arms in a defensive gesture while thumping a foot in irritation. "You remember CoCo? Bald, brown, bitch."

I groaned inwardly. "I hate that canine cockroach."

"Not quite as much as my office furniture does."

"What did she want?"

"She wants me to deliver the message that it's imperative that you go back to her." She grabbed paper towels, blotting up the mess on her desktop. "Now, I've completed my civic duty. Go back to your heartless fiancée, and stay out of my life. I don't have time to deal with this shit right now."

"Apparently, from what just occurred, I might prove handy."

"I forgot to ask why you barged in here in the first place." She glared, stabbing pencils into her penholder, while she lined up a stack of legal pads for execution.

"Vicki asked me to charge in here. Were you going to wait until he started undressing you before you screamed for help?"

Without speaking she pulled a manila envelope out of her stack of legal pads and launched it at me. A single sheaf of photo paper slipped out of its wrapper before I realized what it was. "I'm going to kill her."

Libby smiled sardonically. "No matter what she told you, *that* is not a weapon."

I couldn't laugh at her humor, not that she expected me to laugh. I felt less civilized than a lowlife cretin. "I didn't know she was taking photos of us."

"Once she has that digitally enhanced to make it look like you're batting for the other team, it's going to grace every tabloid cover in the country."

Goldilocks intends on displaying a pound of your naked flesh on the disabled list.

"She won't pay you a second visit."

She leaned over her desk, making me privy to all of her cleavage. "How, pray tell, are you going to assure that?"

"I'll get Fletch on it. He'll think of something."

"Make sure you show him the picture. It's a great shot of your abs. Perhaps Maxim needs a new cover model. Maybe they could even use that shot."

"When something hurts you, you don't always have to resort to sarcasm."

She reclined in her chair and raised that single wing swept eyebrow in threat while she sliced through sealed envelopes with a letter opener like she was slicing through my guts.

"That's why I warned you about the other women."

"You can't be around Cass with crap like this out there." She stabbed her letter opener at the manila envelope on her desk. "Do you have any idea what kids will say to him, if this hits the papers at the same time someone finds out you're his father?" She sighed and her lashes stroked her cheeks. "I appreciate what you've done for Cass this weekend, and this morning, but you're going to have to back off for while."

"Since you're getting your bone marrow, I'm expendable?"

"Why else would I let you spend the weekend with us?" She refused to make eye contact. "With Cass I mean."

"That better not be the only reason."

"You wanted to meet Cass; as a matter of fact it was stipulated in exchange for your bone marrow, remember?"

"You're many things, Libby Tucker, but you're not a coward. Stop lying to yourself."

"I don't lie!" She shot me a look. "Oh, all right. I wanted to know if you've changed, but it hardly matters now."

"It matters to me," I said with clear irritation.

"Fine, you want to know what I think, Sir Chippendale?" She slammed a law book down. "I'll tell you. You're more thoughtful; you listen more, and talk less. Thank God for that. You're calmer. On essentials though, everything is still the same."

"Essentials?"

"You're still arrogant, beautiful, hardworking, spoiled," she made a gagging sound, "and worst of all charming."

I smiled with a sense of overwhelming satisfaction. "I went to see Dr. Seuss. We set up an appointment on Thursday with my doctor to go over everything."

What I didn't tell her was that another match showed up on the registry, some guy in California. I had Fletch look into it, but she didn't need to know about another match unless my transplant failed. I made the decision on the way over here that given her options, she might turn me out. In light of this morning's debacle, the possibility loomed large.

"I'm your man, babe." I winked.

She snorted.

"Like it or not, it's you and me."

"You know you're going to make me regret ever contacting you. I want you," she pointed toward me and then the door, "and all the garbage you've brought into my life, outta here."

She pulled off one of her shoes and clocked me in the side of the head. "Give these to that gripe of a fiancée of yours." I caught the second one before the heel could take an eye out. "She developed a sudden interest in them."

"Did she know I gave them to you?"

"I didn't get why it pissed her off, but I couldn't pass up the opportunity to torment her."

"Now, now, I'm going to start thinking you care."

"I couldn't care less." She was yanking on her half-contained hair, and it tumbled past her shoulders. "Go pick up Barbie Vanderslut and leave me the fuck alone." Her hand made a land speed record to her mouth as if she could pit the words and I snatched her wrist across the expanse of the desk.

"You know, you were doing so well with not using profanity, but now it's time to pay the piper." While she was trying to free her hand, I pulled her by her neck across the desk so I could kiss her. My mouth melded against hers like tires to the asphalt. When it ended, I waited for her to open her eyes and look at me. It took her seconds longer than it should have. She drew in her bottom lip and started working it over, an involuntary groan erupted from somewhere deep in my chest.

I was trying to still my breathing, while she worked her lips and a little smile formed at the corners of her mouth.

During this tussle for the lead, she pulled me by the lapels of my coat toward her, and she drafted onto me like any aggressor would. I was going to have to give her the checkered flag, but I decided to raise the ante.

Her silky knees slipped across the desk and her body collided into mine. I considered tumbling backwards onto the floor where I could roam over more of her body, but she was skittish. A bump and grind on the floor might bring her back to reality.

When I stroked her throat from her ear to her collarbone with my roughened fingertips, her body involuntarily rose to meet me. Each time, I went slower and lower, coaxing her until she was coming up on her knees soliciting me to take my hands lower. I was at the edge of her sexy lace bra in victory lane. When my fingers brushed the rise of her breast over the top of her bra, she involuntarily bit my tongue. I chuckled in my throat while I pulled her hips into mine making sure she understood I was serious about my threats.

Once she noticed the firmness of my intent, she tried to push me away. I responded by running my hands up the inside of her blazer, and when she turned away from my lips I whispered into her ear. I could feel her involuntary shudder. "You and I have unfinished business. I just don't want to complete it on your desk top."

Her focused, fiery green eyes fell on me.

I grinned, before saying, "At least not the first time."

"Aidan, the past is just that—the past." Libby got to her stocking-clad feet, muttering under her breath as she picked up the remnants of the flowers I'd destroyed. "We need to go on. Your life is too complicated for Cass and I. Please let this go."

"I still remember the flowers I brought you the fall before I got you pregnant.

She brought the ruined bouquet to her nose.

"And you do, too. You told Cass."

"That was the first time anyone had ever given me flowers. I thought they were the most beautiful thing I'd ever received, and I wanted to make them last forever." She struggled to her knees. "I thought they meant maybe you cared for me." She laughed at herself. "Up until Saturday's football game, when you walked into your girlfriend's arms instead of mine."

"I knew exactly where you were during the game, but I had no idea that Amanda was going to be there. I was as blindsided as you were when she stepped in my path."

"But you did nothing to send her on her way."

"Our families had been friends for years. I couldn't end it without an explanation. We fought that night and she went home, but by then I had no idea how to find you. I was at the Waffle House with you first thing Sunday morning."

"You left me hanging time after time." She looked up at me through misted eyes. "Now you expect me to depend on you with my son's life hanging in the balance."

"Like it or not, he's our son. This is a matter of life and death, and I won't let you down." I glanced away. "Besides, I'm all you got."

She seemed perplexed by my statement and asked. "What are you talking about now?" She slouched back into her seat, the flowers drooping in her lap.

I ran my hand over my face and I dropped to my knees in front of her. I wanted her to forgive me for abandoning her when she needed me most. "When I went to see Dr. Seuss this morning..."

"You're worried that Cass is someone else's?"

I grabbed her hands, stilling her. "I know he's ours. But I was curious, so when Dr. Seuss went out of the office to check something, I looked at the file. There were two donor I.D. numbers listed."

"What?" she asked, flabbergasted.

"There's another donor, and I had to know who it was."

"You need to tell me the name of the donor before I can decide if I want to cook you and your agent's ass."

"Let me help you and Cass, and forget about the rest."

She narrowed her fiery green eyes again.

"You're an attorney. You know it's strictly confidential information, and I could go to jail if I told you."

"Give me the fucking name, or I'll make you beg for a prosecutor who only handles capital punishment cases."

"You do realize that you just used the F bomb again." I smiled a weak smile, delaying the inevitable.

Her eyes squared and became cautious. "Just say it, for God's sake." She got up and moved around the desk putting distance between her and the information.

"His name is Charles Grover Tucker." I grabbed her around her waist with enough speed to help her make it into a guest chair. "Fletch ran a background check, and the name matched the name on your birth certificate. It could be a total coincidence." She was as pale as a ghost and she closed her eyes. She hadn't passed out, but I considered giving her mouth-to-mouth anyway. As soon as I started to lean into her, her eyes shot open in accusation.

20

DECISION VS. JUDGEMENT

We judge ourselves by what we feel capable of doing, while others judge us by what we have already done.
Henry Wadsworth Longfellow

Libby

All the blood drained from my head, and I heard ringing. I grabbed onto my chair and whispered, "My father."

"Fletch's drawing up some papers for me, and he needed some financial info. This guy's the right age, but he lives in California."

Aidan didn't understand that my father could have lived around the corner, and he wouldn't have bothered to care. I couldn't believe God would play such a cruel trick on me. I had to choose as my child's savior the man who abandoned me, or the man who used and discarded me. I brought the heels of hands to my eyes. "Do you create chaos wherever you go?"

Aidan pulled me into his embrace. I tried not to soak his shirt-front with my tears. "I want to be the one to help Cass. Whatever you want to do about your father, I'll help with that, too."

"I need to think." I pushed away, my breaths coming erratically. "I need time to think."

I calmed as I worked my way through half a box of tissues.

Before I could finish, he took my hands. "I have all the time in the world. This is the best way. You can do your job, and it will be better for Cass because I will make sure he's thoroughly entertained. I can distract him, and make it easier on him than a stranger."

"You're a stranger."

"He doesn't see it that way. He thinks I'm a buddy."

I wanted to argue but Cass adored Aidan, and if that made this easier on him, then I could certainly muddle through my emotions. "You're right," I sniffed.

"Yes, I am." He smiled brightly before kissing my temple. "I have a meeting with Fletch. I'll see you at home."

Then he was gone, and I was free to wallow in my grief for the rest of the day. I didn't think to wonder why he knew who was on my birth certificate until I made the express train, and by then I was lulled to sleep by the swaying of the train as it flew over the tracks.

When my car schlepped down Sheridan Road and up the driveway, my apartment was a beacon illuminated with lamplight. The front door was slightly ajar, and I could hear the quiet notes of classical music coming from the stereo. I stepped into the living room, which was completely organized, and breathed in the scent of spaghetti sauce.

Cass was perched on a stool at the island in a red apron and chef's hat. He was smiling down as spinach leaves made their way over the edge of the glass salad bowl. He picked some up and stuffed them in his mouth. Popeye would be proud.

Aidan leaned over the stove stirring a pot of sauce. He had on a matching red apron and the hat. A little laugh escaped, bringing both of their attentive eyes on me in the doorway. The identical expressions, and the same dimple dancing in their right cheeks floored me. They were so beautiful together they took my breath away.

"How was your day?" Aidan gave me a mischievous wink.

"I got a lot accomplished," I smirked. "I love the hat. A photo of that could buy me an exotic vacation."

He took my briefcase, placing it on the hall table before he peeled off my coat, skimming his hands down my arms.

Cass dropped the salad tongs he was using to conduct the music and came running toward me with an apron and hat in his hands. "Here, Mommy. Put yours on so we can all match."

"I'll wear the apron." I drew in a drag of his little boy sweat, and kissed his head. "No hat, unless I'm the actual cook."

Cass' hand darted out toward Aidan. "I told you Mister Pole-ow-ski." Cass small hand coiled around a five-dollar bill.

I eyed Aidan speculatively.

"Don't look at me, it was his idea."

During dinner, Cass gave me the rundown of his school day. He reiterated three times that Mister Pole-ow-ski picked him up on time. He said they played baseball in the park with Madi. "She calls Mister Pole-ow-ski, Mr. Butthead," Cass belly laughed around a spoonful of spaghetti.

I looked at Aidan and he shrugged noncommittally.

Someone knocked on the front door, and Cass' first instinct was to bolt for it, but he stopped himself. "Ollie's coming over to sit with me." Cass said over a 'you hoo' from the living room. "You need to be Mister Pole-ow-ski's date."

Olivia slipped out of her parka, exposing her long sleeved T-shirt with red Coca-Cola Script that read, 'Enjoy Capitalism'.

"It's a week night," I said.

"I so told you she wasn't going to like it, Old Guy," Ollie said with a triumphed edge. "I'm so not going to be happy if I packed this for nothing." She slammed the oversized backpack down on the table and gazed around the kitchen before zooming in on the sink full of dishes. "That's the clean up?"

"You're being paid top dollar, and all you have to do is a few dishes and give Cass a bath," Aidan said as he slipped away and gestured me out of the kitchen booth. "Keep an eye on Cass."

"All right, all right, Old Guy, fifty bucks. Cash."

Aidan extended his hand, sealing their bargain. "By the way, I'm old hottie to you, and for someone who touts political activism you're a capitalist p . . . "

I elbowed him before he could finish. "Person," he amended, pushing me into my bedroom and quietly shutting my door.

I trailed him to my walk-in closet at a safe distance and stood in the doorway. He pushed my clothes back and forth on the racks before coming to a dead halt. "This is perfect. You can wear it with the new shoes." He tore the plastic wrap back and examined the tags. "Why haven't you worn it yet?"

"I was saving it for a special occasion." It was a beautiful chocolate brown sheath dress, with a low-cut V in the front and a matching patent leather belt.

"A first date." He smiled cockily. "A special occasion."

He shoved the dress at me, when something on the rack caught his eye. He backed up and pulled it from the rest. It was an ancient yellow sundress I hadn't worn in eons. "I loved you in this dress, you wore it the day I came back to school from summer break. Will you wear it for me sometime?"

"I am not wearing either one for you."

He stepped into my personal space and unbuttoned my suit jacket pushing it off my shoulders. "In that case we can stay in."

There was a black stretch limo waiting. Before we reached the bottom stair, David was out of the car opening the door for us. He tipped his hat. "Hey, Boss, how's it going?"

Aidan nodded, chuckled and waited for me to get in.

"Where am I being kidnapped to?" I asked irritably, as I slipped across the leather seat.

He knocked on the roof of the car, and we moved. "We're going to Rusty Connor's Skin Cancer fundraiser at the Black Orchid."

Black Orchid? I tried to place the name, but asked, "The Hall of Fame Rusty Connor?"

"That's him."

"You know the best closing pitcher in Cubs' history?"

"My career isn't over yet. I broke his ERA record last season, and I'm on par to break his record on saves. Maybe I'm the best closing pitcher the Cubs have ever had."

I laughed as we streamed down Lake Shore Drive. There was a harsh breeze off the lake, and I shuddered into my coat. We exited at North Avenue, pulling up to an old brick building and into the line of expensive cars in front of Pipers Alley.

David bowed as we exited the car. "When I picked up Melinda, she asked me to tell you that she wants you to call her. She has some information that might be enlightening."

"Thanks. I'll call you when we're ready to leave."

Aidan latched onto my hand, as he towed me toward the building. The doorman checked Aidan's gilded invitation.

I gawked over the Art Deco lobby. The patterned Saultio tile floor had a five-color sunburst pattern in the center with the lead strips in silver. The raised main lobby had a barrel-vault ceiling that was tiled in a zigzag pattern. Limestone walls gave way to the metal and glass divider that separated the vestibule from the lobby. My eyes went to the gold leafed ceiling and the glorious brass chandelier that together were reminiscent of an illuminated solar system.

Aidan helped me out of my coat, handing it to the coat check girl who trekked him with salacious eyes. When he reached out to take the ticket, the girl had the audacity to rub her hand over his. He hustled me into the elevator, and we regarded each other's mirrored reflections. "Doesn't it bother you that women continuously throw their assets at you?"

"No, it's the ones who won't that trouble me."

"Dream big, and dream often, Palowski." The door chimed open. A sea of people were milling about, with anything from champagne flutes to highball glasses clanking together. Soft jazz music filled the gaps between exchanges of scandalous gossip.

The cocktail waitresses were dressed in forties-inspired halter dresses, torpedo shaped breasts and all. Their fishnet stockings glittered in the lighting. Most of their pillbox hats sat atop their heads slightly askew. Instead of cigarettes, their trays were laden with glassware filled to the brim with beverages that ranged in color from deep umber to crystal clear.

Lost in my admiration of the atmosphere, I stumbled into the rigid back of the man in front of me. He turned toward me. From the spread collar button-cuffed shirt, to the black and gold striped retro tie and hanky, to the two gold double Zoot chains hanging from his waistband that matched his gold leather suspenders, he was retro forties. His expertly coiffed hair was hidden by his black gangster's fedora with a single golden feather.

"Accardo," Aidan managed.

When he recognized me, a smile lit his irritated face. "*Bella*, how nice for you to run into me tonight." He took my hands and kissed my cheeks affectionately.

He extended a hand toward Aidan. "Palowski?"

"I didn't realize you knew my girlfriend."

"*Bella* and I are very well acquainted, aren't we?" Mr. Accardo raised his eyebrow in question and smirked. "But I didn't know she was your girlfriend."

I tilted my head and crossed my arms under my breasts. "Aidan, I'm Mr. Accardo's lawyer." I paused for effect. "And that is the extent of our acquaintance."

I watched as Aidan's shoulders relaxed ever so slightly.

"Now, *Bella*, don't be so modest. At least tell him I tried my best to make you more than my attorney, or Palowski is going to think I've lost my touch with beautiful women."

I looked at Aidan and rolled my eyes. He laughed. Before I could say more, Mr. Accardo's cell rang.

"Excuse me." He turned away. I couldn't hear any part of the conversation, and as his lawyer, I was mighty curious.

"It seems you get around," Aidan said. "I wonder how many other mutual acquaintances we have."

"Very few, I would expect."

"Great!" Tony turned back, he was annoyed but he forced a smile on his face. "This night is going to be a bit more challenging than I thought."

"What's wrong?" Aidan asked.

"Our jazz singer has come down with laryngitis."

I must have looked perplexed because Aidan said, "Tony owns this place. I didn't have the time to mention that."

That's why the name was familiar. It was listed on Tony's assets.

"If you will excuse me, I need to make some calls and see if I can salvage this. Have a great time, and I'll catch up with you." Without a backward glance the crowd absorbed Tony.

I took in the stage where the sixteen-piece band played a snazzy jazz standard. All the band members were in varying colored pinstriped Zoot suits, each with its solid colored tie, hanky, and fedora. The piano sat idle on one side.

Before I could gather my thoughts, one of the waitresses slithered alongside Aidan, batting her false eyelashes at him. "Hi Band-Aid." She gave him a seductive pout of ruby red lips.

"Hi, Candy. How have you been?"

"I haven't heard from you in awhile." The cigarette girl's torpedoes were maneuvering around his upper arm like he was her particular brand of tobacco. "I thought I might once you dumped Vanessa."

He had the decency to step away and made introductions, as if he'd rather be designated hitter for Babe Ruth.

I didn't bother extending my hand. Candy looked at me like I was Sweet and Low, and she wanted raw sugar. Her eyes dilated on pure playboy baseball player sweetness.

"Just keep your back up. There's a reason we call her Vindictive Vanessa." She drew in her lips like she swallowed vinegar and disappeared into the crowd.

Aidan looked at me sheepishly.

"I think you might want to get a safety check—"

"I'm as clean as a whistle."

"Because that Candy's been in a lot of sticky hands."

Aidan took my hand. "It didn't mean a thing."

"Don't bother explaining, it would only incriminate you further," I chortled.

He stuck one long finger into his collar and tugged. "We need a drink." At the bar Aidan ordered me a glass of red wine and he chugged his beer, never letting it touch the bar top.

Then a thought struck me like a thunderbolt. "I need to speak to Mr. Accardo."

21

STRIKING OUT

Good pitching will always stop good hitting and vice versa.
Casey Stengel

Aidan 9 p.m.

Every pitch I'd thrown had hit a bat.

Disgusted with my homerun record, Libby went off to consult with Tony about her light bulb moment. Luckily, Tony was too distracted to put a full court press on Libby, but I wouldn't put it past him to try to give new meaning to attorney client privileges. Tony didn't impress me as the criminal type—too well bred and educated—but there was something about the guy that wasn't entirely above board, and Libby was criminal defense.

The crowd had grown thick. I wandered into the heart of a hornet's nest when I bumped into my ex. I was struggling to get Vanessa's stinger out of my mouth, when I heard the cameras clicking around us.

I faced the viperous reporters head on. "The shows over, folks." I gave them a stare down and they snaked away from the scene. "Vanessa, let's have a word in private."

She stormed off toward the back of the establishment, slamming through the stainless steel door and making several chefs jump. "Banford, you send that lawyer on her way." Vanessa pointed one of her claws in the direction of the party. "How could you embarrass me like this in front of everyone? You want to play around with her, fine, but don't bring her out in public."

I leaned against the door of one of the walk in refrigerators. "Would you like to discuss this like adults?"

"Get rid of that bitch."

I thought my naughty ump spoke my thoughts out loud, when Vanessa's voice registered.

"Libby is my date, and she'll be leaving with me. You're on the guest list because I didn't think to have you taken off. I won't neglect that detail again, if you can't be civil."

She ran her fingers through her hair. She was still wearing the diamond engagement ring. I didn't begrudge her the spoils of my stupidity, but I didn't like what it symbolized.

"I don't need you to receive invitations."

"I understand that, but this is my turf. Why don't you go back to New York, and make this easy on everyone?"

"Make it easier on her, you mean?"

"You don't even register in her hemisphere."

Her eyes blinked, reptilian-like. "When I get through with her, she'll definitely know my longitude and attitude."

Word of the day, Goldilocks has too much to say.

"Stay away from Libby. I already spoke with her building security. You're on their radar. What did you think to achieve?"

"I had to see for myself who you threw me over for, and I wanted to warn her about the kind of damage I can do."

"You do what you have to, I'll do the same. But if you hurt Libby, you'll have to deal with a less reasonable me."

My cell phone rang. It was Libby. She didn't need a special tag for me to know it was her. "Hey, babe, I'm in the kitchen."

"Eating Candy or Vandy?" She gave me a resigned sigh. "Never mind. Can you ask David to run to St. Ignatius?"

Wheels turned in my head; within seconds I caught up with her. She really was brilliant! I turned away from my current pain-in-the-butt to make arrangements.

When I turned back, Vanessa looked ready to strike. "Don't mind me, Asshole."

"I'm glad you think so, that should make this easier."

"Listen, you have two choices, you can come back to me, or I will do everything in my power to ruin you both."

I replaced my phone, looking down at her nose, which three plastic surgeons had worked on to get right. "It's over between us. I'm never coming back. You're expending energy and resources on something that isn't going to produce results."

"I am going to make wince meat out of you."

"You really shouldn't mince words." I winced when I heard her tirade, which involved a pastry chef, ice cream, and garbage cans. I chuckled and moved away from the scene. Finding Libby in the throng wasn't going to be easy.

We met Tony standing in front of the elevator doors. When they opened, Evita was staring out as if she might bottom out in a pit of fire and brimstone, being in a lounge again.

Tony's response: "She's got a beautiful face. Let's see the rest." Her wrap looked like some priest's frock that covered her from neck to toe, but what she had on under it was enough to drive most men to the gates of hell on first class ticket.

The red sequined tube top dress she was shrink-wrapped into was two sizes too small and calling it a dress was an over embellishment. The costume belonged on stage, but wrapped around a pole. From the neck up, she looked like an elegant rendition of a Madonna, but from the neck down Evita emulated red-hot carnal gratification. Regardless of her voice, every guy in the place was going to be mesmerized and mentally tabulating singles available in his front pocket at the same time.

Tony looked at Libby, who had her hand over her mouth before he said, "She's dressed like a hooker."

Evita responded in rapid fire Spanish.

Tony took a belligerent step toward her. "Did you just tell me to go to hell?"

She looked toward Libby. "He speaks Spanish?"

"Obviously."

Evita put her hand on Libby's forearm. "I'm so sorry. Father Ski called some ladies over from the neighborhood and this was the best they could do," she said to Libby.

"I hope you're using the term ladies loosely," Tony said as he gaped from her glossy head to sparkly toes again.

Evita's eyes went from amber to flaming red.

Tony jabbed me in the ribs, drawing my attention away from Evita. I looked at Libby and thought of good intentions paving the way to hell. I winked at Libby.

"It isn't as if they have proper evening attire laying around in a rectory for heaven's sake," Evita said putting her hands on the curve of her hips daring anyone to contradict her.

"Of course not," Libby said.

"She sings the way she's dressed, I'm screwed," Tony said.

Evita's reply was laced with Spanish obscenities, and Libby glared at Tony. "Instead of attacking, why don't you try to come up with a solution?" Just then one of the cocktail waitresses darted by with a weighted down clattering tray. "Tony, are there any more of the cocktail server's costumes?"

"No, the girls showed up dressed."

"I guess there's no other way . . . " Libby walked toward a door that ran alongside the elevators. "What's in here?"

"It's a storage room," Tony replied. "Liquor mostly,"

"Great, unlock it."

He drew out his keys, opening the door. "Happy, counselor?"

"Don't say I don't go the extra mile for my clients." She grabbed Evita's arm and pulled her into the storage room.

Tony and I stood, bewildered. We heard some moving around, a few curses in Spanish, raised mumbled voices, then silence.

Next thing I knew Evita reappeared trying to get Libby's brown dress zipped. She turned toward me to finish it for her, and Tony slapped me out of the way, doing the honors himself.

The door cracked open. "Don't forget the shoes."

Evita was trying to wrangle her foot in a shoe at a hop, as Tony hustled her around the stage to the back of the house.

The thought barely washed through mind. Libby was in that storage room almost naked, when my cell phone rang. "Babe?"

"Can you please send David to your house for sweats?"

"Nope. Put on the dress, or we'll miss Evita's debut."

"I am not coming out of this storage room."

"If you don't want to wear the dress, come out in your birthday suit. I'm eagerly waiting." I hung up.

Her obscenities bounced off the walls in time with my deep laughter. Finally, it grew absolutely silent. Time ticked by. The door to the storage room flung open, before Libby stepped out in the red dress. My heart stopped. "If you say a single word, I'll f'in' kill you with my bare hands."

My mouth wouldn't work if I'd wanted it to. It was too busy manufacturing saliva. My mind was on overdrive, thinking about me, her, and that little slip of a dress. I put my hand out, and gestured with my finger for her to turn around for me.

"Yeah right, give me your coat before someone sees me."

I slipped it off but held it beyond her grasp.

"Aidan, give me that coat right now."

I smiled my sexiest smile, egging her on.

"Fine," she said before she threw her arms up in the air and moved around like a belly dancer.

It was like a thunderbolt to my heart. I couldn't breathe.

I encircled her with my coat and whispered along her ear. "It's a shame to cover up anything this fine in something as meager as Abboud, but if we don't, you might cause a riot."

She caught me with the sharp point of her elbow.

I woofed out the small amount of oxygen I'd been able to get in my lungs.

She turned on me like winter's wrath. "I'll do worse than that if you get fresh with me again."

"I can't think of a more worthy cause to get beaten for."

She stormed off, and I trotted after her like Toto after red glittered stilettos.

"Hey sweetie." Some clown grabbed at her from the crowd. "Come here and let daddy find out what you're all about." I considered decking him, but he was under the influence of a red sparkling testosterone magnet.

When Libby realized he was talking to her, she took his drink and downed it. Her eyes watered. She waved the dry glass in his shocked eyes, before hightailing it toward the stage.

I caught up to her when she took an empty stool at a high cocktail table, where some nerdy-looking guy was sitting alone. The guy looked back and forth between the two of us. "Holy crap. You're on the Cubs." He pulled out an inhaler.

"I'm Palowski; it's nice to meet you." I extended my hand. "Would you mind if we share your table? A friend is going to sing."

"Sure." His breathing went up a notch.

When a cocktail server paraded by, Libby grabbed the girl's arm, and ordered drinks for us.

"Do you think you should have anything else to drink?"

She raised an eyebrow at me and pursed her lips into a tight little O. "One: God only knows how many more of your ex-lovers we'll run into. Two: I'm basically naked, it's worse than the nightmare about showing up nude for the bar exam. Three: my ass is on the line. If Evita can't sing, Tony's going to have me bound, gagged, and fitted for concrete shoes." She pulled her evening bag open yanking out a bag of M & M's with which she occasionally bribed Cass. She plucked a few out before extending them. "Candy? Oh, that's right you already had Candy!"

I swiped the bag from her. "I have every reason to believe she can sing, but I might have you fitted for concrete shoes myself." Our drinks arrived and I tapped my bottle against her highball glass. "Scratch that, I'll just have you bound and gagged."

"That's about the only way you'll get me."

"You're awfully vulnerable in that tube dress. I bet I can have it off of you before we get to Lake Shore Drive."

"You wish."

I was absolutely serious. "Bound, gagged, and exposed. We can create our own special memory of the Magnificent Mile."

"It would take you a lot longer than a . . . "

Our tablemate cleared his throat. We'd both forgotten that we weren't alone. He was beet red, but he took two hits off his inhaler before saying, "The two of you are way kinky." He got up and blended into the throng.

I hadn't laughed like that in forever. I took the stool alongside Libby and pulled hers closer to mine.

I heard Tony at the microphone. "Ladies and gentlemen, we have a very special guest this evening; Ms. Evita is here all the way from . . . " Evita cleared her throat in the microphone loudly, and Tony gave her a glare. "Please help me welcome her to Chicago." Tony's arc of light was extinguished as the applause rose, and a black ebony piano was illuminated with Evita sitting behind it.

Evita began to play softly and the crowd stepped closer to the stage. Then her silky voice started, "At last, my love has come along." There was no hesitation in her crystal voice. "My lonely days are over. And life is like a song." The crowd erupted, clapping and whistling.

Libby's eyes shone with satisfaction. I kissed her temple.

The room was awash in applause, as Tony made his way to us, presenting Libby with a bottle of champagne, and two glasses. "*Bella*, you saved me this evening, she's fantastic. I owe you a dress, any dress you want you just send me the bill."

"You're going to hire her then?"

"I'd be crazy if I didn't."

"I'll have a contract sent over by messenger first thing in the morning. You can pay her cash for tonight. I think twenty-five hundred and then a thousand-dollar wardrobe allowance until we get the details of the contract ironed out."

Tony poured her a glass of champagne. "You're representing Evita, and you want a contract? You're my attorney."

"Yes, but I'm your criminal defense lawyer. Who handles your business contracts?"

"Cyrus Fletcher."

"Then I definitely want an ironclad contract." Libby tossed back a swig of bubbly.

"Twenty-five hundred is too much for one night." Tony looked about, weighing his options. "She's only singing, and I'm betting she's the illegal that's been holed up in the church. It's all over the news. I could lose my liquor license employing her."

"Then I suppose all the guys in the kitchen have green cards?" Libby crossed her arms and tilted her head. "She saved your ass, but I understand. I'll just retrieve her, and my dress and we'll be on our way." Libby moved off the barstool.

"Okay, okay." Tony stopped her with, "Contract, cash, and clothing allowance. Anything else?"

"You have to promise to look out for her."

"Keeping an eye on her won't be a chore."

"Her ex-boyfriend is Enrique Espinoza."

"What?" Tony's eyes, which had been stage bound, flashed to Libby's face. "The Colombian drug lord?"

"Yeah, and you're a Chicago crime boss, right?"

"This is thornier than I imagined." He gazed up at the stage and followed Evita with his eyes.

"If you don't think you can protect her, then we'll just have to leave her locked up at the rectory."

"I can protect her, but who's going to save me from her?"

"Oh, poor Tony." Libby patted his hand.

"By the way, can you take Evita home tonight?" I asked.

"You're pushing me." Tony's eyes focused on Libby in my blazer. "I don't know how you're keeping that dress up without a bra on." Tony laughed before moving away. "I have a party to run. *Ciao, Bella*."

"*Ciao*, Tony. Contract first thing tomorrow, and don't be late for our date with Judge Foreman."

I examined the exposed skin at Libby's neck. "What is holding up the scrap of a dress?"

"We had only one bra between us, and she was going on stage. What can I say? She needed it more than I did."

I stood alongside her and drew my index finger along the lapel of my jacket as close to the edge as I could; my finger lightly traced her pale skin. I put my mouth to her ear. "I want to see you again." And I traced my finger along the edge of the sequins lingering at the indentation between her breasts before she batted my hand away. "I think it's time for me to take you home," I said into her ear.

She shivered in response, but eyed me cautiously. "I think we should stay until she finishes the first set."

"If I give you that concession, what will I get in return?"

"It certainly won't be sex. What's with you? You're acting like you haven't had it in months instead of days?"

"It has been seven weeks, to be exact."

Libby looked puzzled.

I cleared my throat. I really didn't want to get into this.

Libby gave me her cross-examination stare down.

I tugged on my collar. "Vanessa had some work done and sex was out of the question." I threw back some M & M's hoping that was the end of it.

"What would prevent her from having sex?"

I choked out, "She had vaginal rejuvenation."

Libby's face did stunned very well. "Vaginal what?"

"I'm not saying it again." I was as beet red as the nerd and no breathing apparatus would help me. I poured champagne.

"You're telling me that Vanessa Vanderhoff who is, what, twenty-seven years old needed her sna . . . "

I put my hand over her mouth, but she wasn't finished.

"I'm just curious; do you think it was size or volume that made rejuvenation necessary?" She asked straight-faced.

"Libby, I am not answering that."

"Why incriminate yourself? Did you ask for them to fill and rotate the tires too?" She laughed so hard she cried. The alcohol was taking effect because she thought she was hilarious.

I was fuming sober.

And she wasn't finished. "Why would you sleep with someone you know everyone else had?"

I still had some cocky pride. "It makes for great locker room conversation."

She narrowed her eyes at me.

"I was only playing around with her in the beginning, but then she started to grow on me."

"Mold grows slowly," she slurred slightly. "She's a high school drop-out, and you're a Big Ten Academic All American."

"Did your background check list her GED?"

"Generally Educated Delinquent."

"Did it mention that she's going to be a bazillionaire when her dad kicks the bucket?"

"It would have taken all that money to get your children the help they needed to function in society."

The ump laughed so hard that my head shook. Or maybe that was the alcohol, or the direction of the conversation.

"It was her idea," I ground out.

"I get it now." She looked up dawning recognition. "Was she going to give you her rejuvenated virginity?"

I was getting peeved. "I've only been with one virgin in my life, and I didn't know it until a few days ago. As far as I can see, I won't ever be with another one."

She grew stark still. "I'm sorry that my virginity was such a disappointment to you."

"You certainly didn't disappoint me." I shook my head. "I'm frustrated I didn't know how precious what you gave me was."

"Don't get all nostalgic about it, especially since I ended up in the 'Boinking Room'." She scoffed. "Anyway, it seems I can revive my virginity, if necessary. Vaginal re... what did you call it?"

Before I could reply, the guest of honor clapped me on the shoulder. "Hey, kid, how you doing? I would appreciate if you didn't knock off any more of my records."

"Rusty, it's great to see you."

He bear-hugged me. "You dumped my ERA right into the can."

"I was hoping to run into you before I had to leave. Let me

introduce to you my girlfriend, Libby Tucker. She thinks you're the greatest closing pitcher in Cub's history."

"I like this girl already, Band-Aid."

Evita started another song, and the crowd was enthusiastic.

"She's the one," I whispered for Rusty's ears only.

Rusty glanced at Libby, considering her more thoroughly. "I don't know where Mother has gotten off to. She flutters off like she was the superstar." He searched the crowd for his wife.

I moved toward Libby and slipped my hand into the inside pocket of my jacket and drew out my donation. I handed Rusty the check. He unfolded it, and looked at me.

"Now, Aidan, I told you last year's donation was too much, and this is even more generous. Don't give all your money away. This gal here might want you to spend a wad of it on her."

"I want to do this for Mother. She's special, and I know how important this is to the two of you. Take the money and use it well." I put my hand over his fist, closing around the check.

"Those reporters can say all they want about you, but you're one of the best young men around today. You make me proud, son." He pounded my back. "I better get this to Mother, she's in charge of all the funds, and this one's a whopper. We'll talk soon? Maybe you can bring your Libby out to the house before we go to Florida for the winter."

"I'll try my best, sir."

"It was a pleasure meeting you." He kissed Libby's cheek.

We watched him meander his way through the crowd.

"Can I ask you how much you copped the feel for?" Libby asked.

"Your bosom was feeling up my finances."

"Very funny, how much?"

"Don't worry. I have plenty more. I have enough to take care of us for the rest of our lives."

She rolled her eyes. "All I want to know is how much?"

"Fifty."

"Big spender."

"Fifty grand, Libby."

She sputtered through the bubbles of her Champagne. "Fifty thousand dollars? That's not sensible."

"This coming from the woman who gave away the dress off her back . . . and her bra."

"Those I can replace."

"God, I wish you wouldn't."

"Pay attention, this is important." She slapped my arm. "You want to end up like, like, oh-I-don't-know, some broken down old destitute baseball player?"

I drew a hand to my ear. "I'm sorry, did you have a name to go with the speech, because I'm not following along so well."

"You know what? I'm wasting my breath. Why should I speak reason to a man who sleeps with girls named Candy and Mandy? Whose ex-girlfriend needs vaginal rejuv, rejuvena ... "

"Rejuvenation," I said pouring more champagne.

"Rejuvenation. Thank you. A man who gives his money away, who breaks old men's records, and whose trying to break my heart?" She quickly pulled her glass to her mouth to cover her gaff. "I didn't mean that."

"Yes, you did. Let's finish this in the car, so when I take you apart there won't be any witnesses."

The crowd was wrapped around the stage, so it was easier going out than it had been coming in.

I'd almost reached the elevators, when I ran into Fletch. I stopped, and Libby plowed into me. I twisted her along my side.

"I thought you were moving up in the world." Fletch looked from Libby's wild hair to her red glittered stilettos and smirked. "There are hookers better dressed on Rush Street."

Libby took a menacing step in Fletch's direction. "You better fucking watch your mouth, Cyrus."

"I should have washed your mouth out the first time you swore at me, but I lost my head thinking it was kind of sexy."

"Fletch, don't say 'sexy' to Libby. Where's Tricia anyway?"

"The ladies room, where she has been spending a considerable amount of time."

I gave him the questioning eyebrow.

"Morning sickness," Fletch ground out.

"It's the night."

"I know, dumb ass. Don't you know anything about pregnant women?" he asked brusquely before giving Libby a direct look.

"You're surly as hell. What's your problem?" I asked.

"My wife is sick and unhappy, therefore I am unhappy."

"Should've considered that before you knocked her up."

"Did you give it any thought before you knocked her up?"

Libby swayed as she stepped in between us. "Stay away from each other until you feel better."

"As soon as my wife can stop barfing long enough for me to get her horizontal, I'll be as good as new."

"You have officially cemented my image of you as a complete asshole." Libby pushed the button for the elevator.

Tricia came around the corner, looking green except for her bloodshot eyes. Fletch rushed toward her, "How you feeling?"

"I want to go home, I don't think there's anything left, but I want to get off these clothes."

"I'm your man," Fletch smiled and winked at her.

I held the elevator door open and the four of us descended. Libby pulled open her purse again and handed Tricia a sealed peppermint. Tricia looked up at her.

"I keep them in case my son gets an upset stomach."

"Thank you, Libby. I didn't know you had a son."

"If you have a few crackers as soon as you wake up, it might help." Libby smiled. "Fresh air will help, too. Don't worry, it won't last forever."

We got off the elevator and went to the coat check. Fletch helped Tricia into her wrap, while I got Libby's. "You keep the sports coat on." I said to her.

"My coat will be warmer, plus you need your jacket."

"I'm warm enough."

"The doctor said you have to stay absolutely healthy." She slipped off my sports coat and handed it to me.

I tried to stop, but I gaped at her. "We're out of here." I smiled. "Good night, Wretch."

"Don't be late for our luncheon meeting tomorrow, Romeo," Fletch said. "And make sure Juliette's with you. I need to witness her signature."

Libby was ignoring him, but continuing her conversation with me. "I'm not going to risk you catching cold. Do you expect me to put up with you forever?" She asked, tying her belt.

Tricia looked at Libby and I, and then exchanged a raised eyebrow at Fletch.

I pulled Libby's belt tighter, and turned up her lapel before pushing her through the revolving door ahead of me. "Forever and ever, Amen."

Fletch's groan reverberated through the swirling glass.

22

COLLABORATING WITNESSES

Lawyers spend a great deal of their time shoveling smoke.
Oliver Wendell Holmes, Jr.

Libby

We cruised through the tree-lined neighborhood, and the sunlight dappled through the graying branches. There were kids walking hand in hand with parents, older boys on bikes with backpacks, and gossiping girls chitchatting.

I started to get out of the car, when Cass stopped me. "Mister Pole-ow-ski will take me in." He gave me a kiss and went to his door, where Aidan picked him up and carried him on his shoulders toward the building. Several people greeted them, and a blonde woman slid alongside them, chattering away.

Aidan reappeared on the sidewalk, walking with Steve Dubrowski. Once they got to the car, they shook hands. Steve waved to me, as Aidan got in Tank.

"What was that all about?" I nodded in Steve's direction.

"He's going to pick up Cass today after school, and take him home with Madi, and I'm returning the favor next week."

"And when, pray tell, did the two of you become so chummy?"

"Cass introduced us. We had coffee after drop-off on Monday." He pulled back into traffic.

"You had coffee together? How metro-sexual."

He cocked his head and raised the angry eyebrow. "He's a nice guy. He gave me some insight on Cass, and we talked."

I turned in my seat examining at his perfect profile. The faint lines around his eyes crinkled in a smile.

"That's the part that concerns me."

"He already figured I'm Cass' father. Besides, I wanted to know what his intentions were."

"You didn't!" My head was still banging, and with this news, I felt my stomach was going to lurch. How many Tylenol could you take in a four-hour period?

"I asked about the guy, and you gave me nothing."

"I told you we were friends."

"I wanted to hear it from him, and make sure he knows where I'm coming from."

"It would be nice, if you told me where you're coming from first." I sighed and cradled my head in my hand. "Are you going to invade every part of my life?"

"Pretty much." He brushed my hair away, so he could look at me. "I just wanted Steve to know I was going to take care of you, and I hoped that he could understand that."

"What did he say?"

"He said he loved you as a friend, that you didn't want any other relationship with him. He also mentioned he didn't know of any other relationships you've had." He raised an eyebrow.

"Arrrrgh." I stared out the window, as we drove down Sheridan Road. "You never told me why we're meeting Fletch."

"Financial business."

"What?" I choked out.

"Dr. Seuss said I should have all my personal business in order, in case something goes wrong on Friday."

"You never said anything could go wrong."

"It's just a precaution. You know that the recipient is in much more danger than the donor. I just want everything in order before Cass starts chemo next week."

"There aren't any other dangers than those the doctor told us about?"

We pulled up at my office; the plum marble gleamed, and the revolving door never ceased carouselling bodies.

"Don't worry. There are only about three deaths linked to donation in 60,000 procedures worldwide." He looked away. "I'll live."

"Are you sure you want to do this?"

"I'd do anything for him." He watched the pedestrians for a moment, before he looked me in the eye. "Or you."

I don't know why, but I kissed his chiseled jaw. When he turned his head our mouths collided. The corners of his mouth turned up into a relieved smile. "I'll be back at lunch. Check your calendar for tomorrow night. My parents want to have dinner and meet Cass."

I fumbled with the door handle, all nerves after that kiss. "Any more bombs you want to drop on me?"

"My parents want to be here, if I'm having surgery."

"Of course, I should have thought of that."

"Let me help you with the door." He leaned over me to reach the handle and placed his face in my breasts.

A truck laying on his horn deafened any opportunity for a tongue lashing, and as I exited the car, I breathed in the bustling city air to reestablish my self-control.

I'd barely reached Vicki's desk when she spoke. "You didn't fink-tattle-tale, while you were blitzed did you?"

"How do you know I was blitzed?"

"It's almost nine-fifteen and you've never been late."

Again the woman without a watch had better sense of time than a clock. My head throbbed. "I had two wines, a scotch on the rocks, a martini, and...oh yeah, half a bottle of bubbly. It was overkill."

"In your alcohol-induced fog, did you read today's paper?" She examined me under heavy purple eyelids.

"No, why? What's wrong?"

She trailed me into my office; her bracelets sang as she shut the door. I stripped off my trench coat, before she thrust the entertainment section in my face. "Twice in one week. You just might become a celebrity yourself."

There was a photo of Aidan kissing my hand along with other photos of last night's party. I scanned the article stopping on the highlighted message: 'Surprise Performance by New Diva Enthralled All'.

I examined the pictures. Luckily the one of Evita was in profile and grainy; unfortunately, mine was crystal clear.

"This reporter must know about the Cass/Palowski connection?" Vicki probed.

"His first article identified us in Lincoln Park, and Cass was with us. Wonder why he hasn't broken the story?"

"Maybe he wants a comment. He called twice this morning."

"What? Why didn't you say that right away?"

Vicki picked up the paper, nonplussed by my outburst. "That's a very romantic photo of you and Band-Aid. Do dish." It was her turn to smile, and then frown. "Are you sure you can take what you need from him without giving anything back? Are you sure you even want it to play out that way?"

"I know what I'm doing, Vicki." I moved legal pads and file folders around my desk searching for my to-do list. "It's not like I'm liable to fall in love with him again."

"The problem is I don't think you fell out of love the first time. You're an all-or-nothing kind of girl. There's been a lot of nothing for way too long."

"You've been reading your crystal ball rather than your computer screen, and typing on an Ouija board instead of a keyboard." I sighed. "Once Cass is healthy, things will go back to the way they were, and Aidan will go to spring training."

"You're trying to con yourself."

"I'm just making the best decisions I can."

"What's best for everyone might not be what's best for you, Libby. What do you want for just you?"

I put my head on my arms on my desk, willing myself not to cry. "I have no earthly idea," I said, without looking up.

Vicki came over and ran her hand over my hair. "That's what you need to think about. If you want him, you can have him."

"How would I be able to trust him?"

"Maybe this wouldn't have stretched out so long between the two of you, if you had gone to him. You never told him how you felt about him, and you never let him tell you how he felt about you."

"Now you're on charm boy's side, too?"

"Libby, I'm on your and Cass' side, always. But I'm wise enough to know there's a reason you haven't wanted anyone else in your life. Maybe he's the only one for you."

I stared at her like aliens had replaced her with some wide-eyed synthetic monster. "Those are the most romantically idiotic words you've ever spoken."

"I'm an emotional watershed right now." Vicki kissed my head. "Just think it over. Do you want me to get this Winslow guy on the phone for you?"

"Give me a couple of minutes to clear my head."

When Vicki couldn't reach the mystifying Winslow O'Leary, I spent some time reviewing the contract for Evita, putting in the figures, before I had Mohawk Messenger service deliver it.

I made a brief phone call to Evita before I left for the Daley center. I didn't see Accardo until I reached the double wood doors of the chamber. "Mr. Accardo," I said in greeting.

"Don't you Mr. Accardo me! That contract was ridiculous. I won't pay that kind of money for a pain in the cohunes." He tilted his head like he thought I was his witness. "You didn't tell me she had a kid."

"I fail to see the relevance." I nodded toward the bailiff, before taking the defense table.

"Don't use lawyer-speak on me. You didn't tell me Espinoza wants his kid back. I need to keep an eye on both of them."

"You're intelligent. I figured you'd manage things the way you expect me to." I eyed the District Attorney.

Tony furrowed his brow, examining the courtroom. When his eyes collided with Eve Moore's he leaned toward me. "I do find out the most interesting things when I do a little research."

"I have that uncanny ability myself." I glanced at Eve and back at Tony again. "When you give me so many visual clues, I know where to start digging." I slammed his file down on the table. "You seem more concerned about an entertainment contract than you do about the felony charges we're here to face today."

Tony gave me a wry smile, before Judge Foreman entered the courtroom, slipping into his robe. He rubbed his balding head and pushed his gold-framed glasses up his spindly nose. We rose when the gavel dropped, the bailiff read the case number and the stenographer started typing.

Judge Foreman listened to the charges as he thumbed through his notes. "How does the defendant plea?"

"Not guilty, your honor." I looked up from my file.

Judge Foreman cleared his throat. "On all charges?"

"On all those read, unless the DA's office has more to contribute today? Like jaywalking, or speeding, or something else my client hasn't done?"

Foreman gave me a look a look of exasperation over his glasses.

"The defense wishes to inquire why the prosecution has failed to provide us with their entire discovery."

Jax Wagner shuffled through his papers. "The entire discovery was delivered to Ms. Tucker's office."

I looked at Jax and raised a brow. He hesitated and looked away. "Your honor, the prosecution asserts that Mr. Accardo hired a mystery witness to murder one Vincent Serrelli. But the witness is not named in discovery. In order to provide my client with a defense, I need the name of that witness."

"The witness's name was withheld in regard to his immediate safety," Jax countered. "Our office was concerned he might come to the same result as Mr. Serrelli."

"Judge Foreman, I object. If the prosecution asserts Mr. Accardo hired this person to murder Mr. Serrelli, then Mr. Accardo would already know who the man is. The only reason the witness would not want his name in discovery is because Mr. Accardo did not hire him, and once his name was supplied, Mr. Accardo would be able to pursue the witness."

"Pursue the witness, Ms. Tucker?" Judge Foreman asked.

"Sue the man for slander."

Judge Foreman looked irritated and turned on Jax. "Who is the witness, Mr. Wagner?"

"Your Honor, if a witness is in jeopardy then his name may be withheld until we go to trial," Jax retorted brusquely.

I lurched to my feet. "Your Honor, under Federal Rule of Criminal Procedure 12.1, the prosecution must disclose the names of all witnesses that will be called to rebuke the defendant's alibi defense."

Jax rose. "The witness is not rebuking his alibi."

"You're exactly right, he's told the DA's office that he is a murderer for hire, yet you're charging my client with his crime. Furthermore, you're not producing him for cross examination, nor providing the defense with his name, so that we may investigate this person's background, whereabouts, or even his credibility as a witness."

"But your honor," Jax bellowed.

"I'm sorry, Mr. Wagner, it doesn't matter how loudly you yell in my courtroom, you're going to have to answer the interrogatory question in reference to this witness." Judge Foreman held up a hand, warding him off as he threw back a slam of Mylanta. "Mr. Wagner, it is not excessive or burdensome for you to produce this witness's name."

"Your Honor, I want more than just his name now. I want Mr. Wagner to produce the witness in court so that I have an opportunity to ask him a few questions."

"You can take his deposition, Ms. Tucker," Jax replied.

"I could have already done that, if you had provided me with his name," I retorted.

Judge Foreman dropped his gavel. "Wagner, if you wanted to handle this correctly, then you should have produced his name. Now you're wasting our time. Swear the man in, and we'll settle this nonsense."

The look on Jax's face said that he hadn't quite outgrown the possibility of hurling. "Your Honor, he isn't here."

"And why not? I wanted to start this trial today. Why wouldn't you have him in the courthouse?" Foreman bellowed.

Jax hung his head in defeat. "We don't know where he is. He disappeared yesterday." Jax bore a hole in Tony's forehead. He didn't need to speak. The accusation hung in the courtroom.

The judge was none too happy. "Mr. Wagner, you have no witness, your office lost a man who told you he was a contract killer. Why wasn't he in custody?"

Bingo for me, uh-oh for Jax.

"We thought he would be safer outside of jail."

"Since when does the DA's office have jurisdiction over a confessed murderer? I was under the impression that it was the judicial branch that made that decision!"

"Your honor," was all Jax could muster.

"In light of this revelation, and in the absence of a witness to rebut Mr. Accardo's alibi, I am accepting his alibi. It's collaborated by the state's own surveillance detail and by the visitor's log at Mr. Accardo's grandmother's retirement home. I must say it's refreshing that Mr. Accardo spends that much time visiting an elderly relative."

"Your Honor, I object," Jax blustered.

"You can object all you want, but the murder charges are dropped." Foreman dropped his gavel. "Now what else do you have for me in reference to Mr. Accardo?"

"Nothing further."

"Pardon me, Mr. Wagner, I didn't get that," the judge said.

"Mr. Serrelli was our case. I have his depositions."

I jumped out of my seat. "Those are inadmissible without producing Mr. Serrelli for cross examination."

"Would you like for me to produce his corpse?" Jax responded snidely.

"Do you know where the body is?" The courtroom was desolate except for a few reporters who erupted into laughter, which brought the judge's gavel down on my still pounding head.

Then Judge Foreman pointed it at me. "I've warned you, I'd hate to put you in a cell for contempt, but don't push me."

"I beg your apology, Your Honor," I said contritely.

The judge addressed Jax. "I'm sorry, Mr. Wagner, this case has more holes in it than a brick of Swiss. If you don't have any other collaborative evidence, this case is over."

"But your honor…"

"All you've got is a handful of buts, Mr. Wagner. Case dismissed. Mr. Accardo is free to go."

Jax Wagner looked at Eve Moore. She shrugged her shoulders while he assembled his belongings. Judge Foreman turned his gavel on Jax. "I want that man's name, Wagner. I'm issuing a bench warrant, and I want you to personally see that your man is brought in."

Now, Jax was up to his eyeballs in it. I would have felt bad, except Jax sent uniforms to pick up Accardo in the first place.

Jax nodded curtly toward Foreman and then rushed past me as I busied myself, packing my briefcase.

Tony had an idiotic grin on his face.

When the prosecution exited the courtroom, I turned on Tony. "If I ever find out you had anything to do with the murder or the disappearance of the mystery witness, I'll make sure you spend an eternity enjoying cannoli behind bars."

"I don't know you well, *Bella*, but you know I'm not a murderer. I'll have Fletch contact you in reference to Ms. Gutierrez's contract." He stormed around me.

I turned to respond only to find Aidan standing in the back of the courtroom in a snazzy charcoal suit.

He leaned over the railing, greeting me with a kiss. "Babe, you made Accardo mad."

"He doesn't like being saved by the same woman two days in a row." I slipped into my coat as the next case was called. We walked to the elevator, neither of us speaking.

We got into Tank and drove a few blocks, coming to a halt along Adams. The valet came to Aidan's door. "My lawyerdar tells me something is going on. Why do you want this meeting in an exclusive restaurant? You're awfully dressed up."

"You're way too paranoid." He pushed the second valet out of the way to help me out. When I turned in my seat, the side slit of my skirt jacked up, exposing the top of my thigh high stocking. "If you're trying to distract me," Aidan whispered, "that's a great way to start."

"In your wet dreams, Palowski."

He chuckled as he maneuvered me into the restaurant, helping me out of my trench. He leaned into me. "I forgot to tell you how pretty you look today."

He smelled better than the restaurant, and I almost tripped over myself in spite of my lawyers' composure. The maitre d' escorted us to our table, where Fletch was already situated. I admired the buffed white marble floor, the fabulous pale sage green wallpaper, the silk damask round tufted banquettes, and long table cloths sat in puddles around the legs of the tables. The booths encircled a huge ornate vase of fresh flowers. The place smelled faintly of subtle flavors, spices, and fresh flowers.

Fletch concluded a call as we approached. I sat in the booth alongside Aidan. As Aidan ordered a bottle of wine, Fletch glared at me. I rolled my eyes.

"That was Accardo on the phone. He says you sent him a contract with some outlandish requests for that singer."

"Is this the reason for this meeting?"

"We're here to talk about business between you and Aidan."

"Then you can call my office and set up a phone consult on the contract, and not waste Aidan's time."

"Public meeting, very smooth, you must be confident she won't kill both of us in a room full of witnesses." Fletch rubbed his jaw line thoughtfully before looking at Aidan. "You might have misjudged her, though. As just demonstrated, she always plays for the jugular."

I felt the hair on my nape raise and my lawyerdar was I bleeping in my head. What the hell had I just walked into?

Aidan steadied my leg under the table with his hand. "Reassure her no one's out to get her."

"I would, but you're after her, full-steam ahead."

Aidan picked up his menu. "Let's decide on lunch."

I couldn't concentrate on the menu. Nervousness radiated off both of them. Luckily, Aidan ordered something that sounded good, so I said, "The same."

As soon as our wine was poured, Fletch pulled out a legal file and looked at Aidan. "Libby, Aidan has written a new will."

My blood pressure plummeted six stories.

"I'll give you a copy for your records. Basically, it names Cass as his sole heir and you as the executor. On the occasion of his death, Cass will inherit approximately..." he handed me a Post-it note. I tried to count the zeros, but couldn't get my eyes or my mind to focus.

I remembered this morning, as I was toweling off from my shower, I heard Aidan in Cass' bedroom. They spoke back and forth, as if they'd know each other forever. A pang of jealousy hit me. I'd never had to share Cass. And I'd never considered his loving someone as much as he loved me. The thought had been with me for only a second before I'd heard Cass giggle out a belly laugh that was so wholesome that a deep sense of peace washed through me.

"Give or take a few million. Most of the money is currently in trust; it's what he inherited from his grandparents. What he's earned playing ball is invested. Some of that money has recently been liquidated and deposited in a discretionary account for you."

I couldn't hold onto a breath. Aidan's hand slid up and down my thigh. "If you faint in here, we'll have a situation."

"Aidan has made about forty-nine million-dollars in the last eight years from contracts, bonuses, and endorsements." Fletch cleared his throat. "If he had paid child support during this time, it would be twenty percent of his income, which is about ten million. We've liquidated five million to date and once his new contract is paid out, we will get you a check for an additional five-million, plus the six-million you get off the new deal." He paused for some wine. "All in all, you're a very rich lady. I did not extend any of the money in trust toward child support since the interest it earns is put right back into the original investments. If you don't like how I've worked this out, you can take us to court, and you might end up with a few million more or less, but I'll leave that up to you."

I couldn't swallow what was in my throat, I felt more panic stricken than being alone and pregnant. That I could handle. Managing a fortune I could not.

Aidan awaited my reaction stoically.

"No," I was able to choke out a single syllable.

"No?" Aidan and Fletch said in unison. Aidan looked mad. Fletch appeared victorious.

"I don't want your money." I turned toward Aidan, ignoring Fletch. "I did not do this to put my hand in your pocketbook. All I wanted was for you to help Cass physically not financially. You take the money back. I don't want it."

"Babe, it's the money you and Cass are entitled to." Aidan picked up my hand. "I'm his father, and it's my job to support him."

"You signed your parental rights away. Didn't Red Beard tell you don't have a financial obligation to Cass?" I looked at Fletch, who perched on his chair like a long-tailed, red cat with the preverbal canary hanging from its jaws.

"This is my moral responsibility. This way you can do whatever you want with your life. You're free. If you're smart with the money, you won't ever have to work again. I owe you this, I owe Cass this, and it's already done."

It felt like it was my skull dangling from Fletch's jaws. "What do you want in return?" The feathers at my neck bristled.

At that accusation, our food arrived. Aidan and I had chopped salads and Fletch had a side of beef that reminded me that the Chicago cattle yards hadn't been far from here too many years past. I waited for it to moo when he sliced into his meal.

Aidan released my hand. "Let's eat lunch, and then we can discuss the rest of it." He didn't wait for a response. He just picked up his fork and started. I did the same, trying my best to gather my scattered thoughts. Aidan started in on Fletch, "Don't you know that eating like that will kill you?"

"What do I have to live for anyway? My wife won't let me within a yard of her. I thought marriage meant unlimited sex."

I gagged on my salad, and Aidan chortled.

"I'm glad that my pain can bring you so much happiness."

Fletch's fat cat attitude lost its Cheshire grin. "If she isn't barfing, she's crying, or worrying about something."

"Take her away for a few days," Aidan suggested.

"When all hell is about to break lose between you, little Mary sunshine here, and the media? No telling what imaginary tales Vanessa is feeding TMZ, but when they put it together I'll be on overtime, and I might even have to pull in a PR person."

"You're way over-stating this. It will be a five second story, and we're going to keep a low profile. I was thinking of taking Libby and Cass to the retreat, when I get out of the hospital until Cass has to start chemo."

"Cass and I are not leaving town," I said defiantly.

"We can argue about that later, babe."

"I'm not taking your money either."

Fletch was now the arched back cat ready to pounce on an unsuspecting mouse. In spite of his sexual frustration, he looked serene.

"I already set up an account and deposited the money." Aidan took a drink of his wine without looking at me.

"Then un-deposit it!"

"They don't have any un-deposit slips." Aidan grinned like Cass. "Look, the money's a done deal. The will you can review. If you think there's something I should change, we'll discuss it. I want to know that if something happens to me, you're both provided for."

"This is ridiculous. A week ago you didn't even know that I drew breath and now you want to..." I couldn't finish because he was kissing me. He held my chin in place, so I couldn't move.

"That's one way to get her to see things your way."

He pulled away and glared at Fletch but spoke to me. "Don't fight me on this right now. Think it through, and we can discuss it somewhere more private. Tell her the rest."

"I think she might have had enough for one day," Fletch mewled, exposing his perfect canines.

"I'll decide what enough is, you do your job. I pay you five-hundred bucks an hour, get to it."

I looked at Aidan. Uh-oh, this must be bad.

Fletch stared back at Aidan, annoyed but unmoved by his rancor. He moved his half-eaten side of beef away. "Libby, Aidan would like to legally adopt Cass."

I was ready to claw them both alive, it was lucky that cats had nine lives, because these two might need all eighteen of them to learn how to land on all fours.

23

BROKEN RECORDS

Fifty years from now I'll be just three inches of type in a record book. Brooks Robinson

Aidan 1:45 p.m.

"I looked into having the termination of parental rights rescinded, and it can be done, but it would take longer than a simple adoption," Fletch said. "Especially once we demonstrate to the court that Aidan is the child's biological father." He consulted me with a look. "I think this is something the two of you should talk about alone."

Fletch folded his napkin and got to his feet. Libby didn't say goodbye. I focused on calibrating her reaction. I was rubbing my thumb across her palm. I stared into her blazing green eyes and willed words to come to me. "Libby?" It wasn't a name anymore, but an oath. We stood on the edge of a precipice, and if I moved the wrong way, I was afraid of where we'd land.

She closed her eyes and I watched her take in oxygen on gulping whimpers. "You want to buy Cass away from me?"

"Babe, drink this." I handed her a full glass of wine. "Better yet, let's go for a walk."

"I need to get away from you," she squeaked. "Far away."

I settled the check, and then helped her out of the booth. "I promise you everything is going to be good from here on out."

Our bodies collided when I didn't step out of her path. The physical connection went through me and settled in an organ that wasn't best used for thinking.

As we walked toward Michigan Avenue at a clipped pace, the El screeched in the distance; the metal-on-metal scraped as the train turned two stories up. I pulled her through the pedestrian crosswalk while she made a feeble attempt at wrenching away.

I considered a stroll through Millennium Park, but her uncooperative stride told me it might be time to spill my guts. Instead, I started up the stairs of the Art Institute. She stumbled behind me, not paying attention until I reached the top of the stairs and looked down on the pair of oxidized lions which guarded the entrance, 'Stands in an Attitude of Defiance' is on the south end and 'On the Prowl' stands to the north, ironic that their names mirrored our dispositions.

"What are we doing here?" she asked.

"I want to show you where I'm coming from."

I bought her a ticket, while I fished through my wallet for my yearly pass. We made our way to the security guard, an elderly gentleman with a uniform worn so many years it was now a size too small. "Come to sit with your girlfriend?"

Libby stepped alongside me and the guard took her in with startled milky eyes. "By gosh, now it all makes perfect sense."

"George, this is Libby. How's it going today?"

"It had been pretty slow." He tipped his cap at Libby. "I don't think anybody's been in your gallery all day."

The vintage stairwell opened up to a long red-carpeted hallway that galloped along with my increasing heart rate. We entered a dimly lit, unoccupied gallery, where an archway stood on the right. The smaller gallery beyond was painted in a warm cream color. I strung the red velvet rope between two brass stands corroding off the gallery to everyone but us.

Libby moved to the painting on the farthest wall: 'Woman with a Parasol and a Small child on a Sunlit Hillside'. The woman's dainty parasol shielded her eyes and the wobbling toddler in the background was facing away from us, keeping its gender a mystery. The woman's grace and confidence spoke through the canvas, light dappled over her serene face, illuminating the strands of swaying grass. It was as if at any moment the child would fall back on its rump and the woman would laugh. Libby touched the nameplate. "It's the same painting that's hanging in your living room."

She stared at the portrait for long moments before she glanced back over her shoulder to find me leaning against the doorjamb awaiting her appraisal. She went to a cushioned bench that ran parallel with the painting and took a seat.

I paced the parquet floor behind her.

The ump grumbled. **Spit it out, kid.**

I hesitated then continued several more circuits, before I sat as close to her as I could. I rested my elbows on my knees, lost in my observation of the painting as my shoulders collapsed forward. "It's you."

"What?"

"Sometimes, when you come to me that's how I see you. It must have been all that English literature."

She turned her head one-way and then another, scrutinizing.

"A couple of years ago I was at the Bellagio for a baseball show and thought the Renoir exhibit would be an excellent place to hide out from autograph hounds.

"I was mindlessly wandering when I stepped into a small display alcove and suddenly felt your presence for the first time in years. I tried to tell myself I was enthralled with the painting. I tried to shrug off the goose bumps with dinner and gambling, but that night I tossed and turned and finally woke up in a cold sweat. That painting and the unknown child in the background were coming at me."

Libby's eyes flickered across the Renoir.

"I'd worked hard to erase every memory." I picked up her hand and traced the veins.

"But when I saw this painting, my heart raced, remembering what it felt like to be with you. I tried to buy the painting."

Her expression clearly implied she thought I'd lost it.

And I had.

"I visited her in Boston and D.C. Finally, she ended up in my hometown, and I guess from what George said, you know I've sat with her before. I always thought she had something to say."

Libby had to clear her throat to speak. "That's not me."

I brought her wrist to my lips and kissed her gently. "I know that in here—" I pointed to my head, "—but not so much in here." I placed her hand over my heart.

"Now, here's where the story gets strange, and I'd like for it to remain between us. Otherwise, someone might demand a psych evaluation."

Libby chewed on her lip but nodded.

"Last year during the off-season I decided to climb Mt. Olympus, in Washington State. Olympus isn't especially high at eight thousand feet, but it's challenging with the triple peak and heavily glaciated terrain.

"You approach through a breathtaking rainforest wilderness. I was climbing with an experienced team and their familiarity ensured making the summit. But a dense fog set in, and once it lifted, we were blanketed in a snowstorm. We were half way down when we suffered an injury and had to dig snow caves and wait for the storm to pass. I slept fitfully. I was frozen and frayed. I used the last of my battery lamp because I couldn't handle the darkness anymore, and then you came to me."

Libby's green eyes darkened and searched my face.

"I'd been dozing, and you called my name, startling me awake. When I got my bearings, you were sitting at my feet in that dress." I pointed toward the painting. "You came into my arms and a calm rush of heat went through me. You whispered, 'Climb out of this hole, and come find me.'

"When I dug my way out, I located a search party at two-thousand feet. They wanted to take me down, but I didn't think they'd find the camp without me and when we did, the guide and Juan were already dead from exposure."

"The media never caught wind of the story?"

"I refused to be interviewed, I was the only survivor, and Fletch made sure that was the end of it."

"You must have been terrified," she said.

"I was, but not because I was hanging off the edge of the world in a blizzard. I was terrified because I was supposed to find you. Somehow I knew you needed me and facing you was more frightening than freezing to death.

"You're the only thing I've been afraid of in my life." I ran my hands through my hair my mind worked quickly, putting words together in neat little lines. "I've been scared of having you and going on without you. I've failed you when you needed me the most, and I was frightened that if I found you, you'd reject me. But more than all that, I've been afraid that if I can't learn to love you, I'll never love anyone."

Her eyes darted about like a trapped animal before she stiffened her spine. "I need more time."

"I'll wait as long as you need, but don't shut me out. I don't want to be on the outside anymore. I need you, Libby."

She shivered as I pulled her into a gentle embrace, kissing her temple. Our eyes met first, and then our mouths. When I nipped her tentative tongue, she groaned in luxurious surrender. "We need to take this somewhere more private," I whispered.

Her glazed eyes didn't seem to comprehend.

"I would love to continue." I kissed below her ear. "But without video evidence." I brushed my teeth across her neck.

She jerked away so fast I almost didn't make it to my feet.

Instead of exiting the museums main entrance, we took the elevator to the underground parking garage. I spotted Tank parked right where the valet said he'd leave it. I hit the key and the engine roared to life. "I know the perfect place where we can be alone." I hustled her into the back seat.

"Aren't we a little old for this?" She attempted to straighten her twisted skirt.

"Let me help you with that."

Her long ivory legs were sheathed in black silk. I gazed from her black transparent panties to the silky, lace top of her hose. I was on my knees between her legs leaning over her and she was looking up at me. Her face flushed with either excitement or panic. I ran my index finger over the exposed flesh at the top of her thigh highs. Without waiting for her response, I devoured her mouth. I shuddered on her groan as I moved my splayed hand over her belly button, running my fingers across the edge of her panties. "Does your bra match?"

She gave a subtle nod.

I took her mouth again. My tongue stroked hers in a rhythm that had likely stirred men and women's blood since the dawn of creation. I nipped her chin. "Show me."

"Show you what?" she purred.

I reclined in the seat and pulled her legs across my lap. "Unbutton your blouse. Show me the matching bra."

She smiled sweetly. "And if I don't?"

I was staring at her black clad hips, my head jerked up, "You have ten seconds or I'll tear it open."

"This is an expensive blouse." She toyed with the hem.

"Nine."

A button slipped through a hole, she paused, brushing away lint. She undid another button and met my eye, and all I could think about was biting her lower lip. When she was done, there was only a thin slash of naked skin from neck to navel.

"Libby, show me."

She shook her head no.

I smiled, and nodded yes. I used my teeth to pull back the sides of her blouse. "God you're beautiful." I dipped my head, running my tongue along the crests of her breasts. I pulled one cup down and put my ravenous mouth to the rosy, blushed center. She arched, forcing more into my mouth, I greedily accepted as she pushed against me, my hand slid from her abdomen to her center making me aware of her need.

I pulled her alongside me so I could get to her mouth. My

tongue roamed and plunged. One of my hands wandered her breasts, palming their centers until I had her panting. I nuzzled her collarbone while my hand traveled to the edge of her panties.

She whimpered.

"Do you want me to stop?"

She grabbed my starched shoulders and pulled me closer.

"This time, it's about you." I slipped my fingers inside her panties. "Holy mother, you're silky."

I sucked up the pleasure of her cries, where every experienced stroke brought her closer. "Silky and tight." I captured her mouth as I slid my knee between her thighs, applying the slightest amount of additional pressure. She arched against me screaming, "Aidan!"

"You taste good, you feel good, and you smell good. You're going to make me incredibly happy."

She buried her head in my neck. "I don't know the tricks your previous bunnies probably knew."

"I want you, as spontaneous and innocent as you are."

She tensed in my arms.

"You haven't been with anyone in a long time. How long?"

Her eyes shifted examining my tie.

"Libby?" I pulled her head up, the golden flecks in her emerald eyes shined vibrantly.

"Forever," she chewed on that swollen bottom lip.

I crushed her so aggressively that I winded her. "I'm the only one?" I was overwhelmed with feelings of possession but I wondered aloud, "Why are you denying yourself?"

"It just never felt right." She hesitated. "It didn't help that I got pregnant the first time. I thought about other men, but I couldn't do it. I know it sounds stupid, but it just never happened, and I was all right with that."

"How you feel isn't stupid, it's sweet." A grin of conquest overtook me. "No wonder you're bound tighter than a bow string. You have some catching up to do." I flipped her onto her back.

"That shouldn't have happened, we got carried away..."

I pressed my mouth to hers. She fought me only until our tongues met and then she surrendered. When my palm scraped the tip of her breast she was panting as rhythmically as I was. "I'm going to carry you away again."

She bit my tongue. I instinctually ground my wool-clad hips into hers. Her legs fell open inviting the intimate embrace and I pressed myself against her softest recess.

Her fingernails grazed my groin, which prompted me to grind harder. When she moaned, I groaned, literally losing it. "Crap."

She cried out, "Yes." We both lay silent for minutes, she giggled. "When was the last time that happened to you?"

"I don't remember the exact date." I looked at her abashed, "But you'll be happy to know it was with you."

"It's nothing to be embarrassed about. I came all over you. I'm impressed you held out this long."

"I was in complete control . . . until . . . You're making me crazy, all right. I want you so bad that I'm trigger-happy. Christ Almighty." I was glad it was dark in the garage because I knew I was beet red. "Libby, when this happens between us I want to make sure it means something."

"Yeah, it means we're just as physically attracted to each other as we were back then."

"It was more then, and it's more now. I don't know how I'm going to convince you of that, but you can be sure I'll prove it before 'all of it' happens."

The dismissal bell outside Queen of All Saints startled me. While I was waiting for Cass, I was doing anything that could keep my mind off of Libby and I in the back seat yesterday.

A long stretch limo caught my eye as it lumbered down the suburban street toward Tank. The driver opened the door, and Vanessa slipped out of the vehicle.

I gnashed my teeth. Better to be rid of the snake lurking behind the glassy smile, before the opportunity to bare her fangs and strike when I was indisposed in the hospital came.

"You've been trying to reach me?" She hiked her skirt up to get in Tank, exposing her bare thighs. I didn't feel a thing. My libido had recalibrated itself and was now focused on a solitary target.

"A phone call would have sufficed. I'm waiting for someone, and I'd prefer you to be gone before they arrive."

"Has your Libby gone in for concession?"

"Concession stands are in ballparks."

"Whatever," she whined.

"Don't embarrass yourself with anymore full page ads. Breach of Promise is off the books in Illinois, but I'm not opposed to getting a restraining order to keep you away."

"I still have those very interesting photos."

"And I know that Non-For-Profit Wesley Statham set up isn't above board. The company partnering with the Vanderhoff Foundation, CUX, is a front for the mob. Those free discount prescription drug cards, which are supposed to be for low-income families, are being siphoned off by CUX. There might be evidence that they're selling them outright. If not, they're using them to launder money through your foundation. I have a suspicion you've known about it for months.

"One phone call and you'll be up to your neck in federal charges that even daddy won't be able to bail you out of. Not to mention the negative publicity. You know how the press loves to make fun of you."

"You've been doing your homework." She pulled a cigarette out of her oversized bag, fishing around for a lighter. "Did Libby the lawyer find this out for you?"

"Libby's an officer of the court. If she knew, you'd already have federal prosecutors after you." I eyed her. "Don't you dare light that offensive thing in my new car."

She put the cigarette to her lips anyway, but let it dangle there. "What on earth can you possibly want from her?"

"A life full of honesty, commitment, and happiness."

"You'll be boning someone else by the end of the month."

"I've never wanted anyone the way I want her."

"Oh my God." She drew her hand to her face as if I had slapped her. "You're in love with the little nobody?"

"She's somebody to me. What do you know about love? You were screwing some movie producer in San Francisco. Is that your idea of love and fidelity?"

She looked away for a moment, not bothering to deny it. "Whatever I did, I did for my career, including you. Daddy said I needed a respectable husband."

"Slither up someone else's spine. Get out, my charge has arrived." I made my way around the car, opening her door. She was standing at the curb when Cass started up the sidewalk; she looked him over before she looked back at me.

"This is bigger than enhanced pictures." She smiled cat-like. "If you think you can keep him a secret you're crazy."

I pulled her away from the door, slamming it. I opened Cass' door and lifted him. As soon as I picked him up, he wrapped his arms around me. "I missed you, Mister Pole-ow-ski."

"I missed you, too." I looked between my shallowest concept of love and the strongest bond. I was willing to dig deep to keep the latter.

Vanessa continued to wait. "How badly do you want to keep his identity a secret?" she whispered.

"I don't have to hide the things I'm proud of."

As I drove away, I realized I was on the verge of a love affair with my own child. And like any sweet object of affection, he could make my heart sing with anticipation. I was giddy with the excitement of seeing him, of playing with him, of getting to know him a little bit better than the day before. Sometimes when I was with Cass, I felt my late brother Andy's presence. That was another blessing Cass had given my life.

"Mister Pole-ow-ski, that lady has snake eyes. Who is she?"

"Her name is Vanessa, and she used to be . . . a friend."

"Was she your girlfriend?"

"Yes, she was."

Snake eyes, skinny thighs. Small brain, bigger pain.

"You know, Cass, sometimes we give the wrong people too much slack, and the right people, we judge too harshly."

Cass thought for moments. "Judgment comes from experience, and sound judgment comes from bad experience."

I looked at him from the rearview mirror, shocked.

He hunched up his shoulders in an I-don't-know gesture. So through some scheduled lab tests and playing in the park, a six-year-old explained a philosophy that I was just starting to understand myself.

6 p.m.

We met Libby under the red and white neon sign for Italian Village. Cass spun through the revolving door twice before bounding up the white limestone stairs that my parents had been climbing for more than forty years.

Libby was too busy fidgeting with her clothes, buttoning and unbuttoning her suit jacket to notice the maître 'd's admiration as he took her coat.

I pushed her hands away from her waist and took it up myself. "You're beautiful." I draped her hair over her shoulder and kissed her. "I promise they won't eat you."

"They'll probably want to skin me, skewer me, and roast me first," she whispered looking over her shoulder. "They don't eat small children, do they?"

Cass was watching the miniature model of an illuminated Ferris wheel spinning in time with 'Moon in the Sky Like a Big Pizza Pie.' The long narrow interior reminded me of the crowded streets of Rome, but the room opened up like a Piazza with a bubbling fountain in the center of the uneven cobbles. An Italian countryside landscape roved along the wall. Our private booth had an overhanging tile roof, almost as if we were on a secluded veranda of an Italian Villa.

My parents sat on one side of the booth, the back of which ran to the ceiling, enclosing the small room so they couldn't stand.

They both smiled shaking first Libby's hand, then Cass'. My father smiled with his initial perusal of Libby, before he looked at me and nodded his approval.

I leaned across the table, kissing my mother, and then shook my father's hand. "Where's Avery?"

My mother frowned for a moment, drawing her gaze away from Libby. "Your brother decided to take the red eye." She nudged my father to supply an explanation, but he didn't.

My mother studied Cass. I knew she was mentally cataloging the similarities. He looked like me—and Andy. Her eyes misted over; my father gave her a gentle squeeze before pouring wine.

"Cass, I hear Aidan has become your nanny. What kind of a job is he doing?" Mr. Palowski quizzed.

"He's great, Mister—" Cass scrunched up his nose thinking, and then he pointed toward me. "I call him Mister Pole-ow-ski, what should I call you?"

"Call me Mr. Palowski two." He held up two digits.

Aidan's mother chimed in. "Sometimes I just call him old fart, but your mother might not want you to say fart."

Cass giggled. "Mr. Pole-ow-ski is real big on manners, and he might think that's disrespectful. What do you think, Mom?"

Libby almost had her wine glass to her lips and she set it down considering the options. "I think that you could call Aidan, Aidan and then you could call his father Mr. Palowski."

"I think I like Mr. Pole-ow-ski one and Mr. Pole-ow-ski two, kind of like Thing One and Thing Two," I chimed in.

The waiter greeted us in Italian before taking our order, and when he walked away the tiny arched recess grew quiet. My mother broke the silence. "Libby, Aidan said you take a lot of *pro bono* cases. He mentioned that you assisted the young woman seeking asylum at St. Ignatius Church. That's national news."

"I'm still working on the deportation side of it, but that wasn't a *pro bono* case. Aidan paid me to do it. He just hasn't received the bill yet."

My father looked to me, then back to Libby. "'So shine the

good deed in a weary world'." He smiled. "What about your regular practice? Do you enjoy that?" He asked.

"The court room is enjoyable, but the clients are hit or miss. I was hoping to make partner this year, but my boss might prevent that. I'd like to help people in real need instead of the privileged few who can afford our services." She met my father's eye. "No insult intended."

"None taken. What issues does your boss have? He should be ecstatic with the positive PR from such a high profile case."

"Right now he requires oral surgery, thanks to your son." She smiled cushioning the blow.

I ground my teeth together and clenched my hand into a fist. "He's lucky it was only two teeth," I said stiffly.

"You don't mean he's harassing you?" My mother's face was indigent. She lowered her voice to a whisper. "Physically harassing?" she asked appalled.

"Discrimination in all of its varying forms is alive and well in every law firm in this city."

My mother mulled over that for several moments. "I didn't think that kind of thing went on anymore."

Cass was busy coloring on the heavy white paper tablecloth. "Don't worry, Mrs. Pole-ow-ski. My mom can handle Rat Bastard. Aunt Vicki helps her and if that doesn't work..." He pointed toward me. "He'll intimi, intimi, what's that word again?" He turned to me.

"Intimidate."

"Yeah, he'll intimidate him," Cass chortled.

"I agree with the sentiment, if not the exact wording," my mother conceded, laughing along with Cass.

Libby and I exchanged a glance, communicating a need for discussion with Cass about appropriate sharing of confidences. I looked up to find my parents exchanging mirrored expressions.

I was saved from further parental examination by dinner. We talked about baseball, Cass' school, his friend Madi (he did recount the barf story and the fact that I'm now Band-Aid the Butt-Head) and his ongoing love affair with Lori the teacher's aide. My parents were captivated with him and content to question him throughout dinner. When the plates had been cleared, and I wiped most of the spaghetti off of Cass' face, my mother reached under the table. "I have something for you Cass."

"My birthday was awhile ago, Mrs. Pole-ow-ski." Cass tore the paper from the box. He pulled out a Sponge-Bob hospital gown, followed by a Scooby Doo one, both with matching drawstring pants.

"Aidan told me that you're going to be in the hospital for a while; these are made out of flannel, and I thought that you might like them more than the boring hospital patterned ones."

Cass smiled from ear to ear. "They're awesome."

Libby touched the soft fabric. "Where did you find them?"

"I made them myself. Look." My mother showed Cass where his initials were sewn in the collar.

Libby said, "That's so considerate."

"I hope you'll let us know what else we can do to help."

While my father and I grappled over the check, my mother whipped out her credit card and gave it to the waiter.

I thought my parents were going to stay at my house, but they informed us that they had taken a hotel room because they wanted to be closer to the hospital. Translation: they wanted to give us privacy.

As the valet was bringing Tank around, I asked if we could drop them off, but they insisted on taking a cab.

I had Cass in my arms, when I bent toward my mother so she could say goodbye. She pecked Cass' cheek, too.

"See Mr. Pole-ow-ski, moms are kissing machines! Even yours and you're all growed up. You were supposed to help me out of that, not get me more." He smiled his dimpled grin.

My mother's eyes were tear-rimmed. "We'll see you at the hospital tomorrow morning. I love you, son."

My father spun around toward us pocketing his cell phone. "Dammit, I'm going to kill that kid."

I was glad that I had already put Cass in the car. My father rarely lost his temper, but when he did it was a sight to behold.

"I need to go get Avery," he ground out.

"Is he at the airport?" my mother asked.

"No, lockup, courtesy of Chicago's finest."

I turned toward Libby. "You drop my mom at her hotel and then go home with Cass. I'll come home as soon as I can."

She looked confused for a minute then she shook her head. "What if you need a lawyer?"

"If whatever he's gotten himself into requires an attorney, he might be spending the night. I'll explain everything when I get home." I kissed her goodbye as I slipped into the cab my father had hailed.

24

APPEAL PLAY

The truth is always the strongest argument.
Sophocles

Libby

I startled awake as Aidan came into my room, tugging off his jacket and tie. "What happened with Avery?"

"He was picked up for solicitation."

"Solicitation of a prostitute?"

"Technically, an undercover police officer. He pulls this kind of crap just to get under my parents' skin."

"What did your dad do?"

"We bailed him out, but he has to come back for court in a couple of weeks." Aidan sat on the side of the bed.

"I can call in some favors."

"Thank you, but I think he needs to learn his lesson, and the only way he's going to do that is if he takes his punishment." He squeezed my hip in reassurance.

I watched his muscles flex, as he removed his clothes. I questioned my own resolve, but I flipped back the down comforter for him anyway.

Even in the dark I could count each ripple in his abdomen, when I should have been counting sheep. I tried to relax into my pillows, but he reached out for me in desperation.

"We were supposed to tell Cass," he said. "We'll never make it out of the hospital without him finding out, and I would rather he hear it from us."

We'd planned to tell him Aidan was his father after dinner. "I spoke to Winslow O'Leary," I said. "And he hinted he knows. He asked if I'd give him an interview, and I told him I wouldn't, but you would."

"That's fine." He pulled me closer still. "I've arranged the press conference, and I'll make sure Fletch gets O'Leary a front row seat. I had about twenty-five requests for interviews on e-mail, and Fletch said they were coming out of his ears."

"It was naïve to think this could happen quietly."

"I like it when you're naive," he said, as he brushed the hair away from my face. "Dr. Seuss said all the doctors agreed to talk about bone marrow donation."

He kissed my lips. "It's nice to crawl in bed with you."

I cuddled on his shoulder, when he lay on his back.

His hand sifted through my hair and found a chunk to run his fingers through. "I'm going to have to answer a lot of hard questions."

"You don't have to answer questions that are too personal."

"I screwed up. I wasn't accountable for my own actions." He drew in and expelled a breath. "I'm not going to sit in front of reporters like Mark McGuire did when they asked the hard questions about steroids, and take the fifth. People are a lot more willing to forgive you if you admit you were wrong."

"This isn't a congressional hearing, and you're not under oath. You can set the parameters of your own press conference."

He grazed my scalp at the nape of my neck with his fingertips. "I'm going to sit up there and take it like a man."

"Tell them you thought I gave the baby up for adoption; that's the truth. Athletes have done worse, half the NBA's in trouble with drugs, guns, gang-banging, and rape."

"I was the poster child for clean living."

"I'm sorry, I didn't think how much this might cost you."

"Babe, all I think about is what I've gained."

"You know Cass adores you." I kissed his bicep. "He's like you. The older he gets, the more I've seen it. Sometimes he can soften butter with his smile."

He pulled me closer, as if our skin might meld together. "Except his eyes are the colors of yours, and just as devious."

"Speaking of scheming, I'm not taking the child support money. You don't owe me anything, and when this is over, if you want to adopt Cass, he can decide. It's between the two of you."

"You say 'when this is over' as if once Cass is well, I'm going to disappear. I plan on being in this for the long haul."

I tensed. "Or until spring training."

"I signed a contract I need to fulfill."

"You always did have something to fulfill." I pulled away.

"Now we're getting somewhere." He held me still and let out a sigh. "And once you found out you were pregnant you didn't care to be in the same room as me. How's that for dismissal?"

I never once thought he would view my desperate struggle to succeed as a rejection. "I was trying to figure out how to put baby and law school into the same sphere. You were gung-ho for eliminating the problem."

"That's what hurt you the most, isn't it? You think I chose baseball over you?"

"Don't be ridiculous," I sputtered.

"Just because I came from a privileged background doesn't mean that I didn't learn the same lesson you learned: don't ever love anything you can't give up because if you do the world will surely snatch it away. Losing Andy taught me that.

"I was overwhelmed, and the only thing I had to fall back on was my ambition." The shutters filtered moonlight over his face, making his expression shadowed. "I didn't know how we'd make it work with a kid, when I was making you miserable. But baseball had always been there for me. It welcomed me, groomed me, and committed to me, as I had to it. I was a frightened kid, and I didn't know what to do, so I did what I'd been doing all along. I played my heart out."

"I was scared, too, I was sicker than a dog, and I had always been so careful not to make a mistake. Then I found myself in the worst trouble of my life. I thought having an abortion might be the only way out, but I couldn't do it."

"You were going to have an abortion?"

"I went there, but the minute I saw the building, I started throwing up. I couldn't even get out of the car. I heard the echoes of the doctor's words when he confirmed my pregnancy, and I just couldn't.

"What did he say?"

"'However you choose to deal with this will seal your relationship with its father.' And for me it was like the baby was the only thing that was mine, and I couldn't let it go, even for you." Tears ran down my cheeks, and he brushed them away. "I couldn't let that be the last thing between us."

He gathered me into the protection of his embrace. "I'm so happy you didn't. I love Cass."

I tried to wipe my slobbering on my hand, but Aidan tidied my face with his pillowcase before he spooned around me.

The next morning dawned late, and we overslept, having to then rush out of the house. We barely made it to the hospital in time.

"You know, not every guy could pull off the Sponge Bob gown and still look manly," I said, to pull Aidan's eyes away from the exam room clock he'd been watching since we arrived.

He pulled me across his lap. "That manly enough for you?"

He kept me in place with his fingertips on my bare skin, just above the waistband of my jeans, as he rubbed his whiskered jaw along the side of my face. His expression shifted, and became very serious. "After the procedure, you bring Cass to me first thing. If anything happens to me, you tell him the truth."

The doctor entered and cleared his throat.

I moved out of Aidan's lap.

"The process takes about an hour," the doctor said. "When you wake up you might have pain, nausea, vomiting, and sore throat, but we'll give you something for pain management. You might require an autologous transfusion of packed red blood cells from the units of blood we collected last week.

"I'll be using a large-bore needle to aspirate the marrow from the posterior iliac crest, placing it in syringes. The typical collection involves removing about 1.5 liters through two skin incisions. The exact volume has been calculated based on your weight and nucleated cell count. The harvested marrow will then be processed to remove the blood, fat, and bone fragments. It will be put in cryopreservation and frozen to keep the cells alive until Cass' transplantation team is ready.

"The risks involved with this procedure are associated with anesthesia, infection, mechanical injury, and transfusion. We've already discussed your arm."

I held up my hands calling for a time out. "What?"

The doctor looked at Aidan with a raised brow and Aidan met my glare. "This might slow down the healing of my arm."

The doctor cleared his throat. "Palowski, you might never pitch another inning. I can't believe you didn't tell her."

Aidan grumbled, "It wouldn't have changed anything."

I bit into my lip to keep from tearing him apart.

The doctor eyed the door and then me. If I were him, I'd want to escape the tension that filled room, too. But he continued: "Once released you'll need about two weeks to recover. No workouts." He raised his eyebrow, evaluating me. I didn't get what he meant until Aidan chuckled.

I gave Aidan a lethal dose of the evil eye.

"The most important thing is a quiet place to recuperate."

"Yes, we're going away for a few days."

The doctor stood, looking between us. "Good. I'll send in the nurse and I'll be out to talk to you, Ms. Tucker, when the procedure is done. I've also made time for the press conference. I believe Dr. Seuss will be joining us, as well as members of the transplantation team."

The door hadn't even closed in his wake, when I turned on him. "You did not tell me how much this might cost you."

"I'd give up more than baseball to save him."

Aidan looked so hard at me that I wanted to back away.

"Or to have you."

Before I could protest, a heavyset, older woman came in with a scowl on her face. "I'm your nurse. My name is Kratchette." She was the polar opposite of the bodacious blond nurse in the tight dress; she was short, stout and stubbed nosed. "I'll be taking you to the O.R."

I stared until they disappeared down the long corridor, before I headed back to the empty waiting room with my stomach in knots. Every time I thought I had a handle on things, another bomb went off. Aidan might never pitch again. How was I going to live with that on my conscience? I took in the stale, beige walls and scratchy, burgundy chairs and decided I couldn't sit. I paced along a worn trail in the navy carpeting. The television was blaring one of the morning news shows, when I heard a grunt and turned to see a younger, blonder version of Aidan.

A cocky grin plastered his face. "Whoa, this waiting room just added another pleasurable dimension." He looked me up and down, spending a lot of time on the V of my blouse.

I crossed my arms and gave him my best haughty lawyer look.

"Better yet, she's got a temper. You get that fired up where I want you, and we might combust." He ruffled through his hair and gave me another Palowski grin, dimple and all.

"Does that line ever work for you?" I sneered.

His legs sprawled outstretched in front of him. He wasn't quite as tall as his brother, but even at twenty, he had the same ability to command a room. "I'll let you know later." He winked, taking in my body from his new vantage point.

I gripped my arms so I wouldn't flip him off and continued pacing.

"You got a name, babe?"

I glared at his use of the endearment that I had allowed only one man to use. "Of course I have a name. It's Bimbo."

"What more could a guy ask for?"

"I don't know." *Perhaps a brain that wasn't located in the lower extremities?* "You might prefer a gnarly wave, dude?"

"You know what? I like 'em feisty. Is your husband in here?"

"A friend," I ground out.

He smiled through sparkling teeth that reflected his devil-may-care attitude. "My brother's getting his bone marrow sucked out to give to his little bastard that he's ignored for the past six years. The virtuous white knight riding in to save the day, and all that crap."

I swallowed down my angst. "It's miraculous that you come from the same gene pool."

That's when the first flicker of realization crossed his face. "What did you say your name is?"

"I'm Libby Tucker, the little bastard's mother."

"I can see it wasn't a hardship on him to knock you up."

I took up one of the scratchy chairs. "I can see why he speaks so little of you. My six-year-old has better manners."

"Yeah, but I bet he's not nearly as cute as me."

"Once you open your mouth, the California-surfer-stud looks don't mean a thing." I picked up a magazine.

"So you were enough to bring him down."

I put my glasses back on so I could see his face. "Pardon?"

"His Lordship was perfect until this little incident. You must have been some great fu—"

I whipped the magazine at him and the hard edge hit him in the lip. He made to get out of his chair, but before he could move Mr. Palowski's leathery denouncement cracked the air as if on the end of a whip, "Avery!

"Let's go for a walk." It wasn't a suggestion. "Libby, we'll be back in a few minutes, and my son will have an apology and a new attitude."

I nodded, and Mrs. Palowski took the seat alongside me, offering me a coffee. "Where's Cass?" I asked.

"Lori's a candy striper here, and she's giving him a tour."

"He could be conducting the tours."

"Yes, but Lori doesn't know that." She winked at me. "He's going to be quite the charmer, that one."

"That's what I'm afraid of." We laughed.

She became serious. "You'll have to forgive him."

"Avery, you mean?"

"Yes, him, too, he's cast Aidan as the hero and himself in the role of the villainous son." She hesitated. "But I was talking about forgiving Aidan for not being there for you."

"I'm not sure..."

"You don't have to be sure. All you need is hope. Most of what he did was because of us, not because of you. He cares for you. His face lights up when he looks at you. And Cass makes him happy in ways nothing else ever has."

"Regardless of why . . . "

"He wronged you and Cass, but he's always thought he had to be perfect and the best at everything." She looked around the room, ensuring we were alone. "I want to tell you what I know about forgiveness. This will give you insights about Avery, too. We had an older son, Andy; he died in a horrific accident."

"Aidan told me."

"Yes, well, let me tell you the parts of the story that Aidan can only guess at.

"Michael and I separated after Andy died, two years later Michael told me his mistress was going to have a child." She took a drink of her coffee as if fortifying herself. "I thought he was asking me for a divorce. But he wanted to bring the child home for us to raise together. His mistress was a career woman, with no intentions of being a mother. You can imagine how incensed I was."

I swallowed down my own reaction. "What did you do?"

"After I decided not to hire a hit man, I came to the conclusion that life was offering me an opportunity. A chance to have another child made my heart sing. I would get the only man I ever loved back, and my family put back together. I took a chance, and I fell in love with Avery the moment I laid eyes on him. Through that love, I learned to forgive. To forgive God for taking Andy, forgive my husband for turning away from me when I needed him the most, and to forgive myself for gnawing on the wound I should have sewn shut at Andy's death.

"But I had more lessons to learn. I struggled with Avery. Even in infancy, I thought he sensed he wasn't my biological child and so I compensated for his outbursts with coddling instead of the discipline that was so easy for me with my other sons.

"He's always known he's not my biological child. We never lied to him, but liberally to ourselves about his outbursts. That's over now, and he's not happy about it. He contacted his biological mother, she refuses to see him, and of course that's our fault, too. He's in a bad place right now, but deep down, he has a good heart, and he'll come out of it.

"I know the time you and Aidan have together could be limited by Cass' recovery and that once he's better, you might think you don't need Aidan anymore, and maybe you don't. You've done a wonderful job with Cass on your own. But Aidan needs you. He needs you and Cass.

"I can give him almost anything in the world, but I can't give him your love. But don't think you can't give it because you can't forgive him. If you do, he'll use the rest of his life to show you he was worthy of your forgiveness."

I played with a worn spot on my jeans. "How do you figure?"

"Because Aidan is the most like his father, and Michael has done nothing but make me thankful every day that I forgave him. He made the worst mistake, in the worst way possible, but he knew he had to fix it. He doesn't know how he fixed it and neither do I, but I see the gratitude on his face, and I know that loving and forgiving is one in the same. I also had to take responsibility for the part I played in the whole ordeal."

I was used to hearing strangers' revelations, but not those in my immediate world. Although I understood about making mistakes, the larger the mistake and the longer it festers, the harder it was to make amends. I had seen it in the courtroom, in the DA's office, and in my own life. I had seen how just a few simple words, eight simple letters, could change a person's entire perception. Sometimes those simple words—for some, a cliché—were harder to hear than an apology. When one refused to hear the 'I love you', the 'I see you' for so long, he became an accessory to the mistake.

I was trying to wrap my thoughts around Mrs. Palowski's advice, when the doctor appeared. "Ms. Tucker, everything went as expected, and I don't foresee any complications."

"Go." Mrs. Palowski patted my hand. "You can heal him in ways I can't, and I couldn't have picked a person I trust more."

I hesitated before leaving. "How do you know you can trust me, though?" I felt blindsided, but my lawyer's mind worked.

"Cass, of course." She smiled brightly. "I just have to look at him, and I know what a loving person my son chose."

"I'll think about what you said." I slipped away, following the green hallway that led me to the recovery area, where Aidan was in a draped off area. He was still hooked up to an IV and several machines registered his vital signs.

I was counting his breaths. I had never seen him so still.

"He's just fine," Nurse Kratchette said.

"Thank you." I pulled a chair up to his bedside. I took his long fingers, twining them together with mine, careful not to disrupt his IV. I brought his good hand to my mouth and breathed in the scent of him before resting my head on the edge of the bed. My thoughts assaulted me. What did I want today? What had I wanted the first time he crossed my path? Where was all this going, and how much was it going to hurt, when it was done? Kat's words came to me, unbidden. *Take responsibility for the part I played in the whole ordeal.*

The next thing I knew, Aidan was tunneling his fingers through my hair. I smiled. "How are you feeling?"

When he cleared his throat his voice was scratchy. "Like a CTA bus, a garbage truck, and a street cleaner drove over my torso, then backed up and ran over my head." He paused, looking frantic for the first time. "Did I mention I have to hurl?"

I got a pan to him just in time. When he was done, I handed him some water, which he swished around in his mouth before spitting it back out. "In sickness and health, right?"

I tried to smile.

"Come here." He pulled me toward him, scooting over. I lay alongside him, trying my best not to hurt him.

"After we talk to Cass, I want him to leave with my parents." He swallowed down hard a few times. "I don't want him in the hospital with all the media. You don't need to stay, either. It could get ugly."

"Someone needs to take you home. I'll keep a low profile."

"Babe, I think it would be better if I do this on my own. Avery can stay with me. He loves the limelight."

"Of course he does." I squeezed up my face in disgust.

"Please tell me he didn't do anything else."

"Your brother is rude. He called Cass your little bastard." I saw the scowl grow on his face and he bunched up his fists.

"It doesn't matter." I brushed his hands. "Your father showed up and took him for a little talk. What he said has more to do with how he feels about himself than Cass."

Aidan looked perplexed. "How he feels about himself?"

"Your mother told me he's not her biological child."

"He's always known that."

The title bastard put too much blame on the kid, and not enough on the offending parties. I knew this first hand. I felt the brush and sting of it, even as I got older. "He has to think his real mother doesn't love him."

Aidan closed his eyes. "It doesn't matter which parent leaves you, you always think it means they don't love you."

I didn't know if he was referring to his own father, so I asked, "That's what you're worried about with Cass? That he won't think you loved him? That he won't forgive you?"

"I'm holding out hope."

"He will. He's kind that way, and I'll tell him that it wasn't entirely your fault."

"No, Libby, I'm taking all the blame here. I don't want him to consider being angry with you. He needs your comfort. He can take his anger out on me."

Nurse Kratchette reappeared to move Aidan to his room. I followed, my own stomach flipping in anticipation of the coming conversation. One I thought never to have. The wide corridor opened onto the nurse's station, the occupants stared as if a rock star had dropped into their midst. I made my way to the window in his room and stared out over the lake, as the nurse checked Aidan's vitals. She patted his shoulder and told him to try to relax.

I went to the foot of his bed, where I was his sole focus. "Are you sure you're up for all this? You probably don't need all this emotional upheaval, when you're recovering."

"Libby, we can't procrastinate any longer. We've taken as much time as we can to get used to the idea."

Before I could respond, the door opened. "See," Nurse Kratchette said, "I told you your dad was just fine." She patted Cass' head, while he looked from Aidan to me. My son didn't seem shocked by the disclosure. He ambled toward Aidan's bed. "How you feeling, Mister Pole-ow-ski?"

The nurse had solved how to open up the conversation as easily as shoving a cotton ball up a bloody nose.

"I'm doing good, son."

Cass looked at Aidan. "I really am your son?"

Aidan squeezed Cass' shoulder and smiled. "I couldn't have picked a better boy."

Cass' lips had thinned and lost a bit of their color. "Mommy, why did you tell me my dad was dead?"

"I didn't want to explain what happened between your dad and I. And, I never thought we'd see each other again." I fidgeted with the bedclothes, before kneeling at his feet, "I didn't want you to blame yourself because your father wasn't around. I wanted you to feel good about yourself."

"I was an accident, and you didn't want me?" Cass gazed down at his Nike's, before he asked Aidan directly.

"Cass, I didn't know what I wanted then, but I know now. I want to be your father, and I want for us to be happy, together, all of us. You're the happiest accident of my life."

My tears flowed. "I never meant to rob you of each other."

Cass' tiny fingertips brushed away my tears before he looked at Aidan. "I'm not sorry that you're my dad, 'cause I get a funny feeling in my stomach when I'm with you. I feel like I belong to you. I think I knew from when I woke up and found you on my couch 'cause we look alike, and my mom never let a man sleep at our house. So you can be my dad, but I have to know one thing." He hesitated. "Do you love my mommy?"

Aidan's pride seeped through him, filling the room with its strong energy. "I love you, Cass, and you never have to worry about that." Aidan swallowed down and glanced my way. "I've loved your mother from the first moment I laid eyes on her." He looked toward the window to pull himself together; it couldn't have been easy for him to lay open his soul. He looked me in the eye then. "I love you, Libby Tucker, and I'm afraid I always will. You're the only thing that's ever scared me, and the only thing I thought I couldn't live without, until Cass. I hope you won't make me live without you or your love."

Aidan reached out for my hand, but I waved him off. "Let me catch my breath." I stumbled to my feet, as Aidan reassured a worried Cass that I needed a few moments to myself.

In the doorway, I looked back at them together. Cass had placed his small hand inside Aidan's, and this act assured me, not of his forgiveness, but perhaps of his understanding.

Out in the hallway, I literally ran into Suzy coming out of the bathroom. "You're going to worry Cass. And Aidan."

"I feel like I'm on an emotional roller coaster."

"Of course you are." Suzy clucked like a mother hen pulling me back into a family waiting room. "Aidan told Max that your father showed up on the donor registry."

"It's funny, I hardly ever imagine anymore what my life would have been like, and if I'd had a father who'd loved me."

She smiled. "I guess that's because you've grown up, and now you have the one man who was supposed to love you all along."

"No, it's because of Max," I said to change the subject.

"I don't know how a man could live in a world and not know where his child is. It takes a lot of character to admit you're wrong, but even more to try to set it right again. Especially when you loved the person you left."

"Is that what he told you and Max, that he left me because he loved me?"

"No, he told us he left because he was afraid that you'd never forgive him for getting you pregnant. But most of all he was afraid that you didn't love him." She sighed. "Neither of you realized your feelings until it was too late, but you need to stop making Aidan pay for the sins of your father."

"What would you know about her father?" Jeanne stepped out of the shadows. "You think you and Max are her parents, but I'm here to remind you that she has a mother, and you're not her."

"Well, Jeanne, I think Libby's old enough to know whose parenting she wants." Suzy examined Jeanne. "Me versus Bozo."

"You better watch it, Suzy." Jeanne put her hand on her hip.

"What are you going to do? Blow fairy dust up my derriere and hope I magically disappear?" Suzy didn't wait for a response before she huffed, pulling the lounge door open. "Squirt me with one of your water guns?"

The whole thing wouldn't have been comical if my mother wasn't wearing a bright orange, braided wig and a purple top hat.

"The lobby is full of reporters," Jeanne sulked at me. "Do you want them to get a shot of you with those raccoon eyes?"

"It'd be a better headline, if they took a shot of you." I had to giggle, as she stormed through the door and stalked off in the opposite direction of Suzy. I walked around the corner to Aidan's room. Avery had just pushed through the door, followed by David.

Aidan had Avery by his collar and was restricting his Adam's apple. "Avery Palowski, I'm going to give you exactly what you deserve."

"What the hell is in your crawl, big brother?"

"What's 'in my crawl' is your smart-ass, punk mouth. If you ever call my son a name again, I'll ruin that pretty boy smile with one shot to the face."

David shot Avery a sideways glance as he tried to disentangle Aidan's death grip.

Avery spoke sincerely. "I already had this conversation with Dad." He looked back at me. "Libby, you have my apologies."

"Don't play innocent with me, Avery. That only works on Mom, and she doesn't fall for it too often anymore. If you ever speak to Libby the way you did earlier, I'll sand that California tan right off your face with a baseball glove."

"I apologized. How was I supposed to know who she was? It's not like any of us knew she existed before a few weeks ago."

"Don't you have enough problems? You love stirring the stink." Aidan pointed at him when he released his shirtfront. "Don't you even consider speaking!"

When his parents came into the room, his sulking brother sank into a chair in the corner, reading the sports page.

Vicki came in, waving a peace sign and gave my face a once over before introducing Rick, who just happened to be the biggest Cubs fan in Chi Town. Rick stood alongside Aidan, talking sports and dissipating some of the tension in the room. Rick was still in his blue Fed Ex uniform, anxiously watching Vicki. He didn't like having her out of his sight. She stood next to him, and he patted her belly. I thought the baby might be Rick's proudest delivery.

I approached Cass and he hugged me around my middle. Before we could speak, the door opened. Ollie came into the room with Suzy right behind her. Ollie's T-shirt read, 'Support 2nd Base', but the u in support was a pink breast cancer symbol.

Aidan winked at Ollie. "Nice shirt."

"Shut up, Old Guy." Ollie noticed Avery sprawled out in the corner, and abruptly went to stand alongside her mother as Aidan made the introductions between the Rodgers and the Palowski families.

Avery ignored the introductions until he caught a glimpse of Olivia. Then he seemed torn between the sports and staring. Olivia, knowing what she was about, completely ignored him, or made him believe she did, but I caught her giving him the once over out of the corner of her eye.

Fletch and Tricia arrived as Rick was taking Vicki to the cafeteria. Tricia was beaming and Fletch's usual stern face seemed bemused. "If you get that big, Wife, how are we supposed to do what we did this morning?"

The room's audience suppressed their reaction until Aidan said, "If there's a will, there's a way."

Then everyone erupted in laughter. Kat placed her hands over Cass' ears and bright red spots danced on the crest of her cheeks. "I think it's time for us to leave, Cass. Old Fart will teach you how to fish up at the retreat."

"Okay, Mrs. Pole-ow-ski. I mean Grandma Pole-ow-ski."

"How about Grandma Kat?"

"Okay, I like that, Grandma Kat." Cass meandered toward Aidan and leaned in close. "When you and mommy come home, can we all have a big family dinner with Uncle Avery and everybody?"

"That's a great idea, son. But I want you to promise me one thing. No TV."

"No TV got it." He threw his arms around Aidan's neck before he assured me that he would be a good boy. Aidan's parents said their farewells and invited Avery to go with them, but once he had set his sights on Olivia, he wasn't about to leave. Instead, he stood graciously, and asked her if she'd like to walk with him to Starbucks around the corner.

Nurse Kratchette sailed into the room. "Once we get the results of your blood count, we'll get you released."

Mr. O'Leary rushed through the door, his face buried in his Crackberry. He and Nurse Kratchette had a haughty standoff in the doorway. "You're not allowed in a patient's room," she said.

Mr. O'Leary rolled his eyes. "I just came to see if we could begin on time."

"If I don't discharge him, will you send that pack of wolves on their way?" The nurse growled.

"He requested the press conference, Nurse Crusty."

"Obviously, he doesn't know what's good for him because security said there's hundreds of story-hounds downstairs, sniffing around for blood." She charged out of the room.

I cleared my throat. "How many reporters showed up?"

"Last count, about two hundred, but that includes cameramen, sound, and lighting," O'Leary replied.

"What could go wrong in a room full of reporters?" Aidan said a little too cheerfully.

I looked at him over the rim of my glasses. "Disaster, that's what!"

25

UP IN THE PRESS BOX

The press, like fire, is an excellent servant, but a terrible master. James Fenimore Cooper

Aidan
(I'm a little loopy—but there's no time like the present)

Flashes of piercing light and snapping shutters greeted me, as I followed the tail of Dr. Seuss' white lab coat to the raised platform. It was time for me to man up. Fletch was already seated, and as I passed him, he gave me a grin just cocky enough to rile me.

The bullpen, the mound, the locker room, stadiums filled to capacity . . . I was at ease in any one of them, but the energy that filled all the empty spaces around me was a foreign experience. I had never before felt as if the reporters wanted to slice sections of my skin off for dissection. My head was a spinning whirlpool, and my mind was being sucked into its core.

Reporters called out 'Palowski', 'Band-Aid', and 'Aidan', trying to get me to look at their cameras. This was the first press conference where I had my own cheering section, and I wasn't sure if I felt better or worse that those closest to me would witness this from the front row. I preferred locker-room interviews. At least then, I had the barracudas on my turf, even if I was half naked in their midst.

The front row of the audience became crystal clear, all of my bedside visitors, with the exception of my parents and Cass, were here to shore me up. Thank God, Jeanne the clown hadn't entered this three-ring circus. Libby sat at the far end of the row, sandwiched between Tricia and Vicki. So much for her keeping a low profile, but once she knew that everyone else was going to be here, she refused anything other than a box seat.

She smiled with a hesitant glance. Fletch began with introductions, each of the physicians acknowledged the assembly as his name and title was announced. The collar of my new shirt was as stiff as a board, and every time I moved, it rubbed a raw spot along my neck. I was happy I'd look respectable, when my face was smeared across every media outlet in the country.

I had lost track of Fletch's prepared remarks, but I heard him introduce me. "Mr. Palowski has a brief statement and then he will answer a few questions. Go easy on him, folks. He just had a major medical procedure." Fletch glared at the audience.

I cleared my throat, adjusted my microphone, and glanced at Libby. "Some of you may already know that I came to the hospital this morning to donate bone marrow. It was an allogeneic harvest, meaning that I share the same genetic type as the child I donated for. I was a haploid-identical match, which can only come from a parent, and only if the genetic match is at least half identical to the recipient." A buzz rose from the front of the room crashing toward the back wall. I fumbled for air. "The recipient of my bone marrow will be my six-year-old son, Cass."

A twitter rose, and I'd swear wireless connections fizzled through the air of the conference room.

"There are two things I want to briefly speak about, and then I'll answer questions. If they're technical questions, one of the docs will answer them." Shutters continuously fired and the reporters leaned in toward the dais. "The National Marrow Donor Program is a nonprofit organization with the largest volunteer donor's list in the United States. The registry is located in St. Paul, Minnesota, and has more than six-point-three million donors registered, and has helped to coordinate more than twenty-five thousand transplants since its founding in nineteen-eighty-six. You might think that with millions of donors more aren't needed, but you would be wrong. Only about thirty percent of patients with treatable diseases are able to find donors from family members, the remaining seventy percent would have to find a random donor. The chances of two individuals being HLA matched exceed one in twenty thousand. If I had those kinds of odds in my game, I'd be out of a job. I hope you will all visit the National Marrow Donor Program at www.marrow.org and remember that the cost of a bone marrow transplant is about a quarter of a million dollars. In light of recent events, I am setting up a charity called Cass' Game, named for my son, and I will personally sponsor one bone marrow transplant a year for the remainder of my life. After that, I hope Cass will continue this charitable endeavor.

"I've learned more than any parent wants to know about Leukemia in the past two weeks." Before I could finish my thought a flustered looking reporter jumped up and vaulted into a question. "Did you abandon your child?"

"I just recently met my son, but I knew when I went to the minors that a young woman was pregnant with my child."

Once again cameras blinded me.

"Why hadn't you looked for your child?"

"My sole focus was on the sport, and I was so determined to succeed that I lost track of what was important in life."

I swallowed down hard, closing my eyes, willing my vision to clear. Each question felt like a stain on my once-impeccable public image. "I received termination of parental rights papers, and I signed them, wishing to put the whole matter behind me. It is the only thing I've done in my adult life that I truly regret. I'm ashamed of my neglect in this matter."

"So you ended your relationship with Vanessa Vanderhoff so you could have more time with your child?"

"That, and he is more fun to talk to."

The crowd chuckled, dissipating some of the tension.

"There's a rumor circulating that you had arm surgery at the end of the season?"

"There are all sorts of gossip around right now, some are true and some aren't."

The reporter waited for me to say more. He lost his opportunity at rebuttal when another reporter stood.

"Recently a wrongful death suit was filed against you. Did you have anything to do with the death of Sam Landscale?"

Fletch jumped up and seethed. "This press conference is about Aidan's foundation. A man who would go to such lengths to save his son would not intentionally or otherwise hurt anyone."

"Mr. Palowski wasn't involved with Mr. Landscale's death?"

I gave Fletch the calm down look before I answered. "The only thing I had to do with Mr. Landscale's death is that I was on the same mountain, on the same day, in the same blizzard. His death was tragic, but there were six men on that climb, and I was the only one to come out of it alive. I've wondered why, and now I know I was spared because a six-year old kid needed me more than the mountain did." The reporters seemed to lurch backward, as I looked up and made eye contact with as many reporters as I could. "I'll take the next question from Winslow O'Leary. Thanks again for setting this up."

"Mr. Palowski, we can assume your son has Leukemia?"

"Yes, he does. I am not going to talk about the specifics of his case, but you can ask the doctors questions about Leukemia in general, and there is also information in the media packets that will be distributed as you leave today." I thanked my lucky stars for O'Leary, with that one question he seemed to distract the vultures for a time, and I could compose myself. Fletch regained his seat, but he exchanged a look with Libby.

I answered a few questions from several local sports writers about next season. I thought the questions were winding down, when a journalist stood and stated his name. "Albert Rothstein, from the Globe." The Globe, as everyone knows, is a New York tabloid; the room became hushed. Up until this point, all the reporters seemed to expose their claws, but not sink them in. I had a sneaking suspicion this guy could hit a hundred-mile fastball no matter how athletically challenged he looked. I could feel it as clearly as the seams on a ball.

"Mr. Palowski, I don't mean to sound cruel when your son is ill, but it has come to my newspaper's attention that this whole press conference is a cover. Isn't it true that you've been involved with another man for years?"

The other journalists took affront to the New York jerk, who'd come to Chicago to accuse a hometown hero. He obviously did not understand Midwestern sentimentalities, when he continued to speak. "Your ex-fiancée has stepped forward to say she was a diversionary tactic to perpetuate the belief that you are heterosexual, when in fact, you have been in love with a man for most of your adult life. Your response?"

Before I could respond Fletch was on his feet, his voice direct and firm. "Mr. Rothstein, that is a fabrication, and if anyone prints anything of that sort about my client, I will have no other recourse than to sue for libel." A red flush went up Fletch's neck. I was certain that if his eyeballs didn't pop out of their sockets, flames from his furiously flared nostrils would singe the entire first three rows.

I became still. "Mr. Rothstein, as sensational as you think this revelation is, I am not now, nor have I ever been involved in a sexual relationship with a man. I have no problem with homosexuality, but I'm heterosexual."

"So any photos showing you in a compromising situation—"

"If you have any pictures that question my sexuality, I would like to have them carefully examined: for fraud. As for your source, I can only say that Ms. Vanderhoff did not take it well when I ended my relationship with her. So if you received photos from her, seriously consider the source."

"The Globe does have possession of such snapshots, and our experts have determined they don't appear to be doctored."

"I will reiterate, Mr. Rothstein, I have never had a sexual relationship with a man." I looked around the room shooting them a confident smile. "But if you continue in this vein, I'll have no other choice than to assume you're hitting on me."

Mr. Rothstein pulled his eyes away from his iPad quicker than I could say Microsoft. The rest of the reporters started to chuckle before out-and-out laughter took hold of the room. Even Dr. Seuss and Libby were trying to contain smirks.

"If you want to work a legitimate salacious story, why don't you look into Ms. Vanderhoff's free prescription drug discount cards?" A murmur swept through the gathering, and cameras started flashing again, creating a buzz as insidious as flies on horse manure. "I have nothing else to say on the subject of my personal life, and any claims Ms. Vanderhoff has produced should be vetted before publication. As a serious journalist, I'm sure you consider the source. She has been...set aside."

"Didn't you set aside your own child for your career? There seems to be a lot of setting aside from you."

"In an effort to set the record straight, I'll give you insight into my personal life. More than anyone is entitled to know. My son is a wonderful kid, and that's because he has an outstanding mother. I am going to do everything in my power to make amends to both of them. I have every intention of standing alongside them through this difficult time. I hope they can both learn to depend on me the way they have depended on each other for so long; I hope they will let me care for them with the love and kindness they both deserve. I know you want to know all the details of this story, and I'll share what I feel is necessary, but I would ask that you respect my son and his mother and their private lives. It is one matter to chase down athletes for a story, and it's totally another to go after our families. Please remember when you cover this story that I'd set aside anything to protect them."

I looked at Fletch who seemed to be happy with my response, when he called on Winslow O'Leary again.

"Mr. Palowski, when you said families . . . are you planning to make Ms. Tucker your wife in the near future?"

I heard the question but it seemed that the focus of the room had shifted toward Libby. Even though she was seated facing away from the cameras they were snapping photos' of her trying to capture her reaction. Her years of courtroom dramas had schooled her well. She gave no visible reaction.

"If, and when, Ms. Tucker and I decide to marry, we'll be happy to give you the exclusive."

5:00 p.m.

Libby startled awake when we pulled up the gravel drive. "Please tell me this is the lodge down the road from your cabin."

I bent over her to look up. "Nope."

"A cabin is a little three or four room thing."

"It has only three or four bedrooms. And look, it's made out of logs."

Cass came barreling down the covered front porch. David didn't have a chance to open the door before Libby exited the car to greet Cass with a sweet kiss. I wound my arms around both of them. Cass tugged on my arm and Libby looked at him. "Cass, he can't pick you up for a couple of weeks, and you're getting too big to be carried around, anyway."

He sulked, and I frowned at her. I wanted him to be a kid as long as he could, and I would carry him as long as I could.

Before I could say anything, David picked up Cass, put him on his shoulders, and was bounding up the stairs.

We found my mother in the kitchen preparing food. "Mom, I told you to pick up food, you didn't have to do all this."

My father stuck his head in from the back, screened-in porch. "You know your mother. She loves to fuss around in the kitchen." He came in with a platter of barbeque chicken, which he set down on the island.

Avery put the luggage down before he grabbed a chicken leg and put it in his mouth. My mother raised a brow, placed the tray in his hands and pointed toward the dining room. We spent the next three hours being interviewed by Cass. He had a lot of questions; I think he was trying to figure out how he was going to fit in with his newly ascribed family.

David volunteered that he and Avery would clean up, if my mom supervised. I went to the back porch with my dad and had a private pow-wow, while Libby took Cass for a walk on the pier down at the lake. I watched Cass climb into Libby's lap and snuggle up to her in the twilight. When they came back, my mother removed her apron and my dad handed her a jacket, which she slipped into. "Avery, we need to be going." She motioned both David and Avery toward the front door.

"What are you talking about? I just got here."

"We already told Cass, so he won't fuss." My mother kissed first me, then Libby. "We'll see you on Monday."

"I stocked the fridge for you," my father said.

"I'll walk you out," I said as they reached the screen.

"No need, son, you had a tough day. I know you'll take excellent care of him." My father kissed Libby on her forehead.

Cass ran out on the porch waving his goodbyes.

Libby regarded me with an expression of exasperation. "We're out in the middle of nowhere with no vehicle."

"I know. Isn't it great? You have nowhere to run."

Cass giggled. "Mom, Tank is parked behind the cabin."

She stuck out her tongue at me.

"Promise?" I said to irritate her.

My hip was starting to throb, and it was getting late. We needed a good night's sleep. I turned to Cass. "Let's go up. I'll take a shower, while you take a bath."

"At the same time?" Cass asked perplexed.

"Sure, guys shower in the same rooms all the time. We can have man-time. I'll teach you how to shave."

He smiled with enthusiasm. "I don't have no whiskers yet."

"We'll pretend." He turned in the direction of the stairs. "Go watch TV in the family room and relax," I said to Libby.

I let hot water cascade down my body until there was none left, steeling myself until the pain in my hip finally eased.

Cass was still hesitant about his nudity so I helped him into his boxers, before he climbed on a step stool. I sprayed shaving foam into his hand and gave him a plastic shoehorn to use as his razor. He patted the foam onto his face, mimicking me.

"How come you never came to look for me?"

It was like a sucker punch right to the heart. I leaned onto the counter for support. He didn't look hurt, but curious. I should have expected it: he was inquisitive by nature, and he never hesitated to ask about whatever concerned him.

"I messed up, when I found out your mom was going to have a baby. Instead of being happy, I was mad at her."

"You didn't want to have a son?" Again he looked confused.

I wiped off the rest of my lather. "Let's go sit down and have a man-to-man."

"You mean a man-to-boy," he giggled.

I tousled his hair and led him into my bedroom, where his PJ's were laid out. I helped him into them, before we climbed in the bed. "I want to tell you a story."

"Okay. Is it about baseball?"

"In a way, yes. I had an older brother."

"Older than your brother Avery?"

"Even older than me. His name was Andy. Andy was the best big brother in the world, but he died when I was nine years old."

"That's sad. Did he die of Leukemia?"

"No, Cass, he died in a sports car; his car slid off a bridge." I sifted through the catastrophe looking for the pieces that could help explain my deepest thoughts to my son. It was like I was a victim of an eruption, frozen in that single moment, when the burning ash and heat of my brother's death rendered all my petrified memories silent. And like an innocent victim, my baked remains would crumble into ash if prodded to deeply. Libby was the only person I had ever spoken to of Andy, but I shared the memories with Cass as best I could.

When I was done, he was quiet for long minutes before he spoke. "Sometimes life throws you curve balls."

"That's for sure. When I found out your mom was going to have my baby, I was afraid. I was young, and the only thing that's ever scared me in my life was your mother."

"My mommy is not scary, Mr. Pole-ow-ski, she never gets mad at me, even when I do naughty things."

"I know, Cass, but sometimes when big people care about each other they get frightened because they aren't sure."

"You were afraid that mommy wouldn't love you?"

"Yes, and I was scared that if I loved her, I might not be able to have her and baseball. I was afraid of being responsible for another person. I thought I couldn't have a baby, and a baseball career, I was worried my parents would be disappointed. People should be married before they have babies, Cass, they should be committed to each other before they have families."

"I still don't know why you never came to look for me, though. Didn't you wonder who I was? I wondered about you a lot and I thought you were dead."

"I wondered about you, but when you do something wrong, and you hurt other people, every day you let pass is another strike against you. I thought you had a family, and they might not want me to come around. I thought you'd be better off with them than with me. I thought you'd hate me for not being there for you."

Cass rested his head against the back of his pillow, looking up at me. "You big people make everything so hard. I love Lori, how come it doesn't make me scared?"

"Because you never loved anyone you lost."

"But, Mister Pole-ow-ski, I lost you."

"But now we found each other, and when you grow up you'll fall in love with a girl like Madi Dubrowski, and you won't be afraid because you'll know all about love."

"Cause you'll show me?" he questioned.

"No, because your mommy already has."

A wistful smile took his face, before he spoke, "I'm not going to grow up."

His tone picked at my soul. "Of course you are."

"No, Mister Pole-ow-ski, I'm going to be a kid forever."

"Cass, you're going to grow up. Are you afraid of that?"

"No, I'm not even afraid of dying."

I pulled him close to me hugging him. "Cass, don't say that. You can't think like that."

"I don't think it, I know it. I haven't told mommy because she is afraid for me, but you're not scared of anything anymore, so I can tell you."

I looked down into his solemn face and his eyes reflected his old soul. "I won't let you die. I promise."

Cass had his eyes closed, when he patted my hand. "It will be okay, Mister Pole-ow-ski, it will be okay."

I pulled him closer and breathed in the scent of him and prayed that he was wrong. Please, God, let him be wrong, watch over him, and keep him safe. Don't let him die, when I had only just found him. I hadn't loved him long enough to let him go. The God I knew was kind and loving, and he could not be that cruel to me again.

26

RETREAT

To accomplish his purpose, a wise man will even carry his enemy on his back. Panchatantra, 6th century

Libby

"You got one," were the enthusiastic words that woke me from an early Saturday afternoon nap. I reached out wondering where Aidan was, when I suddenly heard him cry out again in happiness in the distance. I jumped out of bed and twisted into a robe before I pulled back the drape. Through the barren trees I could see Aidan and Cass out on the dock. Their fishing poles leaned against the rail, while Aidan wrangled the hook out of a large flopping fish. Cass jumped up and down in victory on the dock.

After I pan-fried Cass' catch, I took him for a hike, forcing Aidan onto the couch, insisting that he rest.

Cass was more energetic since his last medication change, but after a circuit around the lake, I was able to persuade him to take a nap only because his buddy was taking one. I sat on the floor and leaned against the sofa and read a report that Gwen sent me about Espinoza, scanning the highlights: Drug running, age 14. Supplied half the Colombian cocaine smuggled into U.S., worth in excess of 10 billion. 2,000 deaths linked to Colombian drug cartels since 2006. I swallowed.

Aidan startled me by kissing the back of my neck. He nodded at Cass. "How'd you manage that?"

"Ten minutes of your snoring helped convince him."

"I do not snore." He raised an eyebrow and he twisted to sit up, maneuvering his legs on either side of me. The cushions came loose and I saw a flash of hot pink in between them.

I grabbed it, but when I saw the pink lacy contraption I felt as if I'd been served in the middle of the night. The cotton-candy-colored strip of fabric conjured up all sorts of images: an exquisite, lanky, blonde European super model that used her thick accent to lure him to her bosom. Or it could be a leggy dominatrix who wore a leather bustier. I hated her tiny size two Heine.

"How'd your panties get in my brand new sofa?" He grinned.

I wondered if I could strangle him with them.

"These aren't mine." I lassoed them over my head. "A pair of sticky fingers lost her panties."

He grabbed them mid air. "I'm sorry to disappoint the low opinion you have of me, but I have no earthly idea who these belong to. The sick thing is this is a new sofa."

My mind was drawn from the creative expletives I was going to hiss at him to the picture window and the road that lead to the cabin. A set of high beams ambled toward us fast enough to leave a trail of dust dancing in the taillights. "Maybe the pink panty fairy decided to retrieve her under-things."

He raised a single brow. "Not many people know about this place." The wide expanse of his back hid me from view.

Growing more concerned, I looked out at the darkness settling around us. "What about a reporter?"

"No way."

"Vanessa?"

"This is strictly a guy place. Beer, poker, and fishing."

"Did you poker the pink panties?"

"You're starting to sound like an old fish wife." Aidan flipped on the porch light and reached behind the sofa for a baseball bat. "Take Cass upstairs." When I came back, the vehicle had turned into the drive. It was a sparkling silver 600 series BMW.

Before the car came to a complete halt, Tricia jumped out of the passenger-side door. She ran up the wooden porch steps in her stilettos, when one of them got caught, she didn't stop. Instead, she shucked the second one, racing into the house. Aidan waited for Fletch.

Tricia made a beeline into the large knotty-pine paneled family room. With the porch light, and the low burning embers in the stone fireplace, I watched as she got down on her knees in front of the couch and started tearing off the seat cushions, rummaging through the crevices. "Damn. Does Aidan have a maid?"

Aidan followed Fletch in and flipped on the table lamps, Tricia popped up from her knees like a jack-in-the-box.

"Are you looking for these perhaps?" The pink satin dangled off Aidan's fingertips.

Fletch snatched the underpants out of Aidan's grasp. "What the hell are you doing with my wife's panties, Palowski?"

Aidan turned on him with eyes narrowed in warning. His voice dropped to a gravelly tone. "Wrong question, Fletch. The correct question is what are your wife's panties doing in my new couch, in my cabin, in my woods?"

Fletch was as composed as one could be, with guilt dripping from his pores. I had seen the same look on witness's faces when they'd been sweated out in the box. Tricia didn't worry about her husband's distress. She moved into the kitchen and went right for the Beehive cookie jar, she removed the lid, and pulled something red and lacy out before she dove in again retrieving a cookie, which she stuck between her teeth.

"Do you want to explain what's going on?" Aidan asked.

"Not especially." Her voice wobbled around the cookie. "You tell him, Fletchie."

"How many did you hide?" Fletch asked in irritation.

"Obviously more than you could handle, or there wouldn't be any left." She had her hand on her hip and her vibrant red toes were tapping with an equal amount of aggravation.

Fletch took a predatory step toward his wife. "Now you listen to me, Wife, I will be more than happy to demonstrate, right in front of our audience, exactly what kind of a game we had going on the last time we came up here."

Tricia stuck out her tongue before stepping onto the back screened-in porch. We followed in a trail of her cookie crumbs like Hansel and Gretel, afraid we'd lose our way. She bent over the dining table and pulled a black pair of panties from their duct-taped prison underneath the tabletop.

"Have the decency to come clean when you play sex games on my property." Aidan probed. "For heaven's sake, Libby thought I'd done some bimbo on the sofa." A disgusted look crossed his stern features. "You owe me a new sofa." He thought for a moment. "Please tell me you did not do it in my custom-made bed, with the custom-made mattress and sheets."

Tricia winked at Aidan before she spoke to Fletch, "Write him a check for the bed, too."

"For crying out loud," Aidan said. "You didn't have any of your own places to procreate in?"

The tips of Tricia's ears reddened and she bit her lip. "We came up here to make sure everything was in order after that break in. A bad thunderstorm blew in, and we decided to wait until it passed."

She was tapping the toe at an accelerated pace. "It is not my fault, but I happened to ovulate when I was here."

"You're telling me you conceived your kid here?"

"She let me have her wherever I found a pair," Fletch contributed happily.

"For the love of . . . " Aidan's voice trailed off.

"You're all crazy, and I am going to bed," I huffed.

Aidan was pointing to the door. "Out."

"She came for the panties." Fletch indicated his wife. "I came for business."

Tricia followed me up. "Libby, I have a few items up there that I'd better locate, while they talk business."

Aidan and Fletch were speaking in muttered tones as Fletch

pulled his laptop out of his briefcase. Aidan's eyes looked concerned as he rested the bat on his shoulder, but he suddenly looked up, right at me and nodded me on. I felt as if he had somehow installed a GPS tracking device on my derrière.

"How is Cass handling everything?" Tricia asked concerned. "This must be overwhelming for him."

"He seems to be taking it in stride." I smiled as she switched on the light. It was paneled in the same knotty pine. The furniture was heavy and rustic, constructed from rough-hewn logs wrapped together with strands of rawhide. Even the pulls on the drawers were acorns, which coordinated with the plaid comforter and the leaf-patterned drapes in rich fall colors.

Tricia went to the nightstand and retrieved a thong.

"You can't imagine how happy we are that Aidan got rid of Vanessa. She was a continuous pain in the butt. I think she's the reason Fletchie got acid reflux."

"She does have a way about her," I said.

"She wore the most ridiculous dress to my wedding. Aidan was a groomsman and she maneuvered her way into the photos. She was in more pictures than my maid of honor. Anyway, I had her airbrushed out of every single one of them, even the ones that were PG." She fished around under the bed coming up with a black and white plaid pair of boy shorts that had red lace trim and bows; she folded them up like a love letter.

"How long have you and Fletch been married?" I sat on the bed and watched her crawl into the walk in closet.

"Seven months, one week, and three days. I was cold calling on businesses in his office building when I met him. I work for executives, I plan corporate events, arrange diner parties, act as a stylist, and coach etiquette."

"What'd Fletch need?" I asked, curious about how the suave Fletch went about obtaining a wife.

"He was under the mistaken impression that I was a high-priced call girl, and he needed a weekend date in Vegas. He was after some NFL player who wasn't happy with his representation."

"You went with him?"

"You have no idea how much I charge an hour. I maxed out one of his credit cards, and I never let him step foot in my personal space. I despised his arrogant ass from the moment he gave me a shit-eating grin. I made his life miserable for three days, and I'm good with little details."

"So what made you change your mind about him?"

"Simple. He never lost his cool, he never raised his voice, he never put a finger on me, and by the end of those three days he was wound so tight that if a pin dropped in his vicinity he was liable to implode. He never retaliated. He was stalking me so closely, he could probably tell you the number of times I blinked and I had no idea."

"He's never struck me as the patient type."

"He wouldn't have the clients he has, if he didn't know when to lay in wait, and when to pounce." She looked at the panties in her lap. "I think I found them all. I didn't know your name was Libby until the hospital, so I didn't pick up on it."

"Pick up on what?"

"Aidan won't remember, but in February we had a big blowout party before the baseball players take off for spring training. It was a great time, with the exception of Vanessa. All night, she kept going on about the parties in New York. Aidan had a bit much to drink, and by that time she'd alienated everyone else, so when she started in on him, he told her in no uncertain terms that she should high-tail it back home, if she thought New York was so much better than Chicago. Their argument dispersed the rest of our party. She stormed off without a coat. I couldn't stand her, but no coat with the dress she was wearing would have caused third degree anal frostbite. Fletch went after her and took her to a hotel, and I put Aidan in one of the guest rooms.

"He was so agitated that I was barely able to remove his shoes. He was mumbling to himself, and I thought he'd passed out when I was getting him situated. I was talking to myself and said, 'How could you fall in love with someone so shallow?' He sat up in a moment of clarity and said, 'Libby is the least shallow person I know.' I asked who 'Libby' was, and he leaned deeper into his pillows, and whispered in relief, 'Libby's my wife.'

"The next morning while we were talking over breakfast I told them I thought that I would hire 'Libby.' His gaze shot directly at me; his eyes were panicked and all the color was gone from his face. He wanted to know Libby who. I made up some last name, but he gathered up his stuff and left in a hurry. I thought you should know, for whatever it means."

From down stairs, I heard female voices coming from the kitchen: "missionary, doggie, me on top, doggie, missionary, standing, doggie, missionary, on a chair, doggie, in the locker room". When I rounded the stairs, Aidan and Fletch were engrossed with the computer. Fletch was pointing at the screen, and when a voice would go off, Aidan would shake his head yes or no. The no's were about four to one. When Tricia and I were about three feet away, they both looked up.

"Business? I thought we had enough sex-capades for one night," Tricia said in a teasing tone.

Fletch tried to close the screen, but I froze him with an icy lawyer stare. Tricia and I took up their spots. I read the web pages banner: Band-Aids Bimbo Bench. The headline read: *Each of these women insists that Band-Aid is a heterosexual. Read their bios to find out just what baseball's golden boy likes in bed.*

The web page had glossy professional photos of women. When you picked one of them they would giggle and then say a position before going into explicit detail of what kind of sex they had allegedly engaged in with Aidan. I picked 'Candy' from the other night. She said 'doggie', giggled and then said 'missionary' before going into a very detailed description that I listened to for only about ten seconds, before looking at Aidan.

"The vast majority of them I have never even laid eyes on."

"Laid is the operative word," Tricia said turning away.

I couldn't speak. I scanned over the photos, which became a blonde blur until I came to the end. There was a photo of Vanessa, though not a glossy, but a video image.

"That's new." Fletch pointed. "It wasn't on there earlier, when I found out about it."

"It seems that the star appears last." I clicked on her.

It was a tight, grainy shot of Vanessa. She was dressed conservatively in jeans and a Versace T-shirt, with one of her bare feet propped on the edge of her seat, clutching a tissue.

"It was wrong to pretend we were engaged, but after I found him with his lover he was so remorseful. I was devastated, but at least I knew why he wasn't interested in me sexually. He was so apoplectic and I loved him so much that I thought I could help him by pretending that we were a couple. It was his idea to get engaged so that he could keep other women away." The fake tears lasted about five seconds. "Any woman who says she slept with him is either a liar or has more assets than me. Just watch my video or go to Vanessa.com if you want to see all that I have to offer a man." She did a blow kiss, patted her knee and her dog jumped on her lap and she faded out.

Aidan growled. "What are you going to do to get this down?"

"I've already made some calls. That Athletes Gone Bad guy out of Philly is behind this."

"Get him on the phone, and get this pulled. Tell him I'm going to sue him and take him for every penny of porn he's got."

"He's a little difficult to reach. He's incarcerated."

"Find someone to whack him."

Fletch pointed his finger at me. "You did not hear my client ask me to obtain a hit for him."

"I'm too tired to care. Cass gets up early in the morning. I'm going to bed. Figure it out on your own."

"Libby," Aidan whispered in a pleading voice. "This does not have anything to do with you and me."

"You're right. There isn't any you and me." I started for the stairs, and he followed.

"I'll take care of it," Aidan said.

I waved him off and Tricia and Fletch goodbye at the same time. "We'll talk about it tomorrow."

Tomorrow I was going to be as far away from Band-Aid Palowski as medically feasible.

A screen door slamming startled me awake. I tiptoed into Aidan's room. He wasn't in his bed. I imagined he was fishing or maybe netting more women, but I didn't care if it allowed me to find the keys to Tank. I wanted to take Cass home and barricade us in our house. I tore the room apart. No keys.

Cass was still asleep as I slipped downstairs and out onto the back porch. Tank was there, but Aidan wasn't. I thought to go back to my couch in the upstairs den and sleep a little longer, but I decided to make coffee before I dressed, and was grinding the beans, when I felt something silky brush against the back of my thighs. Then, a large arm wrapped around my middle and he dangled a set of keys in my face.

"Were you in my room looking for these?" He rested his head on my shoulder, before he kissed my neck right below my ear.

I turned around; he was standing behind me in nothing except a pair of workout shorts, which hung low on his hips. I took in the view leisurely as he rubbed his taut abdomen, then he gave me the Palowski grin. "You can't get away from me that easily." He put the keys in the inside pocket of the shorts. "Why don't we go upstairs and mess around for awhile."

"Oh, get serious." I turned away.

"You could give me a bath."

"Or I could drown you."

He forced me to face him. "If you did that, you'd remain unfulfilled." Feather light kisses silenced my angry retort. I jumped when the front screen banged again.

"I told you they'd have coffee and . . . "

Aidan blocked the voices and me from whoever it was. I was thankful, as I didn't want to greet anyone in boy shorts and a tank top. "What are you doing up here at six in the morning?"

I put my hands on Aidan's shoulders and peered over them to see Tony carrying an eye-rubbing Manny. Evita pulled up short when she caught a glimpse of Aidan. She took more than one perusal, and I couldn't blame her. "We should have phoned." She elbowed Tony in the side. "We're lucky they're even awake."

"You mean we're lucky we didn't walk in later?"

Evita gave Tony a glare and smiled impishly at us.

"We drove up as soon as the club closed. I tried your cell. I caught Avery at your house and he told me you had Elizabeth up here." He tilted his head to one side. "Good morning, *Bella*." Tony had his shirt sleeves rolled up and his tie hanging in a loose knot around his open collar. "Is there a place where Manny can go back to sleep? We woke him in the middle of the night."

"Yeah, you can put him upstairs with Cass." Aidan moved, but I held him stationary. He looked back at me. "Besides the fact that you drive me crazy without them, here's another reason you need to wear clothes." He bowed, indicating that Tony should precede him up the stairs.

I maneuvered behind them, sulking off into Aidan's bedroom for something to wear. When I got back to the kitchen, Evita was at the stove preparing breakfast. Aidan was setting the table, and Tony was staring anxiously into a cup of coffee.

"What can I do to help?" I asked as Evita shoveled bacon out of a frying pan.

"Eggs. I thought scrambled would be easiest."

I reached for the carton. "Is this a social call?"

"I found something. I showed it to Tony and he thought we should get to you right away."

I poured the eggs into a skillet. "What was it?"

"Before I left Espinoza's house, the man that helped me escape gave me a piece of paper with a number he said I could call if I ever ran into trouble. By the time I called it it had been disconnected. I forgot about it, but when I was writing everything down, I remembered and found the envelope. Another piece of paper was in it." We gathered the platters and went to the table, where Aidan was pouring juice and more coffee.

"Where's the envelope now?" I asked.

Tony took up the conversation. "I have it in my safe."

"What was on the paper?"

Tony glanced at Evita, as she put eggs on his plate. "For future reference, I prefer mine over easy," he grumbled.

"How does that information pertain to me?" she retorted.

Tony shook his head at Aidan. "The women I've been meeting lately have been taking me for granted."

"You're preaching to the choir," Aidan offered back.

"We all know you're no choir boy." I raised an eyebrow. "Tony, get on with it. What was on the paper?"

"An invoice, uniform crate sizes, listed as cases of canned chili peppers. The thing that caught my attention was that they were Peruvian peppers. The ship-to address was some company out of Miami. I did a little digging last night, and you're never going to believe this."

"What?" Aidan and I asked in unison.

Tony bunched up his eyebrows, looking between us. "The crates were being shipped to a company owned by Dick Doyle."

Aidan's hand stopped with a fork full of eggs almost to his mouth. "Dick Doyle?"

I knew that name. Dick Doyle, Dick Doyle.

Aidan continued, "Senator Dick Doyle out of Florida?"

"Holy shit," I said.

Aidan raised an eyebrow.

Tony grimaced. "Holy shit isn't the half of it. The company listed as the sender is out of Yopal, Colombia. Guess whose home town is Yopal, Colombia, and who's the largest employer there?"

"Enrique Espinoza?" I sliced through a piece of bacon thinking that a knife was always a handy weapon.

I frowned at Tony's frown, pointing my knife at him. "And how were you able to ascertain this information?"

Tony looked at Evita, and then smiled. "If you're asking as my attorney, then I figured it out via the Internet, but if you're asking as a friend, I called in a favor at the FBI."

"You have FBI connections? Are you an informant?"

He shook his head. "No, I'm not."

"Are you going to tell me what you are?"

"If I told you more I'd have to kill you." He flashed his classic Italian smile.

Evita chimed in. "Why would you be surprised that a mobster knows people in the FBI? Haven't you watched *The Departed*?"

Tony got to his feet and tossed his napkin onto his half eaten plate. "Aidan, would you mind if I took a shower? I thought since it's fairly secluded, we would stay for the day. Manny could use a day outdoors away from the rectory."

Aidan looked at me, and I nodded my agreement. Company would keep Aidan out of my hair.

Aidan said, "You're welcome here anytime."

Tony looked at Evita a heartbeat longer than he should have, before they left the kitchen.

I looked to Evita. "What's going on between you and Tony?"

She shrugged her shoulders. "He's my boss."

"Bosses don't take this much interest in their employees."

"You're the one who told him to keep an eye on me. He thinks you meant literally."

"Uh-huh." I didn't sound convinced.

"Do you think this information will be able to help me?"

"It just might. But I need to consider all my options before I take the information to the FBI."

"Your state department handles Senatorial misconduct, no?"

"Yes, but my contacts are at the FBI."

We started to gather up the dishes. When Evita's rag was soapy she asked, "Could those contacts find out if Tony is the godfather of Chicago?"

"I don't know." I hesitated. "His family has a long history in organized crime. Did you ask him?"

"Of course I did. I don't want to get invov . . . I mean, I don't want to work for someone like that. I've had enough of criminals to last me a lifetime." She opened the dishwasher. "He said he wasn't the godfather, he actually laughed at that."

"Did he say anything else?"

"No, but I asked him if he had done anything illegal."

"What did he say?"

She looked out the kitchen window absently swirling bubbles around the plate as if she were frightened. "He wouldn't answer, but said he could take care of Espinoza, if he had to."

Did that mean machine guns, brass knuckles or an array of hired hit men? I wanted to say holy fuck! But I settled for, "Crap!"

27

CHARITY CASES

Charity never humiliated him that profited from it, nor ever bound him by the chains of gratitude, since it was not to him but to God that the gift was made.
Antoine De Saint-Exupery

Aidan 3:30 p.m.

Life fell into a rhythm, as I took over Cass' care, giving Libby the freedom to work longer hours. Between trying to balance her case overload, keeping Accardo in line, and Evita in the U.S., she had her plate full.

I stayed at her apartment during the week, and they stayed at my house on the weekends. Chemo was going well for Cass, and my body was recovering. I was looking forward to his transplant, so we could move forward.

The day of the Halloween party fundraiser, it became apparent to me that Cass was going to lose all his hair. I suggested we both shave it all off. I convinced him by saying I had been considering a new look. He laughed, but looked at me skeptically. As soon as Libby went to work, we shaved our heads. Then I prayed a few Hail Mary's that she wouldn't blow a gasket.

She had been courteous and cautious ever since the Internet fiasco, which I was still working on getting pulled. It had hurt Libby, but every once in awhile; I caught her looking at me in a way that sent all my blood to a centralized portion of my body. I knew the time for 'all of it' was drawing closer, and it would be worth waiting for.

Cass and I wore matching baseball uniforms for the party. I took some ribbing about both my hair loss and the bimbo site.

When my family arrived, my mother was aghast that all my locks were gone, but once she saw Cass' head, she understood. Even Avery appeared, dragging his feet and complaining about how lame the event was, until Ollie came in dressed as Elphaba.

I'd given him a lecture last weekend, when he'd wandered into the Rodger's house, when he was supposed to be loading Tank for a Baseball Card show. Obviously, he was not going to heed my warning about Ollie's only being in high school. If she was older, I wouldn't have a beef, but there's a lot of adult experience between seventeen and twenty, and Ollie needed to have those experiences with someone closer to her own age.

Avery assured me they were just friends, but I caught the scarecrow eyeing Elphaba in a way that could quickly move to flying-monkey business, if I didn't keep an eye on him.

Libby said she would get away from the office early and whatever was holding her up wasn't Accardo, as he'd already arrived. He had given me a hefty donation, and Evita and Manny were playing a game of pinball.

Madi was goosing me to get my attention. "Uncle Butt-Head, we want to play Foosball."

"Madi, you know my name's Band-Aid."

She smiled wickedly. "Yes, but you were a Butt-Head first."

You better cooperate otherwise she might call in back-up pixies and we know how you faired last time.

She and Cass were dragging me to the Foosball table. I looked closer at Cass' mouth, as one side of it was distinctly blue. "How much cotton candy did you have?" I asked.

"Just a little and I ate all my carrot sticks." He held up his fingers about an inch apart.

I doubted that was all he ate, so I glanced between him and the bathroom, just to get my bearings. Cass' eyes got wide like saucers right before he puked, so I was keeping a close eye out. "No more cotton candy."

He knew there was no wiggle room. "No more cotton candy, got it." He clobbered the puck right past one of mine to score a point. He'd become quite competitive over the last few weeks. I had to concentrate to beat him, which I occasionally did just to keep his competitive juices flowing, and I could only take losing for so long. The only reason he was able to score off me now was because I was gaping at Libby pushing through the door.

She had a trench coat on, but if the pencils in her wild bun were any indication of what she had on underneath, I might just combust. "Be right back."

I started toward her. She was scanning the guests and smiling at the kids and their costumes, but I could see her three-inch, pastel pink stilettos. After she put her briefcase down, she started to unbutton her coat. I was right behind her when it slipped off her shoulders and I could see the white apron strings, which she was trying to tie. I reached out and steadied her hips with my hands before I kissed her neck, then her ear. "I hope you're here to take my order." I bit into the meaty part of the back of her neck and she shivered in my arms, which were wrapped around her waist. Her top button had come undone and what it revealed made me want to panic breathe. I hissed, "Forget my order, I'll just take you."

She patted my cheek, resting her head on my shoulder. "I need a hug," she said wrapping her arms around me.

"I'm your man." No matter how much I wanted her in the pink waitress' uniform, I sensed that she needed my reassurance more than my lust right now. "What's wrong?"

She buried her face in my baseball uniform. "I'm fine."

I moved her toward a chair in the corner, and I sat down in it never taking my hands off her.

Once she was seated in my lap, she looked up at me, pulled off my cap and ran her fingers over my scalp. "What did you do?"

"Cass and I shaved it off. It's no big deal."

Before I got all the words out, she burst into tears. "But I love your hair," she sobbed.

Okay, there was a major league problem. "Tell me what you're upset about."

Tears ran down her face. I was trying to comfort her, but her tingling touch over my skull shot right through me.

"The hair will grow back. Did something happen at work?"

When she backhanded her nose, I fished around in my pocket for a handkerchief. She took the handkerchief and blew her nose. Her face was streaked with make-up, but she'd never been more beautiful. I asked again, acknowledging Vicki and Rick as they came through the revolving door with scowls on their faces.

"I told you Rat Bastard gave me a pedophile case, and I met with Pervesis." She hiccupped. "I knew the charges were going to stick so I went to the DA and got a plea deal. The charge is aggravated sexual assault with a minor, so he should be getting at least ten years, but the DA's office offered him five with five more for probation."

"It's a good deal, right?" Aidan asked.

"If this creep goes to court, all kinds of things could go wrong including other victims coming forward. Law enforcement estimates that before a pedophile is caught, he has at least twenty-five victims."

"Did he take the plea deal?"

"I met with him this morning, and laid the whole offer out for him. He refused the deal and said he wanted his day in court. I insisted. When I told him he would have to face the victim and listen to his testimony, he said he would relish it. Then he said that he read about my son in the paper and he would love to take a look at him sometime."

Oh no.

"I wanted to reach across the table and strangle him. Then I said I would have to take the matter up with Rat Bastard because I wasn't prepared to take on another lengthy trial.

"He walked behind me out the door and he put his face in my

hair and said. 'It was more than twenty-five before I got caught, so I'll take my chance with the *penal* system.' And he cackled the most heinous laugh. I had to restrain myself from pulling the elevator doors open and shoving him into the shaft."

"What did Rat Bastard say about it?"

"He said if I wanted an easy workload, I should have gone to work at the public defender's office. And that if I didn't want the case, I could quit, there were plenty of other attorneys eager to move up in the firm."

"You finally quit?" That would be a blessing.

She looked at me wide-eyed. "I wanted to quit. But I couldn't do it." Then her eyes flitted over the kids, remembering that there was a party going on around us.

"You don't need to work. And more importantly, you shouldn't be exposed to perverts, junkies, and lowlifes."

"If I quit now, the guy will get an extension to his trial date to find an attorney. I'm already the third lawyer he's had. It's part of the game he's playing, he thinks he can play the system and end up on the right side of the bars."

"The scumbag deserves whatever you have in mind."

"How do you know that I have anything planned?"

"I know you're not going to let him get off scot free. He might have thought that getting under your skin was the way to get rid of you, but he might have just met his match."

"I'm going to make sure he fries. I'm not sure exactly how I can make that happen, but I will."

"Good. Do you feel better now?" I rubbed her back, but instead of relaxing she tensed up and sat straighter in my lap, which wasn't helping me compose myself.

"Urghhh!!!!!" Was all she said as she rose to her feet. I followed her gaze. "Did you invite Jeanne?"

I caught sight of Hildy the Hillbilly clown as she rounded her way through the revolving door. Cass, Madi, and Manny were waiting on this side of it and she went around another time to increase their anticipation. After she came through the door Dr. Seuss was behind her. Cass hooted, drawing my attention away from them appearing together. "Grandma! I'm so happy you came."

Hildy bent low and whispered to the kids.

I rubbed Libby's arm gently. "Be nice." Although Jeanne smiled lovingly at Libby she was blind to it. Whatever was wrong between them flowed right below the surface.

Libby rolled her eyes but spoke to her mother. "Seriously, Jeanne, couldn't you have worn real clothes?"

She frowned at Libby. "Aidan, you need to tell her you asked me to come like this. She thinks this a flashback to her childhood, and I'm trying to embarrass her." She took in the interior for a moment. "I'll set up the face painting upstairs, if you bring her up there maybe I can paint that sour smirk off her face. It might be the only way to get it off."

"I am starting to see more and more similarities." I glanced at Libby. "Don't glare at me. She's doing me a favor by being here. I was going to ask my mom to fill in, but I don't think the French maids costume is PG enough for the kids.

"And my father with nothing on but a butcher's apron. I mean, talk about meat cleavers..." I was going to go on, but then she put her mouth over mine, which was her favorite way to shut me up. When I could feel my tongue again I said, "Now go make peace." I pushed her in her mother's direction, patting her behind.

In response, she swung her hips more than necessary and when she reached the swarm of kids around her mom, she looked back at me, bent forward, and blew me a kiss. A sheen of perspiration rose on my body.

I groaned, as Fletch came up alongside me and put his arm around my neck. "Where did she get that costume? I never considered the possibilities of the diner waitress thing."

"It's not a costume." I smacked him to get his attention.

He whistled through his teeth, "You know all the grief you gave me when I met Tricia, and I was gaga?"

"What about it?"

"You're going to pay for it."

A man with a pair of broad shoulders approached Libby. I couldn't see who it was, and I raised an eyebrow.

"Mitch Ackermann," Fletch chirped happily.

"That rookie punk has a thing for leggy brunettes." I tried to twist away from him, in that direction, but Fletch had a hand on the scruff of my neck.

"Yeah, I bet him a thousand bucks he could take her home." He laughed. "We have business. You can admire his technique from here."

"Fletch, I'm going to twinkle your little star."

Fletch pinched my neck forcing me to turn toward him. "Concentrate. I haven't been able to get Band-Aid Bimbos down yet."

I was listening to him, but I was watching Ackermann bending into Libby's breasts, as if pretending to listen to her. "When will you get the site down?" I asked.

"I tried threatening the guy, but he's already in prison, and doesn't seem to give a shit. Then I offered him money, and he laughed in my face. I have only one other option."

"Uh-huh?" I asked as I watched Ackermann pull one of the pencils Libby had in her hair out, before pulling her order pad out of her apron. I was going to break the guy's fingers.

"Would you cut it out?" Fletch elbowed me to get my attention. It worked. "I'm going to have to hire some hackers to take it down. I tried everything legal. Tony said he knows some guys from Northwestern."

"Uh-huh, Tony knows some hackers." I was busy planning Ackermann's imminent demise, when what he said reached my central computing station. "Are you crazy? If Libby finds out, she'll pitch a fit. She's Miss straight-and-narrow, no way."

"You need to broaden her horizons, or someone else will."

Libby was laughing at something Ackermann was whispering in her ear. I narrowed my eyes. "How many years for murder?"

"Huh?" Fletch cut a look toward Libby. "He's good. He reminds me of you in the good ole days. He'll probably have her out of that waitress' uniform before dinner."

"I don't care how much time I get, it'll be worth it."

"If you kill him, you'll be in jail, and she'll get lonely." Fletch elbowed me again when I ignored him.

"You do that one more time Fletch and I might snap."

"I got a call from Mrs. Landscale today."

Libby toyed with her glasses making the chain swing.

"Yeah? Is she ready to settle?" I asked absently.

"Things are quite settled."

I finally looked at him confused. "Spit it out, Fletch."

"Your little Libby met with Mrs. Landscale and gave her a check for three million bucks. She said Libby explained everything, and she's dropping her lawsuit." Fletch chuckled. "I'm afraid to leave you alone with her."

Ackermann had pulled another one of Libby's pencils out of her hair and her bun fell, cascading down her back. Ackermann stepped closer. I looked at Fletch. "You did this on purpose to distract me?" I said pointing toward Libby.

Hey diddle diddle, that cat played his fiddle. The clown is one hot dame. The little Fletch laughed to see such fun. And Mitch ran away with your flame.

Obviously, I hadn't had enough adult reading material of late.

"I thought Mitch would distract you into going for the hackers, and once you found out about the money, I thought I'd tie up all my loose ends in one grand explosion."

I grabbed Fletch by his lapels. "Where is your costume?"

"I don't dress up for other people's amusement."

"Too busy spending all your time hatching up this little plan to eliminate your complications, but you didn't see it through to its completion."

"I beg to differ. Ackermann's in your crawl."

"I don't care about the money, and if Libby's a problem, Fletch, she's my problem."

He grumbled his understanding. "At least let me have Tony's guys see what they can do about the website."

"Fine, whatever." I let him go.

"Your little problem just cost you three million bucks."

"If it made her happy, it was worth every penny."

Fletch dropped his head and shook it. "You're going to marry her, aren't you?"

"If I can talk her into it."

"And if you can't?"

"A man's got to do what a man's got to do."

"What the hell does that mean?"

"It means if she won't marry me, I'll knock her up, and then she'll have to marry me. Everyone, including you, is going to insist on it."

"Are you out of you mind?"

"This is the sanest thing I've ever done." I started away.

"I'm drawing up papers to have you committed."

Libby's back was to me, and when Ackermann noticed my approach, he smiled broadly. I wound my arm around Libby's waist pulling her into me. "You just lost a bunch of money . . . " I let the statement hang in the hostile air between us. "A knuckle ball to the head will keep you away from my girl."

"She hasn't seemed to mind my company."

"This is my son's mother; she's out of play Ackermann."

"I had no idea."

I took a deep breath. "How old are you again?"

"Twenty."

I looked at Libby. "Babe, seriously?"

She smiled innocently and batted her lashes.

Ackermann leered at Libby and said to me. "You got plenty of babes."

"She's my no-hitter. You want to mess with my record?" I pushed him in the direction of a large group of players. "Go find Exley's wife. She likes all the young players."

Libby followed my eyes, locating the woman. "This is a kid's party. There's more exposed skin on her than your ex's dogs."

"She used to be a Baseball Annie, a groupie. Before she married Exley, she had her way with many boys on the team."

"Please tell me you weren't one of them, or we'll need to run out for a rabies shot."

I raised a brow. "In the time we've spent apart, have you ever seen me with a woman that wasn't top of the line?"

"No they all seemed like Grade A beef to me. Except for Vanessa, she seemed more like rotting fish eggs."

"I believe they call that caviar."

"You can call it by any name you choose, but it's still stinky, rotting fish eggs." She started to walk away.

I grabbed her and turned her back toward me, she had to look up at me even with the stilettos. "I'm in the mood for a perfectly cut filet," I said, as I looked her up and down. "Will you deliver it to my room?" I asked suggestively.

"Maybe you need a little more ground round before you can truly appreciate a prime cut."

I pulled her closer. "Not only can I already appreciate it, I can almost taste it." I put my lips on hers, and when I was done kissing them, I licked them. Then I whispered, "I'll have a fine appreciation of it in my bed on your back, in my car on my lap, in my office on my chair, or just about anywhere."

"Have you been reading Dr. Seuss again?"

I went to take her mouth again, but she put her fingers over my lips. "The children are watching."

I caught a glimpse of Cass and Madi heading our way. "It's only a matter of time before I get all of it."

Libby plucked on one of Madi's pigtails, as she passed her, going to check on Hildy. Madi beamed me with a killer smile. "Since you're like my uncle now, does that mean we can sit behind home plate at the Wiggley Field and get free snacks?"

"If that's what you want."

She jumped up and down with excitement. Cass said, "Mr. Pole-ow-ski, me and Madi need more tokens."

I smiled at him. "Are you ever going to call me daddy?"

He beamed me with a crooked smile and a pinched dimple. "I'm just waiting for when you really need it."

I took his hand in mine; he always had these prophetic ways of answering my questions that were as smooth and sweet as the soft skin on the back of his hand. "Go play." I put tokens in his hand as easily as he put them in my heart.

I located Libby speaking with Vicki, Fletch, Tony, Evita, and a woman I'd never seen before. I took in the woman's practical black square-heeled shoes, her sensible suit, and blond crew cut; it was so precise that it must have been shaved today. Her calm demeanor, as she relayed information to the group, marked her as some sort of high-level law enforcement. Besides, I could see where her bulletproof vest pushed against her suit jacket.

"He's in the process of being picked up by officers out of the field office in D.C." I heard the blonde woman say, as I stepped into the conversation.

My eyes immediately went to Libby's. She seemed to be concerned, but calculating what she wanted to ask. When Libby met my eyes, the woman stopped speaking and extended her hand. "Field Officer Gwen Foley, FBI." I shook her hand and started to speak. She interrupted, "Aidan Palowski, I know who you are.

"We've had Doyle under surveillance for some time now, but when we got your tip, Libby, we started to dig a little deeper. We raided the warehouse you tipped me on. Three tons of cocaine concealed in chili pepper cans. The Justice Department decided to indict him. The Attorney General, Jonathan Gomez, has been a staunch ally on the war on drugs. It's not wordsmithing for him, his kid brother died from a heroin overdose. He's going to try this case personally."

"So what does this mean for Evita?" Tony asked.

"It means immediate citizenship, and the thanks of the justice department. We should have enough evidence that she won't have to testify, but it depends on how things sort out."

"Good," Libby said, cautiously. "Gwen, you could have phoned me with all this. What else?"

"You aren't going to like it, none of you will." Gwen looked around making eye contact with several other agents I hadn't noticed. "We've had Doyle's phone tapped, and he received an interesting phone call from Bogota yesterday. The man never identified himself, but he warned Doyle that he was going to be arrested. We have a leak somewhere, and it's dripping right to Espinoza's ear."

"Shit," Libby said.

"Shit usually slides downward," Gwen said. "So for the interim, you," she pointed to Libby, "and Evita have twenty-four hour surveillance. We don't have a credible threat, but we all know how these men work." She spoke to Tony, and it wasn't a subtle hint.

"I don't want a surveillance detail," Evita said. "You just told me I'm free. I'm a U.S. citizen."

"You either have a security detail, or witness protection, Ms. Gutierrez," Gwen responded.

Evita nodded in reluctant acceptance.

"I have also ordered wire taps on all your phones. Espinoza isn't a well-balanced individual. We can't be sure where he'll strike, or when, but he will. I would venture to guess he knows about Evita's involvement in this. You can't remain at the rectory. I've arranged a safe house."

"My home has more security than you can offer her," Tony chimed in. "She'll move in there."

Evita glared at Tony, but didn't retort before Gwen continued. "You all need to be mindful of your surroundings and if you see anything unusual, you need to call us immediately. As soon as you pick up anything out of the ordinary, do something about it. Try to keep low profiles otherwise, alter your daily activities, and don't become too predictable. We also have your cell phone activity monitored, so don't say anything you don't want the Federal Government to know about." Again, she shot Tony a look.

"Do you think Espinoza is inclined to aid Doyle?" I asked. "Maybe try to get him out of the country?"

"Not a chance. I think he only made the call to play cat-and-mouse with us. He couldn't care less about Dickey boy; he was just a pawn to get his goods distributed here in the States. I'm sure he has a new source in Miami already lined up."

Libby started to speak, but Gwen motioned to the TV's, which were a few feet over head. The screen was filled with reporters sticking their microphones in the faces of two Federal Agents, who were pulling a handsome, but disgruntled, gray-haired man through the throng. The ticker tape at the bottom of the screen read: 'Federal Agents have raided Senator Dick Doyle's office on Capitol Hill and home in Virginia. Initial charges are alleged be conspiracy and distribution of narcotics.'

One of the employees had noticed our interest in the show and had turned up the volume. We congregated around a TV near the bar.

The CNN anchor, Wolfe Blitzer, took coverage over from the live footage. "This just in from our affiliate station in Miami. A search warrant has been executed on Senator Doyle's two homes in Miami and on a large warehouse of which he is partial owner at the Port of Miami." He looked off to his left, to the large screen behind him. "We have a live update from a local reporter on the scene at Doyle's estate in Miami."

A young woman's face filled the screen. "Wolfe, sources close to the investigation have said this afternoon's search on Senator Doyle's home led to more questions than answers. The refrigerator in the Senator's bedroom bar was filled with hundred dollar bills in bricks of ten thousand dollars wrapped in foil and plastic bags. The exact number of bricks recovered is unknown but apparently, it was enough to build a brick wall tall enough to bring Dick Doyle tumbling down. It seems that the Midwest heir to the Bush fortune lost his way along the sunny shores of Miami. Back to you in the newsroom, Wolfe."

"That was local reporter for WPLG, channel 10 out of Miami, Jen Douglass. Great reporting. Stay with CNN for all our latest updates on the arrest of Senator Dick Doyle when we return." Then CNN went to commercial.

I put my arm around Libby and kissed her temple. "It's going to be okay, babe. Don't worry."

28

TRANSFEREE

It is only rogues who feel the restraints of the law.
Joshiah Gilbert Holland

Libby

I nodded to the agent assigned to shadow me today, as I donned my sea-foam green gown, mask, and gloves, the same way I had for the last three weeks. Cass' glass ICU door slid over the track effortlessly, and the air filtration system kicked on, heralding my arrival by sifting through the atmosphere for any impurities I might have dragged in.

Aidan was sitting alongside Cass' sleeping form. He raised a finger to the comical smile he'd drawn across the mask. The book he'd been reading Cass slipped from his lap, as he pulled the other chair closer to his.

I dropped into it and sighed heavily. When he took my hand, I started to relax. "You're here early."

I closed my eyes. My emotions tightened, like a noose around my neck. I felt helpless, threatened by an enemy I was unable to fight, traumatized because engrafting hadn't happened yet, and isolated, even though Aidan was my constant companion.

"How is he today?" I asked.

The long weeks of waiting for the transferred marrow to engraft and his blood counts to return to safe levels were taking a toll on my disposition.

Aidan, however, gave me a cheerful smile, which I recognized because his dimple crested his mask. Through the horrible side effects, the roller coaster ride of one day Cass being violently ill and the next almost normal, Aidan's was the face of optimism to which I turned. This would've been much harder, if not for him.

If I was vulnerable and hurt, I let him carry the weight of it. I had resisted that impulse in the beginning, but after lying alongside him on a three-foot-wide cot night after night, he became my life vest. That security seemed wrapped around me, much the way his arms were so often—tightly, surely, and with such ease, as if they were designed to hold and comfort only me. That thought assaulted me, through countless sleepless nights, when his steady breathing was my only companion.

"He's having an okay day. What about you?"

Aidan was Cass' rock from the moment we'd entered the hospital. When the doctors came to put Cass' catheter in, and he fought them, Aidan insisted on respectful cooperation. When Cass wouldn't listen to my reasoning for a central venous line, Aidan climbed in the bed behind him, wrestled his arms around Cass to hold him steady, nodded to the doctors to do their work, and whispered in Cass' ears.

When the doctors were done, Cass turned to his father and huffed contritely, "You were right. It wasn't as bad as I imagined, nothing like a sword through Arthur's heart."

Through the preparative regimen of chemo and radiation, hours of hydration and evaluation, Aidan was there, talking Cass through it, consoling him when he was weak and irritable. Washing his face when he was nauseous, feeding him ice chips when the mouth sores were so inflamed that food was intolerable.

"I'm okay." I wasn't. We were on day +17 and engraftment hadn't taken place. We were in the most critical two-to-four week period after the procedure, which had taken place in Cass' room, not an operating room. I was terrified of graft-versus-host disease, but the doctors had given him high doses of multiple antibiotics. Until Cass engrafted, we were destined to suffer through blood tests, close monitoring of vital signs, strict measure of daily output and input.

Aidan had barely left the room since day -3. He had stayed in this room for 21 days, a feat for a man who lived for physical exertion. Even the two times he desperately needed an outlet, he went for a run, but confessed later that he ran the outside perimeter of the building over and over.

When we first arrived, Cass had undergone baseline testing of his heart, lungs, and kidneys to check their output and function. Steve had been assigned to Cass' case for psychological observation, but after an interview with the three of us, he told Aidan he knew he wasn't needed. All Cass needed were sweet whispered words of comfort from me, and the constant companionship of Aidan.

Cass and Aidan were holding up under the stress better than I was. It wasn't in my nature to sit and wait. My anxiety about inaction had led Aidan to send me back to work on day plus two. And I had worked hard to occupy myself so I wouldn't think about worst-case scenarios, but that's what a lawyer prepares for.

I slept either here with Aidan, or some nights, after a sparse dinner, Aidan sent me home for sleep. After a week, I realized he was buffering me from many of Cass' nastiest days.

Aidan squeezed my hand to get my attention again. "Let's go for a walk. He'll be asleep for awhile." Aidan helped me strip off the gown and we tossed them in the trash. When he stood straight again, his beautiful blue eyes locked on mine. It hit me hard in that moment, as it did from time to time, just how incredible he was. He said, "What?"

I shrugged my shoulders and headed down the shiny hallway and around the corner to the family waiting room. I walked to the wall of windows and stared out over the lake at the clear brisk day. There wasn't a boat to be seen, Aidan turned back and asked the agent for a little privacy.

Aidan came up behind me and rested his chin on my head. "Dr. Seuss came by this morning. He said Cass' red blood cell count is accelerating. He has every hope that engraftment will happen soon." He wrapped his arms around my torso and gave me a gentle squeeze.

I nodded my head yes, understanding that it was his way of telling me he hadn't given up hope. My arms draped over his and the back of my head rested nicely in the center of his chest.

"What's wrong?" He brushed his whiskered jaw along mine.

I closed my eyes as shivers jolted down my body. I was so tense that the simplest gesture of his body seemed to magnify and explode onto mine. "I quit today." I turned in his arms, looking up to his questioning face. "Before they could fire me, Caster questioned the Pervesis' investigator and once he found out I'd already turned over the list of people he'd interviewed to the DA's office he went ape shit."

He kissed the end of my nose. "You don't need to work."

"I need to take care of myself, I need the insurance, thank God for COBRA, or I'd be screwed."

"You don't seem concerned about the actual job part of it."

"I'm not. I was starting to despise the system. Most of the clients are criminals, the hours suck, I can barely tolerate Rat Bastard, and Pete the Pervert was the final straw. I gave Jax Wagner enough to make sure Pete never hits the street again."

"Everything worked out for the best." He kissed me.

I pulled away. "I didn't get to the good part yet."

"I thought kissing was the good part." He raised an eyebrow. "You want to be a stay-at-home-mom and give me four more great kids?"

"You want four more kids?" That threw the possibility of my being disbarred to the back burner of my brain.

He was nibbling on my neck and he whispered in my ear, "I'm good with any number between four and six."

"You seriously think you could find a woman to do that for you six times?"

"I think I found the woman." He pulled back and looked down at me. "Just imagine how much fun we could have making the six times happen." He eyed me salaciously.

"Oh yeah, sign me up. Since I can't be a lawyer anymore, I might as well become the ultimate baby factory."

He became utterly still. "What do you mean you might not be a lawyer anymore?"

The tears came in a flash flood then. I think it was the fact that he understood how being a lawyer was important to me. That was the biggest change in him from college. He had learned that other people had dreams, too, and he came to consider them as importantly as he did his own. I choked out, "I have to appear before a judge on ethical violations in three days."

He took a chair, and pulled me into his lap. "Fletch can take care of this."

"He's not an attorney-misconduct lawyer."

"If he can't do it, he'll know someone good who can. I promise you, you won't be disbarred. I won't allow it. You're one of the best attorneys in Chicago."

"I haven't heard from Max yet."

"This will be straightened out." He wiped away my tears. "Cass hates it when you're sad. And having my stomach ripped out through my belly button would be more pleasant than watching you cry." He smiled broadly. "Look at the bright side. You get to spend more time with me."

I sniffled. "More time with you only leads to trouble."

"God I hope so." He mumbled into my hair. "It's hard, sleeping with you night after night." He raised a brow for me to catch his meaning as one of his hands roamed along my thigh.

"We are so not going to get busted making out again." I bounded out of his lap, straightening my skirt, as I walked to the two large impressionist landscape paintings hanging there.

He laughed and came up on my left.

I glanced at him. "You did that to distract me didn't you?"

He tilted his head in the same, defiant manner Cass used. "My mom and dad bought a condo downtown. They decided they're going to stay here until Christmas, and they want us to go out to California for the holidays."

I looked at him out of the corner of my eye now. "Cass can't have contact with the general public. No movies, no department stores. I'm sure no airplanes, either."

"That's not the only way to get to California."

"We don't know if he'll get out of the hospital by then. I haven't even thought through Thanksgiving next week."

"My parents are going to take care of that."

"I have my own family. The Rodgers."

"I know, I'm not excluding them." He ran a hand through his hair. "I just want you to include me in your family. I want us to be a family; I want you to be mine."

"It could be up to six months before Cass can resume his activities."

"That doesn't have a bearing on our activities."

"You promised you'd give me time and space."

"You need to take a leap of faith. You need to decide if you love me enough to give me a second chance, because I love you enough to put everything else on the bleachers to be here for you when you need me the most."

"I didn't know we were keeping you from things," I said with enough irritation to make him step back.

"Don't twist my words, Libby. I need you and I want you, but sooner or later, you're going to have to accept all of that or cut me off at the knees." He ran a hand along his jaw line. "Or is that what you want, me on my knees begging you? Because I won't hesitate to do that, if that's what it takes."

Dr. Seuss saved me from a sarcastic retort as he came into the waiting area with my mother trailing in his wake. A smile washed his features as he scanned the print out in his hand. "Good news. Engraftment has commenced."

Aidan and I both stepped into his outstretched arms, before turning on his coat tails and heading in the direction of Cass' room. My mother started chatting in one ear, as I took in the triumphant look on Aidan's face. "Looks like time's up, babe. The only space that's going to be between us is the air between your skin and mine." He patted my derriere. "I, for one, have high expectations that 'all of it' was worth waiting for."

Three days later . . .

I had always avoided pretrial publicity, so I was caught off guard, when Aidan and I arrived at the courthouse to find Fletch conducting a melodramatic press conference right outside the courtroom doors. I stood in the background, watching Fletch orchestrate the crowd of entertainment reporters. He had timed it to occur right before the hearing, ensuring a full gallery.

The look on Matt Caster's face spoke volumes about what he thought of Fletch's symphony. The glee in his eyes spoke volumes about the score he was going to play for the judge. Pete the Pervert scuttled behind him like the weasel rat he was.

Fletch turned, as the reporters started for the courtroom. "In a high stakes legal matter, strategy is everything. I plan on making sure Matt Caster does not come out smelling like roses. And who better to spread the good news than the media?"

Fletch took my other arm, and we sauntered into Marc Marston's courtroom like it was Orchestra Hall. Fletch glanced around the mahogany walls, ornate carved pediments, and detailed frieze and shrugged his shoulders. "Who would've thought?"

The courtroom floors were marble, the seats were fully upholstered in crushed burgundy velvet: the courtroom was your stage when you were the youngest superior court judge in the state of Illinois. I dreaded this trial. I hadn't made many exceptions to the rule of law, but what I had done was for the greater good, and I was honest enough with myself to admit that given the exact same situation, I would've made the same decision. Pete the Pervert needed to be put down, and if capital punishment wasn't an option, incarceration would have to suffice. With a son of my own, I needed to see it done.

Before I brought myself back to the proceedings, I turned to locate Aidan in the gallery. He had two eager entertainment reporters interviewing him in the aisle. Melinda, the girl who'd masqueraded as Vanessa's assistant was speaking in hushed tones to Winslow O'Leary, who gave me a friendly nod of the head.

When Melinda's detailed reporting of Ms. Vanderhoff's behavior hit *US Magazine*, Vanessa required the services of two public relations specialists, and three attorneys. She'd been too busy since to interfere with our lives.

Jax Wagner and Judge Foreman entered the courtroom, taking two seats—on my side of the courtroom.

Aidan must've sensed me watching because he turned away from the reporter, whom I thought might topple over because she was so front-side-heavy. He flashed me a killer smile before heading in my direction. He leaned over the balustrade and kissed by cheek before taking his seat. I heard the reporter sigh; O'Leary chuckled, and Melinda rolled her eyes.

So much for professionalism. Fletch was studying me curiously. "It's a pity they fawn over him anymore."

"What's so pitiful about it now?"

"Before you came along, watching him was fun. He can lay the charm on so thick before you know it you're on a sugar high. I realize now it was all a game to him. On some level, it's always been you, no matter how many women there were, they never captured his attention the way you have. When he said he was going to marry Vanessa, I thought maybe the capacity for gut wrenching love wasn't in his make-up." He guffawed at himself. "It wasn't that he wasn't capable of it, it was that he was already in love with someone. I'd just never witnessed it."

The bailiff entered the courtroom, followed by the judge, and we stood. I whispered to Fletch, "Talk about hiding another side of yourself. You're a closet romantic, Mr. Fletcher."

"No, you were right the first time we met. I was a cave-dwelling-narrow-brow-dim-witted-ass-hole. But the love of a good woman will change both a beast and his perspectives."

I was able to smirk before Judge Marston dropped his gavel calling the court to order. He took in the courtroom. "Mr. Fletcher, Mr. Caster, before we begin this proceeding, I wanted to note, on the record, that

I have met Ms. Tucker before. It amounted to a brief introduction by my wife on the street. We had no conversation except for an exchange of niceties and we never discussed a rule of law or any cases."

Matt Caster positioned himself over his table and twitched his nose like a rat smelling bait. "Your honor, we move that you recuse yourself from these proceedings then."

Judge Marston looked over his glasses at Caster like he wanted to shove some cheese down his throat before he chewed on the stem of his glasses. "Mr. Caster, Ms. Tucker was in your employ. That's much more of a relationship than an encounter on the street. Do you plan to recuse yourself?"

"Of course not. My client is bringing the charges."

"We'll get to those in a moment, but if you're not recused, neither am I," he grumbled. "Additionally, I'm the only member of the State Bar available over the holiday to take these proceedings. I'm sure you want this issue resolved quickly, so your client can enjoy his turkey dinner knowing the law has been observed."

"Your honor, I object," Mr. Caster insisted.

"Mr. Caster, unless you can produce a valid legal argument, a broken rule in the code of conduct, or a genie in a bottle, I suggest you sit down and let me proceed."

A mild muttering simmered in the courtroom. I distinctly heard Aidan chuckle.

Judge Marston looked at the opposing tables. "Gentleman, Ms. Tucker, this isn't a regular trial, but I will ask questions and expect honest answers. You are all under oath, and while this is a more informal hearing, the rule of law still applies to this proceeding. Mr. Caster, we'll start with the charges you filed with the AMA against Ms. Tucker."

"Ms. Tucker engaged in conduct involving dishonesty, fraud, deceit, and misrepresentation. Her actions were prejudicial to the administration of justice."

"Those are heavy charges, Mr. Caster. Can you put them into some sort of a context for me?"

"Ms. Tucker was representing the gentleman sitting behind me,

Mr. Peter Pervesis, under my supervision at Whitney, Brown and Rodgers. In the course of her representation, she negotiated a plea agreement, which she insisted Peter take. When he refused she hired an investigator without my knowledge or advice—"

Judge Marston held up his hand, halting Caster for the moment. "What are the pending charges against Mr. Pervesis?"

"Those are irrelevant to this proceeding."

Fletch stood. "Your honor, we're here today because of Mr. Perv-e-sis." Fletch put the emphasis on Perv much the way Cass put the emphasis on Pole in Palowski. "The charges against him should be part of the record, as they have direct relevance."

"Not only do I agree with you, Mr. Fletcher, I would like to remind Mr. Caster that I am the judge here. I decide what it relevant and irrelevant to these proceedings. Read the charges against Mr. Pervesis into the record."

When Mr. Caster hesitated, Judge Marston, bellowed, "Now!"

"Lewd conduct with a minor and aggravated sexual assault with a minor," Caster chocked out.

The judge cleared his throat. "The charges will be duly noted. Now, Ms. Tucker, you were a junior associate?"

"Yes, I was."

"And in what capacity did Mr. Caster oversee your cases?"

"We had weekly meetings, when I updated him on cases coming to trial, any proceedings, or plea bargains. I never, in the course of my career, reported the minutia of my cases to Mr. Caster, investigative or otherwise."

"And in what capacity did you hire an investigator in reference to Mr. Pervesis?"

"In an effort to find character witnesses, Mr. Pervesis is a Sunday school teacher and a Boy Scout Troop leader, I hired the investigator to interview the people related to these activities. Mr. Pervesis provided me with a list of names."

Caster got to his feet. "That's the point, your honor. Lawyers can be disbarred if they divulge information that can lead to their client's conviction."

"Ms. Tucker, in the course of your investigation did you find evidence that could convict Mr. Pervesis?"

"No, I did not. I had the investigator interview a few children and their parents, and made a list of others that could act as character witnesses. When that part of my discovery was complete, I turned it over to the DA's office."

"Your honor, when Mr. Pervesis asked Ms. Tucker about the investigator, she never replied. Rule 1.4 states that a lawyer shall keep a client reasonably informed about the status of a matter and promptly comply with reasonable requests for information," Caster bellowed.

Judge Marston replied calmly. "If said information did nothing to add or detract from the case, I can understand her classifying it under minutia and moving on. I would think that reason enough for her to set this matter aside when it had no bearing on the defendant's trial." He tapped his papers along his desk. "Now moving along, Mr. Wagner, I see you out there. Are you handling these charges against Mr. Pervesis?"

Jax got to his feet. "Yes, your honor, I am."

"And in the course of discovery, did you observe any impropriety or ethical violations by Ms. Tucker?"

"No, your honor I did not. To be honest, I showed up here today because Ms. Tucker is Mr. Pervesis' third and best-informed attorney. The DA's office is concerned that this is yet another attempt by Mr. Pervesis to postpone a trial date."

The judge rubbed his chin. "I see."

Caster was on his feet again. "Ms. Tucker lacked a competent defense for Mr. Pervesis."

"Mr. Caster, you didn't mention incompetency in your charges. In preparation for this hearing, I obtained Ms. Tucker's employment record, which looks exemplary. As a matter of fact, she has never lost a case she took to trial. Are you insinuating that she was hanging Mr. Pervesis out to dry with her own record hanging in the balance?"

Mr. Caster fumbled for words.

"The attorney acts as the trusted representative of the client, trust is the defining element of the practice of the law. And Mr. Wagner, Ms. Tucker's opponent in this case seems to trust her, so I have to question why you don't." He thought for a moment. "Ms. Tucker, did you speak with your investigator?"

"No, your honor. I read his written report then turned it over to the DA's office."

"Mr. Wagner, have you spoken to the investigator?"

"The report I received was curiously incomplete, so I contacted the investigator. Ms. Tucker is always very thorough and something about the information bothered me. When I spoke on the phone with the investigator, he gave me a modified version of what was in the written report, there were other people he'd spoken to who were no longer listed in the statement. When I contacted them they had less than glowing things to say about Mr. Pervesis."

Caster was leaning over his table, his face red with exertion. "I object," he bellowed.

Judge Marston gave Caster a dirty look and looked back at Jax Wagner. "Now we're getting somewhere. Do you think there was a suppression of evidence?"

"Yes, I do."

"Do you think Ms. Tucker was in any way involved?"

"Of course not. She's always acted above-board, which I can't say about every criminal defense attorney."

"Thank you, Mr. Wagner. Ms. Tucker, who in your office has access to investigators reports and client files?"

"Your honor, almost anyone, but I keep my current cases in my office. I happened to see the investigator coming out of Mr. Caster's office the other day, and after he refused to speak to me, I returned to my desk, realizing the file was gone. When I questioned my assistant, she said Mr. Caster had sent down for the file the day before."

The courtroom started to buzz, but the judge ignored it. "I wonder now, Mr. Caster, what you have to add to this story?"

"Your honor, I . . . "

Judge Marston pointed his gavel at him. "Sit down. I think I'll get further without your babbling. Ms. Tucker, do you have any theories as to why your direct boss has maneuvered around you and is now trying to have you disbarred?"

Fletch and I exchanged looks. "It could have something to do with an altercation between Mr. Caster and Aidan Palowski."

"An altercation about what?"

I shook my head no. I did not want to speak the words aloud because even if I weren't disbarred, a charge of sexual harassment would seal my fate. Law license or not, no firm in this city would hire me. Those kinds of allegations shook the core of the good ole boy network. I had witnessed it first-hand.

The judge looked at Aidan. "Mr. Palowski, please shed some much needed light on this proceeding."

Aidan got to his feet. "Your honor, I had an altercation with Mr. Caster in Ms. Tucker's office that led to him losing his two front teeth."

Judge Marston looked up from the bench. "Would you please share with the court what led up to this altercation?"

I could feel Aidan's gaze digging into the back of my head. He wanted my permission to say it out loud. I nodded my head yes. "I walked into Ms. Tucker's office to find Mr. Caster speaking to her in a vile, sexual manner, and he had his hand on her breast. She recoiled away from him and when he didn't take his hand off of her fast enough I punched him twice, once for his unwanted sexual advances and again for denying it."

"This is becoming crystal clear." Marston gave Caster a venomous look. "Did Mr. Caster file assault charges against you?"

"No, he did not."

"Mr. Caster, since you're such a stickler for the rule of law, why didn't you file any charges against Mr. Palowski?"

Caster looked drawn and pale, his nose twitched nervously like a rat caught in a trap. "Palowski misinterpreted the events."

The judge turned back to me. "Was it a misunderstanding, Ms. Tucker, or sexual harassment?"

I swallowed my career on three syllables. "The latter."

"Did you go to Mr. Caster's superior or to the human resources department in your firm?"

"No, I did not."

"Why?"

Judge Foreman was on his feet. "Marston, she was afraid of jeopardizing her career, she was third chair on Marlin vs. McKinley Donavan Associates."

"The landmark sexual harassment case?" Marston tapped his papers on the bench. "Well that would explain your hesitation. I didn't see that loss in your record."

"I was still in law school, your honor."

"I will give Caster the benefit of the doubt and assume there was no sexual assault?"

I shook my head no.

"Were you made aware of this matter, Mr. Fletcher?"

"When the altercation occurred, I had a conversation with Mr. Caster. I let him know, on behalf of Aidan Palowski, who is also my client, that any further advances on Ms. Tucker's person would include a conversation with the senior partners at Whitney, Brown, and Rodgers and charges filed in civil court."

The judge tented his fingers before he spoke. "I don't even have to go back into chambers to decide this one, Mr. Caster. I think the charges against Ms. Tucker are laughable, and the ones against you disturbing. You're in contempt of my court. You have violated rule eleven of the Federal Rules of Civil Procedure which requires sanction for lawyers and clients who file frivolous or abusive claims in court." Judge Marston nodded toward the bailiff. "Take them both into custody."

When the bailiff started toward them, Pete the Pervert turned and ran. Two additional bailiffs entered the courtroom and handcuffed him. Caster was struggling with the bailiff.

"I won't hesitate to add resisting arrest along to breaking Rule one-point-two. A lawyer shall not assert a position, conduct a defense, delay a trial, or take other action on behalf of the client when the lawyer knows, or reasonably should know, that such action would serve merely to harass or maliciously injure another. Most importantly, you have damaged Ms. Tucker's good name to say nothing of your abuse of power as her direct superior. I hope she files a civil action against you."

The bailiff finally bent Caster over the table and handcuffed him while he bellowed about Miranda Rights, wrongful imprisonment, and other nonsense.

"Ms. Tucker, you have the court's deepest apologies. I will personally make a call to Mr. Whitney, Mr. Brown, and Mr. Rodgers with the developments of this hearing. I would think someone with your credentials is a valuable asset to their firm. I am sure once they are made aware of these circumstances, they will very much like to make restitution. Court adjourned." The gavel hit his desk with a thump.

The reporters crowded around us, but Fletch led them on a merry chase out into the corridor.

Aidan came to the gate, up close to me, and tilted my chin up. "Look on the bright side. Rat Bastard has legal problems up to his ears. Not to mention what the media is going to do to him. Who knows who might come forward once this hits the news?"

Aidan didn't understand how this game was played anymore than I knew about locker room antics. I knew he felt good about what happened, but the reality was my career as a lawyer was probably over. I went into his arms for comfort. My phone vibrated in my pocket, I pulled it out and looked at it. It was Vicki. I looked around the courtroom, realizing for the first time she'd never shown up.

I answered the phone. "Where the hell are you?"

I heard a strangled grunt. "I'm in the gardens at Versailles! Where the hell do you think I am? I'd have to be somewhere pretty damn special not to be at the most important hearing of your career."

"What's going on?"

"Oh, nothing, I'm just at the hospital in labor, alone. My water broke, and my husband is in California at a conference, and I'm going to have a baby all by myself." She started crying.

"Don't freak out. We'll be right there."

The last thing I heard was a startled, "LLIIIBBBEEEE!" before the phone disconnected.

I narrowed my eyes on Aidan. "I don't care what you have to do. Find a way to get Rick here from California ASAP."

"What's wrong?"

"Vicki's in labor."

29

RELEASED AT LAST

Who is so firm that can't be seduced?
William Shakespeare

Aidan (In the nick of time)

Libby pushed through the doors of the elegant shop—Wee, Wee, Babee—with her clipboard in hand. Late last night, Vicki had given birth to Elizabeth "Betty" Davis at six-and-a-half pounds. Surprising, they told me, since she was six weeks early. When I asked Libby how big she would have been, if Vicki had gone to term, she said, "Too big."

Our security guy cough-laughed and Libby smiled at him, and he couldn't resist smiling back. He accommodated Libby's every whim. I ushered him alongside the store's entrance. He was cramping my style, but Libby enjoyed having him as a buffer. I warned Gwen that if we didn't lose the unnecessary security soon, she might lose a federal agent.

With my parents in town, they were with Cass, while Libby lassoed me into helping her and Rick pick up the baby furniture. We were supposed to load it, take it to Vicki and Rick's house, and assemble it. I pulled the gate up on the crib. "This part comes assembled, right?"

Libby rolled her eyes. "No, I'll put up the draperies and do the linens while you guys assemble." She looked toward the front of the store. "I'm sure Dwight will help me, if you're not interested."

I pointed a finger at our agent, who now was on a first name basis with Libby and indicated that he better not move a muscle. I looked at Rick who hadn't slept in two days. He'd had to take three Fed Ex cargo planes and one private charter back to Chicago. He'd barely gotten his hospital gown on before Betty made her screaming entry.

I had been pacing the hospital corridor, my stomach knotted, because Libby had promised to stay with Vicki until Rick or the baby arrived. I was a nervous wreck all night; I couldn't imagine how Libby had gone through that whole ordeal without me, though I thanked God Vicki had been with her. When I mentioned that to Libby, she said it was 'no big deal.' She'd only been in labor for two-and-a-half hours.

"The first one's supposed to take twenty-four hours."

"What can I say? I'm an overachiever in everything."

"As glad as I am it went fast for you, it means next time we might need to put you in the hospital the week before. I don't want to have to deliver a baby in the back of Tank."

She looked around at all the baby furniture, bemused. As if she'd never thought of birthing another child, she smiled shyly. "I think that's putting the cart before the horse."

I slid along her body and whispered, "I'm available for stud services as soon as you're ready."

Rick stumbled up to us, looking at his list. "Do I want to know what a diaper-wipe warmer is?" He looked as if whatever it was might soothe him. His hair was crumpled, his clothes wrinkled, and his five o'clock shadow needed a nap. I didn't think I would be getting a lot out of him other than snoring, when it came to assembling baby furniture. Libby gave him a raised eyebrow and pointed him in the right direction.

"Okay, what's first on our list?" I asked.

"We need to get the crib and dresser numbers so they can pull the pieces from the stock room." She wandered over to a white, round metal crib I read it on the description card, 'French antique in pink-and-white gingham with white eyelet trim.' Libby laughed.

"Vicki put a spell on this, so no one else would buy it." She caressed the blanket folded over the rail.

"Is this the one we're getting?"

"You read the tag, one of a kind, not in our budget. Come on, I'll show you her second choice."

We moved across the showroom, to a plain white wooden crib. It was like a dirt field compared to the friendly confines. She handed me her clipboard. "Write down the style number and I'll dig through the bedding to see if they have what we need."

"What about a dresser or the changing table?"

Libby didn't look up from her heap, but she pointed as if she had some internal mom radar knowing exactly where everything was. It was the first time I thought of her as a mom, because I never saw her with Cass as an infant, I thought of her as a grown-up version of my Libby. While she was Cass' mother, and would hopefully be the mother of all my children, in my heart I couldn't see her as anything other than the most interesting, exciting girl I ever knew.

I didn't think, no matter how she aged, that would change for me. She somehow belonged to me, as if she'd grown inside of me the way Cass had grown inside of her. I wondered if she would grow stronger and surer with every child. It only seemed fair, and I laughed at myself out loud at the realization.

She looked up from the floor, where she had surrounded herself with heaps of baby items. "You find this funny? That I failed in my basic duty as best friend by not giving my friend a baby shower? Her baby doesn't have a stitch of clothes." She dropped her head, when tears started.

I kneeled alongside of her. "Babe, you've had a few things on your mind. And I wasn't laughing at you. When you pointed to what you wanted, just now, it seemed so maternal to me."

"I am a mother, you know."

"And you're one of the best mothers I've ever seen. It's just a little weird for me because I think of you as my Libby. Even though there's Cass, I still think of you as mine first." I brushed my lips against her jaw. "You didn't fail Vicki, and Betty has no idea about what she's wearing."

"This from the man who came out of the womb in Prada."

I pulled her to her feet. "Let's go check out."

"Wait, we need all the numbers."

"I have them in here." I pointed to my temple.

Rick had accumulated a heap of boxed items at the register; the young sales girl was talking on the phone. I went around the register and circled my finger around the pile indicating we were ready, and she immediately hung up.

"I was here for five minutes, and she ignored me." Rick eyed me. "That's the first thing about you I haven't liked."

Libby gave Rick a sideways glance. "Give it time."

I ignored their angst and dealt with the matter at hand. "The antique French bedroom set. If we buy it, do we take it as-is, or do we have to assemble it?"

The girl had a fake French accent to go along with her rude demeanor. "Do you realize how much that ensemble costs?"

"I read the price. Does it come assembled?"

"*Oui.*"

I pulled out my American Express. "We'll take the crib, the matching furniture, and the bedding." I waved my hand over the diaper genie, the diapers, the clothes, the whole kit-and- caboodle. "And all this, too."

Libby blanched. "Do you know how much that crib costs?"

"Will it bankrupt me?"

"No, but it will, me," Rick said.

I turned to Rick. "Listen, you're tired. None of us have had much sleep. Our kids are in the hospital. I don't know about you, but I'd rather spend the day with them than putting together baby furniture. We can load and unload this in no time, and the best part is that Vicki gets her fantasy nursery."

"Libby was going to pay for a lot of this stuff anyway." The only thing holding Rick back from agreeing was masculine pride. "The extra expense is mine. I owe Vicki more than I could ever repay her. She helped Libby, when I didn't. Let me do this for your family to repay the debt."

"I wasn't looking forward to putting all this stuff together." Rick hesitated. "We can get this all done and get back to the hospital by dinner time."

I handed the clerk my card. "Ring away."

We took all the baby items to Vicki and Rick's small bungalow. Rick said the only reason they'd been able to live in Evanston was because the house had been his grandparents' and they'd sold it to him when they moved to Florida to retire. We stacked everything in the dining room against one wall and moved all the furniture directly into the room. Libby and Vicki had painted it before I had known we called the same city home.

We persuaded Rick to take a nap, while we put the room to rights. There were a few items to reattach on the canopy of the crib. I was putting together a swing when Libby came in with a load of clean linens, which she folded on the changing table and then put into baskets and drawers.

She held up a one-piece jumpsuit, which had snaps running from the frilly neck to the crotch and red roses dotting the soft fabric. "Cass lived in these his first few months." And she drew it to her nose, smelling the baby detergent.

"I hope it didn't have roses on it and a frilly collar."

"Of course not." She wrinkled up her brow. "His were blues and tans with dogs and bears. He grew so fast the first three months that some of them he wore only once and then his toes were pushing out of them."

"That's my boy," I said with a chuckle.

She drew herself away from the memory. "I should've come to you for help when he was a baby." She paused. "I was afraid you'd fall in love with him the way I did, and you'd want to take him away from me because of what I couldn't give him."

I became still, frozen with a wrench in my hand. Finally, we were going to have the conversation that could make or break our future. "I wouldn't have taken him away from you."

"I can see that now, but then you were so angry at me, and when you didn't talk to me at graduation I convinced myself you hated me." She turned away organizing the changing table. "That's why I was in such a hurry for you to sign those papers. I was terrified you were going to want to see him." She frowned. "And then I was devastated that you didn't."

"I was a coward, Libby. I was angry, but I knew it wasn't your fault. Deep down, I knew you didn't do it on purpose. I'd had plenty of experience with women. Maybe I did it on purpose. I've thought about that a lot, that maybe it was my way of making you mine without having to ask or risk rejection."

She looked around, as if the words she wanted might be written on the walls and she could just recite them rather than pull them from her soul. "I also stayed away because I was afraid that if you wanted Cass, you might take me along in the bargain, and I wouldn't have been strong enough to say no. That's why I never came to see you. I was afraid I would never know if you wanted me, or if you would've felt obligated. I couldn't live with you, if we weren't equals. You held so many of my dreams. I wanted to know, for once in my life, someone wanted me for me."

I reached for her and she came into my arms easily now, as if she had accepted, understood, that she belonged there. "I want you for you. Not because of Cass, not because of the past. I want you because you're stubborn, and quirky, and sweet, and sexy. I want you because you're on my mind and in my heart and filling my soul. I want you because with you beside me I feel whole, and no one else has ever made me feel that way. I want you because of you. Cass makes us all the better, but the love I feel for him couldn't inspire the kind of love I've always felt for you."

Tears ran down her face. She had cried a lot since I'd come back into her world. In the past she'd always seemed so strong. Now I witnessed the raw, startling, vulnerable side, but it didn't make her weak. It made her more precious to me, and my love for her more tender. And in that lay the crux of everything, the vast expanse of the emotion I felt for her. She could make me seethe with anger and burn with passion. She humbled me with joy and brought me to my knees in gut-wrenching agony.

No one touched my emotions in so many ways. There were never so many triggers, no one made me love the way I loved Libby. I wrapped her in my arms; my chin stroked the top of her head. Her loose hair swept across my hands, and her presence filled my heart with flutters. My mouth found her lips.

In some ways, I hadn't been really living until the day Libby gave me a wake-up call. "You've made me feel things I hadn't felt in years, and I needed to feel them to know something was missing. I've never been benched by anyone but you, Libby. Thank you for making me feel more."

"Bone-deep hatred?" She cry-laughed.

"The first thing I think of in the morning is you and Cass, and you're my last thought at night. I dream of you, and I have since the first moment I laid eyes on you. I know exactly what you smell like, how your skin feels, the texture of your hair, and what you taste like. I care about your happiness before mine. I want you, and more importantly, I need you, and I've never needed anyone before."

She came up on her tiptoes and kissed me. I couldn't remember the times before, when she never came into my arms as willingly as she does now. Life wasn't as simple as it once had been, but it held more promise.

What exactly I had said or done that led to this moment of clarity, I couldn't place my finger on. But I knew things had changed, that we were closer to becoming us. With every step in that direction, I was closer to where I was supposed to be. I had always thought the pinnacle of life for me would be marked by baseball, but I was coming to learn that all the truly momentous events of my life would occur off the field, and I felt content with that truth.

A flash of the ump's face filled my vision, and he smiled. **A wise old owl lived in an oak. The more he saw the less he spoke. The less he spoke the more he heard. Why can't we all be like that wise old bird?**

It was black Friday, and while the rest of Chicago bustled through malls, we had a quiet day in the hospital. My parents arrived about 3 p.m. for Friday movie night.

Libby had a meeting earlier this afternoon at Whitney, Brown and Rodgers. She was wearing one of her kick-ass lawyer suits when she arrived at the hospital. I swear the woman could run in stilettos like an Olympic track-star. I wanted to hustle her out of the building before she realized I was taking her away for the evening.

"Where are we going in such a rush?"

"I have some business you can help me take care of."

She looked perturbed. "I would think, with all the phone calls you've been making, you wouldn't be so busy."

Oh, we were going to get busy. "How'd things go at the meeting?" I asked by way of distraction.

"They fired Rat Bastard, apologized, and offered me a job and a financial incentive not to file a sexual harassment suit."

"What'd you say?"

"Yippee, thank you, no thank you, and how very generous."

"You're not going back?"

"I just don't have the heart for it right now." She sighed. "Once Cass is better, I'll figure out what I want to do. The severance package will give me time to do that."

"That's great. I'm at the point where I might need your help with this project." I pulled out of the parking garage.

She snatched her head out of scavenging inside her bag. "If you've been working on the project for a few weeks, then you're headed in the wrong direction, and you're ahead of schedule."

"Huh?"

"Christmas is weeks away, and Tiffany's is in the opposite direction."

We were headed northbound on Lake Shore Drive. "Tiffany's?" It took me a few seconds to catch up with her train of thought. She thought a ring would be a joke. "I pegged you as more of a Cartier kind of girl."

She gave me an arched brow. "I forgot. There's rich, and then there's really rich." She laughed out loud and the sound was becoming as familiar to me as the beating of my heart. Chuckles were quickly replacing sobs in our daily banter.

"What in particular are you interested in?"

She brought a hand to her mouth and covered it, realization dawning. "I wasn't thinking what I think you're thinking."

"You couldn't possibly have any idea what I'm thinking." I cocked my head seductively.

"I have a sixth sense about you and your thinking."

"Just out of curiosity, what shape would you prefer? I was thinking emerald cut for your eyes."

"See, I knew you were thinking that when I was just thinking jewelry. That's where you got my enamel ring from."

Each of us spoke in circles around the other until I pulled up in front of a glass storefront. Libby looked around, as her eyebrows drew together. "Why are we in Rodger's Park?"

"Come in, and I'll show you." Two construction workers approached me when I stepped inside to ask me a couple of questions. I answered and asked them to locate Sal the foreman.

Libby had wandered to the opposite wall, looking at the floor plans tacked up on the wall. "Where we are right now is the reception area. We're putting offices on either side of this central corridor and then at the very back are a kitchenette on one side and a nursery on the other."

Libby was still thoroughly confused. "Why do you need this large office space?"

"I don't. This is a going to be a legal aid office. I thought you might like to run it."

Her color ran as pale as her silk blouse. "Do you know how much money I make? There's no way this place could bill those kinds of hours."

One of the construction workers turned on a power saw. The floorboards vibrated and plaster rained down from overhead. "But the perks are that it's your own firm, you don't have to report to anyone, and you can come and go as you please. Most importantly you can help people who really need help. If you get the right kind of press, things will pick up and you'll get some high profile cases, paying clients, that kind of thing."

"And you're going to foot the bill for it?"

"It's my early Christmas present to you. You lost your job because of me."

The power saw cut off and sawdust swirled around Libby's silken ankles. "I crossed a line. The only reason I didn't get disbarred is because I had an impeccable record up until then."

Sal bulldozed into the area, he shook my hand, and I introduced him to Libby. We went over his immediate questions about flooring, built-in cabinetry, and his request to replace the front windows with bulletproof glass. Once he realized the office was Libby's, he spoke to her. At the end of our meeting, we had most of the issues resolved to complete the project.

As we left the building, Libby turned back to look at the façade. She smiled slightly, and when she caught me watching her she said, "This is better than Tiffany's."

I kissed her, as I helped her into Tank. "I don't think I can go to California with this going on," she said.

"Of course you can, you can consult with him until we go, and they can do what they can while we're gone. The rest can wait until after the holidays, plus Vicki won't want to go back to work until February. Then there's spring training. I promised Cass he could go with. We'll have to get him a tutor by then."

"Vicki? Spring training? Tutor?"

"Yeah, Vicki. You remember your right hand. Just had a baby? That's what the nursery is for in the back."

"I thought that was more of a play room for Cass."

"We'll hire someone to help with Betty, and she can help with Cass, when I have day games and can't take care of him."

She drew both hands to the sides of her head and then rubbed her forehead. "You have this all planned out, don't you?"

"That's just a basic outline. You can fill in the details or change things as you need to."

She was silent for a long time. I heard her measured breathing. We were in the middle of my block when she looked around. "What are we doing here?"

I pulled into an open spot in the front of the house. "I think it's about time for all of it."

She went stark white and fumbled with her seat belt.

"You want me to carry you over the threshold?"

"That's not funny." She sidestepped me and looked at my front door, as if it were the gateway to the execution chamber. She looked up and down the sidewalk for a way to escape, while pulling her coat around her and knotting the sash. "That's why you got rid of the security detail."

I stepped into her personal space and met her wary eyes. "Nothing's going to happen that you're not comfortable with."

She backed away. "I need time to think, it's all too much."

I took her hand. "Let's go inside and talk."

She wrangled her hand away. "I don't think that's what will end up happening."

I pulled her body up alongside mine. "I need you."

Her voice shook. "I'm not ready. I'm going to go home."

"Libby, you're a beautiful, smart, sexy woman, and you need to figure out why no one could suit you. I'll give you some time, but I can't live in the same world with you without touching you." I wanted to lash out, but not with my temper. I could wait if that's what she needed.

I had overwhelmed her and now she was going to retreat. "I'll pick you up in the morning."

She started off down the sidewalk, forcing her bag over her shoulder, without looking back.

My gut knotted, and my heart lurched, but I knew I couldn't push her. After all this time, when I looked at her, my insides twisted, and I wondered how I'd regain the self control I'd always prided myself on. I was ready to beg for the physical affection I needed so desperately.

I tried a regular workout first, but I let myself become so lost in my fantasy that I didn't know she had come back until I heard the shower door spring open. My left forearm was leaning heavily against the shower wall and my other hand desperately sought release. I turned toward her unabashed.

Her startled eyes went from my face toward my right hand. I spoke on heaving breaths. "This is what I've sunken to."

"I'm sorry." She closed her eyes; even the soft stroke of her lashes a seduction. "I need you, too." She let her blazer ripple past her shoulders like petals lost on a gentle breeze.

I drew her toward me fully clothed. "Come."

"Wait my clothes!" She gasped through the spray of water, as I pulled her under it.

I caged her into the corner and bathed her lips with my tongue in punishing strokes. Fleeting thoughts of gentleness were bombarded with fiendish ones of completion. The way she tore at my shoulders indicated she didn't care what the gentle beast did to her as long as he didn't stop. Her blouse buttons pinged off the walls, as if they, too, were trying to find release. I kneaded her backside, while she squirmed in my hands and bit my tongue. The blouse slipped to her elbows, locking her arms at her waist. She was my prisoner, my captive.

My mind whirled, and my body responded, boring her deeper into the corner. I pulled the blouse down her arms, and her bra found its way to the drain. The silver-beads on her necklace stood on her upturned breasts. She looked like some wild woman in a monsoon in the Amazon, bare to the waist and shameless about it.

I sampled the luxurious surface of one nipple with my mouth and it rippled like rosary beads. When her legs almost betrayed her, she anchored herself with her fingers woven into my hair. As I bent to take more of her, my hand traveled the length of her body to the hem of her skirt, which I dragged up her body, scoring her with my fingertips. Her silky thighs enticed me. My fingers found the back of her knee and drew one of her legs up, parting her body. Mine responded, instinctually moving closer. "I'll make it up to you next time." I struggled for self-control. "I need you now."

Without more than that, I pushed the sliver of silk out of my way. I was at the gateway of the place to which I prayed for entrance with more awe than that of the holiest site. The very tip of myself revered there, waiting for her to accommodate me.

She arched against me, drawing me into her temple on panting groans. When she threw her head back, I sampled the water from her collarbone, lapping it up like a sinner luxuriating in the water of baptism.

As she sucked on my tongue rhythmically, I adjusted her weight and slid into her on a muffled gasp. I closed my eyes and chanted prayers for endurance. Our foreheads were resting together and she stared at me for a long moment as silent and as silky as her depths.

The pointy heels of her shoes dug ruthlessly into the back of my thighs, trying to find purchase. I didn't feel any pain in that moment, because with the sinking of her spikes into my flesh, I pushed into her a part of my soul that I had never shared with anyone. I was willing to burn in sacrifice to worship in her fiery tabernacle.

It was steamy and frantic. I was enraptured, the beating of my heart and my pulsing thrusts pounded out the sprays from the showerheads. In a euphoric moment, she raised her hands over her head, the back of her hands sliding along the slippery tile. It was a simple act of surrender, of giving control of her body to me, that heightened my response, my eager fingers moved to where our bodies were joined. She arched, offering me more, reaching out for my stroke.

"Please." She contorted around me, tensed with her breasts thrust against me. I saw flashes of her erect nipples, as they rubbed against my chest hair. Her head fell back and her mouth opened to the water cascading into it. It wasn't to cleanse, but to fill yet another part of her body.

She became aware of my devotion to her face. I tried to slow my pace. She blinked misted lashes at me before she clutched me so hard I erupted inside her like lightening. I thrust and shuddered, and she squeezed and stroked, creating a frantic frenzy in me. She had succeeded, but in completion, I stood in reverence of her body, knowing that what had transpired was indeed the holiest of sacraments.

I forced myself to focus on her face. "That wasn't how I planned on it happening."

She smiled a shy, yet knowing smile before running her tongue along my jaw line. "What had you planned?" Her laughter made my body respond inside of hers.

"Silk sheets and rose petals," I whispered as I laved her ear, and then nibbled along her neck. "Let me get these clothes off you." I unwillingly lowered her body and turned her toward the wall. I unzipped her skirt, sliding it down her legs, taking off her heels. She stood perfectly composed as I ran my hands up her body to the waist of her panties, which I peeled down her legs along with her thigh-high hose. I licked the back of her knees, the back of her thighs, the cleft in her derriere, the base of her spine. When I reached her neck, I bit into it to hold her in place, with her hands over her head again, I kneaded her breasts. "That was better than the first night, which registered on the Richter scale."

"We're like an earthquake when we're together." She drew one of my large hands toward her sanctuary. Before she grew too excited, I wanted to get her somewhere more comfortable. With reluctance, I changed the momentum of my hands from seduction to industriousness, as I soaped every inch of her exposed flesh. Slippery, she took the soap from me and washed me. Every place her hand caressed rippled red with need.

We were both sudsy, and our bodies slid together, knowing how our puzzle pieces fit together. I was rock hard with need again, and she was panting in my ear. In a few moments, her expectations would demand more.

I pushed us both under the sprayers with deft movements, so fast that I think she became uncertain. Unasked questions rose in her misty eyes.

"I have a few other things in mind first," I explained.

She groaned in my ear, which she bit just enough to send my mind whirling.

"That just gave me a few more ideas." I grabbed a large bath towel and wrapped her in it, then used another one to blot some water from her ropes of hair. I kissed her shoulder, raising goose-flesh. My body, too, shivered in anticipation.

She reached out for the towel. "You're cold." She ran her fingertips across my pecs.

"I'm far from cold." I put her fingers in my mouth and ran my tongue over their wrinkled tips. She closed her eyes. Her towel was slipping away, revealing the edge of her nipple, pebbled and inviting me to taste what was finally mine.

I barely managed to get her onto my bed, dropping the towels along the way. I sat her on the edge of the mattress and got on my knees between her legs. I looked up at her face, pulling her toward me by the neck, and I tasted her mouth. I plunged and I pursued. She pulled my torso toward her center, wrapping me in an embrace of long legs, encouraging proximity between her skin and mine. "Please," she whispered.

"Not yet." I pushed her onto her back going backward with her. I kissed her lips and every inch of her delectable skin between one pair and the next. I feasted on the taste of her, the luxurious lure of Adam's ale. She arched against my mouth and pulled me by my hair toward her. She was so intense, her body hyper aware, that the moment my fingertips brushed alongside my tongue her scream rattled my thoughts.

I worked my way up her body; I hovered over her abdomen.

"Don't," she said pulling me toward her.

I traced the faint fine lines below her belly button with the very tip of my tongue again. "Why not?"

She yanked on my hair to pull me away. "They're ugly." She burrowed her face in my neck.

I pushed her hair away from her face. Her flushed cheeks sent a wave of desire vibrating through me. I swallowed, so I could speak. "Those marks are mine, the physical manifestation striated into your skin for eternity. You bear them because you harvested part of me." My fingertips grazed her abdomen.

She pulled my hand to her breast, molding her hand over mine as it explored. "Yes," she moaned and moved, showing me that her body was mine to use as I saw fit. It was all the invitation I needed to sink deep into her. I could no longer tell where I began and she ended. I moved with the need of a starving man. She panted, bringing me closer. Her mouth was on my shoulder, and when she bit into my damp flesh, my body aligned with hers to bring us both to climax, screaming the other's name. I bathed her neck, shoulders and face with careful caresses until her stilted breathing wavered no more.

I spooned around her, tracing the length of her body with my burning fingertips. Her flesh rose in gooseflesh to greet me. I covered our bodies with soft blankets and listened as her body calmed. She nodded off for a bit, but she was awakened by my gentle thrust into her easily readied body. After her initial gasp, she started to push back against me. I held her hips in place refusing their urging until she surrendered. Then I stroked the length of her body, calming her, relaxing her into the acceptance of my body in hers for a length of time. Without moving to completion, I worshiped there in the deep recesses of her core.

I would wake several times during that night, my body roused by a fleeting touch in her sleep, a whispered gasp on dreams fulfilled or a simple arch of her dreamlike self against mine, proving once and for all that my voracious need for her was far greater and more profound than even I could have imagined.

30

FAMILY PURPOSE DOCTRINE

The owner of a car is vicariously liable for damages incurred by a family member while using the car with the owner's permission.

Libby

By the second week in December, Cass was much improved and was becoming increasingly anxious to leave the hospital. Even Aidan, who was patient, was running out of ways to entertain him. He taught him how to play chess, and he read everything ever written about Star Wars, Cass' new obsession, second only to ESPN Classic, where they watched old baseball games, especially those staring Band-Aid Palowski.

On the way to the hospital, my mother had phoned and asked me to join her for lunch. When I started making excuses, Aidan tapped me on the thigh and encouraged me to go with a brush of his fingertips. I agreed, grudgingly, and then hung up. "I'd rather watch three World Series games than sit across the table from Jeanne today. I wonder if she'll come as Hildy."

"You are going to have to come to terms with your mother. She isn't going to go away, and she doesn't bother anyone other than you or Suzy," Aidan said with a tilt of his head and the voice of a diplomat, which he often used on Cass.

"If only she'd make it easy to ignore her."

"I think she's got something going on with Dr. Seuss, so she isn't going to fade away. What does she want anyway?"

"She wants to talk over lunch at Atwoods in Hotel Burnham. Why can't she send Bozo with a clown-oh-gram?"

It was another one of my mother's empty-headed ideas and in the taxi on the way there I brainstormed what she could want to discuss. If she did have something going on with Dr. Seuss she could only want one thing: to live with me. Crap.

I glanced at the large, plate glass windows with the gold lettering and burgundy café curtains as I stepped out of the cab. When I entered the street-level restaurant, I took in the custom glass chandeliers, the floral arrangements centered in beautifully upholstered banquettes and the white table clothes filled to overflowing with cutlery, china, and glassware.

My mother was facing me, but I couldn't see the person she was speaking too across the table because of the height of the booth. I prepared myself for Dr. Seuss, but when I made the corner it was a man with a superior stature and dark hair with a streak of silver over each ear. When he caught my approach, he looked back and forth between my mother and I, like a trapped animal. I had seen him somewhere before, but when I caught the green of his eyes I blinked. A snapshot I had stared at for hours swilled through my mind.

In the seconds it took me to compute who he was and what my mother had set me up for, bile bubbled in my throat like Liquid Plumber. But I wasn't a clogged pipe, and I certainly didn't need her to repair my plumbing. I was a grown woman, and if I wanted an introduction I would have sought the man out myself. "Jeanne," I plungered out.

She smiled without a qualm. It had taken my mother twenty-nine years to decide she knew what was best for me. And I was prepared to flush her familiar notions down a drain. I dropped into the seat next to her and crossed my arms. The man's green eyes focused on my face. "You look alike," he said.

"Elizabeth, I wanted to introduce you to your father. I looked him up before you found out that Aidan was a donor. He had business in town, and I thought you should meet."

I glared at my sperm donor. He held up his hands in defense. "I didn't know anything about this."

"I have more pressing matters than a family reunion," I regurgitated.

Jeanne latched onto the sleeve of my coat and insisted I stay put. "If you're going to move forward with your life, and be happy with Aidan, you need to resign yourself to putting the past behind you so you don't repeat the same mistakes."

"The only mistakes are the ones you make every time you interfere with my life. Except this time you've gone too far."

"Has Aidan explained why he abandoned you?"

I gave her the death stare. "That's none of your business, Jeanne."

"You might think that's true, but you're the kind of person who always needs an explanation. I thought this was one you deserved. I'm going to sit at the bar while you talk." She pushed herself out of the booth and sauntered to the curved cherry bar.

I collapsed and grimaced. "What pretext did she use?"

"She knew I was coming to Chicago, and she said she wanted to discuss your son. I told her I would be willing to help if he needs another transplant, anonymously, of course."

"Oh, yes, anonymously." I slipped off my coat and took a drink of water. Since I was already here, blindsided, I might as well ask the burning questions, right? But, for the life of me, I couldn't think of one. "What are you doing in Chicago?"

He glanced around the room as if someone might be watching him. Oh goody, he was a secret agent. That's why he'd abandoned me. I might have believed it, but I wasn't a season pass holder to Fantasy Land.

"I came for a plumbing convention."

A chortle erupted. "You're a plumber?"

"No, I sell plumbing supplies."

I continued to laugh. "I see." I looked at him closer. He was still an attractive man, very Middle America, in good shape, dressed in a nice pair of khakis and button down shirt.

"You're an attorney?"

"I'm a criminal defense lawyer." I continued to look him in the eye. I was impressed that he didn't avoid direct eye contact.

"You look like my sisters when they were young, except you're more elegant."

"Yeah, I'm a product of that nature vs. nurture controversy. I wasn't nurtured and the only thing I knew about my nature was that I grew up with a manic-depressive. I'm really self-made."

His smile took on a grim tone. "But you're more like my father. He had the same take-no-prisoners kind of attitude. And he didn't believe in second chances."

"Your needing them might be a character flaw."

"If you smoked a pipe and blew the smoke in my face when you said that, it might be like having him back again."

"Listen, I have no idea what went down between you and your father, but it has nothing to do with my contempt for you. You earned that on your own. Now if you don't mind, I really don't think anything good can come of this."

"Probably not, but don't you want to ask me why?"

It was a question that even few months ago haunted me, but somehow it just didn't matter anymore. "Nope, but if you have this week's Powerball numbers, I wouldn't mind having those."

"You're beautiful and smart. You don't need the sarcasm."

"Did you get that out of 'Daddy for Dummies'?"

"Tenacious, too. You're used to having things your way."

"It's taken everyone else twenty-nine years to know me." The Liquid Plumber that was climbing up my throat was not tasty.

"My sixteen-year-old is about as spoiled and belligerent as you are now." His expression was narrowing slightly.

"But I got this way without any fatherly influence."

He considered me for long moments. Our staring contest was like a tennis match; he dropped the ball just over the net, and he was waiting for me to charge forward and miss it. "Your boyfriend is a professional athlete, and he's your son's father. But you aren't married?"

"Not much on commitment." I smiled. "Now, that I definitely inherited from you." *Eat that Draino man.*

He rested his elbows on the table. "This bullshit isn't getting us anywhere. We probably won't see each other ever again, so why don't you lay it on the line, or walk away."

He had more spine than the average Roto-Rooter. "It all comes down to this: How could you know you had a child somewhere, and not know her?"

"I never wanted a kid." He was solemn, but not contrite. "I didn't want to marry your mother. I tried to be what I was supposed to be, but I felt she was a chain around my neck and you were the ball at the end of the chain." He brought his coffee cup to his lips. "I divorced her, but she still didn't want to let me go. She used you to torment me. I tried to see you, but she thought you were a two-for-one promo."

I wanted to slap him for his utter honesty, but I picked up my water instead and took a drink. Maybe I'd douse him.

"I knew if I stayed in your life, I would have to stay in hers, so I high-tailed it to California. The first couple of years, I was so high I wouldn't have been able to pick my own mother out of a crowd, much less yours. By the time I was sober, you were old enough to ask hard questions. The longer I let it fester, the more cowardly I became. When I got my act together and remarried, I didn't want my wife to know I had been so irresponsible. She knew about the drugs, but if she knew everything, I'd lose her. She still doesn't know. I lost you a long time ago, and nothing was going to change that. But if she finds out, I'll lose her, too."

All the time I'd wasted wondering why; only to find out one intensely selfish individual had spawned me. I thought about all Aidan's acts of selflessness over the last weeks. He hadn't left me because he was selfish, or trapped; he left because he was scared. He was just as frightened as I'd been.

Before I could respond there was a blonde woman with her coat hanging off one shoulder standing at the edge of the booth. She had bed-head and when my examination made it to her feet, her shoes didn't match. Something about her vaguely reminded me of Jeanne as she towered over our table waving her fist in Mr. Tucker's shocked expression. "After all these years! Why, she's young enough to be your daughter! If you were having an affair, why did you bring me all the way to Chicago?"

All the color drained from Mr. Tucker's face. "Clarice, this is Elizabeth," he managed to choke out.

"Don't lie to me." She started to cry in earnest. "I know you came here to meet Jeanne, I read your email. How could you?"

"It's not what you think," Mr. Tucker said.

"I knew something was wrong. You've been acting so strange. You never ask me to travel with you. Why did you feel the need to rub it in my face?"

Jeanne snaked up alongside me and whispered, "I think we need to go, Libby."

"Libby?" Clarice bellowed as she swiped away mascara. "You said her name was Elizabeth."

Jeanne was forcing my coat around my shoulders; she thought we could tiptoe out of here with no one the wiser. I had half a mind to introduce Clarice and Jeanne, but that was his pipe to unclog, not mine. I got to my feet and looked at Mr. Tucker. "Good luck." I turned to leave.

"Halt," his one word sliced through the tension. "Everyone take a seat." His angry expression forced us back into the booth, except Jeanne, who hesitated. "Plant it like a tree with deep roots Jeanne."

Deep roots have been known to do all sorts of damage to septic systems.

As Jeanne's knees bent to sit, Clarice barely glanced at her before she lunged across the table. "Her? She's older than me, for crying out loud." The glasses on the table clanked together and silverware danced across the floor. Every eye in the place focused on our forced family reunion.

Jeanne pulled herself out of Clarice's grasp, but Clarice was scrappy and started over the tabletop, glasses shattered and water ran into everyone's lap. In the next instant two men were towering over the scene, Aidan had Clarice by her trench coat collar, trying to get her back on a leash, while Mr. Tucker was trying to get her hands out of my mother's hair. I looked at Dr. Seuss as if to say. *See what you bought into?*

But the command of the doctor's voice drew everyone's attention when he ground out. "What exactly is going on here?"

Aidan had gotten Clarice back in her seat and now raised an eyebrow in question toward Mr. Tucker. "Does she belong to you?"

Clarice looked at Aidan for the first time. I watched the realization brighten her face. Her dogcatcher was really a God. "Oh my, you. I know you, from People Magazine."

"Can I let you lose now?" He looked at Mr. Tucker. "Has she had all her shots?"

Clarice turned on him. I was certain she was going to bury her incisors so deep that a series of rabies shots would be required. "You're that gay baseball player that abandoned his kid and dumped Vanessa Vanderhoff." Yep, he was going to require a full series of shots.

He glared at me. "Don't say a word." He turned on Jeanne. "What kind of hare-brained idea was this?"

Jeanne refused to speak, and when she wouldn't, all eyes on the table fell on my father. *Gosh, that was weird to say.*

"Clarice, let me make the introductions. If you're going to divorce me, at least infidelity won't be grounds. This is Jeanne," he pointed at my mother. "She was my first wife, and this is Elizabeth, my daughter who I haven't seen since she was an infant. This is her boyfriend, Aidan Palowski, and I'm fairly certain he's not gay."

Clarice skimmed over my mother and I. When her attention fell on Dr. Seuss she asked. "Who the hell are you? Dr. Seuss?"

"A person's a person, no matter how small." He shrugged his shoulders and pointed to my mother. "I'm with her."

Jeanne smiled tentatively. Silence filled the table as everyone took cleansing breaths. The waiter's retrieved broken glassware, righted the tablecloth, and replaced the china. The maitre d' asked if we required any assistance. In other words, he wanted us out of his restaurant during the lunch rush.

Aidan assured the staff that everything was fine. Clarice was the first to speak. "You didn't tell me you had a wife. Which is bad enough, but you didn't have a relationship with your child. You didn't support her. I don't know you." She grabbed the corner of the tablecloth to blot her eyes just as Aidan handed her a handkerchief. She honed in on him, blowing her nose into it. "You carry hankies, and you're not gay?"

Aidan adjusted his stance. "I think this was entertainment enough for one restaurant for one afternoon. Let's go, babe. You four grownups can clear this all up without upsetting Libby." He helped me into my coat and toted me through the café by the wrist; my bright blue plaid wool heralding our departure.

He stepped out onto the busy sidewalk and said, "Okay, your mother is certifiable. And I might compress her in a clown cannon, confetti and all!"

"How'd you know to come?" I asked through the glare of the glass building that was under construction across the street.

"Dr. Seuss mentioned, very nonchalantly, that your father was going to be at lunch, when he checked on Cass this morning. He thought you and your father were estranged—not strangers. I knew it would be a catastrophe, and I wanted to avoid any more crap hitting the fan in public."

I pulled up short and burst out laughing a nerve-filled, tension-relief laugh, but Aidan drew his brows together. I laughed again. "He's a plumber. Can they fix shit on fans?"

Aidan walked to the hot dog vender on the corner and held up his fingers for two. "So, why'd he do it?"

I tried to pretend that I didn't understand, but he gave me the Palowski stare down. "He couldn't deal with my mother; I was a tie he had to sever to escape her."

"So it wasn't your fault."

"I'm not going to be defined by someone I never knew," I said around a mouthful of hotdog. "If he didn't want me, no matter what the reason, it was his loss."

"He left you because he was selfish—he loved himself more than you. I left you because I loved you more than everything else put together, and that scared the hell out of me."

"I just realized that in there." I paused. "What about now?"

His dimpled smile took his face. "You still scare the hell out of me, but I'm not afraid to come onto the field anymore. All I can do is play my heart out, and hope you'll forgive me and stay in the game with me."

"It's good that you're an experienced player."

"When I look at Cass, I think about the moments I've missed, and I wonder how I'll make it up to him."

"This can't be fun for you to watch, either. Thank you for coming to my rescue, even if I didn't need to be rescued."

"I'd do anything to keep you from hurting, even man up to my own mistakes." He watched pedestrian traffic for a few moments while I gathered my own thoughts. "You know I won't ever be able to live without you now." He smiled.

"I lied to myself for a long time about you and my child, but deep down, I was tortured about it."

"Yeah, but all those thirty-two triple D's helped you through," I said to lighten the mood.

"I'm glad to see you haven't lost your sense of humor, because I have something even funnier to show you." He opened Tank's door and belted me in before climbing behind the wheel. He threw his hot dog wrapper over his shoulder into the back, before he pulled out some sheets of paper from under his seat and handed them toward me. "That is going to be on the cover of the LA Times tomorrow morning. Someone at the paper emailed it to Fletch and I, after you missed the breaking news report."

It was a mug shot of a blonde. I scrutinized it closer, realizing it was Vanessa Vanderslut. Laughter became a fountain surging out of me. She looked like pond scum, her hair was atop her head in a stringy ponytail, which revealed hair extensions and reminded me of CoCo. Her white wife-beater was dirty and tattered. Worst of all, her mascara was black oil tracks around her eyes, and her lipstick had taken a sprint off her lips, making new lanes around the edges. I hooted so hard that I thought my sprinkler might spray all over the seats. "That is absolutely her best shot." I continued to laugh, but when Aidan didn't join the rousing cheer, I slowed trying to match his serious expression. "What did she get arrested for?"

"Money laundering, tax evasion, and resisting arrest."

"Resisting arrest?"

"They tried to pick her up this morning, but she snuck out the back of the house and tried to check herself into Cedar Sinai medical center. She claimed to be suffering from a severe sinus infection. The cops didn't appreciate the high-speed chase from one side of LA to the other but TMZ did. It was telecast live on FOX, CNN and MSNBC. It made OJ's orderly parade look like a funeral procession. By the time the police cornered her her Jaguar was practically totaled. She was driving on a flat tire, she had taken out two street cafes, made a garbage truck drive over a sewer line, which sprouted like Old Yeller spewing refuse from the end of one city block to the next."

I bit on my lips so I wouldn't giggle. He wasn't expressing amusement and I didn't want to seem insensitive. "What do the other charges stem from?"

"Fletch turned some pivotal information over to a Federal Prosecutor about the Vanderhoff Foundation."

"Fletch?"

He swallowed. "Yeah, it seems that CUX, the non-profit that was partnering with the Vanderhoff Foundation, was a front for the mob and the free prescription drug cards they were supposed to be giving away to needy families were being sold under the table. Guess who was the one running the show at CUX?"

I couldn't believe that she would be so stupid. "Who?" I asked, calculating how Fletch obtained the info.

"Evan Platt."

"Evan Platt, CEO of 'Sexy, Sweet, Sugar Video Company' and 'Athletes Gone Bad'?"

"One in the same."

"So they we're running a scam. How long have you known?"

"Melinda filled me in the day after she was waiting for us at my house, trying to get a scoop. She knew when she ran the initial story in *Us*, but she didn't leak it because of the ongoing criminal investigation. Evan continued filtering the money through the foundation, even after he was sent to prison."

"Why didn't you tell me?"

"Because I didn't want you to have to lie about your knowledge of it, and I wasn't going to become involved if I didn't have to."

"And why did you become involved now?"

"Because Band-Aid's Bimbos was one thing, but a few days ago I found out she took revenge to a whole new level." He handed me a piece of newsprint. "This is the cover of the next edition of the *Globe*. The story's written by Albert Rothstein, the guy who tried to make me look like raw sewage at the press conference."

I took it with shaking hands. It looked like the anal canker sore was going to have her pound of flesh, even if she hadn't anticipated chewing on it through iron bars. I unfolded the paper on my lap and ran my hands over the creases, steadying myself. I glanced at him, and then looked down at the grainy black-and-white photo. A giggle bubbled through my caulked lips.

He raised an eyebrow and pulled the truck into the parking garage under Northwestern Hospital. "You find this funny?"

That's when the floodgates opened, and I snorted so hard I might have peed myself. It took several minutes before I could speak a coherent word. "First off, I had no idea Fletch was so hairy. Someone might think you're doing an animal rather than your agent. His back has a beautiful arc on it but how did he get his head like this with you riding him from behind?" I turned the piece of paper so I could view it from a different angle as I took in the headline. 'Attorney Client Privileges'. Before I cracked-up even louder, Aidan tried to wrestle the paper away from me, but I had an excellent grip. He was trying to steer so it was easy to pull the page closer to my face.

"Hey, no fair." I pointed to the page. "They air brushed out the dimples you have on the side of your butt. Look." I angled the paper his way still securely holding it.

He tried—unsuccessfully—to snatch it away again. "I do not have a dimple on my butt."

"Yes you do, on both cheeks." I smiled at him seductively. "That's how I'm able to anchor onto you so well."

He pulled into a handicapped spot. "That's it." He lunged for the paper just as I had it small enough to slip into my bra.

I patted the front of my blouse where the instrument of his torture was now safely lodged. "You're illegally parked."

"Do you seriously think that's going to stop me from retrieving the paper, or your goodies?"

I winked, and he lunged over the console this time. He started tickling me, as he planted himself on his knees between my legs. As I wiggled, my skirt slid up my legs, and the top button of my shirt came open, as I twisted another way.

He looked down at my bra. "That's a written invitation." The next thing I knew, the seat started reclining and his hand ran down my tights, pushing my shoe off, so he could tickle me at my most vulnerable spot. "You're going to scream . . . "

I started panting in anticipation and nodded.

" . . . uncle." He slipped his hand up into my armpit.

I was laughing so hard I couldn't draw air and I bellowed. "Uncle, uncle, uncle."

He came to a complete halt, but he didn't remove the finger from my armpit or the ones from the arch of my foot. "Sorry but that's not enough payment now."

"Okay, I'll do whatever you want. Just stop." I laughed.

His fingers froze and his eyebrows questioned. "Anything?"

"Maybe," I said hesitantly for the first time.

"Let's see, first off, you're going to come to California with me for the holidays." His fingertip in my armpit charted a new course that was trailing to the edge of my bra. When I didn't reply fast enough, he used his nails to scratch a path back to my ticklish zone.

"Okay, okay," I wiggled.

"And you're going to let me give Cass whatever he wants for Christmas, no matter how outrageous or excessive."

The tilt of my head riled up the tickle bugs in my arch and I said, "Okay, okay."

"Finally, you're going to pull down your bra for me, so I can retrieve the evidence I need for my defamation lawsuit."

I smiled again. "Lately, you're sounding way too lawyerly."

"Have we reached an agreement?" he asked, his breath washing me.

Once I nodded, he had my shirt unbuttoned. "Peel the bra back nice and slow." I was certain he would watch me, but he was busy unzipping his jeans, which he shoved down his legs before he even glanced at me. "Now, I want you to show me how long you can hang on to those anchors." He raised a brow in challenge.

I did what he told me because as Cass would say, he was the boss of me. It didn't take us very long to reach the point of agreement, and he collapsed on me. I drew in a deep breath. "Was it just me, or did the world move?" I asked.

Aidan's head came up from the crook of my neck with unnatural speed. "Crap!" He was able to get out before I heard the crunch of metal folding onto metal smoothly.

I pulled the sides of my shirt together just as a car alarm went off. The blaring sound was followed by the strobe lights of two parking lot security guards pulling up alongside Tank in their golf cart. I ducked my head inside my coat and let loose with another round of laughter, while Aidan assembled his clothes. He pealed my lapels back to look at me. "There's plenty more of this day left, and I'm not done with you yet."

I opened my car door, got to my feet on the concrete before I stuffed my panties into the front pocket of his jeans. "I know you think your Band-Aids can fix anything, but you need an acme wrap for this. That Beemer's totaled."

He tried to snag me, but I leaped toward the elevators. The two security guys were whistling at me and a particularly nippy breeze washed my backside. The back of my coat was in the waistband of my skirt and the tail of my skirt was in the back of one of my thigh highs. I looked back at Aidan who was laughing his ass off at my costuming malfunction. The two security guards were commiserating with him. I waited until the elevator doors closed, before I was able to laugh at myself, and when I did I realized it was a wondrous thing.

31

CALIFORNIA ZEPHYR

The longest journey is the journey inwards.
Dag Hammarskjold

Aidan 10:00 p.m.

When I came into the bedroom, Libby was laughing so hard that tears crested her eyes. Cass was tucked in, and I couldn't imagine anything that could make her hoot like that. She tried to speak, but was unable to form coherent words. She waved her hands up and down in the air before pointing the remote, the screen came alive and I watched as mirth bubbled through her.

"Oh no," was all I could say as I watched myself swagger around the picture encased in a pink baseball uniform, with six pixies prancing around me throwing glitter and singing a ridiculous theme song. If I didn't have so much to live for, I'd consider dying of mortification.

She stopped laughing long enough to say, "Madi DVR'd it."

"Please no." I tried to wrestle the remote out of her hand to prevent her from replaying it again.

"The best part, besides the corny lines, is how tight your pants are." She wiped the tears off her face. "Those fairies pummeled you. No wonder Madi thought you were a butt-head."

"They're pixies, not fairies. That's the commercial I was shooting when you first demanded a meeting at Gutheries."

She laughed. "That must have been some hell of a day."

"I hate to admit it, but they kicked the crap out of me. That's how I got the shiner. Maybe it was all the fairy dust, but nothing's been the same since."

She smirked and hit the play button again. "When Ackermann and the boys in the clubhouse see this, they're going to make your life miserable." She fast-forwarded the commercial to when I said, "Pixie Power gloves inspire love of the game."

I lunged for the remote, and we started rolling around on the bed over it, she bit me to make me stop tickling her before I pulled her on top of me, she sat up and held the remote over her head, out of my grasp. I looked up the length of her body hovering over mine. All she had on was a flimsy pink tank top and a pair of boy shorts, and the T-shirt was worn thin. My rough fingertips slid up her thighs, and then my eyes refocused, making her chest my new target. Her nipples reacted under my scrutiny, and before she could counter I had a hold of her in a whole new way. She said, "Okay, okay, I'll give it to you."

"Yes, you will." And I forgot all about the television.

1:30 p.m.

We boarded our private train car on track number five at Union Station on a blustery, snowy, early afternoon. While the snow came down outside the terminal in waves, we huddled in our coats and thought of sunny skies and warm breezes of California. The train was a stainless steel streamliner, which reflected a bygone heyday of the forties, where uniformed men whispered eternal goodbyes, their declarations filtering through the smoky atmosphere of crowded platforms.

We were traveling along the transcontinental rail route, the same path the pioneers and gold prospectors traveled. The antique bullet train's historic route would pass through Denver and descend through the Rocky Mountains.

When the chef came in to check on us, he lifted his hands in surrender. "I'm your cook for the duration. I'll do my best to rustle up vittles you'll like." He pulled items out from under his cart and prepared pigs in a blanket for Cass.

Cass belly laughed through his red bandana, which concealed his medical mask, which had been one of Dr. Seuss' stipulations for our taking the trip.

By early evening, not long after sunset, we crossed the Mississippi River. We had dinner under the stars and they seemed to shine brighter and crisper under the clear cool sky of the western edge of the Midwest, which we admired through the famed glass-top dome of our rail car. We folded down the bunks, and Cass and I built a tepee in the center of the car and made Libby our serving squaw. She got into character by braiding her hair down the sides and putting on a long nightgown.

After I had helped Cass get a shower in a bathroom so small that only one half of my body could be doused at a time, I read him a story from a Roy Rodgers book I had picked up for the trip. Then I read him a poem that was on the front inside cover:

The Sandman's coming in his train of cars
With moonbeam windows and with wheels of stars
So hush you little ones and have no fear
The man-in-the-moon he is the engineer

The railroad track 'tis a moonbeam bright
That leads right up into the starry night

So put on you 'jamas and say your prayers

Cass was lulled asleep by the rocking sway of the cars before I had reached the conclusion. Which was fine, because then I lured Libby back into the tepee and showed her how a squaw rode bareback. I fell asleep, exhausted. My squaw was proving to be as insatiable as the desert was for rain.

By the next morning, we had arrived in Denver, and then began climbing the front range of the Rocky Mountains. Cass decided he was going to be an Indian today, while I was a cattle wrestler and Libby was a cowgirl. Cass insisted on having his face painted before breakfast and he wore feathers and a rawhide vest with fringe. He'd refused his shirt, instead applying war paint on his chest. The brilliant orange, blood red, and vibrant blue matched the colors that streamed across the landscape as we passed through the stunning vistas of the Rockies. Barren trees stood stark against rugged crags and crannies, tall cactus stood solitary in vast distances, as if guideposts. Hawks circled over the glass ceiling of our railcar swooping down occasionally, as if we were choice morsels they could easily carry away on wingspans exceeding four feet.

In the afternoon, we made a brief stop at historic Glenwood Springs, which was originally called Defiance, Colorado when founded in 1883. It is situated at the convergence of the Colorado and the Roaring Forks Rivers, and it's the gateway to Aspen. The town had been established from a camp of tents, saloons and brothels, and had been populated with gamblers, gunslingers and prostitutes providing services for the westward expansion.

We played board games, read books, drew pictures, and sang silly songs, which Cass made up, about the greatest 'Sous' Chief who cooked up all sorts of mischief in his spell cauldron for his wandering tribesmen.

The next morning, after we passed through Reno, we climbed through the rugged Sierra Nevada. Then the seven thousand feet traversing Donner's Pass and going through the heart of the Sierra before descending into the fertile green Sacramento Valley. After lunch, we arrived in Emeryville, the original name for San Francisco. Cass could barely control his enthusiasm because he told us that my parents had promised they would take him to see Santa. Libby and I exchanged a look because Cass had restricted public access, and going to a mall was out of the question.

My father helped me unload the bags, and when I reached the top of the stairs, I turned toward my room. He nodded in the opposite direction. "Your mother spruced up your old room for Cass, and we finished the screened in porch for you and Libby. Big Al finished the new bathroom yesterday."

"Dad, you didn't need to do all that. I told you we could rent out one of the inns in town."

"The reason we have this house is because we want you to visit and bring our grandchildren. Your mother is willing to add a wing to encourage you to have more."

"I might have to talk Libby into that." I chuckled.

"You've talked enough, and you've been very patient. I think you might have to take that little Filly by the reins and lead her all the way to the altar, chomping at the bit."

"Dad."

"Do what you have to do, have Cass help you, knock her up again. I don't care what you do, but your mother wants a wedding. And I'm all about giving your mother what she wants."

"Feel free to be blunt about your expectations."

"You're thirty years old and I want you to be settled. I've worried about you, I wasn't the best example of husbandly affection. The love you feel for her seems to pour out of you, and the way you look at each other sometimes... well, it makes me feel like a voyeur."

I put the suitcases on the bed and started unpacking without saying more. I had every intention of marrying her, but as my father said, getting her to the altar might be harder than lassoing a wild stallion.

Cass barreled into the room and started yanking on my father's hand. "Grandma Kat said lunch is ready on the back patio." And he pulled my dad from the room.

"I'm right behind you." When I reached the patio, Libby was having a glass of Sangria, and the table was laden with salads and sandwiches. I caught my mother's eye. "Where's Big Al?"

My mother smiled. "He had to go into town for something, but he'll be around soon enough."

She obviously had him working on some sort of a secret project. I pecked Libby on the cheek as I took the seat next to hers and filled my plate. Cass was already eating, but he looked up suddenly at my mother. "You said we'd go see Santa first thing. I just 'membered, I got my list," he said pulling a wadded up sheet of paper out of his pocket.

Libby cleared her throat. "I'm sorry, we can't go to the mall. We'll have to mail Santa your letter."

"I told you you'd get to see Santa, and I never welch on a promise." My mother winked at him and turned to Libby. "And I'll make sure he isn't exposed to any unnecessary viruses to do it."

Cass smiled, "Grandma Kat doesn't welch, got it."

Before I could probe what my mother was up too, Avery came around the side of the house and plopped into a patio chair.

"You're late," my father ground out.

"You won't believe this, but I have an excellent excuse."

"That would be?"

"Some bozo in a Santa suit is driving down the road with reindeer pulling a sleigh. Real reindeer and they happen to be slower than . . . "

Cass jumped up in his seat and tried to peer around the corner. The long arms of the Spanish Oaks met the sides of the house creating deep shadows and recesses, making it impossible to see the cobbled drive or the front gate from here. "Santa's coming to see me! Santa's coming to see me!"

My mother shot Avery a dirty look before saying, "We will have to wait and see, but we should finish our lunch first."

Avery tried to catch my mother's eye to apologize, but she was focused on Cass. I patted his knee. "Good job, slick." I passed him a plate. "Use your mouth to eat, not to speak."

He narrowed his eyes and then smiled broadly, before turning to Libby. "So, sweet-cheeks, when you going to make an honest man out of my brother?"

"How much community service did Judge Foreman give you for solicitation?" She raised an eyebrow. "And who's the lucky gal who gets to supervise it?"

Cass looked at my father. "Grandpa, I want to look up sweet-cheeks and solicitation on your computer this afternoon."

Laughter bubbled past our lips. Avery gave a cocky nod. "If grandpa won't help you find them, I will sport."

My father eyed my mother. "You did get that bag of coal?"

Before my mother could respond, we heard a very loud, "Ho, ho, ho!" from somewhere at the front of the house.

"Santa's here, Santa's here!" Cass started off the rustic brick paver patio but turned back for his list on the table.

We all waited for him to go first, then my parents. When Libby and I fell into step behind them, and Avery didn't move, I turned back and grabbed him by the scruff of the neck. "Go get the camera, and make sure you don't have any more Santa slip-ups, or you'll be vacationing with Satan, you little minion." I pinched his neck enough to prove I wasn't kidding. He didn't back talk, but he did stick out his tongue at me like a six-year-old.

Big Al was masquerading as the best-looking Santa I'd seen. His coat was cut velvet with fur trim. He was in a legitimate sleigh, which had been pulled in the front yard by two enormous reindeer. My father whispered, "She must've emptied out my 401K to get those beasts up here."

Libby and I laughed as he moved away to help my mother get Cass up into the sleigh. "Did you know?" Libby asked.

"We had Santa on Christmas Eve, but he usually showed up in a Volvo station wagon smelling of highly suspicious eggnog."

Cass was sitting next to Santa and holding the reins, we took some photos, and then Santa took Cass for a ride around the yard several times, before coming to a halt alongside us. "Now, Cass, I heard from my elves you've been extra good this year, so anything you want. The sky's the limit," Santa said as he winked at me, knowing full well I'd get him whatever he wanted.

"All I want this year is two things." He held up his fingers for emphasis. "I want a baby brother, and I want my mommy and Mister Pole-ow-ski to get married so we can be a real family."

Santa was as blindsided as I was, but he covered it with a hearty. "Ho, ho, ho." Libby hurried into the house without a word. I moved to go after her, but my father rerouted me to the back of the house. "Give her some time to think it through." When we were almost around the corner, I heard Cass say, "Mommy said I could ask for whatever I wanted."

"And she meant it, but she probably wanted you to ask for something that was just for you," my mother replied.

Cass' voice dropped several notches. "I've been working on this deal for six years. It's what I'm supposed to do." I could imagine my mother chewing on that. She had already asked me if I noticed the strangely prophetic things that Cass sometimes said.

The next three days were hectic and tense; we took turns staying with Cass while others went shopping. Libby and my mother spent an entire day in San Francisco and didn't return that night until everyone else was asleep. She'd been doing her best to avoid me and the discussion prompted by Cass' Christmas wish, but by the night before Christmas Eve, I followed her up to tuck Cass in, and then into our room. "Okay, I think it's time we clear the air. My parents are expecting a lot of guests tomorrow, and I don't want them feeling uncomfortable."

"I'm fine, I just feel bad that Cass put you in such an awkward spot in front of your family."

"What are you talking about?"

"I know you don't like being backed into a corner. I told him he couldn't say things like that in front of other people."

"Why can't he?"

"Because you've been acting weird ever since," Libby said.

"I thought you were freaking out about getting married."

A look of shock crossed her face. "You think I'm grateful enough to marry you."

Glare from a fly ball in the sun would have cleared my vision faster. "No, I thought . . . forget it."

"Tell me."

As if she had no idea what was on my mind! As if every time I told her I loved her, and she didn't respond, it didn't hurt me! I was a jock with a big ego, but even I couldn't stand repeated rejection. "I thought you loved me enough to marry me, not for

Cass, not for Christmas, and not because it's what everyone else around us sees."

"I never told you I loved you."

"What is this then?" I raised an eyebrow. "Contrary to how you feel about emotions, they aren't like dental surgery for everyone. I love you, and either you love me and marry me, or you don't love me and won't marry me."

"Everything's happened so fast. I'm not sure."

"It's not me you don't trust. You don't know if you should give anyone your love because you're afraid that they'll use it and throw it away. But I'm not asking for your heart on loan, I'm asking for forever... maybe that's what you've needed all along." I ran my hand through my hair. "Let's just get married."

She looked over her shoulder at me as she unbuttoned her sweater. "That's the best you can do? 'Let's just get married'?" She plopped down on the bed.

I came around the bed and dropped on my knees in front of her. "In the scenario that played out in my head, you yelled accusations about my mental stability, when I asked you."

"Now you'll never know how I would have reacted, if you would have given it you're all."

I re-buttoned her sweater. Then I grabbed my cell and dialed. "Yeah, meet me at the entrance in five minutes."

Before Libby could question me, I silenced her with a kiss and tugged her behind me and out of the house. We headed in the direction of the storage caverns, Big Al was already there, he handed me a candle and we walked behind him, every time I sensed that Libby was going to ask the questions that I could feel bubbling through her, I quieted her by squeezing her hand.

When we arrived at the end of the tunnel, Al and I both blew out our candles. Libby flinched into my arms, which I wrapped around her. Al was known throughout Sonoma Valley for his personal wine tours, which ended with him singing Ave Maria a cappella. As he sang now, I could feel the gooseflesh rise on Libby's arms. The stirring performance left my hair standing on end. His deep baritone reverberated off the silent walls making the moment seem sacred. In the black quiet, I heard his footfalls disappear.

I struck a match, relighting my candle. I pulled a red box with gold embossed fretwork out of my pocket and placed it in her hands. "Does it look like I'm messing around?" I dropped to my knees in front of her.

She looked down for long minutes. "Where'd you get it?" The vein in her throat was pumping blood faster, flooding her face.

"Cartier, in Chicago."

Her eyes, which had been staring at the box shot to mine. "You bought it before we left, before you knew what Cass wanted for Christmas."

"I bought it on black Friday before 'all of it' happened."

"But why?"

"Because I was absolutely certain that you were supposed to be my wife from the day we played pool in McCreary's, through all the hours in the library, through all the food you fed me from the diner." I squeezed her hands. "From the first night you let me know your body, and through all the times I've loved it with such desperation since 'all of it' happened. Even during all the time we spent apart, I knew that you were the one."

"If that was true, why didn't you come looking for me?"

"I was afraid. I didn't think you would forgive me for forcing you to give your child away. I thought I'd lost you and our child. It wasn't as if all the time we were apart I realized something was missing, it was just that there was pain and longing, when I thought of you. It hurt, and it made me mad. But once I saw you again, I knew something was missing, something very important, and I wanted it back. I love you, Libby, and I don't want to live without you."

She swiped away a tear.

"Will you make me the happiest man in the world, Libby?"

Her eyes found mine again before she shrugged. "I don't know. It depends on how big your surprise is."

"If you want a bigger one . . . " I tore the box open.

"You must really love me." Tears started down her cheeks, she backhanded them away. "I'm tired of fighting loving you, it's exhausting." She looked me in the eye. "I've loved you, Aidan, from the first time you kissed me." She laughed. "When you fell in the pile of books, you thought I laughed because you knocked over the bookcase, I laughed because I thought it was senseless to love someone who would never love me back."

I slid the ring onto her finger, and her eyes came alive. "And now?"

"Now, I hope I can love you as much as you love me."

I smiled. "I don't mind showing you the way every day."

She fell into my arms and my stomach settled for the first time in months. I had everything and more a man could want. And I knew the tranquility of peace.

Chicago Closer Closes a Lifetime Contract
By Winslow Davis

Ladies of the City you might need hankies because Band-Aid **PALOWSKI** is off the market, and as promised, you heard it here first. I spent New Year's Eve on the west coast, where the **NUPTIALS** took place at St. John of God Catholic Church in San Francisco. The small church isn't much larger than a chapel, but its stucco exterior, heavy carved wooden doors, and rose window over the entrance mark it as one of the quaintest sanctuaries in California.

The bride arrived in a horse-drawn carriage in a Vera Wang gown, which inspired thoughts of elegant movie stars of the forties. The groom wore an Armani tux. The groomsmen were the couple's son, Cass, who is looking healthy, the groom's brother, Avery Palowski (lookout, ladies, there's another heartthrob in the making), agent Cyrus Fletcher, and Aidan's old college friend David Allen. The **RESPLENDENT** bridesmaids were Madi Dubrowski (Cass' sweetheart of a friend), Vicki Davis and Jenny McQuire, the brides close friends, and her niece Olivia Rodgers.

The interior of the church was spectacular, illuminated by candles and overflowing with California wildflowers. The ceremony and Mass were among the most touching I've had the honor of attending, and the love flowing through the sanctuary and its fifty-odd guests was apparent.

The reception took place in the Marina District at the Palace of Fine Arts. The bride and groom arrived via gondola from the lagoon flanked by two white swans as they glided across the glassy expanse of calm water, as if their feathered choice of lifetime commitment guarded the other pair to their destination. Monterey cypresses and Austrian eucalyptus trees fringed the path to the towering Corinthian colonnade walkways, which led to the single remaining Romanesque rotunda dome, where dinner was served by candlelight.

A quartet serenaded guests to beautiful classic ballads which seemed in perfect harmony with the purely romantic Roman ruin, overgrown, mutilated, and moody like a Piranesi engraving. One couldn't help but notice the freely interpreted sculptured frieze and allegorical figures that dance around the outside of the structure seeming to support the dome. The weeping ladies represent Contemplation, Wonderment, and Meditation, which the groom's father, Mr. Palowski mentioned in his toast as tools worthy of consideration of any groom throughout the course of his marriage.

As to plans for a honeymoon, they were not disclosed. What more could have been demonstrated about the depth of their love for each other and their child than the sweet embraces and whispered words that only they shared as they left the grounds hand-in-hand-in-hand.

We'd stayed longer than expected in California, with the wedding, and we were all eager to return home to start our new lives together.

Dr. Seuss gave us clearance to fly back, and now I was in first class with Libby asleep leaning into Cass and me draped over part of her lap lulled by the hum of the engines.

I had made to-do lists and arrangements for Libby's apartment to be packed and moved into my house. We had talked about putting Cass back in school and opted to continue with the private tutor, who could come to spring training with us. I had already promised Cass he could come, as long as he received a clean bill of health from Dr. Seuss at next month's check up. He hadn't seen any obstacles, when he examined Cass at our wedding; he'd come as Libby's mother's guest.

Libby was barely speaking to her. In time, it would align itself. Jeanne wasn't about to give up trying to show her daughter how much she loved her.

That was the thing children didn't realize until they were adults. A parent shows love in the way that makes the most sense. If the child interrupts that form of love as too demanding and interfering, they reject it as not love at all. But I was learning that love was a lot more about showing and listening, than telling and demanding, and Libby would learn that lesson in her own time.

With nothing but time on my hands, I flipped through the pages of the book about The Palace of Fine Art, which my father had given to us as a wedding present, along with some of the most incredible wedding photos I'd ever seen. My father had selected the photographer, and he had captured the emotion of the day in a way I wouldn't think a stranger could.

The page I flipped open in the book was about the architect Bernard R. Maybeck who was fifty years old when he'd designed and built the Palace. When asked later in life what should happen to his masterpiece, which had fallen prey to vandalism and decay in the sixties, Maybeck said, "I think the main building should be torn down and redwoods planted around—completely around—the rotunda. Redwoods grow fast, you know. And as they grow, the columns of the rotunda would slowly crumble, at approximately the same speed. Then I would like to design an altar, with a figure of a maiden praying, to install in that grove of redwoods. I should like my Palace to die behind those great trees of its own accord, and become its own cemetery." But by the time of his death at ninety-five, he had changed his mind and was enthusiastic about the palace becoming a tourist attraction.

Maybe Maybeck had decided it was all about his legacy.

I was happy it hadn't taken me ninety-five years to realize the importance of legacy. I was fortunate enough to be young enough to change what I had thought mine was. It wasn't statistics crunched into a book somewhere, but memories created by those I loved stamped indelibly across every cell of my consciousness.

The ump made a call. **Finally! He stripped off his mask. You got your dame, now I can retire this game.**

32

GOING TO A HIGHER COURT

First-Chill-then Stupor-then letting go-
Emily Dickinson

Libby

January had bled into February with my heart overflowing, and I didn't think I could love any two people more. Cass grew stronger and more like his childish self. Aidan was my constant companion, and our lives melded with sweet simplicity. I was happier than I'd ever been.

Around the distant fringes of my mind, I sensed that nothing this fine could last long, and now I knew I was being summoned to a reckoning of accounts as old as my birthright.

It was a glaringly bright day with a sky so blue it reminded me of Aidan's eyes when he was especially mischievous. The sun reflected off the piles of glistening white February snow as I rushed across the garage. The parking lot caution yellow lines vibrated against the asphalt. In the covered bay, an ambulance's lights were throbbing red and white in warning.

Once inside, the intense florescent lighting reflected off the slick tile floor of the emergency room. The walls were glaring white but dotted with red, pint size hearts for Valentine's Day. My vision blurred as I rushed onward, the hearts smeared becoming bloody streaks down the walls.

A doctor stopped me, refusing to let me go further. The splattering of blood on her lab coat reminded me of a spider's web, perfectly proportioned, but abstract. The chaos of instructions and instruments as their sounds collided against the walls, added to the symphony of noise accelerating the tempo of my panic.

The doctor caught the attention of a nurse, who dragged me to a waiting area. My heart was beating in the piercing rhythm of a siren, so that my eardrums refused any other sound. Aidan started toward me, speaking words I couldn't comprehend, because my muffled, erratic heartbeat was thrumming in my head with the urgency of a code red. I saw the rising welt on the side of his face and reached out to him. My eyes rolled back in my head and my world went blank.

When I came to, I was in Aidan's lap in an ugly burlap chair. "Sweetheart, you're scaring the death out of me."

"Where's Cass?" I looked around frantic.

"They took him to the OR."

I tried to calm my breathing, I was certain I was going to throw up, but I swallowed down, willing myself to pose a coherent question. "What happened?"

Aidan ran his scraped hand down his face. "It happened so fast, I'm still not sure." He looked at me. "We were done with Cass' check-up and got the all clear. I promised him and Manny that I would take them to McDonald's for ice cream, if the doc said it was okay. We came out of the building heading toward Michigan Avenue. An Escalade plowed down the sidewalk right at us. I barely pulled the kids out of the way, when the car corralled us against the building; two guys stormed out of the vehicle. One of them he hit me in the side of the head with a gun, and I went to my knees. They took off with the boys at full speed, and I started running after them. In the next block, one of the passenger doors opened and they tossed Cass into the street without slowing down."

I started shaking and raised my hand to the welt on his temple, as I searched his face for answers. "They took Manny?"

"Yeah, the cops are looking for the car." His hand shook as he ran it over his chin. "They were Hispanic, and I don't know much about guns, but I'm pretty sure it was an automatic rifle."

Two police detectives came into the waiting area. Deahl had his badge hanging around his neck over a sloppy sweatshirt, and the second officer flashed his badge before slipping it back into his tailored suit pocket. Aidan extended his hand, making the introductions.

"Wait a minute, one of the guys, I've seen him before." He held up his hand, as if tabulating. I willed him to remember. He looked up wide-eyed. "The bartender at my Halloween party."

"You're certain?" The officer asked.

"I'm positive."

"Espinoza?" I mumbled.

"The son of a bitch has been watching us all this time."

"Where are Evita and Tony?" I asked.

As if I summoned them, they rushed into the waiting room. Evita screamed, "Where's Manuel?"

The second detective held up a boy's red knit cap and Evita wilted. "Ms. Gutierrez, we found an abandoned black Escalade, tinted windows with no plates on I-94 near O'Hare. We have the crime lab going over it, we might have a couple of prints."

"Oh my God, he took him." Her hand was over her mouth.

Aidan said, "They were after Manuel and once they found out Cass wasn't him, they dumped him."

I swallowed down and my legs almost collapsed like pasta in a colander. Aidan maneuvered me to a chair and the four of us sat, while the detectives went over everything that had led us to this place. We were working through the story, when Agent Gwen Foley swept into the small space with two other agents. She met eyes with the detectives and the group stepped away. A short argument ensued before the group came back. One of Gwen's colleagues fired off queries as the other detectives paced. I answered them as best I could with Aidan's help, but I was numb, as I watched the time slip away on the clock over the entrance, I stared at it as if it could give me some news.

When we were finished with the interview, Gwen approached

me. "Libby, I'm so sorry. I should've extended the security detail, but I was certain it was a moot point."

"We weren't very cooperative. We didn't think we needed it any more than you did. We all underestimated his reach."

Gwen set off with the agents at a determined pace.

There was nothing to do but wait. Evita and I walked the length of the corridor like zombies. We stood blank-eyed, staring down beige walls. We sat together in silence, where tears of fear were the only sounds. Occasionally, Aidan or Tony would step out of the waiting area to take or make a call. They spoke in murmured words and did their best to keep us comforted.

Every fifteen minutes, I walked to the nurse's station to hear the same thing that they had told me the fifteen minutes before: someone would come to us as soon as they knew more.

Aidan brought me a meal and I chewed, but I couldn't swallow the first bite. Evita refused food, too, but Tony coaxed her into going to the cafeteria for coffee.

"Babe, you need to sit down, or you're going to pass out."

Aidan reached out and took my hand, drawing me back. I sat there, lying across his lap while he ran his hands through my hair, soothing me. A thousand scenarios ran through my mind. Most of them I never wanted to face.

"He's going to be all right, right?" I choked out.

"He only had a bloody nose. Of course he's going to be all right." He was able to shudder out, but the consternation was tight across his brow.

We both knew there was more to it; otherwise he wouldn't be in surgery. "This is all my fault," I mumbled.

"Come again?"

"If I wouldn't have gotten involved with Evita and Espinoza, this would have never happened."

"Babe, Espinoza might be behind this, but if he is he's after Manuel. Cass just happened to be in the way." He kissed my temple. "If it's anyone's fault, it's mine. I was with them, and I couldn't stop them. And I pushed to lose the security detail."

"They had guns, if they started shooting I can't imagine who might have been hurt."

"I wish it was me in that operating room," he sighed.

I breathed in his scent to calm myself. "I'm scared."

"Me, too." He gently kissed me.

I heard heels tap and the female doctor stepped into the lounge, and Dr. Seuss was with her. She didn't smile, neither did he, and their combined expressions crushed my expectations. I closed my eyes and willed myself to listen. "Aidan, Elizabeth, this is Dr. Bolyard, she's the surgeon who operated on Cass."

I got to my feet and teetered. I forced myself to make my weedy limbs cooperate as we shook hands; hers were ice cold and the chill took hold of me and stole its way from my fingertips to the heels of my feet. "What's going on? Where's Cass?"

Dr. Bolyard spoke, "We have him in ICU. You can see him in a few minutes. I did everything within my power for him, but he had massive internal injuries. His body was weakened from his transplant and I don't expect him to wake up. I'm sorry, but we've done what we can for him." She dropped her head and walked away.

My entire body convulsed and the only thing that came out was a wail. If Aidan hadn't caught me, I would have hit the floor. Dr. Seuss bent and helped Aidan right me. "Elizabeth, listen to me. You need to be strong now. Cass needs you. If he does wake up, you want to be able to talk to him." Dr. Seuss spoke with quiet determination. "I know you're strong. You can do this. I'll take you to his room."

I tried to pull myself together, but it was too harsh of a reality for me to fathom. I was certain I would break into pieces so jagged and sharp that they would impale everyone around me. Aidan's jaw was set so firm I thought it might break off, and then the dam of icy tears he was suppressing would run like a frozen torrent. He held my hand and squeezed, it was the only thing that kept me moving in that direction when I wanted to run away. Dr. Seuss pushed through the ICU doors and past the nurse's station, they all stalled for a moment when they saw us.

We walked down the wide corridor, and we came to a room, the glass door was closed and the drapes that lined it were drawn in somber silence. I paused before the door and turned toward a rack with gowns, grabbing one and started putting it on with jerky movements. Dr. Seuss stopped me. "You don't need a gown."

"Of course I need a gown and a mask. We don't want to expose him to any viruses. He has a weakened immune system."

"Elizabeth, the gown won't help him now." Dr. Seuss' solemn clarity pierced me. A stab in my heart would have been more merciful. I wanted to scream. I bent with the pain of it, as Aidan took the gown out of my hands.

"It's going to be okay," he said as a tear slid down his own tortured face, assuring me that it was never going to be okay again. He twined his fingers in mine, and we went into the room. The room was shuttered from the twilight. The only light in the room was coming from the many machines keeping Cass alive.

Cass was reclined and propped up on pillows. He looked serene, and if not for the oxygen mask across his face and his pale complexion, I would say I'd seen him look the very same way many times before. I went to his bedside, Aidan flanked the other side, and Dr. Seuss stood at the foot of the bed. "He's not in any pain. He might wake up for a bit sometime during the night. I'm not leaving the building. Ask the nurses to page me, if you need something." He quietly disappeared.

I looked at Cass and then Aidan, whose tears now ran free. He shook, trying to remain upright.

"He doesn't have his own PJ's," I said. It made me sad to see him without them. The spoken thought brought Aidan to his knees. He crumbled on his side of the bed, clutching Cass' hand. His shoulders shuddered and quaked, the pain so acute that it overtook his body making his limbs spasm. I couldn't comfort him. My own pain was so sharp and raw that its serrated edges twisted into my flesh.

But I was humbled, and I slipped to my knees. I had fought and struggled through life. At times, I thought I had failed, but now I knew those were life's pop quizzes and this—my baby boy dying right before my eyes, when I had done everything in my power to save him—this was my final exam.

I can't imagine their thoughts when Evita and Tony came into the room, but I saw their sorrow and anguish. I gave them a brief glance before they joined us on the floor. Evita took my hand in hers, her face palling with new tears. Tony's head was bowed in solemn reverence. I don't know how long we knelt there, it might have been minutes or a millennium, but with the steady rhythm of the heart monitor, Evita started to sing a Spanish lullaby. The sweet melody filled the room as she sang it over and over again with the machines' hypnotic accompaniment. It was angelic, an offering fit to lie at the feet of God. Though her own son was missing, she sang for mine, as if her sacred chorus would open the gates of heaven to receive him.

Father Schimkowski came into the room. When Aidan moved to get up, he gestured for him to stay where he was. He went to the head of the bed alongside Aidan and quietly gave my son Last Rites, anointing him with holy oil and prayers for salvation.

I was glad Evita continued singing. I didn't want to hear the words that would deliver my son to heaven, when I so desperately wanted him to remain on earth. When Father Ski was finished, he knelt and spoke to Aidan quietly. Father Ski blessed each of us before he left. I was the last and I almost flinched away, angry with the Father's master.

The door sprung open. I looked up to see Ollie's face frozen in fear, her torment came out in a one-word scream. "NO!"

Suzy and Max pulled up short at the sight of us. Evita got to her feet and Tony did the same, they took Ollie out of the room without a word.

Suzy took Evita's place, and she squeezed my hand. Max, silently watched, and then crumbled to his knees. The man I thought had made the world revolve on its axis, bellowed. His cry tore me apart anew; it was a wild wail of a large animal skewered through the heart. Max's large hand settled on Cass' leg before he rested his head on it, his tears marking the sheets.

I crumbled, my face meeting the cold tile. I wrapped my arms around myself to stop my heart from taking on any more anguish, and I sobbed. Suzy tried to get me up, but I wasn't coherent enough to move, even with clear instructions.

As surely as I had fallen, I had failed. I had failed at the most important thing in my life. I didn't protect my child. I didn't save him. I wanted to scream the words, I wanted to rant and thrash everything in the room, but all I could do was sob, as the strangling sorrow clogged my windpipe.

I felt strong hands on my arms and under my knees as Aidan lifted me. He took me to a chair and held me in his lap while we cried. He tried to calm me, to soothe me, but he cried as hard as I did. I felt Max's large hand on my head before he muttered into my hair, "Libby, we're here for you, and we love you." And then they slipped out of the room.

Time became an otherworldly thing through the night. Vicki and Rick came, Vicki sat on the mattress with Cass and she recited the prayer she'd taught Cass when he was a toddler. It flooded me with images of a time I thought was so difficult, but now only seemed full of joy.

I never moved from Aidan's lap. I cried in waves from whimpers to violent bouts of hysteria. Aidan wiped my tears away, while his fell slow and steady into my unbound hair.

In the depths of darkness, we both came awake with a startled jolt when we heard, "Mommy?" from a raspy voice.

When I got to his side, he was looking around with concern.

"I'm here, Cass." I took one hand and Aidan took his other.

Cass smiled and I moved his oxygen mask out of the way to kiss his sweet lips. "I heard an angel singing," he whispered.

Tears ran down my face. "Yes you did."

Cass looked at Aidan. "You remember what I told you today, I'll come tell you when she's ready."

Aidan put his hand on Cass' forehead and bent toward him and murmured in his ear, before kissing him. "I love you, Cass."

"I know you do, Daddy."

Aidan choked out a cry and the weight of it slammed into my chest, it was the first time, possibly the only time, he would ever call him daddy. Tears I was certain I had exhausted flowed through me creating puddles of remorse.

Cass reached toward me. "Hold me, please." I climbed into bed with him and pulled him into my embrace. Aidan took up the other side and he cradled us both. There were no sounds in the room except Cass' labored breathing and the rolling of tears.

I shuddered on every one of his measured breaths, praying, hoping beyond reason for another. Aidan's thumb brushed across the back of my hand, where it rested on Cass' abdomen. Cass drew in a startled breath, and then he spoke with calm clarity. His voice was not the voice of a little boy any longer, but deep and strong and sure. "Mommy, make sure you show Daddy your love everyday for the rest of your life. Your love makes life worth living." And then there was nothing but deafening silence.

I came awake when the doors slid open. It was just past dawn and a dreary light was filtering around the edges of the blinds, the sky was a gray as my heart. Aidan was already on his feet speaking in a low tone to two orderlies that had come to take Cass away. The thought of them taking him to some cold metal locker stole my composure. I raised my arms to hold them off and screamed incoherently while I clutched Cass' lifeless body in my arms.

"Libby, sweetheart, we have to let them take him now," Aidan spoke the traitorous words calmly.

I fought him off and screamed, "No!"

He unwound my arm in determined grace. "Please, Libby, you're killing me. Let me help you."

I pulled Cass away from them and into an empty corner of the bed, like a mother lioness pulling her wounded cub by the tuft of his neck, away from danger. "You!" I pointed to Aidan. "You put him on the Gurney. Don't let them touch him. He's ours, and I don't want them to hurt him." I watched as Aidan unwound my arms around the only thing I treasured in this world. Aidan carried

Cass' still body tenderly. I threw myself back into his pillow, gasping his scent, pulling the pillow into my arms, as if it could be my baby, as if it wouldn't have to be the last time I held him. Through my tears, I watched as Aidan bent over Cass and kissed his forehead. When the orderly went to pull the sheet over Cass' face, Aidan stopped him.

"I have to take care of some paper work. I'll be right back." Aidan went to reach for me but instead ran a hand through his hair. "Promise me you won't leave until I come back."

I nodded from the depths of the pillows. I must've dozed off for a few seconds, or minutes, or hours. Time had no meaning and no one came to interfere with its passing. I startled awake and stumbled to the bathroom. My mind was lost, but my basic bodily functions seemed to go on. They were my only reminder that I'd been alive for the last eighteen hours.

"Shit!"

I opened the bathroom door to find Aidan staring at the empty bed, his arms outstretched like wings.

I cleared my throat. "Aidan."

He whirled toward my voice. "You scared me." He pulled me into his arms. "I thought you might've gone home."

"We don't have a home anymore without him."

He held me steady and bent to stare at me, eye-to-eye. "Of course we do. We'll always be each other's home."

When I started to speak, he put a finger over my lips. I swallowed the words: no matter how much I loved Aidan, I didn't want him as much as I wanted Cass. I would give up anything, Aidan included, if I could have Cass back. I knew the cruelty of it, as its truth. So I let his fingertip stop any more pain from being caused by words that would help no one.

Outside it was pouring rain. Before he could go for Tank, I tromped into the storm. "I want to feel something." I drew in the damp, tepid air. Rain was unusual in Chicago in February, but it was as if even the heavens opened up and shed tears.

He didn't dissuade me, but pulled me under his arm. By the

time we arrived, my hair lay in ropes of frozen icicles. The car emanated stagnant emptiness and we drove in silence.

When we got home, a trembling stillness greeted us. "Babe, let me carry you inside. You're soaked through."

I stepped into the rain and raised my face to its pounding rhythm. "I can walk." If I got sick, maybe I'd die. We were drenched and shaking with cold, but when we stepped into the kitchen, we both pulled up short.

A toy ambulance Cass had gotten for Christmas from Aidan's father was blocking our path. I heard the echo of Aidan's voice from yesterday, when he told Cass to put it away.

In my mind's eye, I saw the ambulance in the emergency bay, its lights spinning red and white, glaring loud in warning. The room spun around me. Aidan moved for the truck, but when he saw me start to crumble, he dropped the toy and reached me before I hit the floor. He swept me up into his arms. When we reached our bedroom, he stood me in the center of the room, steadied me with one hand while the other stripped off my wet coat. "Babe, your lips are purple." He started on the next layer.

"I'm so cold." But I didn't feel pain, there was too much of that on the inside to pay much attention to the vessel that was holding it.

He didn't waste any time before he had me stripped to the skin, and into the bed, pushing me into the pillows and draping the covers over me. He searched for another heavy blanket and threw it over me before I watched him take off all his clothes. The closed blinds shuttered us in; he turned off the phone, then got into bed and gathered me into his arms.

He stroked my cheek in the quiet darkness, where the only sounds between us were our heartbeats. We lay face to face with each of our hands cupping the other's face. There were no more tears, no words, just us. He kissed his own fingers before placing them on my lips. "Sleep," he whispered. But my body heard other things in his voice and responded by moving closer.

When I kissed him, it was tentative, only because I was afraid to let him know how desperately I needed him. He kissed me back with the same painstaking tenderness until something needy unfurled within me. My body, again, knew what I wanted and needed: to prove to myself that I was still alive. His body did not require encouragement for the instinctual flame of survivor's lust to take over and rule his body.

There was not an inch of my skin he did not brand with his touch, not one moment when I felt there was anyone other than the two of us alone in a world of our own making. Every utterance of love branded me feverishly. While he did not take me where I wanted to go, he took me to the edge. When I cried out in protest he said, "Not yet, love, not yet."

When I felt I couldn't go any farther, he pushed me beyond the point where the end must be. He brought his face close to mine, and licked the tears that swelled along my cheeks. He came into me with a thunderous plunge. His lips brushed along my ear. "Now, Libby, now."

I cried out his name with equal parts of relief and remorse.

Strong arms encircled me and tender words filtered through me. "Sleep, my love, I'm going to take care of everything. Hush, love, don't cry anymore, sleep."

And when the tears were exhausted I followed their lead and disappeared into oblivion.

When I woke, I was cold and alone. I sat up on a strangled cry lodged in my chest, the room spun and my stomach heaved. I barely made it to the bathroom. Before I was finished being ill, Aidan was there with a washcloth, pulling my hair away from my face and wrapping a robe around me. "God, Libby I hope you're not sick," he washed my face and I slid down the wall.

For the first time since I ever laid eyes on him, he looked wrung out. Bags hung heavy under his bloodshot eyes and his smile, usually so vibrant, was too grim to reassure.

"I am sick, Aidan, sick at heart."

He got down on the floor alongside me. "I know babe, we all are." He brushed his fingertips over my bare thigh. "Let's take a bath."

"What time is it?"

"Seven." He tried to smile for me. "You slept most of the day. I don't know how you did with all the traffic that's been through this place but I'm glad you did." He moved toward the tub and started the water. He pulled his T-shirt over his head and I watched his body move with the elegant enduring grace of a man. Cass would be forever a little boy in my mind, but if he had grown into a man I knew very clearly what that man would have looked like. How strong and durable he would have been, how gentle. The reminder of the future pulled me to my feet. I stepped into the warm water and sat down.

Aidan brought me a cup of hot tea. "I'll feed you when we're done." He slipped in behind me.

His arms came around me and I shuttered as I sat back against his chest. "The tea will settle your stomach," he said as his hand rested on my abdomen. "Feeling better?"

I nodded yes, and we sat in quiet as our bodies were lowered below its surface. "I never used this tub before you were here, well you know about me and the shower, anyway, I'm glad it's here for you." He used a washcloth to dampen my scalp and then he shampooed my hair. "My mom and dad will be here tomorrow. You're mom is staying in your apartment. Good thing we didn't take everything out of it yet."

I drained the teacup and put it on the rim of the tub. "No more brandy in the tea, okay?" The question had been thrumming through me since I awoke; the question I asked every time I woke up since the morning he was born. "Where's Cass?"

"He's at the funeral home, tomorrow night we'll have his wake and then the next day a funeral mass and his burial."

"Family only."

"Libby, I don't think that's possible. It's made national news. I have to speak to the media tomorrow morning. I initially declined, but Tony asked me to do it, so we can bring attention to Manny's abduction. I couldn't say no, they have no idea where he is, living or dead."

I shuddered. "You're right, that's what Cass would want us to do. What church did you arrange?"

"Father Ski is going to preside at St. Ignatius, it's the only place large enough. I think you might know every attorney in Cook County. Vicki's been working the phones with me, but I sent her home with a list of calls to make. I don't know if you wanted flowers but I asked for donations for Cass' Game."

"You should have woken me up so I could help you. You're taking on too much of this." I felt relieved that I had no decisions to make, but guilty that I wasn't doing it myself.

"You've already had too many sleepless nights. This is something I could do for you, and it kept me from going crazy. We can go over all of it later, and we can change anything you want." He paused and ran his hand down the length of my hair as it trailed into the water. "We need to get him a suit, but I can take care of it in the morning."

It didn't seem right to bury him like that. I imagined him tugging on the collar of his tux at the wedding for eternity, and it seemed cruel. "No, no suit. He would prefer the baseball uniform and the new Nikes you gave him."

He crumbled onto my shoulder. I reached behind me to soothe him. He cried into my hand and his tears streamed down my arm and into the water. When he had emptied his heartache into the basin, I lathered a washcloth and turned to him.

He took up the rag and washed me before running the sprayer over my body to rinse away the soap. If only he could wash away the anger, injustice, and loss with as little ease. When he was done he drew me against him again, surrounding me in the shelter of his strong arms, and buried his face in my neck, laving at the water there before his hands involuntarily came up to my breasts. I didn't mind, but he squeezed them a little too roughly. I flinched away.

"I'm sorry. I didn't mean to hurt you."

"You didn't." I turned to get to my knees.

His fingertips brushed the crest of my cheek. "I never want to see you hurt again. It's like someone digging in my chest with a shovel."

"I know Aidan, I know." I got to my feet and he followed wrapping me in a towel. I sat at the vanity; my legs were too shaky to stand. He kissed my shoulder to steady me before he was gone, and all I could do was stare in horror at my reflection. I had deep blue circles under my red-rimmed eyes.

Aidan was dressed in loose fitting work out pants and a T-shirt. He put another robe around my shoulders and handed me a bowl of oatmeal, my stomach grumbled out loud.

"I heard that," he said. It was exactly the right thing to do and I closed my eyes, thankful once again that there was at least one person in the world who could anticipate my needs.

The phone rang in the distance. "We'll call them back." He picked up the brush and started working through my hair. "Eat your porridge, Sleeping Beauty, I'll wrangle these knots out."

I took a spoonful and was surprised I could actually swallow it. Even if I didn't really want to eat, or couldn't taste it, I knew I needed nourishment. "Did anyone tell Madi?"

"Steve came by, she knows. I told Steve to come early with her, that way she can see him alone, and Steve won't have to curtail her reaction. Plus Steve's devastated; he needs to be comforted but I don't know how."

I studied his reflection. "That was kind of you. It will be better for Madi if she sees him on her own terms."

"It's the least I owe them for everything they did for Cass, when I wasn't man enough to do the job myself." Tears streamed down his face. "I missed so much of Cass' time. Steve probably knew him better than I did." He shook in agony.

I reached up and caressed the side of his jaw. "Aidan, no one, not even me, knew him the way you did. I loved him and knew him from his first breath, but you and he connected on a level that went way beyond father and son. You know that, right?" Words were the only comfort I had to offer.

"If that's true, then it's because when I looked at him all I saw was undeniable proof that the love we felt for each other was greater than either of us ever realized." He dropped to his knees nestling into my center. "Cass didn't show me how to love. He made it seep from my pores. He made it irrefutable. Not that I would turn my back on it, but he made certain I'd never be able to deny it again."

I discarded the bowl and ran my hands through his thick hair. "What did Cass want you to tell me?"

He hesitated several moments. "Yesterday, when we were waiting to see Dr. Seuss, he told me he had fulfilled his purpose for being born. I thought he was kidding, so I chuckled. He said he meant it, that God had sent him for only one reason." Aidan smiled a weak smile before he rubbed his tears away with my robe.

"What did he think the purpose was?" But I knew Cass had a soul deeper and older than even my own.

The doorbell rang and Aidan glanced that way. He kissed the end of my nose. "He said he would tell me when you were ready to hear it." He ambled to his feet.

"But how will he tell you?"

"I'm not sure, but I have every faith that he will when he's ready." He kissed my temple. "Are you up for visitors?"

I said yes to the visitors, and yes to the fact that Cass would let his wishes be known where and when he became ready, because either in this world or the next, Cass would come to me again. I knew it.

I had convinced myself that I could do this. I could say good-bye to my son. I told myself the worst of the grief was past, until I walked into the funeral parlor with a small hand clutching mine. Madi walked between Steve and I, holding on so tight that my fingers ached, which was good. The pain allowed me to feel something more than the gaping hole in the center of my chest where my heart used to be.

I hadn't seen Cass since the orderlies took him away. Aidan had asked if I wanted to look in on him when we first arrived, but I decided to wait for Madi. I had never avoided anything in my life, but I didn't want her to arrive because I never wanted to look at my son is a satin-lined box. That shouldn't have been one of my last images of him: still, sweet, and silent.

Madi climbed up on the kneeler in front of the coffin and I took in Cass' calm serenity. He looked like a beautiful angel, as if I could reach out and shake him awake.

"Daddy, he's not dead, look how pink his cheeks are." And she reached out to touch his cheek. When their skin connected, she quickly drew back her hand. The tears she had so bravely held back crested her eyes and ran to her chin.

Cass looked charming in his baseball uniform, his hat off to one side, keeping his precious face visible. Madi was right. His cheeks held a blush that wasn't even skin deep. He had his mitt on one of his hands and his bat resting in the other. The dark blue pinstripes of his white uniform stood out against the pale blue silk that lined the rich mahogany casket.

Madi started digging in her frilly white blouse, she pulled out a chain. "Look Daddy, Cass is wearing his necklace, the one Mister Pole-ow-ski said would keep us safe." She started crying in earnest. I ran my hand over her silken ponytails.

I bent toward Cass' body. The silver St. Christopher medal rested on his Cubs blue T-shirt.

"It's okay sweetheart," Steve managed to strangle out. "Cass went straight to heaven. He's probably already with Saint Christopher."

Madi pounded her foot on the kneeler to get her father's attention. "No, Daddy, Mister Pole-ow-ski promised that these necklaces would keep Manny and me safe, and that Cass wouldn't die of cancer." She stomped her foot again. "He lied to me, and he lied to Cass, and somebody stole Manny from us. I don't like him no more. Everything was fine before he came around, it was me and you and Cass and Auntie Libby. I want it like it was before, and I want my Cass back," she bellowed.

My knees went out from under me, and I collapsed onto the kneeler as her words echoed through my soul.

I want my Cass back.

Steve helped me steady myself, as he spoke to Madi, "This is not Mr. Palowski's fault. He loved Manny, and Cass and he loves Libby just like we do. I think that he loves you a little bit too, or he wouldn't have given you that necklace."

Her tears were running freely. "But Cass was supposed to grow up to be the boy I loved."

"Sweetheart, you already loved Cass," Steve said. "And for some reason, God needed him more than we do. I know it's hard to understand, we don't even understand, and we're grown-ups. Mr. Palowski hoped and prayed that the necklaces would keep you safe, but God had another plan."

Madi turned her body and put her arm around my neck. "Aunt Libby, does God have plans for everybody?"

I smiled to reassure her through my tears. "Yes, he does." I prayed that He would reveal mine to me.

The sound at the back of the room signaled Aidan had come in with his parents. We got to our feet and started in that direction. Aidan moved faster than his mother was ready for. She pulled up short. Her face mirrored mine, the loss palatable in her eyes. Up until now, I hadn't thought about what this moment would do to her. She had held me at home, and we had cried together, but nothing prepared me for her look of agony. It was for Cass, but there were traces of the pain of Andy in the creases of her brow. She had already buried a son, and I didn't know how she could face burying her only grandchild, but if she could make it through this day, and all its recollected pain, then so could I.

When Madi got about halfway up the aisle, she dropped our hands and ran to Aidan. When Aidan knelt, she flew into him, almost knocking him back. "Mister Pole-ow-ski, the necklace didn't work," she wailed again as she rubbed her tear streaked cheeks into his lapel.

"I'm sorry, Madi, I'm so sorry."

Madi backhanded her nose. "God had a plan for Cass, Mister Pole-ow-ski," she said matter of fact. "And you know what?"

"No, what?" He drew a handkerchief out of his breast pocket and dabbed her cheeks.

"Even all our love couldn't keep him here." Aidan took Madi into another embrace, as his tears ran free. "I still love you, Mister Pole-ow-ski, even though you were wrong."

"And I love you, too, Madi, and Cass loved you very much," Aidan said reverently.

That night when I desperately sought sleep as an escape, that exchange was the only coherent conversation I remembered because the hundreds of others that followed seemed to be ghosts and echoes of the one so simply explained by a six-year-old. I didn't know that night, or even the next day, or even the weeks, or the months that followed, but that night Madi showed me that forgiveness is a four letter word: Love.

She drew me a portrait of it, vividly splashed across my consciousness with the feelings straight from her heart, but I'd have to open that conversation and watch it over and over again before the colors of its lesson were raw and exposed on the canvas. And like most great works of art, whose value is sometimes not renowned until long after the signature is dry, so were the truths that I was yet to learn.

33

BURIAL MOUND

To understand is to forgive, even oneself.
Alexander Chase

Aidan 2:30 a.m.

As I approached the gate of the cemetery thunderstorms broke open the night sky. A bright flash of light fizzled along the sky, as if searching for something to electrify into oblivion. It had rained every day since Cass passed away, as if all the angels in heaven shed tears for him.

I felt as if I hadn't breathed through my constricted lungs for days; the dull cinching in my chest did nothing but tighten. Nothing before—not even losing my brother—had made my body ache with such misery. I felt as if my torso might explode, as if my heart were the conductor through which the crackling light that blazed the sky would surge through and destroy.

During the wake, the groundskeeper had called to say that the plot was frozen. They had dug as deep as possible; enough to clear the top of his casket, but the balance would have to be hand-dug. I knew his casket needed six feet of earth over it—if only to keep me from coming back and digging it out, so I could hold my son one more time. I didn't want anything to lure me to the barren, snow-covered cemetery until the mound was flattened and perhaps the grass had started to grow over it.

So after all the prayers were spoken, when all the condolences were given, when everyone left and after I rocked Libby to sleep, I stole away here on the blackest night of my life. I wanted nothing more than to parachute from a towering skyscraper or swim the icy waters of Lake Michigan during a tempest, but duty awaited no man's pleasure.

I vaulted myself over the fence with enough ease to imagine myself a track star. My camp lantern threw strange distortions across headstones in the windy rain and intersected with faint wavering lights from nearby mausoleums. I knew my way around Ascension Cemetery. Andy was buried here, and I couldn't comprehend putting Cass in the cold dead ground at all, but at least I could place him alongside my brother. The two people I should have understood better, both gone before I had the opportunity to demonstrate the depths of my affection.

By the time I reached the grave, I was soaked to the bone. The temperature was hovering at thirty-six degrees, the rain falling at a steady pace. The chilled temperature did nothing except keep me from combusting. I should have been freezing, but my anger was so hot that it rose off me in still blocks of steam.

Each chunk of frozen earth I pulled from the mud was a testament to my fury. I purged all my recriminations for Andy who lay listening in cold silence. They were as raw and as rigid as the frigid soil. Any tenderness I had left, I used to hold Libby. She was delicate, she hadn't been able to keep much food down, and I watched her constantly. I knew at some point she would collapse, and I wanted to be there to catch her.

I schooled myself from taking her again. I was afraid the livid monster just below my surface would unfurl itself, and I didn't want to hurt her. I wanted her with a whole new sense of desperation, and it was foreign from the tender way I usually took her. I knew she would go where I led physically, but gentle caresses would heal her faster. And so, I took my anguished body and put it to good use—digging a tomb.

I excavated half-gallon chunks, which I hurled out onto the deserted field of markers. I raised the pickaxe and pictured Espinoza's face in the bottom of the hole as I slammed into the earth, imagining blood spurting from gaping eye sockets. My desire for recompense wouldn't require a weapon. I could kill him with my bare hands. The idea of murder suddenly became palatable. I threw back my head and shrieked, the drizzling silence and grumbling thunder my only reply.

The deeper I dug the more frozen the earth. I had rainwater up past the ankles of my boots, when I slipped and landed on all fours. I dropped the shovel and dug into the loosened soil with my bare hands. I tore through the terrain, throwing rock and roots, and decaying leaves. My hands should've hurt, but all I felt was an acute sense of loss, the grief as thick and cold as the mud, took away my ability to breath.

Tears pounded with the rhythm of the rain, and then sobbing filed along diligently in the parade of pain. Why did I waste so much time? Why did I wait so long? Why had I refused to feel the love Libby had so generously laid at my feet back then? Why had I avoided happiness in my life?

If I had those years with Cass and Libby, I would have more memories to live off and cherish. I would have the exact smell of him burned into my consciousness, but as it was, it was already fading. I had been carrying around one of his t-shirts with me, sealed in a plastic baggie. I stowed it in my underwear drawer, and I'm not ashamed to say that I had gone to that drawer and pulled it out and taken deep mouthfuls of it many times today, to steel myself, to steady my resolve. I wondered how many times I'd do it tomorrow, and how many times I could do it before it was nothing more than a plastic-smelling little boy's T-shirt.

I managed to rise from my knees and drive the pick-axe into the grief-soaked soil again, loosening another section of earth, which I hauled onto the pile, ignoring the pain searing through my arm. I heard heavy feet sloshing through puddles of muck, rapidly approaching me, when the man came up alongside the hole he stopped.

"What are you doing here?" I asked.

"Penance." Tony climbed into the hole with me.

I swiped my sleeve across my brow, clearing my vision. "This isn't your sin, it's mine."

"Come on, Palowski, this is a hell of a lot more my fault than it is yours. Your kid's dead because I didn't calculate how far the guy would be willing to go to get his back."

"How'd you know I'd be here?" I asked

"I overheard your conversation with the caretaker." He pressed his shovel into the earth with his foot, making it sink up to the neck.

"If I was a better man, maybe neither one of us would be here." My voice was loud; it carried over my shoulder and into the macabre night.

"I would have ended up here, one way or another. There's always collateral damage with the company I've been keeping."

"What exactly have you been doing?"

"Trying to right a wrong," Tony said over his shoulder.

"Then you have nothing to apologize for."

He turned up large chunks of soil. "You do when you let your pursuit become vengeance."

I contemplated that in the silence of the never-ending rain. "Napoleon said vengeance has no foresight."

"He was right." We bumped shoulders and continued to dig, and after a moment, he spoke, "*Bella* says stuff like that."

"Like what?"

"She has this way with words, the words you need to hear." Tony set his shovel aside, wiped his brow, before gripping my shoulders. "This is not your fault. I know you blame yourself, but what both of you did to help Evita was a good thing. I'm familiar with the kind of man who thinks there are no repercussions for his actions, and I should've anticipated what he might do."

I met Tony's eye. "If the law doesn't make this right, you'll help me."

Tony dropped my gaze and started to turn away. I grabbed a fistful of his jacket. He turned back and slowly raised his eyes to mine. "I will personally make sure he pays."

We dug into consecrated ground as heartache wove through me, the head of its needle piercing me with the regularity of a sewing machine, but this thread didn't bind together. It frayed and disintegrated, like old bones beaten into dust.

5:42 a.m.

Dawn was breaking when, showered, I slipped in bed alongside my wife. I had a new reverence for what that meant and how desperately happy it made me to know I had her to come back to. To hold and to love. Today might be the hardest day I would ever face, the only thing I could imagine being worse would be losing her. She turned to me in her sleep. I felt tears twisted in her damp hair. I kissed her brow gently, and she came awake.

"Where have you been?"

"Sleep with me." I ran my raw fingertips over her jaw.

She flinched away with their roughness and examined my hands. "What happened?"

"Nothing." Even in her grief she was the most beautiful woman I had ever laid eyes on. My hands encircled her waist, resting on her hipbones, which were much too thin. I made a mental note to feed her more often.

"It looks like you beat the crap out of someone."

I looked at my blisters and welts. Even the blood boil didn't hurt as I flexed.

"Did you decide to become a third shift lumberjack?"

I nodded my head no.

"Good thing we're already married because if you asked me now I'd have to cite failure to communicate as a reason to decline." She placed her face into my chest and drew a deep breath. "You smell good," she said on a sigh before she drifted off again.

10 a.m.

During Mass, Libby was as agitated as Cass had usually been; she hummed with nervous energy. The sanctuary was full, but the security I had hired had made sure that only those on my list would be allowed in. The only welcome member of the media was Winslow O'Leary. I would have given Melinda a green light, but she was in LA covering Vanessa's pre-trial publicity.

As I kept an eye on Libby, I caught phrases and lines of the speakers. *'When we lose God, it is not God who is lost.'* Madi sang a song with Evita, which touched everyone, but Libby remained stoic. *'He who kneels in front of God can stand in front of anyone,'* echoed across the coiffure ceiling.

Steve gave the eulogy and his carefully chosen words reverberated between the pews. Libby asked me to deliver it before she had asked Steve, but I didn't think I'd be able to get through it, and I wasn't sure if I had the courage to stand in front of all the people who loved him and tell them about his life, when I had chosen to be absent from so much of it. *'Peace is not the absence of affliction but the presence of God.'*

We were standing for the last time, and Father Ski was giving his closing prayer. After Cass was buried, I didn't have a plan. Up until the moment he died, I'd had a plan. It was a map, a charted course, and Cass was the needle on the compass. Libby and I were the arrows pointing the way. Now the compass was broken, and I didn't know which road to take. The revelation overcame me. I was completely and utterly uncertain for the first time in my life. "When we put our cares in His hands, He puts His peace in our hearts," Father Ski's final words for Cass.

In the vestibule I steered Libby toward her mother by the small of her back. Jeanne hugged Libby before directing us to the corner where Dr. Seuss was waiting. He had been good for Libby's mother, regardless of what Libby thought.

"I don't know what your plans are in the near future, but I didn't want to bring you all the way to my office to tell you what I could simply say now."

Libby didn't speak.

"I don't understand," I said.

"The last day I saw you in my office," he cleared his throat. "The day Cass died we had drawn blood for normal blood work."

He pulled out a printed lab results. "The lab brought this to my attention." He extended the paper toward me.

I looked at the form, and then at Libby.

"The lab ran the tests, even though we already knew Cass had died. They didn't want to close Cass' file until everything was complete. The blood work revealed Cass' cancer had already returned and had spread to his lymph nodes."

I looked up from the results and Libby grabbed onto my arm for support. "What does that mean?" I asked.

"It means that if he wasn't thrown from a moving car, the cancer would have spread through his system in a matter of weeks. It was very aggressive, and I'm surprised he hadn't complained of any pain."

Libby brought a hand to her mouth. "Oh, my God."

A few heads turned toward us.

Dr. Seuss took her hand. "I wanted you to know, so you wouldn't blame yourselves, or even each other. Cass was going to die, and there was nothing any of us could have done. It doesn't make it easier, but the cancer would have caused more suffering. So when your priest says God works in mysterious ways, He does."

"Thank you Dr. Seuss," Libby choked out.

Dr. Seuss caught her easy dismissal and reached out to halt her retreat. Like any good disciple, he continued to sell his story. "We couldn't have saved him, Libby. Not my science, or your love, or even your strength, Aidan. None of us are to blame because we all did our best. I hope someday this will make it better for you." He'd started to move away, but turned back. "When I was a child, my father used to say, 'Don't cry because it's over. Smile because it happened.' I didn't know it was a saying from Dr. Seuss until he had been gone many years. I never told you, but he died of cancer."

We left the church and all the way to the cemetery, Libby twisted a handkerchief in her hands. She would spread it out flat in her lap, then fold it up into a neat square, then wring it out. Finally, I put my hands over hers to still them.

I held an umbrella over her as she walked toward the casket.

Snowflakes started to swirl around her booted ankles. When we arrived under the white canopy, she moved to her seat without acknowledging Cass' mourners. When everyone was assembled, Father Ski started with a prayer and then a simple child's Bible verse. Then the assembly filed by one by one, piling pieces of frozen earth on the top of his casket, Libby didn't move when everyone had walked past. I searched her face but I couldn't read her eyes behind her glasses. Her hand was full of soil, but she held steady.

Father Ski said, "God is subtle, but He is not malicious."

A moment after he had made that simple statement, she extended her arm out in front of her, ground the soil through her fingers and laughed. It was anger-filled and must've come from somewhere deep within her.

"God is not malicious!" she screamed. "If God is not malicious, why did he do this? Why did he take the life of a small, innocent boy? What could he be to God that was more than what he was to me? God is not malicious! If this is not baleful injustice, I don't know what is. God has been malevolent from the moment of my conception. Your God is spiteful and cruel!"

People rushed to comfort her, but I waved them off, speaking under my breath to her. "That's enough, Libby."

Max moved along her side, assuring me of his assistance.

I nodded my head at the groundskeeper, who lowered the coffin into the grave. When it was below the surface, Libby dropped to her knees and clutched at the side of the hole, as if she could stop its descent with the strength of her will alone.

She tore at the edges of the grave with her bare hands ripping away soil, trying to reach the coffin.

I got on my knees alongside her, pushing the mud back in the hole as easily as she tore it away in clumps. Her fingers clawed away until she caught sight of my hands, now damaged and dirty.

Her eyes swung to mine. "You! You dug this hole deeper." She pummeled my chest with her muddied hands. "I didn't want it deeper." She pushed me away and her hands smeared down the front of my once white shirt. "I don't want Cass in there. Why did you dig this out? Why?" She sullied me with poisoning phrases as she beat on my chest like a crazed woman.

I caught her wrists to steady her and stop her violent assault. I shook her once to get her full attention. "I did what needed to be done. I did it for Cass, and I did it for you. Even when it hurts like hell, you have to do the right thing for the people you love. Pain is a small price to pay for loving. Years ago, you paid that price for my career and let me go. I had gained all and lost myself, while you lost everything, but gained yourself. You taught me this."

She brought her muddied hands to her face and I pulled her into my chest. Everyone melted away. She cried, and finally it wasn't with anger, but laced with remorse. I stroked her back while she emptied the bottled-up emotions. I dug out another handkerchief and wiped at her cheeks before I helped her up. She looked down at the coffin, opening her purse and dumped the contents over his grave as a final offering: gum balls, M&M's, and Skittles pinged and popped over its mahogany surface.

5 p.m.

After Libby's outburst, she was finally able to grieve, and she huddled in a corner with Ollie, who was taking the loss of Cass as if he was her own brother; with Vicki who thought of him as her own child; with Suzy, Jeanne, and my mother who grieved the loss of their grandchild together. Whenever I tried to approach, she waved me away. I respected her space, weaving my way through the throng of the room.

When the room cleared, I couldn't locate Libby. I went to the kitchen where my parents were working together at the sink. They looked up from whatever heated exchange they were having.

"You don't have to clean up, the cleaning service will."

My father cleared his throat. "We don't mind. It gives us something to do together. If you don't think you need us, we're going to go back to California tomorrow."

"Unless you'd like us to stay," my mother chimed in hopefully.

When my father gave her a look of warning, she turned back to the sink and let the subject drop.

"Have you seen Libby?"

"She went out the back door awhile ago without a coat," my father said, "but she promised me she was just going to walk around the house. I thought I heard the front door open."

"That must have been someone else leaving." I didn't bother with a coat. As I went out the back door, I sensed that she was gone. I couldn't feel her. I jogged around the house, then to the garage. Both cars were still in their spots. I ran back into the house, threw the front door open, yelling her name. We searched the entire house, but she wasn't here, I couldn't fathom where she went without a word, but she had vanished from under my ever-watchful eye.

34

DEATH SENTENCE

No one ever told me that grief felt so like fear.
C.S. Lewis

Libby

Once I staggered outside, I couldn't go back. I couldn't choke through the weight of any more strained sentiments or well wishes, even if I knew of their sincerity. Now that he was gone, buried in an icy, unmoving mound, alone and cold, all I wanted was escape. Fresh air soothed my nauseous stomach and my spinning head. I took my coat from the garage, before I sulked off alone down the alleyway. I ventured a trip around the block, but when I met the first intersection, I kept walking north.

It would be light for several more hours. I marched as if the journey would bring me to a destination where the pain ceased. I hiked for a few miles, and then thought to take a taxi. My feet hurt, but I had no inclination to even give a stranger the location where I would huddle and lick my wounds. My cell phone rang incessantly. I turned it off and dumped it in a trashcan. I wanted to be alone in my grief. For three days I had shared it, and now I wanted to wallow in it all alone, I wanted to go to my own bed and lie there and pray for death to take me to my son. I knew, intellectually, I wouldn't die, but I wanted it. In spite of everything that I had to live for, I wanted the kind God, whom Father Ski tried to convince me, loved me, to grant me death as his final mercy.

I walked into the street without looking. I ignored the cursing milkman, and the bus driver who laid on his horn, and I continued to walk. I must've been walking at a steady pace for several hours by the time I reached Sheridan Road.

I dragged my limbs until my feet were numb and I was certain I would drop into oblivion. I stumbled up the stairs, feeling along the doorframe for the extra key. Then I looked inward and felt along the edges of my heart for a spare memory of my child. I couldn't focus on his face as tears crowded my vision. I didn't bother with a light. I didn't want anyone's company. I sat down on the sofa in the dark and I cried.

A knock on the door made me push the reminiscences away and listen. I sat perfectly motionless; hoping whoever it was would disappear.

Then I heard a man's voice say, "Elizabeth, I saw you go in. Answer the door." There was a prick of recognition with the voice, but the face wasn't coming to me. Anyone who knew me well enough to be pounding down my door called me Libby. I sat quietly, hoping whoever it was, would give up and go away. I was sick to death of the media, and their questions, and it could only be one of those lechers who would be callous enough to want an interview now. "Elizabeth, open this door."

Something compelled me to stumble to the entry. I cracked the door with the chain still in place. "What do you want?"

"Let me in, and I'll tell you."

I backed up and unchained the door, a burst of dizziness swept through me, and the world swam before my eyes as I slid down the door into a heap of blackness.

I came awake with a sudden jolt. I was lying on the sofa, and the lights were on. A large figure hovered over me before he spoke. "That was not one of the reactions I anticipated." He passed me a glass of water and I focused on my father's face.

"Were you expecting a welcome home party?" I asked wryly. I scooted into a sitting position. "What are you doing here?"

"I saw the press conference on TV about Cass, and I wanted to see if there was anything I could do. I went to the cemetery, but they wouldn't let me in."

"So you've been hiding in the bushes? I don't live here."

"It's not like Aidan Palowski's address is posted on the Internet. I figured someone would show up here sooner or later."

"So you've been waiting here for me all day… why?"

"Because I wanted to make sure you were all right."

I laughed to myself. "I am at the worst place in my life, and you think there's a possibility that I might be all right? You're more heartless than I thought."

He ignored the dig. "I thought you might need me."

"Need you?" *Seriously*? A burst of rage seeped through me. "I needed you when I was four-years-old and my mother dropped me with strangers all over town, as if I was a puppy to board. I needed you when I was six and wanted to learn how to ride a two-wheeler. I needed you when I was fifteen and my mother was sleeping around. I needed you when I was twenty-two, pregnant, alone and broken-hearted. But I'm twenty-nine years old, and unless you can raise the dead, I don't need you and your fucking guilty shit in my life right now."

His arms were resting on his knees, and his head hung between them, his shoulders slumped further. He stared at his loafers for several moments before he raised his head. "I thought I could tell you what I've learned about life."

"I have just lost my only child, and I don't have the inclination or the energy to deal with you right now. I can't imagine what you thought to gain by coming here."

"Life isn't about the high notes or the low tides. It's about the day-to-day living and loving. And I know you're surrounded by people who love you, but maybe they love you too much to be straight with you."

"You think this is a low tide? This is a fucking tsunami!"

"I thought I could help you straighten out your feelings, maybe explain that losing your son wasn't any more your fault than not having a father around." He rose to his feet. "I can see you're not ready to hear what I have to say." He put a card on the table as if this were a business meeting. "When you're willing to talk, give me a call."

I got to my feet and teetered like a Weeble and I heard, 'Weebles wobble but they don't fall down.' My mantra: no matter how close I came to falling, I always caught myself before the ultimate tumble. "Don't wait by the phone," I bellowed.

The front door swung open and I met Aidan's concerned face. "Babe, you scared the crap out of me. I've been looking everywhere for you. Why didn't you answer your cell? I would have brought you here, if you wanted to . . . " His eyes, so concerned for me, followed mine and he noticed we weren't alone. "What the hell is he doing here?"

Mr. Tucker looked shell-shocked, as he swallowed.

I looked back and forth between the two men who should have cared about me more than anyone else in the world. "Aidan, you remember my sperm donor. Mr. Tucker, my husband."

Aidan's anger eyebrow shot up. "Our son just died. Don't you think that's enough turmoil?"

"My only intention was to help Elizabeth."

"Her name is Libby, but you wouldn't know that because you haven't been around for the last thirty years," Aidan bellowed.

Mr. Tucker's head shot up from his chest. "I named her Elizabeth, while you were still in diapers, Band-Aid. And from what I've been able to piece together, you don't have a much better record in this game than I do."

Aidan lunged with his forearm across Mr. Tucker's throat, pinning him to the living room wall. "In case you didn't get the live feed, I'm here for her, and she's more my wife than she'll ever be your daughter."

"What the hell is going on up here?" Max was bellowing from the open doorway. "Did someone break in?" He examined the confrontation between Aidan and a man unknown to him.

"Aidan, let him go," I ground out. "Dr. Maxwell Rodgers, meet Mr. Charles Tucker."

Max looked confused. "As in your father?"

"Biologically speaking."

"Does your husband need assistance killing the whoreson?"

I twisted in shock at Max; I had never heard that kind of language or sentiment from him. Aidan stepped next to me and wrapped his hand around my angry fist.

"I didn't come here to cause more heartache." Mr. Tucker was straightening his clothes avoiding Max's angry stance. "I thought El . . . I mean, Libby, might need help. I can see now she doesn't. If you'll excuse me, I'll get out of your hair." He scrutinized me and nodded to Aidan before starting for the door.

Max stepped into his path. "Let's you and I have a few words down at my house."

"You want to talk? Or murder me?"

"I'm a lawyer. Do you think I'd be dumb enough to kill you in my own home?" Max opened the door and gestured. "After you."

Aidan's arms came around me. "Babe, I'm sorry."

I was trapped in his coat and struggled to get out. "I want to go to sleep I'm tired."

"Let me get you in bed." He pulled me back to my old bedroom, helped me get out of my clothes, and found me a T-shirt. Aidan took off his coat, and started to pull his shirt out of his slacks. "You had us worried. Don't run off like that again. How did you get here?"

"I walked."

"Libby." He closed his eyes and took a deep breath. "That's a long way, and its cold out." He used the irritated dad voice. Then he softened. "Please, you're scaring me."

I watched him loosen his tie. "What are you doing?"

"I'm getting undressed, so we can go to sleep. I'm beat."

"I came here because I wanted to be alone for awhile."

"Libby, please?"

"Please go home."

"Wherever you are is my home," he said somberly.

"Go home to your other home. I need some time. I want to sort things through by myself for awhile." I wanted to crawl in the deepest, darkest place I could find and fade away.

Pain washed his face, and he froze as if he was perilously standing on an island of fragile ice in the middle of a darkened lake. Blind-sided, he hesitated, first to move toward me, then taking a step back, his hands moving away from his clothes. I turned away. When he sat down, his hand came to rest on my hip. He squeezed. "I need you."

I placed my hand on his to reassure him, but I knew there were no assurances in life. "I know, but I need to be alone."

"Babe, we need to be together. That's the best way for us to get through this."

"That might be what's best for you, but what's best for me is some time alone. Please don't make me beg for it."

"I loved him, too, Libby."

"Yes, but I loved him from the moment I knew about him."

"You grieve for all that you had and lost, and I grieve for all that I wasted and will never be able to get back." I heard him shudder out a few inhalations. "I grieve the misery of regret, like your father." He moved over me and his warm breath washed my face before he kissed my temple. "Please don't shut me out, not now. Not after everything."

Tears started to run down my face. I wanted to wallow in them without witnesses. "Please give me time to get where I need to go, this is something you can't give me."

I could hear his emotions battling in his wavering voice when he spoke. "I'll go, if you promise not to go anywhere."

I sniffled out a yes.

"I'll call you in the morning." He kissed my temple again and ran his lips from there along my hairline to my ear. "I love you, babe."

I didn't respond. I was torn between wanting his love, which I had always dreamt of having and pushing it just beyond the grasp of my fingertips.

"Libby, I know you're hurting, but I love you so much."

With a raw, wounded heart, his love didn't seem to faze me, my father's concern didn't seem to register, all the whispered encouragement couldn't fill the gaping hole left by the death of my child. All I felt was the sharp loss of Cass. I couldn't choke out words of reply; they would have been hollow memories my grief had sucked dry. What could I say of love, when all the real love I had ever felt was buried six feet under the frozen earth?

35

BIGGEST DOUBLE OF MY CAREER

Grief knits two hearts in closer bonds than happiness ever can. Alphonse De Lamartine

Aidan 4:30 a.m.

"Daddy?"

I came awake with a start. I was sure I had heard a voice, and I thought maybe Libby had decided to come home after two tortuous weeks. I barely slept, and when I did, it was neither for very long, nor without suffering. I rubbed my eyes trying to adjust to the murky dawn.

"Daddy, it's me," a childlike voice whispered.

Another voice said, "You don't have to whisper, Cass. No one else is here except us and your dad."

I zeroed in on where the voices were coming from at the end of my bed. My instinctual reaction was to back away.

"It's okay, Daddy, it's just me."

I locked eyes with the eerily translucent figure at the foot of my bed. His eyes were the exact color of his mother's. How I could see the green depths in the dark I couldn't explain. He was wearing his baseball uniform, exactly as I had last seen him and his hat was slightly off kilter the way he liked it best—he'd said it was cool that way. "Cass?"

"It's him. Are you going to pay attention? We don't have much time."

I focused on the other figure and almost jumped out of my skin. My brother was standing next to Cass in a Florida Marlins uniform. His face hadn't aged since I was nine-years-old. The pain of it struck me to my core. "Andy?"

He smiled. "You still remember me?"

This was a serious delusion, but at least it was a pleasant one. "Of course, you're my brother." I looked back and forth between them. "Why are you with my son?"

"Daddy, Uncle Andy is my guardian angel. He takes care of me in heaven." He smiled his crooked toothed smile. "'Member when I told you that you should tell mommy why I was sent to earth? You need to go and tell her now."

"But I don't know why."

"Think, Daddy. Think."

"I'm thinking."

"Think harder," Cass insisted.

With those words, the truth I had never considered washed through me.

"You got it now, Daddy?" He smiled.

I did. "But she won't see me."

Andy said, "Set aside your pride and your hurt feelings."

"I don't understand."

"Go see her this morning, Daddy. Get her out of bed and make her eat. If she doesn't, the babies are going to die."

"The babies?"

"Mommy has two babies in her pocket." Cass smiled proudly. "Didn't you get my signs? 'Member you said if the player doesn't see the first sign, you should send more. First, I made mommy sick, I didn't want to, but Uncle Andy said I had to. Then I made her faint, 'member?" He looked down at his cleats and then he looked up at me blushing. How on earth could blood rush to the cheeks of a delusion?

He wasn't from this earth any longer, and my mind dipped past the stupor and came up with the only conclusion available. Cass dug into the carpet with his shoe. "Member how she hurt when you touched her somewhere? I know you didn't mean to hurt her, but be extra gentle with her body now."

"Libby's going to have a baby?" I asked.

Andy nodded and held up two fingers before he put his hand on Cass' shoulder. "This is your single, and now you got a double. Are you going to try to hit for the cycle?"

"We're going to have twins?"

"I told you that." Cass smiled. "Mommy has a boy baby and a girl baby in her pocket. There frat . . . frat . . . what's that word Uncle Andy?"

"Fraternal."

"Yeah, fraternal twins, that means they aren't exactly alike. But you got to make mommy understand."

"Get Libby to understand, got it," I said as I started to get out of bed and move toward Cass.

"I love you, Daddy, I only get to come and see you this one time." He smiled. "Don't worry, Daddy, I'm happy where I am."

I stumbled and tried to reach him. "I love you, Cass."

"I know, Daddy." He started to fade, then became blurry and slipped away. It hurt that in one moment I could hear his sweet voice, and in another I realized I'd never hear it again.

Andy was still there. "If she won't listen to reason, make her mad. She's as pig-headed as you are, and we have other people we need to take care of. We can't come back, but if you don't get her out of this funk she'll exist only in your dreams." He started to fade away. "You've turned out to be a good man, Aidan. Make her see what we all see."

"I love you, Andy. Thank you."

"You're welcome, little bro. I've got my work cut out for me on Avery. Later." When he was nothing more than tiny particles of light, he whispered, "I love you, too."

I had been torn up about what to do. I was trying to be patient, but she could try the patience of a saint. I was hurting, too, and she was the only thing that made me better, the only comfort in the world to me.

7:00 a.m.

It was time to play hardball. When I called Max from my cell on the way to his house, he agreed on my course of action. "I'm probably going to have to break the door down."

"Aidan, at this point do what you have to. She barely takes our calls. The only person she's cracked the door open for was Ollie, and she wouldn't let her in. Aidan, you need to prepare yourself. Ollie said she looks like hell."

"Why didn't you call me?"

"Ollie didn't see her until last night, and Suzy called afterwards and threatened that if Libby didn't come out that she was going to come in." He chuckled to himself. "The one person you never want to piss off is my Suzy. Libby tried to cry her way out of it, but Suzy let her know that yesterday was the end of the pity party."

"I've played into for too long."

"I've been impressed with your restraint, I couldn't have lasted a week."

"You didn't doubt me?"

"In the past, yes, but not anymore, I've never seen a man watch a woman more closely than you did Libby after Cass died. Even through your own pain, she was foremost in your mind. Not too many men love like that, but those who do are the lucky ones." Max cleared his throat. "Before I forget—any word on Manny?"

"No, nothing. I think Evita might be desperate enough to go to South America to see if she can find him."

"Espinoza is probably hiding him in plain sight. I'll call Tony and see what I can do. Evita might be signing her own death warrant if she touches South American soil," he sighed, disgusted. "Maybe that was Espinoza's plan from the beginning."

"I want Espinoza to pay for what he's done."

"Get in line," Max said as he hung up.

I was glad Max was up to speed on the situation. I wasn't in the right state of mind to help Evita. And after this morning's spiritual intervention, Libby's health was my top priority. Vengeance would have to wait. I pulled up the cobbled drive and mentally prepared myself for the coming battle.

I grabbed my Walgreen's bag, a couple of moving boxes and the pickaxe. I wasn't quiet coming up the metal stairs. I put everything on the landing and decided it wasn't worth it to knock, so I took the head of the pickaxe and hammered it into the lock, after three whacks, the deadbolt fell.

I picked up my bag and went to her bedroom door, which was closed and locked. I banged on the door with my fist, no more Mr. Nice Guy. I was a big leaguer. "Libby, open this door, and let me in," I said in my angry voice.

"Go the fuck away."

"Libby, you know how I feel about that language."

"I'm not a mother anymore, so I can say whatever the fuck I want."

I knew she wasn't going to open the door so I went to my bag and got out the tools as I continued to talk. "Open the door because one way or another you're getting out of bed today."

Something slammed against the door. "Get the hell out of my apartment or I'll call Max."

The first bolt pinged onto the floor from the top hinge. "Max isn't going to take your side, you call him and see. He was planning on sending the fire-breathing Suzy up here."

I could hear her thrashing around. "Just go away."

"Sorry, babe, time is up, and I came to give you good news." The second pin wouldn't slip from the hinge so I used the crowbar, pulling away pieces of the doorframe. I moved the door out of the way. The room was pitch dark and quite honestly rank. Libby was wound up in the covers in the bed facing away from me. All I could see was the dark mangled mass of hair. I leaned over the bed and started untangling the covers.

She resisted, but after a considerable struggle, I had all the covers torn away and her lying on her back. She grabbed me by my T-shirt, which was exposed under my jacket, and pulled me into her. She wasn't sweet when she bit into my neck and opened her thighs to embrace me. "Take me," she said.

I wanted to, despite of her greasy hair, body odor, and stale breath. I wanted her with a vicious intensity that made me harder than hard. I ground my body into hers before I heard Cass' whispered words in my mind, 'be gentle with her body'.

"Maybe later." I pulled away. "After you shower."

I had never been as blind-sided as when her open hand met my left cheek in a resounding whack. "If you don't want to fuck, then get the fuck out."

Andy said to make her mad and she was furious, her eyes glistened with raw anger and if I didn't know deep down she was sweet and innocent, I would say she was feral. "I want to 'fuck you' as you so crudely put it, every minute I'm with you, and most of the ones I'm not. But that's not what you need right now." I held her hands back on either side of her head.

She struggled against me and tried to knee me.

"Listen, Libby, you need to stop this temper tantrum right now. It's not good for the babies."

She became perfectly still. "What are you talking about?"

"Surprise, you're pregnant."

"I am not pregnant, I have an IUD."

I narrowed my eyes. "You never told me that."

"You never asked. Do you think I'd be dumb enough to let that happen again?"

"It's not the same. We're married, and you're pregnant."

"I am not," she said but she looked around frantically.

I let go of her and grabbed my plastic bag. "Well, we're only minutes away from finding out."

"I am not pregnant."

"The last time you had your period was in the beginning of January. I remember because I was disappointed you weren't already pregnant."

"Extreme stress can mess with your cycle." She thrashed around in the bed giving me her back. "It's common with an IUD."

"Had you ever missed it before?"

"Only when I was pregnant with . . . " She couldn't finish the sentence, her mind putting the pieces together.

While she was lost in her thoughts I started dragging her to the bathroom. "You can't keep much food down." I turned on the shower water. "You fainted," I said as I pushed her back toward the toilet handing her a Dixie cup. "Pee in the cup and we'll find out." I tore the pregnancy test open. My hands shook and I prayed that I was right, that Cass and Andy had led me down the right path.

She took the cup but stood stock still, her eyes like large green marbles bulging from her gaunt, sunken cheeks. She did look like hell, but a few days of food and love would take care of all that. "Pee in the cup, Libby. Then you can shower."

She pointed toward the door.

"No way. We're in this together, from beginning to end. Plus, I've seen all your pretty parts already."

She lifted the toilet seat. "Go f—"

I covered her mouth. "If you say that, I will wash your mouth out with soap. God knows you need it." I pulled her panties down to her ankles and pushed her onto the toilet.

She complied, and when she was done, handed over the cup with a shaking hand. "I am not pregnant."

"We'll see." I set the cup on the sink. She was staring at the urine sample. I moved toward her and put my hands on the hem of her tank top pulling it over her head. "And, as the last piece of evidence, counselor, we have larger breasts, tender to the touch." I ran my fingertips over them and they pebbled under my caress. I stepped closer to her and she crossed her arms under her breasts pushing them up toward me. "The color of your nipples has gotten much darker, Libby." I placed a gentle kiss at the top of each breast before I pulled back the shower curtain for her.

She stepped in without a word, but I could almost see her thoughts racing. "You did this on purpose to trap me."

"Isn't that my line?" I narrowed my eyes.

"You did it deliberately."

"Yes, I did." I smiled and closed the shower curtain over her face, which had the first inkling of acceptance. "You said I could give Cass anything he wanted for Christmas."

I peeled the plastic paper off the pregnancy test and dipped the thing in the sample. "They're painting your name on the door at the Legal Aid office today." The urine seeped up the stick to the little window.

"The security system has been installed." The first pink line lit up the window.

"Vicki's had the whole place painted. The office furniture arrived, the daycare rooms are finished, and she hired a daytime nanny. Good thinking on her part, 'cause that nanny is going to earn every penny I pay her. I might have to pay her more, taking care of two infants and a toddler, don't you think?"

The second pink line appeared slowly, parallel to the first. My heart raced with joy. I said a quick prayer, to Cass and Andy, too. She'd have no other choice but to join the land of the living now. I grabbed the receipt out of my bag and scribbled two smiley faces and 'I love you' on it. "Read the results on your own. I'll make you something to eat." I slipped out of the bathroom.

There was nothing else in the cabinets except oatmeal, and cereal and the milk was sour in the fridge. Libby stayed in the bathroom longer than I expected. From what I could gather, she hadn't eaten more than saltines for the last two weeks.

I gathered the empty boxes from the landing on the front porch and carried them into Cass' room. I smiled at the place where I'd first laid eyes on him. Even with the joy of this new surprise, I yearned for him. Starting with his dressers I packed everything except photos.

From Libby's room, I heard dressers opening and closing; at least she was getting dressed.

I went to the kitchen and reheated the oatmeal. It wasn't going to be that tasty, but it would sustain her.

Back in Cass' bedroom, I continued with the next drawer of his dresser. At the bottom was a piece of artwork. I traced the lines of the drawing, it was a family, a woman with long brown hair and green eyes, and a man, each of them were carrying a bundle in their arms. I smiled, swallowing down the tears, knowing Cass was happy. He had told me so only hours ago.

"What the hell are you doing in here?" Libby vaulted herself into the room.

"Packing up Cass' stuff. The Cancer Federation is going to come by next week." I handed her the bowl of oatmeal.

"You have no right to do this."

"I have every right. I'm his father. You're his mother. That makes us equals."

I was across the room, when she launched the bowl of oatmeal at me like a missile. I barely ducked before the bowl shattered against the wall and the oatmeal slid to the floor in a glob.

"I've had enough of your angry outbursts," I ground out.

"Well then, run along. Isn't that your response to a pregnant woman?"

"I haven't been the one running for the last two weeks." I sealed up another box and stacked it atop the first one.

Libby kicked at the boxes and they toppled onto the floor, the top one broke open.

"I know you're hurting, and you're mad, but if you weren't pregnant, I'd want to beat you within an inch of your life."

"I wish you'd kill me!"

"Babe." I stepped toward her, pulling her into my arms. "We're going to make it through this." I coaxed her to sit on Cass' bed, and I knelt in front of her. "I love you, and I miss you. Please come back to me. I need you."

Tears raced down her cheeks. "I don't need you, I don't want you, and I don't love you."

"What about them?" I spread my hand over her abdomen.

"Those pregnancy tests are wrong all the time."

"Are you going to try to convince me you don't love our babies?"

She fell forward, her elbows on her knees. "Just go away. I don't want to be with you. You remind me of Cass. And I don't want to love you."

"That's unfortunate for you, but you're my wife and you already love me."

She looked up at me. "Aidan, don't make me hurt you."

"You already have by shutting me out, by trying to disregard our future."

"I don't love you, and I don't want any more kids."

I smiled. "You lie, Libby. For all your declarations to the contrary, you're lying to yourself. You're hurting, and you're angry. You love me, and you have from the beginning." I waited for the words to sink in. "The same way I've loved you. You can deny it, but it doesn't make it any less true or any less real. And speaking untruths now isn't going to ease your pain. It's only going to make you feel worse later."

She leveled her gaze at me. "I hate you." She could have knocked me over with a feather with that. Even though I knew it wasn't true, it hurt me, but on some level, maybe she wanted to test the love that I had so easily and often professed.

"You hate what's happened to us, and so do I." I reached for her hands. "But life is going on, and we need to go on. We need to pack this place up, and then get on a plane to Arizona. I have to go back to work, and we need to find you a good doctor. We both need to heal, but the best way, the only way I know how, is to do that together."

She pulled her hands out of mine. "Of course your precious baseball career awaits," she screamed.

I remained calm; one of us needed to be. "The only things precious in this world to me, Libby, are you and our children. I can't stop the people I love from dying, but I can love the ones I have left all the more."

Her body racked with the tears. She could fight me, if I was angry, but if I was tender, she had no defense. "Just get out. Go to Arizona and don't come back."

"Libby, I know you feel anguish, heartache, and grief, but you're killing me from the inside out. I can't eat, I can't sleep, and I can't think straight. All I can do is take one day or one task at a time." The tears I'd been holding back started to run down my cheeks. "I need you."

She raised her chin with defiance. "I don't need anyone."

"Yes you do, Libby. Everyone needs someone who is more important to us than ourselves."

"My someone died on Valentine's Day."

"Are you trying to rip my heart out with your bare hands?"

"Will that make you go away?"

I looked around the room as if there was some shred of hope for me to grasp onto. I threw the only pitch I had left. "Cass wouldn't want this." I showed her the drawing.

She became fiercely angry and hurled accusations in my face. "How would you know? When did you become such an expert on what he'd want?"

"When he told me, I listened," I threw back at her without thinking before I composed myself. "You remember when he said to tell you his purpose for being born? He came to me this morning, and he told me it was time to tell you. He said he's happy."

"You're delusional." She put her hands over her ears. "I won't hear this."

I fought her hands off her ears and held them steady in her lap. "Too bad. It's what you need." I hesitated gathering my thoughts, organizing them, hoping beyond hope I could reach her. "Cass told me he was born to keep us together, and when that didn't work, we needed a reminder."

"I hate you, Palowski, and I hate God. What kind of God would use a little boy to force two people together who were so completely unsuited for each other?"

"A merciful one, one who knew what each of us needed from the other."

"I don't need anything from you or anyone else."

"You're hiding behind a lie because you're scared. I know you, Libby. You're not a liar, and you're not a coward."

"I don't love you, Aidan. I'm sorry."

She thought she knew her own heart, but right now it was filled with so much anger and pain she wasn't feeling anything else clearly. "It's good, then, that I love you enough to forgive you for this right now." I got to my feet. "You're the only woman I love, the only one I'll ever be with again, and the only one who'll ever carry my children. And you're the only woman I'll forgive without you even asking."

"Don't count on it."

I lifted her chin, so she'd have to look me in the eye. "Don't count down the fact that I'm planted in your heart as deep as my children are planted in your body. Don't count down the fact that every time your body changes, or the babies start to move, or whenever you're reminded that something bigger than either of us is growing inside of you, that you'll see my face, and you'll hear me say I love you in your mind. Every memento is me pulling on your heart strings, pulling you back to me."

"I gave you up once before—for him—and I'd do it again in a heartbeat, if it would bring him back."

"Not everything in life is a trade off."

"Do you think I can replace one child with another? Is that what your merciful God thinks?"

"Maybe we're tied together in a cord that's stronger than either of us. Maybe it's a reminder that we're a family, that you are as much a part of me, as I am, you."

"The only thing that ties us together is binding arbitration. Don't fool yourself into believing we're in control, we don't even get to sit down with the opposition and plead our cases. Unfortunately, sometimes we walk away from the table with less than we bargained for, and some, like me, we end up without anything left."

I kissed her lips tenderly, as if I could brand my words into her. "I love you, babe, and I'll be waiting."

I backed away as stillness seemed to envelope her. I pivoted myself, a man with an axis again, and I forced myself to make determined strides. Then suddenly, like an eruption, things started flying about Cass' room with resounding clunks. She screamed curses from the top of her lungs.

I drove away, clamping down on a raw surge of pain. I had done all I could do for now. I instinctively knew that forcing more on her now would send her into a tailspin. Last time I thought I could force her hand she hadn't come back when she desperately needed me.

But now, she didn't need me. I'd given her the money and the freedom to decide, which in turn was the gift I'd given myself. If she came back now, it would be permanent testimony of her love for me, as tragic and as flawed as I am.

I'd have to live on the love we had shared in the past few months until she was able to forgive me for not saving Cass, until she was able to forgive herself, until she'd allow herself to feel my love again. I'd have to live on the hope that as our babies grew, so would her realization as to the depth of my love and devotion to her.

Batter up, the ump said solemnly. **I'm glad she knows how to take strikes.**

36

RIP: REQUIESCAT IN PACE

Grief fills the room up of my absent child, lies in his bed, walks up and down with me, puts on his pretty looks, repeats his words. Shakespeare

Libby

I dumped drawers. I emptied cabinets. I shredded the linens. I threw books. My head hurt, and I was dizzy by the time I collapsed in quiet contemplation of the gaping hole that once was my bedroom door. Aidan had ripped the framing away, the way I'd desperately tried to rip him out of my heart.

A flutter in my stomach prompted me to close my eyes. Cass had been to see Aidan, in a dream. A common phenomenon, the dead visiting, settling accounts, and assuring ourselves that the one we lost goes on without us.

Why had he chosen Aidan? Why not me?

I needed more time to grieve, but now a new life growing inside me would take that time away. I had to live, or risk injuring *them*. There was more than one. 'Babies.' Aidan had smirked as he spoke, as if he'd thrown a no hitter.

A shadow crossed the doorway. "What the hell happened here?" I heard a baby's babble and looked up. Vicki stood in the doorway with a baby carrier in one hand, and a shopping bag in the other. Her long, patterned coat was dragging off one shoulder courtesy of an expensive diaper bag.

Vicki set the baby carrier down and unbundled the gurgling Betty. "Cat got your tongue?" She tucked Betty into her elbow, placing small cardboard boxes of Chinese food directly in front of me with chopsticks on top. "Eat. You look like shit."

The smell of the food came at me, and my mouth watered. I opened the container and started to eat, as Vicki sat down on the end of my bed offering Betty her breast. "You haven't returned my calls."

I shrugged noncommittally.

"Time's up, Libby, no one is going to tolerate this bull-hockey any longer, especially your husband."

I stuffed a stick full of fried rice into my mouth, speaking around it. "I sent him away."

"You're trying to put the kibosh on the best thing that's ever happened." She murmured to Betty, "Aunt Libby might need an extended stay at the Looney bin. Jeanne's finally rubbed off on her." Betty's fist hit her mother's breast, and Vicki's knowing eyes fell on me. "This isn't just about your pain. He loves you, and you're punishing him, as if this is his fault."

"I can't stand to look at him. It's Cass' face, the same crooked smile, the eyebrows, and the dimple."

"News flash for you, Lib, but it was his face first. And that's the face of love for you. Why would you deny it?" She reached into her shopping bag and handed me chocolate milk.

"I don't want to love him."

"His love can fill the gaping wound you're letting fester."

I shrugged, digging in another cardboard container.

"You always have been too blind to see." She ambled to her feet; she had lost most of her pregnancy weight. When had that happened? She handed Betty to me. "Burp her. I have to pee. For the life of me, I think my bladder is ruined."

I gathered Betty onto my chest. When she murmured, it sent an ache into my own breasts. I patted her back in a steady rhythm while she sucked on her fist. All of a sudden, she let one rip and it wasn't from her front end. I moved onto the floor, pulling the diaper bag behind me. I was fairly confident I still knew how to do this. Betty flayed her arms, pumping them up and down as I took off her shoes and her fleece bottoms. "Wow, that's quite a doozy." She cackled at me in response.

"We call her Betty Poop." I almost jumped when I heard Vicki's voice. "I guess you can see why."

"She seems to be an over-achiever in that department. Does she get that from your husband?" I laughed. I laughed!

She chuckled, too. "You must have gotten this from yours."

I looked up to see the white pregnancy test dangling from her fingertips. "I can't believe you didn't tell me. I'm your best friend, for crying out loud."

"I just found out." I pulled Betty's pants on. I didn't bother with the shoes, but scooped her up and blew raspberries on her protruding tummy. "I'm surprised Mr. I'm-So-Proud-of-Myself-I-Knocked-Her-Up-Again didn't tell you when he sent you."

"He didn't send me."

I raised a brow, trying to hand off Betty.

Vicki refused to take her. Instead, she sat on the edge of the mattress, before clearing her throat. "Cass sent me."

I was concentrating on Betty's little toes, trying to get her sock back on. My head shot up and I wondered if I looked as confounded as I felt. "What?"

"Aidan called me and told me to bring you food, but Cass is the one who sent me."

I looked at her with skepticism. "Did he phone or text?"

"No, this was old world, biblical communication. At least I think it was a dream."

"Vicki, this is a little over-the-top, even for you." I kissed Betty's head and it was as soft as down and smelled sweeter than anything I could recall. Then I remembered...as sweet as Cass' hair on a sun filled day.

"Do you want to know what happened, Miss, excuse me, Mrs. Analytical?" When she moved her arms dramatically, all her bracelets jangled. "For once in your life, just listen. The night before last, I fell asleep nursing Betty. You remember that nice French nursery your husband furnished for me?"

I raised an eyebrow again.

"I came awake when a blast of hot air rushed over me and receded. Cass was standing at my feet. He was so beautiful. He had on his baseball uniform and he was kicking his cleats into the carpet. He was made up of these tiny particles, almost like floating glass, on one side they were his image and they danced back and forth as he moved, like a floating light boy.

"Cass broke my train of thought when he said, 'Does she remind you of me, when I was a baby, Aunt Vicki?'

"I said, 'She poops more than you.' And Cass cackled."

I couldn't speak because the tears were welling up.

"Cass said, 'You've got to save mommy from herself. She's going to ruin everything with daddy, and you got to make her stop. You have to convince her that I'm okay, and I have to know she's okay, or I can't finish my trip. The only way is if she's with daddy. Will you go and see her and tell her?'

'Why don't you go to her, like you're here to see me?'

'If I go before she's ready, she won't be able to see me, and I only get to go once. Will you go for me?'

'Yes, I'll go.'

'Thank you, Aunt Vicki. Tell Betty about me when she grows up, I'll be watching out for her. I love you.'

"I reached out for him, 'I love you too,' but my hand felt like it was going through static energy. It shocked me on the wrist and woke me up."

Vicki's eyes, which had become larger in the course of the story, met mine. "Do you remember when Cass was about four and he painted my wrists with glue and glitter, while I was taking a nap? And I was so mad at him?"

I smiled at that memory I hadn't thought of it in years. "He was in his Sheriff Woody phase."

Vicki laughed. "Yeah. A couple of days later, when I still

couldn't get all the glitter off my wrists, he said, 'Why would you want to take off my handcuffs? I put them on you because I love you so much, Aunt Vicki.' When I laughed, he spoke with the conviction of a philosopher, 'When those wear off, you'll meet someone new to love, but I'll still be wrapped around your wrists. My love is like that glitter. It may fade away, but its smallest speckle will reflect our love.'" Vicki started to cry, and my own eyes welled up with tears.

"It was three weeks later, and I was still rubbing it away at my desk, when Rick walked up to me the very first time. When he held out his computer, I took it with both hands. He looked at my wrists, then into my eyes, and asked, 'Love handcuffs?'

"From the first time I held Cass, I knew there was something special about him. I wasn't his mother, and I'd never given much thought to parental love until he was born, but from the time he came into my life, I felt this unconditional love. He did that for me, and he did that for you."

Tears streamed down my cheeks for several minutes.

Betty sighed in her sleep.

"You might think its all new-age mumbo-jumbo, but I know Cass came to remind me." Vicki got up and she pulled up the sleeve of her sweater up. "I tried touching him with this hand." She held out her wrist for me. "He left me this reminder. He must have known you'd need proof."

I latched onto her wrist like it was a lifeline and pulled it to my face. I turned it in the midday sunlight and admired a diaphanous band circling her wrist like a diamond bracelet. I ran my finger over it. It wasn't glitter on the skin, but under it, threaded into her flesh.

"Where would we be today if it wasn't for him? Maybe we thought we worked so hard and achieved so much for him." She took Betty from me, and bundled her into her snowsuit, before putting her in her carrier. "Maybe not."

I couldn't speak. My mind raced with memories as sweet as any I could recall, and I let the tears flow in testament to their beauty as they filled my wounds.

Vicki got to her feet and I shuffled behind her. When she was at the front door, she moved it, and the sun lit her from behind. She looked like a goddess lighting the path for the righteous. "We have work at the legal aid office, so I'll pick you up at eight tomorrow morning."

I nodded. I wasn't sure I was ready, but I felt I needed to go somewhere. Maybe I could help someone else since I wasn't helping myself, wallowing around here. "I'll be ready."

"That's my girl." And she disappeared into the sunlight.

I lay back on the sofa in the suns warmth and closed my eyes. I wasn't asleep, but I startled, when someone created a shadow in the doorway. My mother-in-law was smiling. "I just spoke to Vicki, but someone sent me here to see you."

"Cass?" Disappointment seeped through me. *How many people had he deemed more worthy than me?*

"No, I had a dream about Andy. He had a little boy with him." Her hand went to her mouth. "That was Cass."

"What does Andy want me to know?"

"He said to tell you that since he died, you're the first person Aidan has given his whole heart to, and to remind you that he's hurting too." Her eyes welled up. "It's the first time I've ever dreamt of Andy since he died. It must be why I was unaware of Cass. It was so vivid, like he was in the room with me. I think he came now because of Cass."

"How so?" I pushed the sofa cushion out of my way so I could see her face as she sat alongside me.

"I don't think I really let go of Andy until Cass died. I still clung to bits and pieces. I was always bartering. Even after all these years, I thought I could somehow earn him back. Hanging onto him, even if it was only in the abstract, was preventing me from living. I've wasted so much of my life trying to stop the pain of losing him, or trying to go back and make another decision to save his life, that's prevented me from living in the moment."

Kat wrapped her arms around me. "Libby, you were a wonderful mother for Cass, and you're an incredible wife for Aidan, and you're a good daughter." She kissed my forehead. "What's most important to know is when to let go, really let go. Keep the memories and the laughter and the happiness you shared with Cass, but everything else needs to fade away, and you have to resign yourself to the fact that he is never going to come back. Nothing you could have done would've saved him. The only thing you can salvage now is the love between you and Aidan. Cass wanted you together. Somewhere inside he knew what was going to happen, and he wanted you to have each other."

Before my tears had subsided, she kissed me and was gone. I blew my nose on the tail of my T-shirt.

I walked to my bedroom to get another shirt, the room smelled rank. I opened a window to clear out the stench. I walked across the hall and did the same in Cass' room to catch the chilly cross-breeze. I picked up the box Aidan had been working on and started reassembling it.

He was right, I needed to pack this stuff up and give it away, or it would be tied around my neck until I did. He was right about a good many things, but I needed to sort through them before I'd be able to admit that to him. I made another box and went to Cass' closet, opening the door. I heard a sound and I looked up to find Suzy standing at the foot of Cass' bed.

"What can I do to help?"

"I'm attacking this closet. You can fold while I'll sort what's worth giving away to charity and what we should toss."

"Let's get after it." She smiled. "I'm happy to see you've gotten out of bed. I was going to have to resort to extreme measures if you didn't come out on your own."

"No fear there. Aidan did that early this morning."

"You're lucky he's been as patient as he has, most men would have broken down the door days ago."

"You mean Max would have broken down the door days ago."

"Well, yes." She folded a red, long-sleeved Rugby shirt while a thoughtful expression took hold of her face. "Have you ever wondered why I brought you into my home and helped you so much when Cass was an infant?"

"I thought old Mr. Rodgers asked you to take care of me."

"He did, but that's not why I did it." She had a strange cadence to her voice that I had never heard from her before.

"This conversation doesn't have anything to do with a dream or a spirit since Cass died?" I asked passing her more clothes.

Her head shot up from her chest and she became very pale. "I did have a dream about a baby crying, but I've had it before. It's a recurring nightmare of mine."

"I don't understand."

"There's a reason I helped you, and there's a reason Max was so incensed about what Aidan did to you in college."

I rubbed my arms trying to calm the baby hairs.

"I'm going to trust you with this story because I think you need it now. You know I was an undergrad at Loyola when Max and I married before I graduated. Everyone thought we were so in love, but that's not really how the story goes."

"What?" I almost sucked all the fresh air from the room.

"When Max and I met, I was a junior and he was a senior. It was the early seventies, and there was a real push for woman's rights. Max had the lingering mentality that a woman had her place. He told me once that I was too ambitious for a woman. Ultimately, it was the reason we stopped seeing each other.

"I was part of a group that was protesting the war in Vietnam. I went to Washington the summer after Max and I parted company. I started seeing a senator's son there.

"When I returned to Chicago to finish my senior year he promised to come see me, but he never did. He sent me letters assuring me of his devotion, but in September I found out I was pregnant. I was naïve enough to believe if I told him, he would marry me and take care of me. Of course when faced with the news, he accused me of sleeping with other men.

"Roe vs. Wade was a raging battle, and I was trapped in the middle of it. Nice girls didn't end up in situations like the one I found myself in. If they did, then the fellow took responsibility. But the senator's son had political ambitions, and while my family had money, we didn't have the right connections. He told me I was more of a liability than an asset. With those words I decided to have an abortion. While they were legal then, they certainly weren't easy to come by.

"I went to a party with friends and ran into Max there, who was in his first year of law school at Northwestern. He sensed something was going on with me, and he kept hounding me to tell him what was wrong. I ate something that didn't agree with me, and I got sick, and I couldn't stop throwing up. Max insisted that he take me to the hospital. By the time we left the ER, he had discovered the truth, along with my parents. My parents assumed that Max was the person who was responsible for my pregnancy, and Max never denied he was the father. He just signed the paper work and left my father ranting in the lobby of the hospital.

"I told Max what I was prepared to do, so I could go to law school. I knew that my parents would insist that I have the baby and give it up. Max didn't tell me what to do.

"I was still asleep that afternoon when he appeared in his best suit, a dozen red roses and a diamond engagement ring. He offered to marry me and raise the child. All he asked in return was that someday, when I was ready, I'd give him more children and put aside the idea of law school until he finished it himself."

"But that baby wasn't Ollie? She would be much older."

"Max and I married, and when I was seven months pregnant I went into labor. The baby was stillborn. By then I wanted that baby because I knew it was the only part of the man I loved that I would ever have.

"I'd graduated, so that summer I started applications for law school. When Max asked what I was doing, I told him that we should divorce. Of course he had a fit. At the end of the tirade I knew I would be his wife for the rest of my life. Because I knew he loved me and wanted me not for that child, but for me. And somehow that became more important than a law school degree."

I didn't know what to say. I stood, frozen, with clothing in my hands, while Suzy worked to keep her shaking hands busy.

"So years later, when Max's dad asked us to help you, we did so. Max did it for you because he had always regretted taking my law school dreams away. I did it because I didn't think that anyone should give up her aspirations because she fell in love with the wrong man."

I moved toward Suzy, who had always been more of a mother to me than my own, and wrapped my arms around her. I had always thought her so happy; content with what life had offered her. She hugged me back and ran her hand over my hair, consoling me, as if I were indeed her child.

She pulled away and smiled at me. "The difference between your story and mine is that you fell in love with the right man at the wrong time. And he loves you, the true kind of love. The kind Max offered me from the start."

"Maybe Aidan's confused how he feels about me with how he feels about Cass."

"And maybe it's just as simple as he always loved you, but he was scared. He isn't scared anymore." She cuffed my chin. "What about you?"

"I don't know."

"When we love, we love with our whole hearts, and when we grieve, we grieve with them just as vigilantly. We've all lost children—you, me, Kat . . . even Jeanne feels that loss. Your mother not only lost her grandchild, but she feels she's lost you, too."

I started to cry. "It's hard to imagine anyone else in pain, when you're hurting so bad yourself."

"Fresh grief, like any new emotion, is overwhelming, but it's the only one that fades away with time." She picked up another box and started filling it.

Chills ran up my spine and my eyes met hers. "Who was the father of your baby?"

Her face was devoid of all emotion.

"You don't have to tell me, if it's too personal."

She thought for a moment. "Richard Doyle."

The goose bumps went from my arms to the base of my skull,

and then crept up the back of my head. "Senator Dick Doyle, who I helped put behind bars?"

"He ended up where he belongs." She went to the closet as I taped the box ... and my mouth—shut.

"What's this?" Suzy asked.

I looked up and saw Aidan's black Armani sport coat, the one he was wearing the day I met Evita. It was the first time I'd spared my new friend a thought, and I chastised myself for my selfishness. Our first meeting seemed like a lifetime ago now. "It's Aidan's."

"You should return it to him." She extended it toward me. Something fell out of the pocket, and Suzy bent to retrieve it. It was a packet of envelopes tied with a blush colored ribbon.

As I took the envelopes and the blazer, I remembered he'd wrapped Cass in it when he had gotten sick at the retirement home. It must've been hanging in the closet since that day. I looked down at the bundle tied in ribbon. My name was scrawled over each of them in Aidan's script. I'd know his handwriting anywhere. The red trimming that held them together seemed brittle, when I slid it free from the envelopes.

Suzy's voice traveled on a whispered breeze. "There's an old saying, 'The word that is heard perishes, but the letter that is written remains'."

October
Dear Libby,

I'm on the road again and missing you. You weren't in the library last night, and I didn't get to kiss you goodbye. I wonder sometimes why I miss you and wish you were with me, when I haven't seen you in a few days. I wonder why, when you're quiet, I become desperate to know what you're thinking. When you smile, I hope I'm part of the reason. If you're sad, I hope I can find a way to make it better. When I don't expect to see you, and then I catch a glimpse of you, I wonder why I can't breathe.

Last week, one night after I walked you to the library exit, I sprinted up to the third floor and watched as you walked away from the building, your long hair trailing behind you. I stared after you until you disappeared, and I stood in that spot, hoping that if I remained still, my longing would change your course and you would come back to me. Even if you just sit alongside me, it's enough.

I want you in a way that is so foreign. Physically, to be sure, but the ache I feel when I go without you a few days is in my chest. It makes it hard for me to breathe. I want to feel the rhythm of your heart beating in time with mine. I want to take you into the stacks and kiss you until you can't whisper 'stop', until you can't move because your knees go weak with trembling, and you can't speak because you start to giggle.

I want more, I feel more, I need more, but if you're sitting in the same room, I can live off the hope that someday you'll be mine. —Aidan

November
Dear Libby,

We're on the road somewhere between Milwaukee and home. The night is so dark that I can barely see the stripes on the pavement. I try to study, but my thoughts stray back to you as the yellow lines hypnotize me as if they are the yellow brick road drawing me back to you.

It snowed during the last three innings of the game, coming down so hard at one point we had a fifteen-minute snow delay. In the dugout, I stared into the distance and I imagined you standing there. Your hair falling over your shoulders, your eyelashes covered with giant snowflakes. The green of your eyes beckoned me, but when I reached out, you slipped away into the swirling snow.

I wonder if you're curled up in bed already. I wonder at my desire to crawl in alongside you and wrap you in my arms. I lay awake wondering what sounds you'd make, if you would let me touch you the way I was meant to. I wonder what it would feel like if you let me become part of your body, in those moments when I can't garner air for the thought of my wanting our joining. I want to feel your body wrapped around mine so that it awakens me deep in the night. I know you don't want me to feel that way about you, but I do, and the more I try to squelch it, the more desperate it becomes in my dreams. I dream of it now, even when I am fully awake. It's much more than lust, but I don't know how to speak the words of tender yearnings. How often I think of forgetting everything for the sake of lying in your arms, breathing in your scent, tasting your sweet, silky skin, or staring into those emerald eyes until you shudder.

I've tried to forget you and because of my efforts, you've become more vivid. You storm my sleeping mind. I've tried to replace you. I've tried not to want you. I've tried not to love you, only to find myself hopeless and helpless. I will pursue you until you can no longer deny what we see when we look at each other, as if not another soul exists. In this world, you are the only thing that did not come easily, the thing I don't think I can live without. You're irreplaceable. If I could show you my feelings as plainly as the words on these pages, the world would be simple, and you would be mine. —Aidan

February
Dear Libby,

I'm scared. For the first time in my life, I'm terrified. I'm sure you are, too. I'm angry, and I want someone to blame, but I know where the blame lies, even though I lashed out at you. I know you didn't do it on purpose, but I feel trapped, like I have to choose between you and what I worked so hard for all these years. How do you choose between what you're supposed to be, and what you should do?

What I should do is take care of you and beg for you to forgive me. I should take you home and marry you, not because you're going to have my baby but because I can't live without you. I can't imagine a world where you're not in it.

But you won't talk to me.

Yesterday you blamed me, and you were right. This is my fault, I should have done something to prevent this from happening, but I wasn't thinking of consequences. It was the only time I hadn't thought through exactly what could happen. But that's what you are to me, you're the freedom to stray from the plan, to act impulsively because when I'm with you nothing else seems to matter, and that scares me.

I've wanted you, I've had you, and now I don't know how I can go without you. You won't talk to me, and you won't let me touch you. You're suffering, and you won't let me help. Scarier still, you won't look at me.

You must hate me for ruining your life. I can't bear to think it, but I must disgust you. Please, Libby, look at me, and see my love for you. See me. Release me from my suffering with just a single kind word.

And I beg of you find it in your heart to love me. —Aidan

March
Dear Libby,

Yesterday you didn't show up like you promised. You won't talk to me, and I can't imagine what you're thinking. I thought you didn't want the baby, and that's why you agreed to go with me to Indy. So we can end this misery between us.

I've looked everywhere for you. Your apartment is empty. Vicki showed me your vacant room, but she knows more than she's telling. She knows where you are, and I'm pissed. I went to the diner and begged Mr. Rodgers for your home address. He told me if you wanted me to know, you would have told me yourself.

Isn't that true?

Finally, he escorted me out the front door and told me if I came back he'd call the law on me.

Why are you punishing me like this? Tell me what you really want so I can give it to you. I would give you anything, or do anything, to make you happy. But now I can't even tell you that.

All I can do is write letters that can never be sent. I should have mailed all the others, long ago; I could have slid them under your door, or slipped them in your book bag. Now all I want is an address. I want to spill my guts and I don't care if you laugh in my face, I want you to know what I feel is real and frightening, and I want you to go on the journey with me.

I want to tell you more than anything else. I'm done trying to fight what's already a lost battle. —Aidan

Graduation Day
Dear Elizabeth,

I graduated today... and so did you. I didn't know you were going to graduate, but that's because you never told me. Looking back, you never told anything, you were one big mystery and maybe that was part of your allure. Maybe I wanted you so bad because I was never going to really know what was going on in your head, so I'd have to settle for your body.

But we both know it wasn't because I wasn't willing to listen, it was because you couldn't bear to reveal yourself. You hide behind whispered words and secrets.

I think now that you wanted to make me suffer and pine for you. All these months, you've been hiding somewhere nearby, away from me, but right under my nose to prove once again you're smarter than me. All my suffering has been in vain because you were near at hand and could have staunched it. All my recriminations could have ceased, if you would have called or came to see me, face-to-face. You wanted me to suffer and hurt.

But I have never suffered more than I did today, when I watched in shock as you walked across the stage with our baby beneath your gown. Your body carries part of me. A body I know as well as my own, a body so vivid in my mind that I could almost feel you breathing as you walked across the stage with your air of intellectual superiority. You are by far the smartest girl I've ever known, but you are also the cruelest. You walked down the aisle, and I watched your measured advance. You refused to look my way, and I know you knew where I was. I could feel your stoic determination not to crumble where I, or anyone else, could witness it. I saw it all, all your pain, and all of mine washed through me. What I wanted more than anything in that moment of insanity was to take you. I didn't want to be tender, I wanted to unfurl all my anger, and lust at you. And perhaps if I could keep from killing you, I would be able to be tender and love you the way you needed to be loved.

But I wouldn't touch you, when you hadn't spared me a stray thought in all these months. Could I speak a single word to you without putting my hands on you? No, so I stalked away. I wouldn't meet your gaze, though I could feel you begging me to do so from across the expanse of a parking lot. I didn't want to see you then, to know I couldn't have the one thing I had wanted more than my own happiness.

I didn't taste my expensive food at lunch. I didn't hear my father's speech about success. I didn't feel my mother's pleasure at my achievement.

I'd been bottle fed on pride since the moment of my birth. I've never had to swallow it in my life, and I didn't feel inclined to do so at the hour of your choosing. So I walked away.

I saw you after lunch on the square in the center of town tossing pennies into the fountain. It hurt me to watch how beautiful you were when you placed your hands on your stomach in reassurance.

Sooner or later, you're going to have to need me, and until you really need me for more than a conversation, we'll never be together. I want you to need me. I hope your suffering and fear will finally make you humbly accept my love. Perhaps, if there is any glimmer of hope, you can admit to yourself that you love me, too. —Aidan

37

FINAL APPEAL

Do the right thing at the right time for the right reasons.
Leonard Chitunhu

Libby

I looked up from the case file I was working on when Vicki strolled into the office at eight-thirty. She set Betty Poop's car carrier on my desktop before she threw the *Tribune* over the brief I was reading. I raised an eyebrow.

"Page thirteen."

I ignored the paper and blew kisses at Betty, who gurgled in response. Her baby sounds made two babies do cartwheels in my abdomen, as if they were eager to have her as a playmate.

It was the end of May, I was four months pregnant, the Legal Aid office was thriving, and the Cub's home opener had come and gone without the closing pitcher paying me a visit. He was trying to make me suffer, by refusing my phone calls and ignoring my notes. Either way, I wished he'd show up, so we could get the confrontation over with.

Fletch hand-delivered each signed payroll check for Vicki and I. I hadn't caught a glimpse of Aidan, but I had a feeling he was laying in wait. "What's on page thirteen?" I asked.

"An article about your husband and a Hollywood starlet."

I refused to lunge. "That's not exactly news."

"You might want to read it before you weep." Vicki's eyebrow arched so sharply I thought its inky end might reach out and lash me until I was as red as the other strands of her hair.

I pretended to concentrate on the brief as Vicki pranced away. I eyed the newspaper out of the corner of my eye. I tried to ignore its lure. I didn't want to know what he was doing because it would make it harder for me to stay away. I had hurt him so bad I didn't know if he would forgive me, babies or not.

I gave in, grabbed the paper and turned to page thirteen.

There was an entertainment article from Winslow O'Leary:

CHICAGO'S CLOSER NO CLOSER
TO CLOSING THE DEAL

It has come to this reporter's attention, and most of the fans in this city, that our all-time best closing pitcher is in a slump. He hasn't completed a single inning since opening day. When he's out on the mound, he just doesn't have it anymore. We all know about the tragic loss he suffered early this year. But rumor has it he and his wife, **LIBBY**, are expecting twins. So, Band-Aid Palowski should have reasons enough to turn his game around.

Although, his wife has been missing from the family section at the friendly confines, no one has spotted her anywhere other than her new legal offices in Rodgers Park. Mrs. Palowski's too busy defending the downtrodden to sit through endless innings on the North Side.

There are rumors, that **AIDAN** has become quite attached to Darcy Crooner who came to town first to help with a Public Service Announcement for his charity, Cass' Game, and several times since as a gesture of friendship. When questioned as to her intentions, she stated, "Aidan **NEEDS** a friend right now, and that's all that we are."

They were seen dining at Darcy's hotel, but it seemed to be a business meeting. When she took the elevator to her room, he drove away from the hotel. I've never doubted this man and his love for his wife but **YOU** never know someone until you walk a mile in his shoes. So for **NOW**, we can hope for a speedy reconciliation between the hometown hero and the game.

I read the highlighted words. '**Libby, Aidan needs you now.**'

Tears flowed down my cheeks and my guts wrenched. I couldn't blame him. I'd sent him away.

"What the hell are you going to do?" Vicki pointed to the paper as she collapsed in her office chair across from me.

"What do you want me to do? It's not like I didn't drive him to it. It's been two months."

"You're giving him an out, if he's been unfaithful?"

I hesitated and my eyes filled with tears. "If he has, isn't my fault? Didn't I break the vows first? Aren't you supposed to cling unto one another in times of need?"

"Okay, so if he was unfaithful, you'll forgive him, but you're not going to see that it doesn't go on?"

I couldn't meet her eyes. "What should I do?"

"What should you have done weeks ago? You're going to put your perfect little pregnant body into the sexiest thing you have." She froze for a moment, one of her hare-brained ideas taking root. "No, no, that little yellow sundress, the one you wouldn't let me give away to charity. The one you said Aidan asked you to wear sometime."

"That will no longer cover these boobs."

Vicki winked at me. "That's the whole point."

"What am I going to say?"

"You're going to choke out a sorry, tell him how wrong you've been, and beg for forgiveness."

"He won't listen."

"Then you're going to tell him you sleep with his letters under your pillow, call out his name in your sleep, and place your hand over your belly when anyone says his name. You're going to tell him he's the only man you've ever loved. And then you're going to tell him losing Cass was the worst thing in your entire life, and you only survived because you loved him just as much as you loved Cass. And all that will be the truth, right?"

I lowered my head. "Yes, that's all true."

Vicki got up and pulled me to my feet. "Go see him."

"Now?"

"There's no time like the present. He has a noon game, go change, go to the will-call window at the ballpark and tell them who you are. After the game, someone will show you where the players come out."

I made it to the ballpark by the middle of the second inning. My stomach was rolling, and my breasts were aching from the tightness of the top. Once I put it on, and looked at myself in the mirror I broke out in hysterical laughter. In another month the thing wouldn't wrap around my breasts. I had to wear jeans under it because it was too short and worn to go otherwise. A tan sweater wrap helped cover the overflow.

When I found my seat, several beautiful women sitting alone smiled at me knowingly. A couple of them had small children sitting alongside them and over the course of the game I could name their fathers, based on their banter.

Aidan wasn't pitching. Butterflies pirouetted in my gut. He was close-at-hand. Even if I couldn't see him, I certainly felt him.

When the game came to an end, one of the women introduced herself and showed me where to wait for the players after the game. We walked down the concrete ramps of the stadium to the deepest level; I stood against the cold gray wall and thought about what to say. As time passed, the crowd of those waiting diminished. Finally, I was alone, except for one other woman, who moved closer and closer to the locker room door as the others dissipated. It would have been difficult to ignore her, even if she wasn't well known, both in the music industry and the movies. She also had a thing for professional athletes and had as recently as today been linked to my husband.

The tight knot in my stomach doubled. I wished I could disappear. The fact that I felt like a small whale didn't help. I was only four months pregnant, but I looked larger. I watched as she tossed her chestnut, waist-length hair over her shoulder when the locker room door opened. From where I was standing, no one would see me if they didn't turn around.

My heart stopped beating when I saw Aidan's profile. He smiled at Darcy and she waved tentatively. Then as another person exited the locker room, a grin spread across her face. She jumped into the second man's arms. Mitch Ackermann had finally found his own leggy brunette.

The steel reinforced wall held me up. I wanted to chisel out the mortar and crawl into a crack. I was shaking. In an instant, I decided it was better if we didn't meet like this. I didn't want him to think I had come back for the wrong reasons.

Mitch and Darcy started away, hand-in-hand, and Aidan followed behind them a few steps. He came to an abrupt halt, shaking his head, like he was shedding rainwater. The lovebirds didn't notice he wasn't trailing them. He let them get several yards away before he turned and focused on my exact location, as if my GPS had set off his internal tracking system.

I jumped.

As he walked toward me, his eyes traveled the length of my body. His eyes settled on mine. When he was an arm's length away from me, he stopped and drew in a deep breath. He closed his eyes, and when he opened them I could almost hear his silent prayer for patience.

"What brings you here, Mrs. Palowski?" His clipped tone was mildly condescending. "Come to check in, or see if I was remaining faithful to the wife who abandoned me?" He had worked himself up to seething mad in a matter of seconds.

I swallowed down. When I had enough courage, my gaze sought his. "I wouldn't blame you, if you hadn't been faithful."

"Did you come to give me permission?" He was shaking, I assumed, from barely contained rage.

I winced. Under his intense scrutiny, my eyes wandered to his highly polished shoes. I raised my head. "You've always been free to do as you choose. I'd hope you remained faithful to me because you love me." I strangled the words out. "I hope you still love me, and can find it in your heart to forgive me."

His hands went to his lean hips. "You're not here because I've been begging you to come back to me. You're here because of the crap you read in this morning's paper."

"No, that's not why."

He waited for me to continue without speaking.

"I miss you desperately."

"I'm glad you've learned about desperation."

"Aidan, please, I'm sorry." I wanted to pull him toward me by the ears and make him listen.

"Not good enough, Mrs. Palowski."

I pulled the last trick out of my bag. "Cass wouldn't want this. He'd wanted us together."

"What's standing between us now has nothing to do with Cass." Aidan's eyes shot to mine. "It's about you and me. When you get that, I'll be around."

He turned on his heel and didn't look back, even when I started to cry. I wanted to rant and rave, but all he wanted was to know that I loved him. He was done telling me first.

So I was going to have to suck it up and tell him, by the time I'd worked up the courage and was ready to scream it from the top of my lungs, he was gone. I made my way out of the stadium. I'd go see him at home later. I was determined to resolve this with him today, and he was in for it because I had other ways of getting to him. I had certain charms he couldn't resist, even if he wanted to, and I had never unleashed the full extent of them on him before.

When I arrived back at the office I walked in on a dispute between two Hispanic women in the reception area. I had no idea why Vicki hadn't already resolved the issue. Fights were hardly unnatural events, and we were starting to become a little flippant about it.

Vicki flounced up the hallway. "Evita's in your office."

I looked up from the mail. "What's going on with them?"

"They're your next clients." She narrowed her eyes. "You don't have the glow you normally have after a rendezvous with your husband."

"He's playing hard-ball. I'll dazzle him tonight. If he sees me in this dress and nothing else, he'll cooperate."

"You promise."

"Don't worry. Now, try to make sure they don't murder each other, and I'll be ready for them after I speak to Evita. They're acting like they're fighting over the same man."

"They are. He's married to both of them."

Oh Geez. I started into my office and I was shocked after my first perusal of Evita. She looked like death frozen over and she had lost at least twenty pounds. "Hey, how are you?" I greeted her with a hug, searching her sunken cheeks up close.

"I came to say good-bye. I'm going to Colombia."

"Does Tony know?"

She smiled grimly. "Yes, he knows."

"Is he going with you?"

"No, he forbids it."

I raised a brow. "Forbids?"

She laughed herself. "As if he thinks that will stop me. I knew you'd understand. You might be the only person who knows how far a mother would go for her child."

I pulled her into the chair next to mine. "I do, but Tony has to be afraid for you. If you get close enough to Espinoza to get Manny, he'll be close enough to kill you."

"That won't be necessary. He assured me he doesn't want me dead, he just wants me back. For whatever reason, I believe him." She folded her hands in her lap in acceptance.

"You spoke to him?" I got up and shut the door.

"He called me. He knows where I am, and he said that Manny is fine. And if I want reassurances, I only have to come back. I can live the rest of my life with Manny under his watchful eye."

"You can't go back. He'll kill you. You have to know that."

"I can't believe you're concerned about me. If I would've stayed where I belonged, your son wouldn't be dead."

"I haven't had a chance to talk to you. If Cass hadn't died that day, he would have passed by now, anyway. His cancer spread."

"I'm so sorry." She wiped away tears. "Either way, I'm dead. It's only a matter of time. At least this way I can see Manny one more time. Enrique will want to play with me for a bit before he disposes of me."

"So that's it? You're going to sacrifice yourself?"

She smiled and patted my hand. "Wouldn't you?"

I swallowed down. She was right in regards to how I felt for Cass. But now I had another reason to live—times two. I smiled at her. "I'm going to have a baby. Actually, two babies."

She smiled and tears crested her eyes before she hugged me, "I'm happy for you and for Aidan. I had wondered, but I didn't want to impose on your privacy. I wish I would've known. I would have delayed my flight for another day to celebrate."

"It's all right. Your good wishes are enough."

She handed me two envelopes. One was sealed, and the other was open and full of cash. "What's this?"

"That should cover your legal fees. I've stayed this long because I wanted to repay you before I left."

I forced the money back into her hand. "Where you're going, this might be the difference between life and death. I don't want it, and I don't need it." I forced her fingers around it. "What's this other one for?"

"It's for Tony. When you find out what becomes of me, give it to him. If Espinoza dies or goes to jail, ask Tony to find Manny for me. Tell him it was my wish." She moved to her feet, pushing me away as I tried to slow her exodus.

"Evita, I don't get it. What happened with Tony?"

She didn't respond at first, but I followed her down the hall. "It doesn't matter now, *Bella*. It doesn't matter." And she blew me an air kiss as she threw her bag over her shoulder.

I closed my eyes and drew in a deep breath. Vicki was ushering the two fighting women into my office. I scanned the waiting area, where a bearded man struggled to his feet. He was wearing a heavy trench coat and something about the way he moved was familiar. I stepped behind the desk and felt along the edge for the panic button. The inner office door opened, and an elderly man in an old baseball cap and bow tie stepped into the reception area. My eyes locked with his, before I looked back at the bearded man who was lifting a sawed-off shotgun. His identity came to me with a dawning realization—Rat Bastard.

The elderly man in the baseball cap said, "Cass sent me," just as a round went off, shattering the ceiling.

Rat Bastard had my attention. I trembled. "You, bitch, have ruined my world." He took aim at me.

Everything I ever loved flashed before my eyes. I quivered when I remembered that less than an hour ago I didn't tell Aidan that I loved him. Now, I'd never get another chance. I thought of seeing Cass again, and as pleasant as that would be, I wasn't ready to go to him. I screamed, "No!"

The door opened again. Evita stepped back in at the exact moment the second shot went off and sailed past my cheek, so close I could feel the heat of it before I started my descent to the floor.

Rat Bastard took aim at Evita, but I'd already closed my eyes when the third round went off. I heard the elderly man's authoritative voice say, "You're out of here." Then the scuffling of feet as the gun discharged again. My head clunked on the corner of the desk, and slowly, blackness swallowed me.

38

BOTTOM OF THE NINTH

If you could kick the person in the pants responsible for most of your trouble, you wouldn't sit down for a month.

Aidan 4:07 p.m.

When I came out of the University Club, I had 22 urgent voicemails. I smiled, thinking she was finally going to thoroughly cave. She was at my mercy. Before I could even fantasize about begging and making up, the phone rang again.

Fletch said, "I'm on my way to Northwestern, get your ass there. Chicago PD called ten minutes ago to tell me there'd been a shooting at the legal aid office."

I froze in mid stride. "Who?"

"I don't have all the details, but—" I heard him swallow. "—It's bad, one fatality, three injured."

There were only four people usually there, Libby, Vicki, Betty and Jeanne. I strangled out a cry.

"Aidan, let's see what were dealing with before you jump to conclusions." I nodded into the phone, but I had already bounded past disastrous conclusions and sunk into recriminations.

4:29 p.m.

I pushed through the emergency room doors. "Where's my wife?" I bellowed at the first nurse I saw, I had been here once before and I wasn't leaving empty handed—this time.

I ran into Fletch in the parking garage and had easily outstripped his pace. "Calm down. We'll locate her."

A minute without Libby was like an hour in hell. "Libby," I screamed.

The center desk was frenzied. Doctors and nurses were rushing out of exam rooms. It wasn't the calm environment it had been the day I'd run through the doors, carrying Cass. "Libby!" I bellowed. Two cops and hospital security pushed me against the wall, which sent Fletch's hackles up to his shoulders and out his mouth in a violent cursing fit.

I was ready for an all-out brawl, but I caught a flash of faded yellow, the exact color of the dress Libby had been wearing earlier. I saw her standing in the doorway of an exam room with a compress at her forehead. She leaned against the frame for support. I caught sight of her bare legs and feet.

She gave me a tentative smile. "Would you please stop yelling? I have a terrible headache."

I vaulted over the cops and Fletch and ran to her, catching her around the waist, which was larger than I remembered. "Don't use that I-have-a-headache line on me." I gathered her into my arms and kissed her.

She kissed me back, patting my cheek. "I love you." She rubbed her temple. "But you're acting like an idiot. Stop screaming, or they're going to toss you out of here."

"I'd like to see them try." I watched Libby put her hand at the arch of her back. "What's wrong?"

"My back hurts."

I picked her up and put her on the bed. "Is everything okay with the babies?" My heartbeat picked up again.

"The doctor is coming down to make sure, but their heartbeats are strong. I only hit my head."

"What happened?"

She gathered her thoughts. "It all happened so fast. Rat Bastard, fatigues, beard, sawed off shot gun, revenge."

"I'm going to kill him."

"He's already dead. He was sitting in the reception area when I came back from seeing you. He said he wanted to kill me for ruining his life. Some old guy in a beat up umpire's uniform showed up out of nowhere. I think he's the one who stopped him. Evita was shot in the leg. Stray pellets from the shotgun."

"Some old guy?"

"Yeah, oh my God!" Her hand went to her mouth. "I just remembered, he said Cass sent him. He was wearing an old-fashioned baseball cap. Do you know him?"

I felt thunderstruck.

Fletch stepped into the room. "Police say some unidentified man shot Matt Caster after they struggled over the gun. It went off into Caster's gut. He died at the scene. Evita is doing well, but she's going to need surgery this afternoon, she might have some nerve damage. Tony's raising hell. Vicki suffered some cuts from exploding glass. Your mom is in the waiting room, she's shaken up, but okay. Betty's sound asleep. Everyone else and God is on their way here to make sure you're okay." He turned to Libby in irritation. "Where the hell is your cell?"

"In my purse."

I handed her the bag, in which she fished around and pulled out her phone. "Sorry, I forget to turn it on."

Fletch gave her a dirty look but spoke to me. "Please instruct your wife that having the phone on, and in working order, in her line of work is imperative."

"I'll tattoo it on her backside." I raised an eyebrow at her. "Or maybe her forehead."

Fletch's phone rang again. "I'll deal with everything else. You keep an eye on her, so she doesn't get in any more trouble."

"You aren't going to give me any more trouble?" I asked.

"I surrender, I was so scared." Tears crested her eyes.

I handed Libby a handkerchief and she gave me the same look she had the first time I handed her one the elevator. "I don't know what your complaint is I carry them around for you."

Fletch passed a woman stepping into the room. "Well, Libby, this isn't the kind of special visit I like from my patients."

"Dr. Osborne, this is Aidan Palowski, my husband."

"Nice to meet you." She put down her chart and pulled on some gloves, while she examined me from a distance, assuming I was a wayward husband. "Let's see how these little monsters are doing." She turned down the lights, smeared some goo on Libby's abdomen, and applied a wand to it while she stared at a small screen. At first I couldn't make out anything, then suddenly I could see them lying side-by-side end-to-end.

I took Libby's hand and smiled. The sight was more amazing than Wrigley Field filled to capacity on a home opener.

"They look good." The doc turned. "Your son is sucking his thumb." She swiveled the monitor, so I could get a better look.

I was awed. "What's the other one doing?"

The doc pushed her gray hair back over her shoulder and looked at the monitor. "She's reading a book." She bent closer to the screen. "I think it might be Shakespeare."

I bent closer to the fuzzy image and both of the women laughed at my expense. "Libby, I want you to take it easy for a few days. Got it? No work, no stress."

Libby nodded, but I wasn't convinced, myself.

Dr. Osborne said, "You have my permission to tie her to the bed, if she won't stay in it." She winked. "You can get your clothes on and I'll get you discharged as fast as I can."

It was more than two hours before they managed to discharge Libby, but we had plenty of visitors. Time passed quickly and I was content to sit there and hold her hand even though I wanted to get the conversation that we needed to have over. So we could make up. When we were free to go I said, "I'll take you home."

She nodded her head yes.

I was confident she knew I meant our home.

In the parking garage, her cell started ringing. When she was digging for it, a stack of envelopes tied with a ribbon fell out of her purse. I picked them up, while she reassured her mother again that everything was all right.

Once she'd hung up I asked, "Where did you find these?"

"In your black sports coat that you left in Cass' closet."

I shook my head. "I tore apart my house looking for these. I thought they might prove something to you."

She hesitated and looked around to make sure no one was nearby. "I came to see you this morning because of what I read in those." She extended her hand, asking for them back. "What I believed you meant when you wrote them."

"When did you find them?"

She frowned. "The day you dragged me from death's door, kicking and screaming."

"If you believed what they said, what took you so long?"

"I needed time to digest it," she said as she folded her arms across her body with the letters close to her heart.

I snatched them out of her hands deftly, and with my body, I pushed her into the concrete wall and boxed her in with my arms, her spine flat against cold surface. "And what did the letters say that my words hadn't?" My breath washed her face.

Gooseflesh rose on her skin. I wanted to kiss her and smack her with equal amounts of intention. I looked in her eyes and saw the raw emotion, the anguish, and the fear.

"Those letters made me believe you would love me even if I think I'm unlovable and my behavior, inexcusable."

My torso rubbed against our children. I looked down at her abdomen, before staring into her eyes. "Have I proven my love and devotion to you?"

"Yes," she hissed.

The sweet smell of her made my fingers itch to stroke her face, but I didn't move. "How do you intend to prove your love for me, Mrs. Palowski?" I stared intently at her lips.

The question startled her and she met my eyes. "I came back to you, didn't I?"

"I was with you from the moment I knew you needed me, and that wasn't proof enough for you, cutter."

She bit into her lip. "What would you like me to do, jock?"

I moved my face even closer to hers but I still remained a fraction of an inch away. I whispered raw words into her ear. "Open your sweater, and show me what you're wearing."

She let her bag fall to the ground, untied the sweater, and pulled it open, revealing the yellow sundress.

My eyes lingered on her breasts, which overfilled the cinched top. I swallowed down on an indrawn gasp. My single fingertip ran across the swell of her breasts from one shoulder to the other. "You might be missing a bra, Mrs. Palowski."

Her breasts lifted in anticipation of my caress and her eyes went from my finger, to my eyes, to my finger again, as it swept over the swell there. I swallowed and waited. I removed my finger grudgingly and then pushed off the wall and paced back and forth in front of her.

"I enjoy your body, Mrs. Palowski, but I believe I've went without it longer than I've possessed it." I stopped and stared at her. "What do you intend to do to set that right?"

"Give it to you whenever you like."

I narrowed my eyes. "Whenever and wherever?"

She swallowed and nodded.

I smiled victoriously. "Take off the sweater."

"Here?"

"Whenever and wherever, remember."

She let the sweater drop from her shoulders.

"Now, whenever and wherever are good but, what about whatever?"

"You're pushing it, Palowski."

"We'll get to that a little later." I winked and smiled. "Raise the hem of your dress for me."

She pulled up the hem of her dress exposing her ever-increasing middle. When the expanse of her stomach was revealed, I dropped to my knees in front of her. I whispered words to her abdomen, and I caressed her with my hands, then my jaw and then my lips. I stood and swiped at my knees as I considered her. "I'll take you back, but it's no longer your way or the highway. From now on we run this show together."

She reached out to seal our bargain with a kiss. Her lips were only a hairsbreadth away, but mine formed a perfect smile as I backed away and raised a brow.

She rolled her eyes. "You're the boss of me, got it."

I pulled her behind me by the wrist, hustling her down long concrete labyrinth and into a fenced underground parking garage. I didn't see anyone else, but the parking area still had several cars and it took me awhile before I located Tank. I hit the automatic starter and the vehicle came to life, as I hustled her along to the rear side door. I opened it and helped her in.

"Move over."

She slid away. I stopped her with a hand around her ankle. I removed her shoe, and threw it in the cargo area. "No more heels. You're pregnant, you might fall."

"Shoes are definitely a safety hazard," she reiterated, nodding her head obediently.

I tossed the second one as I bent over the seat searching the center of her body. "I like barefoot and pregnant." I felt for the waistband of her jeans, when I realized that they didn't have any zippers and buttons I chuckled. "Very convenient," and pulled them down her legs still standing in the open doorway of the car. I tossed them and stood back, widening my stance before I leaned on my forearms against the frame of the car and dipped my head in. "Take off your panties."

She pulled them down the length of her body. When she threw them at me, I caught them without drawing my gaze away from her. I shoved them in my front pocket.

I climbed in alongside her and kissed her passionately. Because I knew she'd give me anything I wanted and because she knew the same, the mood shifted to a tender loving embrace. We sat in bowels of the building that had given us equal parts heartache and hope. We whispered for hours. And after all these years, we made a plan together on what our lives would be.

I laid her back against the seat and wound myself around her. "I love you, Libby, more and more." I kissed her. "And I'm especially fond of fondling you." One of my hands found her breast and the other reveled in all her other secrets.

The ump faked mock disgust. **Forget the game, I'm retired. And you, Palowski, your one hell of a baseball player but you're a much better man.**

I hadn't heard from him in so long my head jerked up. He smiled at me through the rearview mirror. I said, "Thank you."

"You're certainly welcome," Libby responded, "but don't you want to finish first?"

"I'll never be finished with you, Libby Tucker."

She smiled coyly. "I'll tucker you out sooner or later."

39

OUR PARTING IS SUCH SWEET SORROW

Where there is sorrow there is holy ground.
Oscar Wilde

Libby

A sound awakened me in the darkest part of the night. I sat up, watching the rise and fall of Aidan's chest through a slit of light in the blinds. He was sound asleep, wound around me like a shelter, with one of his hands under my short nightgown resting on my abdomen protectively. He was the life preserver, the place where I could unload my burdens, the thing that was always right where you knew it would be. It was exact in its placement, consistent, and affixed to me, so that no one person would be able to remove it—or his love—from me. I felt it as surely and was attached by it as strongly as the love I felt for Cass.

As if by magic, he was standing at the foot of my bed. I almost jumped away at the flash of instantaneous sparkling light. "Mommy?"

"Cass?" I moved toward him.

"I was wrong. You look pretty with babies in your pocket."

I smiled and reached out to him. He came to me, folding his little body into my lap; he was dazzling as the current that seemed to run through his body. "I miss you."

"I know, but I'm happy and nothing hurts where I am and you know what else?"

"No, what?"

"I hit all my balls out of the park." He paused thinking. "Daddy said I have baseball in my blood. I hope you don't mind 'cause I want to be a jock just like daddy."

I tried to squeeze him tighter but my arms moved through his body. "I love you, and you can be whatever you want."

"I gotta go. I just came to tell you that I love you and I'll always be with you."

"Oh, please don't go yet."

And he didn't move away, but circled my wrist with his small angelic hands. "I circle your hands, I circle your heart. I mark with my brand, while we're apart. I sparkle in both your joy and laughter, because I'm part of you ever after." And instead of disappearing or fading away the little particles of shining glitter that made his iridescent form fluttered and stirred closer toward me and then through me, filling my chest cavity. And then I was sitting alone at the end of the bed with only Aidan's gentle snore filling the contentment of my heart.

40

PLAYING CATCHER

The best ballplayer's the one who doesn't think he made good. He keeps trying to convince you.

Aidan 5 months later

Libby screamed, "Hurry!" For the tenth time since we'd gotten into Tank. The word rang through my head with the strumming regularity of the busy signal on the phone. I was torn between watching her anguished face and the road ahead. Watching the road was useless, since the blizzard left visibility to about two feet. We were lucky there were no others cars on the road, the temperature was hovering at about thirty, but she was sweating, and she turned the heater down as she dug her feet into the dashboard as another contraction hit her.

"I should have let them admit you into the hospital after the last office visit, when they said you were already dilated."

"I would've sat there for two days."

"At least we wouldn't be stuck out in this."

"This is a freak storm. It never snows in October."

I turned my head and looked at her like she was crazy. She was technically right, but looking around at the pounding snow proved she was obviously wrong. Another contraction hit her. She dug her fingernails into my arm, and as she did, a gush of water rushed down her legs. "My water just broke."

I looked at her in wide-eyed terror. "We aren't going to make it to the hospital, are we?"

She shook her head as I pulled into a deserted Dunkin Donuts parking lot. I set the heater before I opened the backdoor and folded down the seats. I helped her into the back.

"Everything's going to be fine." I assured her, but I could see my panic mirrored on her face. "Emergency services are still busy." How the crap is it busy? A gust of frigid air and snow swirled into the opening. I shut the door, and spread out a blanket we'd used for a picnic at Ravinia Park last week. "Tell me what to do," I said with the phone wedged between my shoulder and my ear.

Libby steadied me. "We can do this. Thousands of women had babies before there were hospitals. I can do this." Another contraction hit, forcing her onto her back in a contorted heap.

I wrestled items out of my baseball bag before I shoved it under her head. I tore through my tackle box looking for anything I could use. I was holding a glove in my hand when the pain subsided enough for her to focus on me again. "No matter what they told you in birthing class, you can't catch a baby with that."

I smiled at her and started tearing the laces out of the glove. The glove I had used while winning the divisional championship. "We can tie off the cord with this."

She reached out and stilled my hands. "You'll ruin it."

"Libby, our babies are about to be born. I couldn't give a crap less about this mitt."

Another contraction hit her and her hands went to her abdomen. I expected her to cry out or scream, but she just met my eyes firmly. As the pain rolled over her and away, she shook her head. "Soon, it's going to be soon."

"Crap." I tore my sweatshirt over my head, removing my shirt and T-shirt before replacing the sweatshirt. "Let me get your clothes off."

Another contraction hit as she tried to help me lift her hips. She was wearing a dress, so all I had to remove was her panties. I pulled them down her legs. I smiled. "Thank goodness for your affinity for those thigh highs. At least your legs won't be cold."

She smacked at my arms drawing my attention away from her incredible legs. "Yeah, they've gotten us into trouble more than once; it's about time they bailed us out."

"It's only right that the babies are born in here." I chuckled. "I bought this thing for our kids and we did an awful lot of practicing in here."

She clutched my arm as I pushed her hem past her knees so it met her belly. I looked between her legs for the first time, then back at her. I thought I'd be freaked by what I saw there, but I was amazed. "The baby has a lot of hair."

"Oh my God, you see the head?" She had no other choice than to push, her feet lodged against my knees. I pulled her toward me, as she groaned.

"Good job, babe. The heads completely out." The baby's airway was clear, and it was breathing on its own. "One more push, and he or she'll be out."

She squeezed my forearms as another contraction hit her and the baby slid out. "It's the girl. You would deliver her first." I smiled at her with so much enthusiasm my face hurt. "She's beautiful." I held her in my hands, while she bellowed at me, her little fist raised in warning. I had just been put on notice by a newborn that there was a new sheriff in town. I placed her on my shirt, tied off her cord and then cut it with wire cutters from the tackle box. I gazed at her one more time, before I laid her alongside Libby.

Libby admired her. She had the curliest hair I had ever seen. "Are you sure this blonde came out of me?" she asked. "At least we already know you have a small affinity for them."

As if the baby knew we were watching her, she blinked open her eyes, the bluest I'd ever seen. Then she yawned and closed her eyes again serenely. Libby said, "Yep, she's yours, makes a grand entrance, then falls fast asleep."

I wanted to hold the tiny little bundle and tell her that her mommy didn't really mean it, but I was afraid that another contraction might hit Libby and she needed me to focus on that.

I met Libby's smiling face. "One down, one to go, babe."

She nodded her head in agreement before resting.

I had finally gotten through to 911. I was telling them where we were, what had happened so far, and if there were things that I should have done that I hadn't ... The operator assured me they were on the way, and then started congratulating me for winning the division. I had just had the most amazing experience of my life, delivering my own child, and this idiot thought a game was important!

Libby's body contorted, I laid the phone down and caught my son as he slid onto home plate. He was beautiful, a bald, green-eyed monster. I wrapped him in my T-shirt and commiserated with him. "Our team only has two boys, and we we're outnumbered because your sister and mommy have fiery tempers," I said as I counted his toes. He blinked his eyes suspiciously and furrowed his brow. "Maybe we just leveled the playing field after all."

I smiled at Libby. "I was thinking Duncan."

"What? You never mentioned that name before."

I eyed the parking lot signage. "We could call her Donut."

Libby touched the baby's hair. "Very funny."

"You never told me where Cass' name came from."

Her lips formed a perfect little pout. "He's named after you."

"Huh?" I looked up from admiring my son.

"Cass is short for Casanova."

I burst out laughing and startled my son into a crying fit. I shushed him as I gave Libby a slow smile. That was the thing; she could talk to me about Cass. It hurt still, probably always would. But that burden was ours to share, and we never had to soften blows with each other the way we did for others. It was our love that made him, our love that missed him, and our love that would never let us forget.

I beamed at Libby. "You did it, babe, and not a single curse word. I'm so proud of you." I kissed her lips.

"Rule number one, no cursing for mothers."

"Amen to that."

So that's what we learned—loss with its unlimited power to destroy—could be overcome with love. And love was the thing that bound us together. It wasn't arbitrary; it was contingent upon the soul's discretion and once found it wasn't easily abandoned.

OTHER CONTEMPORARY NOVELS

CUTTERS VS. JOCKS

On the idyllic campus of Indiana University, Little-Libby-Nobody clashes with Band-Aid All-American-Athlete and fireworks explode, spiraling Libby and Aidan into a collision course of love at first sight versus lust you can't fight. Libby believes superstar jocks don't take cutters to Rose Well House, at midnight and pledge their undying devotion beneath its sparkling dome. And Band-Aid imagines there's no place in the major leagues for a small-town waitress. As the game plays out and their affection grows, they realize that labels like cutters and jocks can't extinguish what's between them.

"There is a gritty reality to this story that is compelling and addictive. There is profanity and sexual situation and conversation which are really the angst of the story."
~The Book Runner

STAINED
CARPETBAGGERS, REBELS, & YANKEE SERIES BOOK 1

What happens when your darkest truth is revealed to the world?

Scarlett Marbry was just sixteen when her mother, an acclaimed Sacred Harp singer, committed suicide in front of her, sending her running from rural Alabama and the darkness that pushed her mother over the edge. Now, after five years of building a fragile cage around her heart to protect herself, she must return to Crossroads for her grandparents' funeral. There, she'll not only be forced to deal with the reality of her deep Southern roots, but she'll have to face the one she left behind.

Revell Marshall is used to working with fragile objects. He's built a life and career around reassembling the delicate stained glass windows that have put Crossroads back on the map. He's also been pining for Scarlett all these years . . . Determined to win her heart, he helps her piece together the facts of her mother's past. Except these revelations, once exposed, could set Scarlett on the downward spiral she barely escaped the last time. Especially when the truth that stained the past may be the same one that shatters her faith in the one person she thought she could trust . . .

ABOUT THE AUTHOR

Windy City writer, Elizabeth Marx, brings cosmopolitan life alive in her fiction—a blend of romance, fast-paced Chicago living, and a sprinkle of magical realism. Elizabeth resides with her husband, girls, and two cats who think they're really dogs. She grew up in the city, has traveled extensively, and still says there's still no town like Chi town. You can contact the author at elizabethmarxbooks@gmail.com or visit her website at www.elizabethmarxbooks.com.